The Barrington Brothers

JULES BENNETT

MILLS & BOON

First Published in Great Britain 2018
by Mills & Boon, an imprint of HarperCollins*Publishers*
1 London Bridge Street, London, SE1 9GF

THE BARRINGTON BROTHERS © 2018 Harlequin Books S. A.

When Opposites Attract... © 2014 Jules Bennett
Single Man Meets Single Mum © 2014 Jules Bennett
Carrying The Lost Heir's Child © 2015 Jules Bennett

ISBN: 978-0-263-26866-9

05-0718

MIX
Paper from
responsible sources
FSC™ C007454

Printed and bound in Spain
by CPI, Barcelona

WHEN OPPOSITES ATTRACT...

JULES BENNETT

This entire trilogy is for my amazing agent, Elaine Spencer, who, when I mentioned a horse series, said, "Horses? I'm more familiar with dogs, but go for it." From one animal lover to another, thanks for holding my hand during this journey.

Also, a special thank-you to F.J. Thomas, my Twitter buddy who answered many questions regarding the world of horses and racing.
Any mistakes are mine alone.

One

With a nice, round backside greeting him as he stepped over the threshold of the fancy stables, Grant Carter was more certain than ever that accepting this film project was not only a chance of a lifetime, it was a gift from God.

He might be looking to settle down and calm his ways, but to ignore the perfection displayed before him would be a sin. Besides, Grant knew his place, and he hadn't worked this hard in Hollywood to blow it just because temptation seemed to be glaring right in his face. Literally.

Temptation would have to wait, because producing a film revolving around horse-racing icon Damon Barrington was an opportunity he couldn't pass up...no matter the nightmares that followed him here.

The shapely woman in front of him might be a slight distraction, but that's all she could be. The new clause typed up in his contract had been reinforced before his arrival at Stony Ridge. Apparently, fraternizing with anyone involved in this film was a no-no. Shame, that.

Besides, even without the clause, nothing could cripple him more than being thrust back into the world of horses. But he could compartmentalize and he could be a professional on set. He simply couldn't let personal conflicts pass the barrier he'd built around his heart.

Grant eyed the round bottom hugged by tight black riding pants. *Damn clause and personal demons.*

The familiar smells of the straw, the feed, the leather saddles; the sight of beautiful Thoroughbreds... The combination brought back memories—memories that had no place in his life. Especially now.

Concentrate on the backside. A body like that could surely cure all ails. Even if she was off-limits, he had already taken a mental picture to fuel fantasies.

"Excuse me. Can you tell me where I can find Tessa Barrington?" he asked, carefully stepping farther into the stables, straw crunching beneath his new boots.

The petite, yet curvy woman stood up, turned and slid the vibrant red ponytail back over her shoulder. And he'd be a complete liar if he tried to deny the punch to the gut he felt when those sapphire eyes landed on him. In an instant, he wondered how many times she'd used those intriguing eyes to lure a man into her clutches.

Between the body and the face, she was a stunner, but he wouldn't be as clichéd as to say so. No doubt she had men falling all over her, and he refused to be so predictable.

"Are you the producer?" she asked, setting aside the brush she'd been using on the horse.

"One of them. Grant Carter." He closed the gap between them and extended his hand.

"I'm Tessa."

Surprise slid through him, but he prevented himself from dropping his jaw...just barely. So, he'd been admiring the beautiful jockey. Interesting.

When she propped her hands on her slender waist, just above her flared hips, he nearly swallowed his tongue. That sweet little package all wrapped in denim and plaid? Who knew he had a thing for country girls? Of course, Tessa Barrington was hardly just a country girl. This woman put the fear of God in most male jockeys, trainers and owners, if rumor served correctly.

"My father said you'd be arriving today." She gripped his hand, her gaze sliding down to his feet. "Pretty shiny boots you got there, Slick. We'll have to scuff those up a bit."

He couldn't help but smile at her piercing glare, her judgmental words. A woman who didn't hold back and wasn't throwing herself at him? He liked her already.

When she pulled her hand from his, Grant hated how such delicate features had calluses on them, but he knew this jockey took her lifestyle seriously. She didn't get to be the number-one contender in the country by sitting on the sidelines sipping mint juleps and wearing oversize hats.

"It's a pleasure to meet you," he told her, offering a smile. "I have to say, you're quite impressive."

A perfectly sculpted brow lifted as she crossed her arms beneath her breasts.

Grant laughed. "That didn't come out right."

Seriously? Was he in high school and suddenly unable to form an intelligent sentence?

"What I meant to say was I'm impressed with your talents."

Damn it. Nothing was working for him right now.

"I'm assuming you mean because of my racing," she replied, her brow still raised.

Relieved that she'd let him off the hook, he tilted his head. "I know you have a busy schedule—"

"It's beyond busy, Mr. Carter."

"Call me Grant," he told her, cutting off that curt tone. "We'll be spending a great deal of time together over the next couple of weeks."

Tessa turned, picked up the brush and stepped back into the stall with the stud. "Mr. Carter—"

"Grant," he reminded her with a grin.

Her eyes darted to his, then back to the horse she'd been brushing. "Mr. Carter, my schedule is pretty tight. I came up with a spreadsheet so you can see when I'm practicing, when I'm working in the stables and when I have time blocked off for you. Your area on the sheet is green. I would like to stick to this spreadsheet, but if you have other engagements during our time, I can attempt to rework it."

Grant tried his hardest not to burst out laughing. She was

starting to sound like his oh-so-organized twin sister...or at least how he remembered his sister before her accident.

Seeing as how Tessa still hadn't shown a hint of a smile, he assumed she was dead serious. Wow, this woman would be tough to crack. He loved a challenge, but something told him she wanted nothing to do with this movie. Most people would be thrilled to know Hollywood wanted to make a film around their life and on their property. The majority of the women he knew would give their entire shoe collection to be associated with a Bronson Dane movie with Max Ford as lead actor.

Grant watched as Tessa stroked the horse's mane with precision and care. This woman was obviously not impressed with him or this film. She seemed to be in her own world of details and structure, from the spreadsheet to her perfectly placed low ponytail. He had a feeling the beautiful Tessa Barrington rarely had her feathers ruffled.

And he'd so love to ruffle her. But beyond coproducing this film, he couldn't get swept back into the world that had ruined his family's life. He had to keep any personal emotions off this set. His next goal, of starting his own production company, was within reach, and he'd be damned if he'd let his guilt and fear hold him back.

"When is my first time slot, Tessa?" he asked, propping his hands on his hips as he took a step back from the open stall. "My team will be arriving in a month, and I plan on outlining the sites for the order of filming after I visit all the locations. But I'm flexible. I'll work around you."

With perfect ease, she turned, tapped the brush against her palm and tipped her head. "I know my father agreed to have me help you, but my racing has and always will come first. I should make it clear I'm not happy about this film and I don't endorse any part of it."

Grant couldn't help but grin. Apparently Tessa wasn't a fan of having her work disrupted. Actually, she was a refreshing change from the women who stumbled over themselves to get his attention because of his celebrity status and his bank account. Tessa was obviously impressed with neither, which only made her even more intriguing.

"I understand you're a busy woman," he repeated, hoping to use a little charm to get on her good side. "I'll try not to take up too much of your time."

"I only agreed to let you shadow me because I refuse for this film to be anything but accurate. I don't want my father's life spun into something ugly or devious."

Interesting. Clearly, Tessa had had an unpleasant experience somewhere along the way, and now Grant was in her path of anger. Lovely. Nothing like spending the next month working closely with a bitter woman.

"I will make sure this movie is done to everyone's satisfaction and is the best film we can produce," he promised.

"Looks like we'll both be getting our way, then," she said with a tight smile.

Both get their way? His eyes roamed over her delicate frame. Oh, the possibilities. Slipping that tight ponytail down would be the first. Unbuttoning her stiff shirt would be next.

And making use of that empty stall would be another.

Yeah, this would definitely be a long month.

Tessa knew when a man was attracted; she wasn't stupid. And in all honesty, she found this hotshot producer pretty sexy, but she'd built up an immunity to sexy, smooth talkers.

Besides, the last guy who'd captured her attention was a city boy through and through. His polished shoes, designer suits and perfectly coiffed hair hadn't bothered her. What bothered her was when he'd decided to use her name and finances to further his small-business venture.

There was no way Tessa would let herself get sidelined by some captivating, powerful stranger from Hollywood just because he made her heart beat a bit quicker with that one-sided smile and those heavy-lidded eyes.

Most twenty-five-year-old women were getting married and

having babies. Tessa opted to chase her own set of dreams—the Triple Crown.

There was no time for serious relationships when she lived in a stable, training most hours of the day. And she most definitely thought more of herself than to let go of her innocence for a quickie.

Besides, she'd learned the hard way how cruel relationships could be and how the word *trust* meant different things to different people.

"I need to take Oliver out for a ride," she told Grant, hoping he'd take those sultry eyes and be on his way for now. "I assumed when Dad said you'd arrive today, it would be later, so I had blocked out a two hour window for you after lunch."

He checked his watch. "I can come back, but it may help if I have that spreadsheet, so I know when not to disturb you."

Tessa sighed. He was mocking her. That was fine; she was used to it. But the last guy who'd decided to make a joke of her had found himself out one girlfriend and a whole lot of pride by the time she'd finished with him. Of course, his mocking had come on a whole other, more painful level.

She moved to the next stall, where Oliver, her beautiful Thoroughbred, waited for his warm-up. Oliver wasn't her racing horse. No, he was her baby, and she loved him as dearly as she would her own child. He was a bit finicky, a bit hyper some might say, but Tessa and he understood each other. And they pretty much both loathed outsiders.

"I'll bring that spreadsheet to our meeting," she told Grant as she slid open the stall. Oliver, restless as usual, started his bucking dance, his way of letting her know he was more than ready to go. "I can meet you back here in two hours—"

One second she was talking and the next she was in Grant's arms. She hadn't seen him move, but suddenly he was pulling her away from the opening in the stall.

"What are you doing?" she asked, looking up into the most impressive set of dark, near-black eyes.

Grant stood frozen, his arms wrapped around her, his eyes

now wide and focused on Oliver. With his attention not directly on her, she could take a moment to appreciate the strong jawline beneath the dark stubble, the tanned skin, his firm grip on her, giving her the opportunity to learn that he had fabulous muscle tone beneath that new gray flannel shirt.

And he smelled so damn good. Perhaps she was just glad to be inhaling something other than hay and horse poop, but Grant Carter's aftershave, cologne or the combination of both was masculine, strong and sexy...just like the man.

"Grant?" she asked, sliding from his grasp.

His gaze went from the stallion to her and held, before he shook his head as if to focus.

"He jumped when you started to step in," Grant told her, taking a step back and raking a hand through his short, messy hair. "I didn't want you to get hurt."

Still confused at his overreaction, but a little touched by his instant ride to the rescue, Tessa crossed her arms. "Hurt? I won't get hurt tending to the horses, Grant. Oliver is always like this. That's why I'm the only one who handles him."

Grant shrugged. "My apologies. I'm just not used to horses."

She tilted her head, still trying to get a feel for this newcomer into her world. "Are you going to be okay on this set?"

"I'm fine." He sent her another killer, knee-weakening smile. "I didn't want you hurt, that's all."

The way those dark eyes held hers, and the soft, yet firm tone of his voice washed over her like a warm, protective blanket. She didn't want to feel anything for this man. But that protective streak, and an underlying secret vulnerability, made him even more attractive in her eyes.

"I don't think that's all," she commented, calling him out on whatever seemed to cripple him. "I don't want to be rude, but you are working on a film about horses. Shouldn't you know something about them?"

That sexy smile spread wider across his face as Grant eased forward with a slow, easy stride any cowboy would envy.

But this man was from L.A., the city of sin and silicone. If it weren't for the newly purchased clothes, which were so fresh looking they might as well have the tags dangling, Tessa would swear he lived on a farm.

But he was in the film industry. He probably always looked the part. Appearances were everything to shallow people.

Grant stopped when the tips of their boots nearly touched, and she had to either stare at the way his dark gray flannel stretched across his firm pecs, or glance up and meet that dark gaze. Either body part would tempt a nun, and Tessa was finding it hard to remember what she was saying when he towered over her and looked straight down into her eyes as if he could see her deepest secrets.

She'd been tempted before in her twenty-five years, but never this fast, this hard. Tessa feared she might be in over her head with Grant Carter because they'd been in each other's presence for mere moments, which was barely a blip on the radar in the grand scheme of things.

"Learning all about horses is why I have you. I've waited years to get a project of this caliber." His eyes roamed over her face, from her eyes to her lips and back up. "And when I want something, I find a way to make it mine."

Why did those arrogant words hold such promise? And why did she delight in the way chills raced over her body?

Had she not learned her lesson? Pretty words and attractive men were all around her in this industry. She'd been naive enough to fall for a smooth talker, had nearly taken his ring while dreaming about their future. She wouldn't make that mistake twice.

And she certainly had no room for overeager hormones. She had races to win and titles to collect. Nothing could come between her and her goal...not even if it was wrapped in chiseled muscle and a white-knight attitude.

But she couldn't deny the man tempted her more in these few moments than her ex had in the months they'd been together.

Tessa was proud she still had her virginity. Some women

might be embarrassed by the fact, but she felt that was just another layer of her strong will. And a promise to her late mother.

But Grant did make her hyperaware of desires she'd never fully engaged in.

Good grief, why did she have sex on the brain? She'd just met this man, but those broad shoulders and mesmerizing eyes, combined with his protective streak, made all her lonely girlie parts perk up and wonder exactly what she was missing out on.

"I'm not interested in anything other than my racing and my horses," she told him, damning her voice when it didn't sound as strong as she'd wanted. "Don't waste your fancy charms on me."

One corner of Grant's mouth lifted in a mocking smile. "Oh, my fancy charms aren't going to waste, Tessa. You're just as attracted as I am. It's natural to see a beautiful person and allow your mind to wander into fantasy. There's no need to deny the facts."

Tessa laughed, took a step back and crossed her arms over her chest again. "If your ego is going to be the third wheel, we may have to adjust the spreadsheet to accommodate. But I'm afraid my time can't be stretched so thin, so check it at the door, Slick."

Grant laughed and, damn him, she just knew if she was going to lie around him, she'd have to be more convincing. There was no way she could let her guard down, or she'd find herself falling directly into his seductive, high-class world.

Two

The wide, curved staircase leading up to the second-story balcony overlooking the entryway would be the perfect place to shoot the opening scene. Grant wanted to begin the movie with the early years of Damon and Rose Barrington, and since this home was the focal point for their family, this would be where they began.

Taking mental notes as he walked through the main house at Stony Ridge Acres, Grant could already picture Max Ford, the lead in the film, leaning over the balcony, watching two little girls frolic in the open floor plan.

Of course, Max was playing the younger version of Damon Barrington, when he had first started making a name for himself on the racing scene.

Grant couldn't help but smile at the image of a young Tessa running through the house, which had been handed down to Damon from his own father. Even as a child, Tessa probably had had the whole family on a tight schedule, from lunch breaks to riding times.

"Grant."

Turning toward the wide side hallway, Grant smiled as he moved through the open foyer to greet Damon. The tall, thin man with silver hair had a presence about him that demanded attention and respect. Grant was more than happy to devote both, considering this film would take him to the next level of his career plan.

Directing had always been a passion. Grant loved the up

close and personal contact with the actors, loved the level of trust they built with each other.

But now he was ready to take that next step, and coproducing this film would only add another monumental layer onto what he'd already attained.

"I apologize for not being here when you arrived," Damon said, slapping him on the back. "I trust you found Tessa in the stables?"

Bent over, looking sexier than she had a right to.

"I did," Grant confirmed, keeping his carnal thoughts to himself. "I'm meeting her in a bit to go over a few preliminary questions. She has a schedule for me."

Damon's robust laughter filled the foyer. "That girl. If she's not on a horse, she's at her computer with color-coded schedules."

That woman needed to relax, and Grant fantasized about making that happen during his month-long stay here on the estate before his team arrived. Of course, he had to maintain his professional manner because of that clause he was growing to hate more and more.

Stupid "no fraternizing" section. He'd had one slipup a few years ago. Okay, so he and the makeup artist had drunk a bit too much and had made headlines, but that was in the past. Yet he was still paying for his sins.

And he refused to get in deeper than lust. Tessa was sexy as hell, but her world and his did not and could not mesh.

Besides, he wasn't ready to settle down. In the future he wanted to have a family, but right now he didn't have the time. No reason he couldn't get Tessa to relax a little and enjoy herself, however. They would have weeks together, and he didn't intend to spend them looking at his watch and checking some damn spreadsheet to see when he could take a bathroom break.

Flirting while he was here would help him keep his mind off his real issues.

"Apparently my allotted times are in green, but I've yet to see the schedule."

Damon sighed, raked a hand over his face. "She is her mother's daughter. My late wife had labels on everything, each day scheduled to the minute. Used to drive me insane."

"I'm hoping when Lily arrives for the filming, the two of you can talk," Grant said, referring to the A-list actress playing the role of Rose Barrington in the early years. "She's been studying your wife's biography and looking at the pictures you supplied, but I know it will help to have a firsthand account from you."

"I look forward to speaking with her." Damon beamed. "I still can't believe a movie is being made of my career and life."

"You're a remarkable man, Damon, and you can't deny you have an incredible dynasty here. Not only did you win the Triple Crown, you now have a famous daughter who is a jockey and another daughter who is a trainer. Everything in one perfect family. Some may say you're the luckiest man in the industry."

"Luck has nothing to do with it," Damon corrected with a slight grin. "Life is all skill and patience. Remember that and nothing can stop you."

Grant had a feeling there was so much more to this man than racing and owning a prestigious horse farm. While those elements were key, Grant got a true sense of family loyalty here. Besides the countless framed pictures hanging along the walls in each room, celebrating various family milestones, Grant had seen the pride in Damon's eyes when discussing his girls, and that same pride and protection in Tessa's eyes when she talked of her father.

Being part of this film thrilled Grant more than he'd originally thought. Family meant everything to him...which was why he could never face his sister again after ruining her life.

Shaking off the haunting memory, Grant focused on the film. When Anthony Price and Bronson Dane had first approached him, he couldn't say yes fast enough. The big break he'd been working for, fighting for, was finally here, and he wouldn't let anything stand in his way...even a beautiful, sexy jockey. She might be totally opposed to this film, but she really had no say over the matter.

Of course, she could make these next several weeks difficult, but he'd find a way to crack her outer shell. She might be immune to his charm, but she was attracted. He'd seen the way her eyes widened, the pulse at the base of her throat sped up, and more than once he'd seen her gaze dip to his lips.

Yeah, she was cracking already.

"Listen, I've got to head out and meet a man I'm thinking of hiring on as a groom. But I shouldn't be gone too long." Damon checked his phone, then slid it back into his pocket. "Please, make this your home. Look anywhere you like, and Tessa can show you around the grounds. I assume you got your stuff into the guesthouse?"

"I did," Grant replied. "I appreciate the use of it. Though I'd be perfectly content in a hotel until the on-site trailers arrive."

Damon waved a hand. "Nonsense. We have two extra guesthouses, other than the one my oldest daughter, Cassie, and her baby live in. They're a bit on the small side, but they're better than any hotel or trailer."

On that Grant would agree.

"I'll be back later if you need me, but I imagine Tessa will have everything under control."

Laughing, he nodded. "I have no doubt."

When the elderly man walked out the front door, Grant continued his stroll around the house. He'd been through it before, but now he was looking at even finer things and really thinking of each scene, each facet of Damon's life.

Several scenes would be shot at various horse parks before and during the races, but he would mainly stay here, directing the shots from the estate. Bronson and Anthony would be more on location, traveling with their wives and kids.

Bronson Dane and Anthony Price were half brothers and a force to be reckoned with in the film industry. And Grant was beyond thrilled they'd asked him to coproduce this movie about the Barrington dynasty.

Glancing at his watch, he noted he had about five minutes until his scheduled time, so he headed out the front door and toward the stables. Wouldn't want to be late and have to be rescheduled to—gasp—the yellow slot.

Grant smiled as he walked across the lawn, calculating all the ways he could throw off Ms. Spreadsheet. How could he not want to have a little fun with this? People who were that uptight missed out on all the joy in life.

He totally understood the need to be serious, when the time called for such actions, but wasn't life supposed to be fun and enjoyable? A spreadsheet for daily life? Who actually lived that way?

Tessa stepped from a stall just as he came to the entrance. Sliding her hands into the pockets of her very slim, hip-hugging, mouthwatering riding pants, she headed toward him.

"Punctual," she said, closing the gap between them. "I think we'll get along just fine."

Grant allowed his eyes to roam over her face. A fine mist of sweat covered her flushed skin, and damp tendrils of hair clung to her forehead where her riding helmet had rested.

"Why don't we go inside, get some water and talk?" he suggested.

Tessa crossed her arms over her chest and offered a smile that flashed a dimple just to the right of her full lips. "City boy can't handle the heat?"

He laughed. "Actually, I thought you may need a break."

"I don't take breaks," she told him, tilting her chin in defiance. "And a little heat never bothers me."

Unable to stop himself, he stepped forward and slid a stray lock of hair behind her ear, letting his hand linger a bit at the side of her face. Tessa's swift intake of breath pleased him. He had a feeling nothing much set her off her game.

"Good to know you can handle activities that work up a sweat," he murmured, mentally cursing himself for crossing into carnal-thought territory. Thoughts led to actions, and he didn't have the time or the authority for such shenanigans.

Tessa reached up, put her hand in his and smiled. "You're going to have to do better than that, Slick. Clever innuendos won't work on me."

Grant couldn't help but grin. "Oh, I'm just getting warmed up, Country. Throwing you off your guard is my main goal here."

Keeping her eyes on his, Tessa tilted her head. "I thought producing and directing this movie was your main goal."

He leaned in, close enough to smell her musky scent, feel her warm breath on his face. "I'm an expert at multitasking."

She patted his cheek as if he were a little kid, and laughed. "It's good to have goals, Slick. Now, what do you say about grabbing some lunch? Your two-hour time slot just narrowed down to an hour and fifty minutes."

She sauntered around him, while Grant stood there looking like a complete moron as he watched the sexy sway of her hips in those taut riding pants.

But from the heat he'd seen pass through her eyes, and that frantic pulse at the base of her throat, he knew she wasn't unaffected by him.

This project had just got a whole lot more interesting.

Three

Tessa let herself in the back door of her father's home and nearly wept at the refreshing, cool air that enveloped her.

She'd gotten overheated outside, though her rising body temperature had nothing to do with the unseasonably warm spring day and everything to do with the hotshot city slicker who thought he could get under her skin. And if she didn't get some distance, he just might.

A whole month? She'd spent only a few minutes with the potent man and he'd pretty much touched every single female nerve she had. How on earth could she survive a month of Mr. Tall, Dark and Tempting?

The last thing she wanted was to, well…want him. Wasn't he technically the enemy? At least in her world. Sexy, fast with the seductive words and lingering glances…

The thought of this movie, of being thrust into the media, made her stomach churn. And there was no way she could be blindsided by another charmer, who was probably used to women trailing after him, hoping for a sliver of his affection.

She dealt with enough media, being a female jockey and Damon Barrington's daughter to boot. But a movie was a whole new level of limelight she really didn't want to enter into.

And she'd had enough types like her smarmy ex to last several lifetimes.

As Tessa grabbed a bottle of water from the refrigerator, the door behind her opened and closed. She straightened and turned to see Grant leaning against the counter, arms crossed over his wide chest, his eyes on her. Those eyes visually sampled her, and Tessa refused to enjoy the shudder rippling through her.

"Water?" she asked, holding up the bottle.

"No, thanks. What hours do you put into riding?"

Horse talk. Much safer ground.

Uncapping the bottle, she took a hefty drink. "Waking hours. But right now, I also tend each horse and clean stalls, until Dad hires a new groom. There's always work to be done. I'm at the stables from morning till night. And on the nights I can't sleep, I come over and ride to relax. I've been known to sleep in the barn."

"You live close, then?" he asked.

Tessa nodded. "My property is the next one over, but it's not near as big a spread as this. All of my horses are here."

"Your dad mentioned your sister lives in a guesthouse."

"Cassie and her baby live here." Tessa rested her elbows on the granite island and squeezed her bottle. "She moved back onto the estate when her jerk husband left her, right after Emily was born."

A muscle in Grant's jaw ticked. "Not much of a man, leaving his wife and baby."

Tessa warmed at his matter-of-fact statement. "On that we can agree. And since her ex was the previous groom, we obviously need a new one."

"A female trainer and jockey," Grant murmured. He held her gaze and smiled. "Isn't that very unusual?"

This was a common question from people outside the racing world. "Yes, but we're both good at what we do. There was a time not too long ago when women weren't allowed to be trainers. My dad used to tell stories about how he'd sneak women into the stables early in the mornings, to help train his stock. He swore they were better for a horse's demeanor, because men tend to be harsher, more competitive."

Grant shifted his weight, leaning against the counter as if

processing all she threw at him. "I read that in his bio. That's quite intriguing, actually."

Intriguing? Tessa didn't want him using that word when he was staring at her with such intensity. Did the man ever blink? Or just mesmerize women with that heavy-lidded gaze?

"Cassie is the best trainer I've ever seen," she told him, circling the conversation back to the reason for this little meeting.

"She's older than you, right?" Grant asked.

"By three years."

"She never had the itch to become a jockey?"

Tessa nearly laughed. Cassie was so gentle, so nurturing. She was much better left in the stables, where she could tend to the horses...many of which needed her gentle touch.

"No. She's more a behind-the-scenes type." Tessa took another drink of her water before replacing the cap. "My dad taught us every aspect of the racing industry. I was practically raised in a saddle. Cassie is more delicate. She's perfect as a trainer. Me, on the other hand, I love the fast-paced adrenaline rush of the race."

Grant smirked as he moved closer, stopping and resting his elbow on the counter beside her. "I wouldn't think such a perfectionist, and someone who holds on to their control the way you do, would be such a fanatic about adrenaline rushes."

Tessa turned her head, cursing herself when those dark eyes shot a shiver of arousal through her. "I have several layers, Slick. Don't try to uncover too many at once."

A corner of his mouth lifted, and she found herself staring at his dark stubble. How would that feel beneath her hand... her lips? Why was she letting him get to her? There were so many things she needed to focus on right now, and the feel of a man's facial hair was nowhere on her list. Yet her skin still tingled, and she couldn't help but wonder what would happen if she actually touched that dark stubble.

"I'd like to uncover as many layers as possible," he murmured.

How did this man come onto the scene, literally hours ago, and already have such power over her heart rate?

"You sound hesitant," she told him, holding his stare, refusing to be intimidated. "Not that I'm complaining."

Grant laughed. "There's a small annoyance in my contract."

Tessa stood straighter, bothered that even with him leaning on the counter, she was shorter than him. Being petite was an advantage and requirement for a jockey, but right now she wished for a few more inches.

"Something in your contract?" she asked with a grin. "And what does it say? No flirting or charming while filming?"

"More like no seducing while filming," he corrected, a hint of amusement lacing his voice.

Tessa swallowed hard. She was quickly drowning in deep waters. "Seducing? Is that what you are trying to do?"

His eyes dropped to her mouth, then moved back up to meet her gaze. "Oh, if I was seducing you, you'd know. Flirting is harmless, isn't it?"

Was it? She wasn't so sure anything about Grant Carter was harmless. Not his dark eyes, not his naughty grin and certainly not his smooth words, which washed over her, through her, like a breeze on a warm summer day.

In no time he had sent shivers down her spine, made her smile, attempted a rescue and had her questioning why she was hanging on to her virginity. None of that had happened with the last guy she'd dated and considered marrying.

The timing couldn't be worse. Between the film and the upcoming races, she just didn't have time to wonder why Fate had decided to dangle this all too alluring man in front of her.

And why she had to be so attracted to someone with the exact qualities of the jerk she'd just dumped a few months ago? Had she not learned her lesson when he'd tried to exploit her and when that failed, he'd tried to ruin her career, just so she'd be forced to marry him and move to some overpopulated, confining city? Had he honestly thought she'd hand over money for him to get his newfound business off the ground?

If he had truly loved her, respected her career, she would've gladly supported him in any way. But he'd laid down ultimatums, and in the end Tessa had pointed him back to that city he loved so much.

She thanked God every day that she hadn't tumbled into bed with him. She'd assumed they were getting married, and she'd wanted to make their honeymoon special.

Thankfully, she'd made a promise to her mother to wait for real love and marriage.

"Do we need to add that to the spreadsheet?" he asked.

She shook off thoughts of her ex and met Grant's hard stare. "What's that?"

That wicked grin of his widened, deepening his dimples. "Flirting. Is that something you need to figure in, or should I add that into my two-hour time slot? I am a master at multitasking, you know."

"So you've mentioned before."

"I think I'll keep my two hours to work, and throw in a little flirting when you least expect it."

Had the heat kicked on in here? Tessa resisted the urge to undo a button on her shirt for some extra air. She also refused to rub her damp palms along her pants. She would not give Grant the satisfaction of knowing he was getting to her.

"So I need to be ready for you at any time?" she asked, forcing her eyes to remain locked on his.

"Ready? You could never be ready, Country."

She studied his tanned face, his chocolate eyes beneath thick brows. "Why is it I have a feeling you have a problem with controlling your hormones?"

"Oh, I can control them," he assured her. "Because if I couldn't, I would've already kissed you."

That simple declaration weakened her knees. She leaned back against the counter and took a deep breath. If she couldn't avoid the roller coaster of emotions, she may as well enjoy the ride.

"Then it's a good thing you have control, because kissing me would be a mistake."

Yeah, that was a gauntlet she knew he'd pick up. Why was she flirting, purposely provoking him? She did not have time for this. Beyond that, she didn't like him—or didn't want to like him—and she sure as hell didn't like this whole movie idea. But there was nothing she could do about it at this point.

Damn, she was attracted, and she hated every blasted nerve that sizzled for him.

"That so?" Holding that mesmerizing smile, he inched closer and whispered, "And why would kissing be a mistake?"

"For one thing, I'm not comfortable with this movie."

His lips turned up slightly. "Anything else?"

"I don't have time. In case you're unaware of how the season works, I'm gearing up for the first of many races, which I hope will lead me down the path to the coveted Triple Crown."

"I don't think a kiss would throw off your rigorous routine." He laughed, still continuing to invade her personal space. "And I'm more than aware of how the season works. I did thorough research for this film."

"You don't seem like the type of guy who would do thorough research on anything," she retorted. "You seem too laid-back."

In a flash, his hands came up, framed her face, and he had her all but bent over onto the island. The hard planes of his body molded against hers. Sweat trickled between her shoulder blades as she waited to see what he would do. And that wait only made her more aware of just how sexy, how powerful this man was. Her breath caught in her throat as his face hovered mere inches from hers.

"Baby, I'm thorough…with everything."

His mouth slid over hers, and Tessa was glad she was wedged between his hard body and the counter, or she would've withered to the floor. The full-on attack sent shivers through her entire being, affecting areas never touched.

And there it was. That click. A click of something so perfect sliding into place, but Tessa couldn't focus on it because Grant was consuming every bit of her thoughts, her body, with one single kiss.

He coaxed her lips apart with his tongue, leaving her no choice but to accept him. How could a kiss be felt in your entire body? Such a simple act sent tremors racing one after the other through her.

A slight groan escaped her as Tessa gripped his thick biceps.

Before she could revel in the sensations sweeping through her overheated body, Grant lifted his head, met her gaze and smiled.

"Sorry. Guess I can't control my hormones."

"What about that clause?" she asked, cursing her breathless tone.

That sultry grin spread across his face. "I didn't come close to violating the clause."

Grant walked out the back door, and it took Tessa a moment to realize that she still had over an hour left in the time she'd allotted for him. And she hadn't given him his copy of the spreadsheet.

With a sigh, she sank onto the nearest bar stool and came to a conclusion. Grant Carter had caught her off guard, and he'd been right. She would never be ready for him.

Four

Grant glanced at the spreadsheet on the kitchen counter in the guest cottage he was staying in. Although "cottage" was a loose term for the two thousand square foot home, complete with patio overlooking the stables and a massive walk-in shower in the master suite.

As he raked his eyes over the colorful paper, he took another sip of the strong coffee he'd just made. Little Miss Country Organizer would be pissed. He was already five minutes late…which may or may not have been on purpose.

Of course, she'd given him the spreadsheet a day late, so it wasn't as if she had a leg to stand on in her defense.

Yesterday, after he'd lost control and kissed her, he'd walked around on his own, and by the time he returned to his guest cottage, she'd taped the schedule to the front door.

But in defense of his tardiness today, he'd had an early-morning call from Bronson Dane regarding a hiccup in the crew's plans for arrival, and he'd had to deal with that. Grant took another sip of the coffee and placed the half-full cup back on the counter. No time to finish it, and he had a feeling Tessa wouldn't care about his excuse for being late.

Why did he feel as if he was heading to the principal's office? She was a grown woman, she had no control over him and he wasn't going to get suspended. So why get all wrapped up in the details of a color-coded piece of paper?

Grabbing the house key and shoving it into his jean's pocket, Grant headed out the door and made his way toward the massive two-story stables. The stone building, with its dark wood trim and weathered wooden doors, would make an impressive backdrop for many scenes. It suggested power and wealth, much like the great Barrington patriarch himself.

When Grant stepped over the threshold, he saw Tessa heading toward the opening of the stables atop a Thoroughbred. Without a word, he stood still and admired the scene, both as a producer and as a man.

She had her dark red hair pulled in that low ponytail again. The crimson strands slid back and forth as her body shifted in the saddle. Her simple white shirt was tucked into jeans that looked perfectly worn in all the right spots. Grant's palms literally ached to feel those slim hips beneath them. For someone so petite and delicate looking, she had curves that would make any man drop to his knees and beg for anything and everything she was willing to give.

"Are you just going to stand there or are you coming in?" she asked without turning around.

He couldn't help but smile. "I'm actually observing right now."

Throwing a glance over her shoulder, Tessa quirked a brow. "Observing the barn structure or my rear end?"

Unable to stop himself, Grant laughed. "I was taking in all the structures."

"Are you going to make an excuse as to why you're late?"

Grant shrugged as he moved along the side of the aisle and closed the gap between them. "Do you care about an excuse?"

"No."

"Then I won't offer one."

"Perfect." Taking the lead line, she moved the Thoroughbred toward the open door to the riding ring. "I assumed you weren't coming, and I was going to take Romeo out for a run. But if you want to talk, I'll put him up."

Grant didn't want to talk, didn't want to ask questions. He found himself wanting to watch her work, watch how she moved so gracefully and efficiently. The woman had a rare talent, and she was so damn beautiful. Stunning women were everywhere in L.A., but the majority in the circles he ran in were surgically enhanced. None had that porcelain skin, deep blue eyes, a cute little dimple and dark red hair. None of them wore cowboy boots with body-hugging jeans and Western shirts. And none challenged him the way Tessa did.

For once in his life, he was the pursuer.

"I'm ready to work if you are," he told her.

She turned the beautiful horse around, dismounted and led him back to his stall.

After her saddle was back on the wall, she took a brush and started grooming the animal in large, circular strokes. "Romeo is going to learn to race. His father was a winner, and I can't wait to see him fly."

There was love in her tone, Grant noted. "How long will he train before he can race?"

"Cassie'll have him ready to go next year. He's not quite there yet."

With ease and care, she moved around to the other side and repeated her motions. Her delicate hands were so gentle, and if he'd stop fantasizing about those hands on him, Grant might actually concentrate on the fact he was here to do a job.

The world of racing and horses was certainly glamorous to some, but not to him. Nothing about this sport appealed to him…except the sexy jockey in front of him.

If he didn't start compartmentalizing soon, Tessa would suck him under, and he honestly didn't think he was strong enough to climb back out.

"Do you have a favorite track?" he asked.

Her eyes met his over the back of the horse. With a wide grin she replied, "Yeah, the one where I win."

Grant stepped closer, but still remained outside the stall. "How old were you when you started racing?"

"Officially? Eighteen. But I've lived and breathed horses my entire life." With precise motions she swept the brush over the horse's side and toward its flank. "I didn't play sports, didn't even go to my prom. I much preferred to spend my time right here."

Hooking his thumbs through his belt loops, Grant shifted his stance. "I imagine there's not a place on this farm you haven't ridden."

"You'd be right. If I'm not training, I'm riding for fun."

Grant smiled. "Care to show me around?"

"I'd love to, but since you were late, your time is less now, so we won't be able to go over as much of the estate."

"When I got here you weren't ready, either."

"Because I thought you were a no-show."

He stepped even closer, still watching her over the side of the horse. "Not all of us can live by a schedule."

Tessa stared for a moment, then turned and put the brush away. Grant had a feeling he wasn't scoring any points with her, but it was fun to get under her skin, and especially fun when she had no comeback.

"Follow me," she told him as she stepped from the stall and headed toward the front of the stable.

Grant turned and gladly followed those swaying hips. "Which horses are we taking out?" he asked, dreading her response, but refusing to succumb to fear and let his vulnerabilities show.

"No horses," she called over her shoulder.

Grant released a deep breath. He couldn't let the fear cripple him, but he was relieved they were leaving the horses in the barn. He followed her into another large, two-story barn on the property and smiled.

"A four-wheeler?" he asked.

"Stick with me, Slick. I'll show you all the cool country toys."

Oh, the possibilities of comebacks with that statement. But Grant knew it was probably best to keep his mouth shut.

Tessa threw her leg around the seat and straddled the device, then sent him a saucy look. Damn woman. She was teasing him on purpose, and he was a sucker, falling for her antics.

Maybe separate horses would've been safer.

"You don't have a problem with me driving, do you?" she asked with a grin.

Mercy. With her legs stretched wide over the seat, her body leaning forward to grip the handles, Grant knew he needed to take control, and fast, before this vixen completely made a fool out of him. She was mocking him, taking his attraction and blatantly throwing it back in his face.

And he deserved it. But two could play at this game.

Grant slid on behind her, making sure to tuck in real tight from torso to hips, gripping her thighs with his own. His hands slid around her tiny waist and his mouth came in close to her ear. "I don't mind this one bit," he whispered, pleased when she trembled.

Tessa turned her head slightly, enough to meet his gaze, her lips nearly brushing his. "Don't make this weird, Slick."

Grant flattened his palms on her taut stomach. "*Weird* was not the word I was thinking."

She fired up the four-wheeler, turned her attention toward the opening of the barn and took off. Grant literally had to hold on to her because the force with which she exited nearly threw him off the back...which was probably what she wanted.

Oh, this little excursion was going to be fun.

Did he have to hold on so damn tight? He was practically wrapped around her, and instead of feeling trapped or confined, Tessa felt...aroused and anxious.

This man kept her on her toes, and she never knew what he'd say or do next. But she did know one thing: she refused to fall for charms or let her hormones control her. After all, what did her hormones know? She'd never fully used them before.

Another city boy who exuded power and intensity would not deter her from what mattered most—winning the upcoming races and making sure Slick didn't get any ideas about exploiting her family or spreading rumors. Nothing else mattered.

And she had to keep telling herself that, considering the way his hard chest pressed against her back, those strong thighs fit perfectly down the length of hers, and his size made her feel so delicate and protected. She didn't want to feel any of those things. Tessa was quite happy with the way life was right now, before Grant had stepped into her stable with those heavy-lidded eyes and that day-old stubble that she knew would tickle her palm.

As she headed out beyond the buildings and guesthouses, she frowned at her sister's cottage and the empty parking space in front. Cassie had texted earlier to say Emily was running a fever and she was running her to the urgent care facility. Hopefully, it was nothing serious.

Cassie had a full plate, being the trainer for Stony Ridge and now a single mother. All the more reason they needed to hire a new groom. The timing couldn't be worse for being one man short. They'd tried a replacement after Cassie's ex left, but that groom had ended up moving out of state, so here they were, waiting on their dad to find another.

Tessa sped up, moving down the edge of the property line toward the most beautiful place on the estate. She knew Grant would love it, and she had no doubt at least one part of the film would be shot at this location. So many memories were held here, and she figured he'd want to know the special history of her parents.

Even though her mom had been gone for a while, Tessa felt every day the indescribable void she'd left. There was always an ache, an emptiness in her chest that had settled deep when Rose had passed. Nothing and no one could ever fill that gaping hole.

She and her mother had shared so much. Rose had always stressed the importance of not giving away love or your body to just anyone. Both were too precious to throw around.

Tessa had always promised her mom she'd wait for the right man. He just hadn't come along yet.

She highly doubted the man molded to her back was "the

one," but he certainly was more tempting than any other guy she'd ever encountered.

Tessa cruised over the rise and came to a stop so Grant could take in the view.

"Oh...that's...wow. Tessa, that's beautiful."

Up ahead lay a valley with a large pond surrounded by evergreens. The water always seemed so vibrant and glistening. A part of her was thrilled that his reaction was all she'd hoped.

"I always ride out here to relax," she told him. "It's so peaceful."

Turning slightly to see his face, she watched as his eyes roamed over the land, as if he'd never seen a more beautiful sight. She wanted to study him, memorize everything about him, but what would be the point? He wasn't staying, and even if he were, she didn't have time for a relationship, didn't want a relationship and certainly didn't intend to start one.

They'd technically just met, so all either of them was feeling was pure lust. Lust would get her nowhere but on a road to heartache. She was totally out of her element here.

Added to that, she highly doubted she was Grant's type. He probably wasn't too keen on virgins. Kissing was her limit until she found someone she truly felt a deep connection with, and if Grant ever knew that... Well, he would never know that, because this whole train of thought was coming to a crashing halt.

Seriously, this whole string of ideas only led down a path to a dead end.

"Want me to take you down there?" she offered.

"Please."

She revved up the four-wheeler and took off down the slight slope toward the pond. Once at the water's edge, they couldn't be seen from the main house in the distance.

Grant slid off the seat first and offered a hand to help her. As much as she wanted to bat it away, she accepted it. Hey, if a sexy man was going to play gentleman, she was going to take full advantage of the situation.

He dropped her hand once she was on her feet, and Tessa smiled as his eyes roamed over the wide pond.

"My father used to bring my mother out here for picnics," she related. "I remember her telling me and Cassie about them."

Tessa glanced toward the water and sighed. "I never got tired of hearing about their romance. I think it's important for children to see their parents in love, to know what they should look forward to, and not settle for anything less."

Grant turned his attention to Tessa. The ends of her ponytail danced in the breeze, her eyes were focused off in the distance and her arms were crossed over her chest. He knew she was trying to visualize the moment her mother had told her about, knew Tessa was more than likely a romantic at heart.

"And is that why you're single?" he asked. "You're not going to settle?"

Glancing over to him, Tessa quirked a brow. "No, I'm not. I shouldn't have to. I'm not looking to marry right now, anyway. I'm a little busy. What about you, Slick?"

Grant laughed. "I'd love to settle down. My parents aren't much different from yours. And I agree it's important for parents to show their love. I plan on having kids and I want them to see how much I love their mother."

Tessa's eyes widened, her mouth dropped.

"What?" he asked, stepping closer so that he could see the navy specks in her eyes. "Didn't expect me to have goals in the marriage department?"

"Actually, no, I didn't." She stared at him for another moment before turning back to look at the lake. "I ride Oliver when I need to get away. I get on him and he just automatically comes down here. Recently..."

She shook her head, and Grant waited for her to continue, but she didn't. He didn't like the sadness that slid over her face as she gazed at the water.

"The racing getting stressful?"

"No more than usual. But it's something I love, so the stress is mostly self-induced."

Tessa eased down onto the ground, pulled her knees up and wrapped her arms around them. "Go ahead and have a seat, Slick. Unless you're afraid you'll get a grass stain on your new designer jeans."

He didn't tell her his jeans weren't designer or new, but he did plop right down next to her, a little closer than she was probably comfortable with. But she was trying to get under his skin, so he damn well would get beneath hers.

A smile spread across her face. "Spend much time in the country?" she asked.

He'd grown up in a modest home surrounded by fields and wildflowers in the heart of Kentucky, but she didn't need to know that. She already had an opinion of him, and he'd break it down by his actions, not his words.

"Enough," Grant told her. "Much more peaceful than the city. But there's a reason for both, and some people just aren't cut out for the other."

"What about you?" she asked. "You're all city boy. Are you going to be able to handle the next few weeks here with me?"

Unable to resist her jab, Grant reached up, slid a stray strand of her hair behind her ear and allowed his hand to gently roam back down her cheek in a featherlight touch. She trembled beneath his fingertips.

"I think I can handle it," he whispered, purposely staring at her mouth, waiting for that dimple to make another appearance.

Her eyes widened before she turned back to the pond. She might be all tough exterior, but Grant had a feeling the lovely, intriguing Tessa Barrington had layers upon layers to her complexity. He wanted to peel each one away and find what she truly had hidden inside.

"Do you have other special areas on the property?" he asked, circling back to the fact he was indeed here to do a job, and not seduce.

"All of the estate is beautiful," she told him. "There's a wooded spot on the edge of the property that has this old cabin. It was the first home on this land, built long before my dad lived here. He never tore it down, and Cassie and I used to play there when we were kids. It's also where my dad proposed to my mom."

"Show it to me."

Grant hopped to his feet and extended his hand to help Tessa up. She resisted for all of a second before slipping her delicate hand into his. Before she could fully catch her balance, Grant tugged her against his chest, causing her to land right where he wanted her.

What the hell was he doing? He knew better than to play games like this, but damned if his hormones weren't trying to take over. That whole chat he'd had with himself about compartmentalizing had gone straight to hell.

But each time he was with Tessa something came over him, something he couldn't explain, and he was drowning in confusion and...her.

Tessa's breath caught, and those bright blue eyes held his. With her body molded against his, Grant had no clue what to do now. Well, he knew, but he was supposed to be a professional and not get tangled up in this world on a personal level. Mentally and emotionally, he couldn't afford to.

Besides, the last thing he needed was to get kicked off the set before filming even started.

Yet, as usual, lust controlled his actions.

"What about you, Tessa?" he asked, eyeing her lips. "Are you all country girl or could you handle the big city?"

Something cold flashed through her eyes before she pulled away and glanced at her watch. "You only have twenty minutes left, Slick. Better go see that cabin."

Whatever trigger he'd just hit on, Grant had a feeling he would annoy her even more before he figured out what he'd said that upset her. Because he knew their body contact hadn't gotten her so angry. No, he'd seen desire in her eyes, maybe even confusion—a glimpse of an internal battle, but not anger.

He followed her back to the four-wheeler and climbed on behind her. This time Grant held on to the back rack instead of Tessa. He was treading on thin ice as it was.

Five

She rode effortlessly, with captivating beauty. The way her body controlled the stallion, the strength she possessed, the determination on her flushed face… Grant could watch Tessa Barrington for hours, and was well on his way to doing just that.

Tessa turned the corner and headed toward him. With all the laps she'd made, there was no way she could've missed him standing here. They'd already spent the past two days together, and he had no time scheduled with her today. But that didn't stop him from wanting to see her, to learn more. And this sexual pull was dragging him into this damn world he'd worked so hard to put behind him.

"She's amazing, isn't she?"

Grant turned at the sound of a voice and found himself looking into another set of bright blue eyes. "Yes, she is. You must be Cassie." He glanced to the baby asleep on her shoulder. "And who is this?"

Cassie's smile widened. "This is Emily."

Grant took in the pale blond curls peeking beneath a bright green hat, and wondered if the little girl had those Barrington blue eyes.

"How old is she?"

"Just turned one last month."

Cassie turned to watch Tessa round another curve, and Grant studied the woman's profile. She was beautiful just like her sister, with her blue eyes and bright red hair. But there was something more fragile, almost sad about Cassie. He'd learned enough about this family to know Cassie's ex used to work in the stables but had left shortly after the baby was born. Anger bubbled within Grant at the thought of a deadbeat dad ignoring his kid.

But as he watched her, Grant realized there was another layer of emotions in Cassie's eyes as she focused on her sister. Concern.

"You worry about her," he said, not bothering to ask.

"I do." Cassie shifted the sleeping toddler to her other shoulder. "She pushes too hard at times. Strange coming from me, since I'm her trainer. We already practiced today, but she and Don Pedro are made for each other. They're happiest in the ring. Of course, that passion is what makes winners, but her biggest competitor is herself."

Grant could see that. In the few days he'd been here he'd seen Tessa out of the stables only during their "allotted" times.

"Does she do anything for fun?" he asked.

"You're looking at it. She lives for this."

On one hand Grant admired Tessa's drive and determination. He had more drive for career than anything himself. But on the other hand he found it sad that this was her whole life.

And from a purely personal level, the thought of her spending more time on her horse than off flat out terrified him.

Her career stirred up so many haunting emotions. Not that they weren't always there, but having the lifestyle thrust in his face all day only made the memories that much more hellish.

Yet the attraction was something he hadn't planned on… and couldn't ignore.

"She doesn't date?" he found himself asking before he could keep his mouth shut.

Cassie spared him a glance. "She just got out of a relationship, which is another reason she's pushing herself even more."

Bad breakup? While Cassie didn't say it, the message was implied. And there was a story there. Grant never turned away an intriguing story.…

"So when will the rest of your crew arrive?" Cassie asked.

"A few weeks." He caught her smile and laughed. "You seem excited about this."

She shrugged her free shoulder. "What's not to be excited about? My father is an amazing man, a prestigious horse owner and winner. A movie about his life will be awesome."

"You forget you and Tessa are a huge part of his success, and in continuing the Barrington tradition." Grant glanced at the track as Tessa came flying by again. "I don't think your sister feels the same."

Cassie nodded. "Tessa and I don't always agree on things. Besides, she has her reasons for not being so thrilled about this film."

"And you aren't going to share those reasons, are you?"

Cassie laughed. "Nope."

Emily started to stir on her shoulder, and Cassie patted her back. "I better head back inside and get dinner started. It was nice to officially meet you, Grant."

"I'm sure you'll be seeing more of me."

She walked away, and Grant turned back to watch Tessa, but she was out of sight. He took his boot down from the rung of the fence and headed into the stable.

He found her in the last stall, pulling the saddle off Don Pedro's back and hanging it up. At some point he'd quiz her on the reason behind the horse's name, though he had a pretty good idea.

He knew enough Shakespeare to know Don Pedro was a prince in *Much Ado About Nothing,* and her recreational stallion's name, Oliver, stemmed from the villain, who later repented, in *As You Like It.*

Apparently Miss Barrington had a romantic streak. So why was she fighting this obvious attraction?

Straw shuffled beneath his boots as he made his way closer. Oliver shifted in his stall and Grant froze for a half second before he forced himself to keep walking.

He would not revisit that time in his life. Fear was only a state of mind, and he'd be damned if he'd let it overtake him.

"I just met your sister," he said as he moved in closer.

Tessa didn't stop her duties, didn't even spare him a glance as she picked up a brush and started her routine circular brushing.

"Emily is adorable, but she slept through our meeting." Grant tucked his hands into his pockets. "Cassie seems pretty excited about the film."

Maybe that comment warranted a grunt, but he wasn't sure the noise was directed at him or the fact that Tessa was reaching up to brush the horse's back.

"It's a beautiful day—"

"What are you doing here?" she asked, tossing the brush into the tack box with so much effort it bounced right back out.

Grant paused. "Working."

"No, here in the stable. Right now. What do you want?"

Her eyes were practically shooting daggers. Okay, something had pissed her off and he had a sinking feeling that "something" was him. How did women get so fired up, when a man was still left clueless?

"I was watching you train," he told her honestly. "I'm just amazed at your talent."

Tessa moved around Don Pedro, coming to stand in front of Grant. Propping her hands on her hips pulled her shirt tighter across her chest, and he had to really concentrate to keep his eyes level with hers and not on those tiny strained buttons.

"Don't you have a film to be working on instead of ogling my sister?"

For a second he was shocked, then shock quickly turned to a warmth spreading through his body. She was jealous. Best not to laugh or even crack a smile. But damn, he liked knowing he'd sparked some emotion from her other than disdain for his occupation.

He could have fun with this morsel of information, but he was never one to play games...especially with women. He may have dated his fair share of ladies over the years, but they always knew where he stood with their relationship. Besides, he was ready to start settling down, making a home and a family, after this film wrapped up.

For now, he wanted to get to know Tessa on a personal, intimate level, away from her racing lifestyle. He had interest in the woman, not the career.

"Actually, I was watching you *and* working." He crossed his arms and met her icy stare. "We'll be shooting here, and I was watching as the sun moved in the sky, to see where it is at certain times and how the shadows fall across the track. Your sister came up to me to introduce herself, since we hadn't been formally introduced yet."

A bit of heat left Tessa's expression, but Grant couldn't resist. He stepped closer and bent down until her eyes widened and her warm breath feathered across his face.

"And if you're not interested in me, Country, then it wouldn't matter if I was flirting with your sister or not, now would it?"

He turned, walked out of the barn and kept going until he was back in his guest cottage. Damn woman could make a man forget everything but the thought of kissing her senseless and finding a better use for that smart mouth.

Since she was raised a well-mannered lady, for the most part, Tessa found herself standing outside Grant's cottage. The sun had long since set, and she'd been in the stable, talking to herself and trying to find a way out of groveling and apologizing.

There was no way out.

After a gentle tap of her knuckles on the mission-style door, Tessa stepped back and waited. If he didn't hear her knock, she'd leave. At least she could say she'd tried.

A large part of her hoped he didn't hear.

But a second later the door was flung open and Grant stood there, wearing only a towel, chest hair and water droplets.

"Tessa." He hooked an arm on the half door, causing his muscles to flex and her mouth to go desert dry. "What are you doing here?"

"I...I came to apologize." She tried to focus on his face, but dear mercy, all those bare muscles were distracting her. "Um...for earlier."

Grant smiled and opened the door wider. "Come on in."

"Are you going to put clothes on?"

Laughing, he stepped back to let her pass. "You want me to?"

She came face-to-face with him and nodded. "I think it's best."

He closed the door behind her and went toward one of the two bedrooms. Tessa hadn't been in this cottage forever, but it had the same layout as her sister's. Open floor plan, with the kitchen and living area in front. Grant had thrown a shirt over the back of the sofa, running shoes sat by the door and the smell of a fresh, masculine shower permeated the air.

Between that clean scent and those muscles he'd had on display, Tessa was having a hard time remembering the reason for her visit.

Grant strolled back into the room, wearing knit shorts and pulling a T-shirt over his head. "Care for a drink?"

"No, thanks." She twisted her hands and remained in the doorway, because if she moved any farther into his temporary home, she feared she'd want to move further into the world she'd sworn off. "I just wanted to apologize for being rude earlier."

"Rude? I didn't think you were rude." He leaned a hip on the edge of the sofa and crossed his arms over his broad chest. "You were honest. I'm flattered that you were jealous."

Flattered? He might as well pat her on the head like a good little girl and send her off to play with her toys.

"I wasn't jealous." She would go to hell for lying. "I'm just protective of Cassie, and I know your type."

The corners of his mouth threatened to curve into a smile.

If he was mocking her she'd beat him with her whip. No, wait...he'd probably enjoy an aggressive woman.

He'd been so playful when they'd first met, so quick with his wit and his smiles. Her instant attraction had worried her, but now her feelings for him were growing.

Which begged the question, what did Grant like in a woman?

"What is my type, Country?"

"You think your city charm will win you any lady you want," she told him. "Cassie has her hands full. I realize she was introducing herself, but I just didn't want you getting any ideas."

He straightened, then slowly crossed the room until he stood directly in front of her. "Oh, I have ideas. None of them involve Cassie, though."

Tessa tried to ignore the shiver of excitement that crept over her...tried and failed. She didn't want to find him appealing, didn't want to spend any more time with him than necessary. She didn't trust him. He oozed charm, and in her experience, that led to lying and deceit.

Backing up, hoping to make an escape, she reached blindly for the handle on the door. But as she retreated, Grant stepped forward. His fresh-from-the-shower aroma enveloped her, and his damp hair, hanging in a tousled mess over his forehead, practically begged for her to run her fingers through it.

"You could've apologized when you saw me tomorrow," he murmured as he came within an inch of her face. "Why did you need to stop by now?"

Because she was a glutton for punishment. There was no other excuse.

"I wanted to clear the air before I saw you again. I didn't want anything to be uncomfortable."

One hand came up to rest on the door beside her head as a grin spread across his tanned, stubbled face. "I prefer to clear the air, too."

In one swift motion, his head dipped down to hers and his

free hand came up to cup the side of her face. Tessa's back was firmly against the door, and she had nowhere to go...not that she wanted to go anywhere, because Grant's mouth was so gentle, so amazingly perfect. Instead of pushing him away, she kept her arms at her sides and tried to remain in control of her emotions. But she did open her lips at his invitation, She was human and couldn't resist temptation, after all.

Slowly, his tongue danced with hers and chills spread from her head to her toes in a flash. Before she could get too wrapped up in the moment, Grant stepped back. Tessa lifted her eyelids, meeting his dark gaze.

"Since we don't want things to be uncomfortable," he told her, his hand still framing her face, "you should know I plan on doing that again."

Tessa couldn't speak, could barely think. How in the world did she end up with zero control here? She'd just wanted to apologize, and instead she'd gotten the most tender, yet toe-curling kiss of her life, and an amazing view of Grant's bare chest.

"What about—"

"The clause?" he asked, intercepting her thoughts. "Seeing as how you're attracted, too, I don't see why we can't pursue more. Behind closed doors, of course. No one would have to know, Tessa."

"I'm not interested," she told him, lying through her still tingling lips. "Save your attraction for another woman."

Grant dropped his hand. "Then it's my turn to apologize. I assumed by the way you look at me, the way your pulse beats at the base of your neck, the way you catch your breath when I touch you, that you were interested in me, too. And the way you participated in that kiss... But apparently, I was mistaken."

He leaned right next to her ear, so close his lips brushed against her lobe when he whispered, "Or you're lying."

Tessa tugged on the door and moved out of his grasp. "Good night, Grant."

Like the coward she was, she ran away. Nobody made her feel more out of control, more internally restless than this infuriating man.

Surely that didn't mean...

Tessa sighed as she climbed into her Jeep. She had a sinking feeling that Grant Carter was the man her mother had told her about. The man who would come along and make her question how she'd gotten along without him in her life.

The one man she'd been saving herself for.

Six

Tessa slid out of her worn boots and set them beside the back door. Then she hung her heavy cardigan on the peg and moved through her kitchen toward her bedroom. Spring had arrived early, but the nights were still pretty cool, and she wanted to relax in a nice hot bath after her late-night ride. She was a creature of habit, and her raspberry-scented bubble baths were a nightly ritual and the only way she allowed herself to be pampered.

As usual, she hadn't been able to fall asleep. But this time, instead of having horses and racing on her mind, her thoughts had been full of a certain Hollywood producer who had kissed her so gently, yet so thoroughly, she couldn't even remember what kissing another man was like. Not that she'd kissed a slew in her life, but enough to know that Grant Carter knew how to please a woman.

And that was the main thought that had kept her awake. If he could cause so much happiness within her body with just a kiss—and a tender one at that—then what would the man do when he decided to really take charge and not hold back?

Her antique clock in the living room chimed twelve times. Midnight. The same time every night she found herself getting back home from her ride on Oliver. He always stuck his head out of the stall when she returned to the stable late at night. It was almost as if he knew her schedule, knew she'd be back for one last ride to wind down her evening.

Tessa padded into her bedroom, undressing as she went, so

when she made it to the hamper she dumped in all her clothes. When she entered her bathroom, she paused.

Grant Carter was consuming way too much of her time, both in person and in her mind. She plucked the short cotton robe from the back of the bathroom door and went to the old desk in the corner of her bedroom to boot up her laptop.

For a man she'd met just two weeks ago, a man who'd kissed her like no one ever had, she really should learn more about him.

Of course, the internet gave only basics, but that was certainly more information than she had right now. He had a whole file on her life, her sister's and her father's. Grant and his crew knew way more about her childhood and the entire backstory of the Barringtons, so Tessa felt it only fair she level the playing field.

Clicking on a link, she quickly learned that Grant was a twin, but there was no other mention of this sibling.

She glanced at his birth date. A Christmas baby. Tessa's eyes widened as she stared at the screen, inching closer because there was no way she was seeing that number correctly.

He was ten years older than her? As if her virginity, his obvious experience, her country life and his city life weren't enough major blockers between them, he was ten freakin' years older.

With a groan Tessa moved to her bed with the laptop and sagged back against her plush pillows. Grant was out of her league. She could tell by the way he'd kissed her, by how he flirted and his laid-back mannerisms, that he was more experienced with life than she was. But ten years was a hell of a lot of time.

She ventured into the area of pictures. Image after image she clicked through showed a smiling, sometimes heavy-lidded Grant, and in most of the pictures he wasn't alone. Beautiful women were his accessory of choice, apparently. Surprise, surprise.

So, what? Was his kissing her just passing time while he

was here? Did he choose a woman on each set to keep him company? No, he had that clause that prohibited that. But she had a feeling Grant Carter was a rule breaker when it came to getting what he wanted.

Hollywood was a far cry from Dawkins, Virginia, and the fast-paced city life was something she just couldn't—and didn't want to—grasp.

Another man, another city charmer with smooth words, flooded her mind. But he'd had hidden agendas: marrying her for her family name.

The hurt of betrayal still cut deep. Hindsight helped, because she could admit that she'd never loved him…at least not the way she thought she'd love the man she would marry.

Tessa's eyes slid back to the screen, where Grant's dark gaze held hers. Stubble covered his jaw, and she knew from experience how that felt against her palm, her lips.

Now more than ever she was convinced she needed to keep her eye on him. He was a slick one, probably expecting her to turn to putty in his hands. She wouldn't be played, and she wouldn't fall for another man just because of physical attraction. He couldn't be the one for her. Tessa was merely confusing frustration for lust.

She honestly didn't think Grant would do anything underhanded like Aaron had done, but she had to be cautious. No way would she be blindsided again.

But she also had to be honest with herself and admit Grant pulled emotions from her that Aaron hadn't even touched on.

Groaning, she shut off the computer and returned to her spacious adjoining bathroom. Her bubble bath was calling to her. She had to be back in the stables by seven, so didn't have time to waste online…no matter how intriguing the subject.

After several days at the stables, today they were changing up the precious spreadsheet. Grant couldn't wait to spend the majority of the day with Tessa away from Stony Ridge. She was taking him around town to show him various locations, such as the old feed store and the church. Grant was banking on shooting a few scenes in the quaint, historic community.

The script already had several locales specified, but Grant wanted to get a good idea of lighting during different times of day, possible angles, and the atmosphere of each place.

Last night he'd been unable to sleep, so had emailed Bronson and Anthony all the notes he'd taken thus far. The grounds and main house were going to be the primary focus, as well as tracks to showcase the actual racing and practicing.

While drafting his email, he'd seen headlights cut through the darkness. When he'd peered out his window, he'd noted Tessa's Jeep parked next to the stables, and had smiled.

Every part of him had wanted to go to her, had wanted to get her alone in the night. He'd had to conjure up every bit of his strength not to go see her, kiss her and discover just how far they could take this attraction.

But he'd refrained, because he had work to do and only a narrow window of time to get it all done. Besides, he wanted to keep her guessing about his motives, because in all honesty, he had no clue what the hell he was going to do about Tessa. She held too much control over him, and he didn't like it. Never had a woman posed so much of a challenge and appealed to him all at the same time.

There were moments when she seemed so sultry and sassy, and other moments when his words or actions seemed to take her by surprise in almost an innocent way.

Added to that convoluted mess, that damn clause was going to come back and bite him in the butt if he wasn't careful.

Was Tessa Barrington worth all this flirting, seducing and sneaking? Seriously, was he willing to risk this film on a roll in the sack with her?

Hell no. But he hadn't bedded her, and if he did...well, he'd have to make sure no one ever knew.

And bedding her was all he could do. He was already treading a thin line, emotionally, where the beautiful jockey was concerned. Her life revolved around horses, and his...well, it was in the city, far away from the risk of horses and the life he'd once known in a small country house in Kentucky.

Some might say he'd run to one of the biggest cities in America to get away—and they'd be absolutely correct.

Grant left his cottage and made the short walk to the stables. He'd purposely left thirty minutes early to throw Tessa off even more. Damn spreadsheets. He had his lying on the kitchen table, but hadn't looked at it since he got it. He was always allotted the same time bracket each day: two hours after lunch.

Except for today, when his green column was wider and took the slots from nine to three. Six hours, and he was going to make the most of them...both professionally and personally.

Tessa was heading from the stable to her Jeep as Grant neared. Once again she had her hair tied back in that ponytail—he had yet to see it any other way—and she had on a long-sleeved plaid shirt tucked into well-worn jeans and battered knee boots.

She might be prim and proper, but her wardrobe was nothing new. Tessa wasn't a spoiled princess who just looked the part of a jockey. She was all jockey, and her appearance proved it. He'd never seen her fuss with her hair or worry about her appearance. Hell, he'd never seen her with makeup on.

And yet she still stole his breath each time he saw her... which just proved his point of how fine an emotional line he was treading.

"Let's get going, Slick," she said, not missing a step as she got to the Jeep and hopped in.

Grant bit back a smile at her abrupt tone. She was something. Most people, women especially, would be tripping over themselves to please him because of his celebrity status. Yet somehow, with Tessa, he felt as if he had to work to gain approval.

And that was just another layer of her complexity. She couldn't care less about his status, and that suited him just fine. Caused more work to get her attention, but still suited him. At least this way he could keep his feelings separated and not go any deeper beneath Tessa's very arousing surface.

Grant hopped in the passenger's side and barely got his seat belt clicked in place before Tessa was speeding down the driveway.

Her white-knuckle grip on the steering wheel and her clenched jaw were telltale signs she was agitated. And being angry only made her sexier.

"Want to tell me what's wrong?"

She spared him a glance before gripping the wheel even tighter and turning onto the two-lane country road taking them toward town.

"That kiss," she muttered. "It won't happen again."

Um...okay. She'd seemed to be a key player in the exchange the other day, but something had ticked her off, and apparently she'd spent a lot of time thinking about this because she'd worked up a nice case of mad. One step forward, two steps back.

"You didn't enjoy it?" he asked, knowing he was on shaky ground.

"My enjoyment doesn't matter," she countered, eyes focused on the road. "I won't be the one you use to pass the time while you're working here. I'm too busy, and I'm not into flings."

Confused, and working up a good bit of irritation himself, Grant shifted in the seat to look at her fully. "I don't use women to pass the time," he informed her. "I'm attracted to you, and I acted on it. I wasn't in that kiss alone, Tessa."

"You're ten years older than me."

Why did that sound like an accusation?

"And?" he asked.

"I'm...you're..."

She let out an unladylike growl, and Grant again had to bite back a smile. "What does age have to do with attraction, Country?"

"When I started kindergarten you were getting your driver's license!"

This time he did laugh. "I believe we're all grown up now."

"It's just not right. Your life experiences, they're levels above mine, and I won't be played for a fool."

The word *again* hovered in the air, and Grant wanted to know what bastard had left her full of doubts and insecurities. But he refused to let himself cross into anything too personal.

Tessa's shoulders tensed up as silence settled between them. Grant didn't want her angry. He wasn't even sure what had spawned this, but he was here to work and there was usually enough drama on sets. He didn't need this on top of it.

"I read you have a twin," she told him, breaking the silence. "But I never saw anything else."

Tension knotted in his belly. "My family isn't up for discussion."

"Seriously? You know everything about mine and you—"

"Not. Up. For. Discussion."

Tessa shook her head and sighed. "Looks like we're at a stalemate then."

Stalemate? No. He refused to discuss his family—his sister—but he also refused to let this attraction fizzle because of a past nightmare that threatened to consume him at any moment.

"Pull over."

She jerked her gaze to his briefly. "What?"

"Pull over."

Once she'd eased to the side of the road, Grant waited until she'd thrown the Jeep into Park before he reached across the narrow space, grabbed her shoulders and pulled her to meet him in the middle.

A second later his mouth was on hers, and she all but melted. Grant indulged in the strength of the kiss for long moments before he let her go.

"Don't throw stumbling blocks at me, Country. I'll jump them," he told her. "Don't lump me with whatever jerk broke your heart. And do not downgrade yourself by thinking I'm using you simply to pass the time."

She lowered her lids and sighed. She was exhausted. Physically and emotionally. No wonder Cassie was worried. Guilt tugged at Grant's heart. Damn it. His heart had no place in this.

She didn't want this movie made, didn't want him here and was fighting this attraction. He wanted the movie and he wanted Tessa.

Grant hated to tell her, but she was fighting a losing battle.

"What's really bothering you?" he asked. "I realize you're uncomfortable with...whatever we're doing, but that wouldn't have you this angry."

When she met his eyes, she shook her head. "I'm not sure. It may be nothing, but I'm just so paranoid lately."

"Tell me what it is, and I can help you decide if it's nothing. That way you won't drive yourself insane with your internal battle."

"Too late," she said with a smile. "My dad hired this new groom a couple days ago. We needed to fill the slot, but this guy...I can't put my finger on it. He almost looks familiar. It's his eyes, but I can't place him. He's really quiet and keeps to himself."

Squeezing her shoulder in reassurance, Grant said, "I fail to see an issue."

"It just seems like every time I turn around he's there. I don't know if he's spying on me or what." She paused, bit her lip and went on. "I know this sounds silly, but what if he's out to harm the horses or sabotage my training? We don't know this man and the timing..."

Grant didn't think this was a big deal, but if Tessa was concerned, he'd definitely look into it. Because she was right, the timing was perfect if someone wanted to ruin her racing season. Better to be safe than sorry. And he sure didn't want anyone to screw up this film before it got started. This was his big shot at producing with the biggest names in the industry. No way in hell was someone going to come in and ruin everything.

"He passed the background check, and from what I can tell he's a very hard worker." Tessa blew out a sigh. "Maybe I'm just paranoid because of Cassie's ex. We thought we could trust him, too."

Grant cupped Tessa's cheek, stroking her soft, delicate skin. "I'll keep an eye out for the guy and do a little digging of my own."

"Really?" she asked, her eyes widening.

"Yeah. I mean, I can't have some random guy wreaking havoc on the set. Best to get to the bottom of this now before my crew arrives."

Tessa nodded and pulled from his grasp. Putting the car back in gear, she drove back out onto the highway.

Grant realized his words may have hurt her, but he wasn't quite ready to admit he was falling for her a little more each day. So there was no way he could tell her that he'd be watching this stranger like a hawk to make sure he wasn't out to take advantage of Tessa or any of the other Barringtons.

He may have told her it was all about the movie, but that was a lie. A good portion of it was because he refused to see Tessa hurt.

Damn. There went that heart of his, trying to get involved. But a little voice whispered that his heart was already involved.

Seven

The feed store showed promise. Maybe not for an entire scene, but most definitely for a backdrop or even during the opening credits.

But the little white church, complete with bell in the steeple and a picturesque cemetery amid a grove of trees, would without a doubt be in at least one pivotal scene.

"This is where my parents were married," Tessa told Grant as she pulled her Jeep to the side of the gravel road. "It's small, but my mom wanted an intimate wedding. She was very private."

"Sounds like someone else I know," Grant said, throwing Tessa a smile before stepping out of the vehicle.

She came around and joined him as he stared up at the simple structure. Tall, narrow stained glass windows adorned either side of the arched double doors. A narrow set of steps led up the embankment toward the church, and Grant could easily see Damon Barrington and his young bride marrying here.

With a director's eye, he could see a smiling, maybe tearful couple exiting the church, while rice sprayed them and lined the path to an awaiting car.

Key to the start of the movie was the whirlwind romance of Tessa's parents. They'd known each other for only six weeks, but according to Damon, he didn't need to know Rose a moment longer to be sure she was the woman he wanted to spend his life with.

Unfortunately, she'd passed all too soon.

Grant's eyes drifted to the cemetery, then back to Tessa, who was also looking toward the graves…and he knew.

"You want to go see her?" he asked softly.

A brief smile spread across Tessa's face as she nodded. "You don't have to come, but I can't drive out here and not go visit."

Without a word, Grant slid his hand into hers and headed up the slope. He let her take the lead and found himself standing in the shade of a large oak tree. The sunny spring day had a bit of chill to the air, so he slipped his arm around Tessa's shoulders.

Or that's what he told himself. Honestly, he wanted her to know she wasn't alone, wanted her to know he was here. He couldn't fathom the heartache of losing his mother. Nearly losing his sister had crushed him, leaving him in a world he couldn't even describe.

"This never seems real," Tessa whispered. "I should be used to not having her, but I always feel… I don't know. I guess I feel something is missing."

Grant stared down at the polished black stone with a single rose emblem beside the name Rose Barrington.

"I can't imagine the void that slips into your life," he told her. "Nothing replaces that."

The hole in his heart for his sister had never been filled… never would be unless he faced her.

"You just learn to cope," Tessa said softly. "There's no other choice."

Grant let the gentle breeze envelop them, allowing the silence to take over. He had no idea what to say, so he said nothing. There was no need to try to fill the moment with useless words.

Tessa bent down, rested her hand over her mother's name and whispered something. He took a step back to allow her more privacy. Other than his sister, his heart had never ached for another woman until now.

Even though her mother had been gone fifteen years, Tessa

was obviously very torn up. More than likely coming here for her was both comforting and crushing. And seeing Tessa so vulnerable wasn't something he'd planned on.

At one time Grant's family had been close, had had a bond that he'd thought nothing could destroy. But he'd murdered that when—

"You okay?"

Grant shook off his thoughts and realized Tessa had come to her feet and was studying him.

"Fine," he told her, refusing to let past demons haunt him. "I wanted to give you some privacy."

She moved on through the cemetery, and he followed, taking in strangers' names and various dates. Some stones were obviously decades old, and others were fairly new.

"This area holds a lot of meaning to your family," he commented as Tessa moved in behind the church.

Large trees shaded the entire area, providing a canopy over the stones. Grant could hardly wait to show Bronson and Anthony the stunning scene.

"I hope to marry here someday," Tessa said. "I still have my mother's wedding dress. It's old, but it's so simple and classy, I want to wear it."

Grant could see her with her auburn hair pulled back in a timeless style, and wearing a vintage gown. She'd make the most alluring of brides.

He wasn't too happy thinking of another man waiting for her at the end of the aisle, but it was hardly his place to worry about such things. After all, in a few months he'd be out of her life.

"I bet you have everything all planned out in a color-coded spreadsheet," he teased as he stopped and turned to look down at her. "I'd guess you have each detail, down to the shade of each flower."

Tessa narrowed her eyes, tilted her chin. "Maybe I do."

Grant laughed. "Nothing to get defensive about, Country. Some people are just wired to never relax."

"I relax," she countered, crossing her arms over her chest. "I'm relaxing right now."

He took a step forward; she took a step back. They danced that way for a few moments until Tessa's back was up against an old weeping willow.

Grant rested an arm on the trunk above her head and smiled when she had to tip her head to look up at him.

"You're relaxed?" he asked. "The only time you've fully relaxed with me was when my mouth was on yours. You never take downtime, and you work yourself too hard."

"That's not true," she said, her words coming out almost a whisper.

Grant took his free hand and traced a line up her neck, right over her pounding pulse. "Really?"

Tessa continued to hold his gaze, never wavering. And he wanted to keep her guessing what he'd do next.

"Then in that case—" he leaned down, coming within a breath of her lips "—have dinner with me."

Her eyes widened. "I don't think that's a good idea, Slick."

"Sure it is." Grant eased back, just enough to give her room to breathe. "You pick the day and time. I can work around you, but I want to have dinner with you, and I want you to take one evening to do absolutely nothing."

"I'm training," she insisted. "I have way too much to do and…"

"And what?"

"And I can't think when I'm with you," she whispered. "I want things, things I shouldn't. I can't get involved, Grant."

"With me or with anybody?" he asked, resisting the urge to kiss her until she lost her train of thought. But she was torn, and emotional right now.

That made two of them.

"Anybody." She placed her hands on his chest and eased him farther away as she straightened from the tree. "Besides, we couldn't be more different, and when the film is over, you'll be gone. I already said I won't be the one to help you pass your time here."

Grant shoved his hands into the pockets of his jacket. "I asked you to dinner. I'm not asking you to have a wild, torrid affair worthy of headlines."

Not yet, anyway. Damn that clause. He had to get creative here, to protect not only his career but his peace of mind. Sex was all he could afford, all that he wanted.

Yeah, keep telling yourself that.

"Dinner only?" she asked.

"Unless you find me irresistible and can't keep your hands off me," he countered, offering her a smile, hoping to lighten the mood. "In that case, we'll have to keep it a secret so I don't get fired."

"I'm pretty sure I can keep my hands off you, as long as you keep those lips off me."

Grant winced. "Ouch, you really know how to drive a hard bargain. But I want you to relax, so I'll keep my lips to myself."

She raised a brow and twisted her lips as she contemplated. "Fine. Dinner. One evening and nothing more."

"What night and time?"

She slid her phone from her pocket and searched. No doubt she had her spreadsheet on that damn thing, too.

"Tomorrow at seven."

"Perfect. Don't wear anything too fancy, and come by my cottage."

"You're not going to pick me up?" she asked.

He shrugged. "I don't want you thinking this is a real date. It's just dinner, remember?"

"As long as you remember, that's what matters."

Grant suddenly felt as if he'd won the lottery. Of course, a miracle had been performed. Tessa had not only agreed to spending downtime with him, she'd agreed to relax.

And he might have to keep his lips off of her, but she'd said absolutely nothing about his hands.

Eight

Don't wear anything too fancy.

Tessa nearly laughed. Oh, she had fancy clothes for uppity events she was forced to attend, but those gowns and dresses lived in the back of her closet, more than likely collecting dust on the shoulder seams that were molded around the hangers.

After working in the stables, helping Cassie clean stalls, Tessa did shower and throw on fresh jeans and a white shirt, rolling up the sleeves. She shoved on her nicer black boots and grabbed a simple green jacket to top off her "not a date" outfit.

The air outside had been a bit chilly, and she knew she'd be cold when she came home later.

She groaned as she grabbed her keys from the peg by the back door. How the hell had she let him talk her into this? Intriguing as he was, she simply couldn't allow herself to sink deeper into his world…a world of class and glamour. A world she'd narrowly escaped a few months ago, along with a man who'd claimed to care for her.

But something about Grant seemed to pull her. He had no qualms about the fact that he found her attractive, but he also seemed genuine, and at the cemetery he'd been supportive and caring.

He also guarded his family…that had been evident when she'd brought up the topic of his twin. And while his instant raised shield intrigued her, leaving her wanting to know more, Tessa could appreciate the value of privacy. Ironic, considering she loathed the idea of this movie, of virtual strangers invading her space, her life.

But Grant seemed to be truly concerned about her feelings. He'd gone out of his way to assure her he'd portray her family in the best light.

He understood family. And, she had to admit, was starting to understand her. He was a Hollywood hotshot, used to elegance and beauty surrounding him. Yet he was blending just fine here in her world.

She didn't want him to have so many layers, because each one threw her off and made her wonder about the possibilities beyond those kisses.

No. Tessa shook off her thoughts as they started down a path she wasn't ready to visit.

If Grant knew she was a virgin, he'd probably give up his quest...or he'd see her as a challenge he needed to meet.

Dinner. He'd only said dinner. Added to that, he'd promised to keep those talented lips to himself. A part of her was disappointed that she wouldn't feel them, but the logical side of her knew this was for the best.

Each kiss made her yearn for...well, everything he was willing to offer, which scared the hell out of her. She'd never desired so much from one man, never considered giving in before.

But somewhere along the way, she felt as if they'd crossed some sort of friendship line. She found him easy to talk to, and as much as she hated to admit it, she wanted to spend more time with him. She really didn't have friends outside her racing world, and Grant was refreshing...kisses and all.

That friendship line they'd crossed held a lot of sexual tension, and Tessa worried one day all that built-up pressure would explode.

Which was why she had to stop this roller coaster of hormones before it got too far out of control. The two different worlds they lived in would never mesh, so why even add something else to her list of worries?

Besides the upcoming season, as if that weren't enough stress, she really wasn't comfortable with the new groom. When she'd mentioned this to her father, he'd waved a hand and told her she was imagining things and was probably just still skeptical because of Cassie's ex.

Yet the stranger had made a point not to get too far away from her and Cassie as they were cleaning stalls earlier. He'd been working hard, but still, Tessa had a gut feeling he'd been trying to listen to their conversation.

But that was a worry for another day. Right now, she had to be on her guard for her dinner "not date."

Tessa hopped in her Jeep and made the short trip back to Stony Ridge Acres, her heart beating a bit faster. Why was she getting so worked up? This was dinner. They had to eat, and were just doing it together.

When she pulled up in front of his cottage, he'd turned on the porch lights. The sun was at the horizon, but in no time it would be dark.

Before she could knock on the door, Grant swung it open and...

Tessa laughed. "What are you wearing?"

Grant wiped his hand on a dishrag and glanced down. "An apron. Don't you wear one when you cook?"

"I thought we were going out," she said, trying her hardest not to stare at him in that ridiculous apron, which looked like a woman wearing a grass skirt and coconut bra.

"I never said that," he countered, taking her hand and pulling her inside. "I said we were going to have dinner together. And I'm cooking. Besides, how can you relax if we're in public?"

Would've been a hell of a lot easier than in the lion's den.

Something tangy permeated the air, and Tessa's gaze drifted toward the open kitchen. "If you're cooking anything associated with that smell, I'm impressed."

Grant headed back to the kitchen, leaving her standing at the door. "It's just barbecue chicken, but it's my mother's sauce recipe. I also have some baked potatoes and salad. Hope all of that is okay."

"My mouth is watering already."

He threw her a glance, his dark eyes traveling down her body. "Mine, too."

Tingles slid all over her, through her, and Tessa had no clue how to reply to that, so she took off her jacket and hung it on the hook beside the door. After dropping her keys in the jacket pocket, she headed to the kitchen.

"Want me to set the table or anything?"

"It's done and so is the food," he said, removing the ridiculous apron.

Apparently, he'd taken full advantage of the very well-stocked cottage.

In no time he'd set the food on the small round table, covered with a simple red cloth. Thankfully, he hadn't gone to the trouble of romantic flowers or a candle. This she could handle. The sultry looks and kisses...well, she could handle them, but they left her confused and, okay, aroused.

Tessa concentrated on her food and prayed he had no clue where her mind had wandered, though she feared her face had turned a lovely shade of red.

Small talk during dinner eased her a bit more, and she nearly laughed at herself. Had she expected him to pounce on her when she arrived?

Tessa picked up her empty plate and stood.

"Leave the dishes," he told her, reaching across to place his hand on her wrist. "I'll get them later."

"I can help with them now. You cooked, so at least I can help clean up."

"You're my guest. I'll get them."

Because she never backed down from a fight, she carried her plate to the sink. "Technically, you're our guest, since you're on Barrington grounds."

She'd just turned on the water and was rinsing the dish

when Grant's hands encircled her waist. His lips caressed her ear.

"You're not relaxing," he whispered, his breath warm on her cheek, her neck, sending shivers down the entire length of her body.

The dish slipped from her wet hands and into the sink. "I'm relaxed." Any more and she'd be a puddle at his feet. "I just wanted to help."

Strong fingers slid beneath the hem of her shirt, gliding over goose bumps.

"And I promised you a night of relaxation."

Did he have to whisper everything in her ear? Could the man back up a tad and let her breathe? Because if he didn't, she feared she'd turn in his arms and take that mouth she'd promised herself never to have again.

"Grant..."

"Tessa," he murmured, his lips barely brushing against her neck.

"You promised not to kiss me."

Soft laughter vibrated against her back from his strong chest. "I'm not kissing you. I'm enjoying how you feel. There's a big difference."

"I can't... We can't..." She couldn't even think with the way his fingertips kept inching around her abdomen. "Wh-what are you doing?"

The bottom button of her shirt came undone, and then the next. Grant splayed his hand across her taut stomach and eased her back against him. "Relaxing with you."

Unable to resist, Tessa allowed her head to fall back against his shoulder, her eyelids closed. Reaching behind her, she raked a hand over his stubbled jaw. The roughness beneath her palm aroused her even more. Grant was all male, all powerful, and yet so tender.

When had a man held her in such a caring, yet passionate way? When had she allowed herself to enjoy the simple pleasures of being wanted?

Tessa wasn't naive. Well, physically she was, but mentally she knew Grant wanted her body. He'd told her as much, and she knew he wasn't asking for her hand in marriage or even a committed relationship. But right now, she could be open to this moment and relish it. They were both still fully clothed, both just enjoying the other.

As his hand inched higher, her shirt traveled up, as well. The edge of his thumb caressed the underside of her silk bra and her nipples quickly responded to the thrilling touch.

Tessa's breath quickened as she turned her mouth to his.

When he didn't respond to her kiss, she pulled back.

"I promised," he murmured.

"I'm letting you out of that verbal contract."

Grant's mouth slammed down onto hers, and Tessa lost track of everything else around her. His touch consumed her, making her ache in a way she'd never thought possible.

Grant's hand slid from beneath her shirt and she turned around, pressing her chest against his as one hand held on to the nape of her neck and the other gripped her bottom through her jeans.

Being wedged between the hard planes of Grant's body and the edge of the counter was a very wonderful place to be.

Tessa wrapped her arms around his neck and opened her mouth wider, silently inviting him to take more.

What was she doing? This wasn't why she'd come here. But now that she was in the moment, she didn't want to stop to rationalize all the reasons this was wrong. Because her tingling lips, aching body and curling toes told her this kiss was very, very right.

Grant's mouth traveled from her lips to her chin and across her jawline. Everywhere he touched, everything he did to her had her wanting more. The man certainly knew exactly how to kiss and where to touch. Everything to pleasure a woman.

And that revelation was the equivalent of throwing cold water on her.

Tessa wriggled her hands between them and eased him

back. Those heavy-lidded eyes landed on hers while his lips, moist and swollen from kissing, begged for more. But she had to stop. This kissing and groping was as far as she'd ever gone…so anything beyond this point would be a disappointment to him.

Tessa met his gaze, refusing to be embarrassed for who she was, the values and promise to her mother she desperately tried to cling to.

When she'd been with Aaron, she'd been tempted, but she'd assumed they would marry, and she'd wanted to wait.

But the level to which Aaron had tempted her didn't come close to the fire of arousal she felt right now with Grant.

Her eyes held his, and as she opened her mouth, he held up a hand.

"Don't say you're sorry," he told her.

Tessa shook her head. "No. I'm not sorry, but we can't do this."

"We can and we were," he countered. "What happened? Something scared you."

Yeah, the big city playboy and the country virgin. Could they be any more clichéd? Why couldn't she be this attracted to someone in her league, or at least in her town?

Moving around him, because she needed distance from his touch, his gaze and his masculine aroma, Tessa walked over to the sliding glass doors and looked out into the darkness. Mostly all she could see was her own reflection, and that was worse than looking at Grant. What she saw was a coward.

"Talk to me," he urged as he stepped closer, but didn't touch. "I'm not going to push you into anything, Tessa. But I want to know what happened."

He stood behind her, their eyes locked in the reflective glass. Tessa sighed and turned, crossing her arms over her chest.

"When I told you I wouldn't be the one to help you pass the time on set, I meant it." He opened his mouth, but she held up a hand. "And I didn't say that initially, or now, to offend you. I said it because you need to know where I stand, where we stand. The differences between us, Grant...they're huge."

"Is this the age thing again?" he asked, stepping forward to brace his hands on her shoulders.

"That's one reason," she confirmed, hating how vulnerable and defensive she felt. "I've never been with a man before, Grant. Ever."

She waited for the words to sink in, waited for him to drop his hands and take a giant step back, as if she'd just drawn a line in the sand and on her side was the plague.

"Tessa, you're not a virgin."

"Yes, I am." She tilted her chin, refusing to be ashamed of what she was just because society felt she should be another way. "I promised my mother I'd wait for love. My body is something I value, Grant. I want my first time to be with someone I truly care about, who I know cares for me.

"I won't lie," she went on, when he remained silent. "I've never before been kissed in a way that made me forget everything and want to give in to all my desires." She took a deep, steadying breath, bringing her hands up to grasp his wrists. "But with you, I want more."

"I value your morals," he answered. "I probably respect you more for them. But you know there's something here. This is more than just lust, more than just sex. You need to let yourself live."

Shifting his hands, causing hers to fall away, he slid the pads of his thumbs over her bottom lip. "A woman with as much passion as you have, as much desire lurking in those eyes, has never fully committed to another man?"

Tessa shook her head, not knowing what to say next. This was the part when a man turned totally weird or ran out the door...not that there had been many men to begin with. Her ex had certainly thought he could persuade her. Now she was even more thankful Aaron hadn't convinced her.

Since Tessa was at Grant's house, she figured this was her cue to go. Shoulders back and pride intact, she stepped around him and went toward the door. She'd barely pulled her jacket from the hook before a hand closed over hers, another at her waist.

"Don't leave."

With his strong body surrounding her, and those two simple words that held so much meaning, Grant engulfed her.

"I can't stay, Grant. I'm not ready to give myself, and even if I did, you'd be disappointed."

"Look at me."

Forgoing the jacket, she dropped her arm and turned. But instead of seeing confusion or disappointment in his eyes, she saw tenderness, plus a heavy dose of desire. And determination.

"First of all, no matter what you did to or with me would ever be disappointing," he told her, framing her face between his hands so she had no choice but to face him head-on. "Second, the fact that you're a virgin doesn't scare me away, if that's what you were waiting on. And if it scared other guys before, then they're jerks and don't deserve you. Whether we sleep together or not is completely your call, Tessa. I enjoy you, I enjoy talking with you, learning from you and, yes, kissing you. But the ball is in your court. If you don't want to take the next step with me, I totally respect your decision. But don't expect me to stop kissing you at every chance I get."

At his warm smile, Tessa found herself grinning. "I wouldn't mind you kissing me whenever you want. I can't promise I'll ever be ready for more with you. Not that I don't want it, I just can't give myself, knowing it would only be a fling."

Grant's lips touched hers briefly before he pulled back and looked into her eyes. "You're the strongest woman I know."

"I'm not feeling strong," she retorted with a laugh. "I'm feeling like I want to forget the fact you're not staying, and throw aside all rationale."

"Country, you know where to find me." He stroked her lips

once more. "But I'm not giving up. You're so passionate and I want to be the one to uncover that hunger you've kept hidden."

Well, that declaration certainly wasn't helping matters. Besides the fact she'd be seeing him every single day, he'd been so understanding, so comfortable with the news that she was a virgin. Which would make him even harder to resist.

But on the flip side, he would try harder, be even more charming and irresistible. Her mother had always told her the right one would accept and understand her values, and try not to push her.

And without hesitation, Grant had accepted her. Which made him all the more tempting, and quite possibly...the one she'd been waiting for?

Nine

How the hell did he cope with this bombshell? He'd never been in this situation before and honestly had no idea how to react, let alone what to say.

Had he said the right thing?

Running a hand down his face, Grant stared out his patio door toward the pasture, where a few horses grazed off in the distance.

For the sake of his career, here he was, in a world he'd sworn off, finding himself drowning in a woman he wanted just sex from, only to find out she was a virgin.

Grant laughed at the irony that was now his life. The damn film hadn't even started yet, and he was sinking deeper and deeper into worlds that threatened to leave him weak and vulnerable. Way to stay in control of the game.

He glanced at his watch, noted it was time to head to the stables, and sighed. No matter his personal feelings—and he couldn't deny there were very personal feelings involved now—he had to remain on task and get the job done. This was still his livelihood, still his reputation on the line if he wanted to move on up in the movie industry.

As he headed out the door, his cell phone rang. After shutting the door behind him, Grant stepped off the narrow porch.

"Hey, Bronson," he said.

"I hope you're sitting down, man. I've got news for you."

Freezing in his tracks, Grant gripped the phone. "Good news or bad news?"

"Beyond good. Marty Russo has been in contact with me and Anthony. He's willing to back your production company if this film takes off like we think it will."

"Are you kidding me?" Grant asked, suddenly seeing his dream spiraling closer toward reality.

On the other end of the connection, Bronson Dane laughed. "Not at all. If this movie is a hit like we all believe it will be, Russo Entertainment wants you to come on board and branch out with your own company."

Grant could hardly believe this. He'd been a director for years, had worked his ass off to get to the point of producing, and now, before his production debut, he might already have a chance at starting his own company?

He'd been fortunate in the past several years to have some major deals, which set his name on the film map. But his own company would take his career to a whole new level.

"Man, that's great," Grant said. "I don't even know what to say."

"You deserve it," Bronson replied. "Marty was going to call, but I wanted to be the one to tell you. I'm sure he'll be calling you later today."

Grant had worked with the man several times. Being the CEO of Russo Entertainment, Marty often had a direct hand in the company's films, and was a very hands-on guy. Grant respected the hell out of him and had every intention of not letting him down.

"Anthony and I are wrapping up at Churchill Downs today. Between there, New York and Maryland, we've covered the main tracks and have some amazing areas for scenes. We should be arriving at the end of next week."

Grant continued walking his path again as he and Bronson discussed the church, cemetery and other local places that had meaningful ties to Damon Barrington's past.

By the time he disconnected the call, he was beaming. The sun had risen, the spring day was beautiful and promised to be warm, and he had the chance of a lifetime right within his reach.

But his smile faded and fear set in when he saw Cassie running alongside the fence and Tessa on a horse, barreling faster than he'd ever seen seen her go.

Fear flooded him, and he had to force himself not to over-react. Another time, another woman flashed in his mind and nausea threatened to overtake him.

Especially when Tessa kept pulling back on the reins and yelling, alarm lacing her voice.

Grant ran to the fence, having no clue how he could help or even what the hell had happened.

The horse seemed to reduce his speed, barely, but then reared up, after which everything seemed to happen in slow motion. Tessa screamed, slicing a new layer of dread straight through Grant. When she fell off the back of the horse, he leaped over the fence, not giving a damn about anything but getting to her.

He crouched down beside her as she was rolling onto her back, gasping—whether in pain or because the wind had been knocked out of her, he didn't know.

"Tessa, honey." He ran his hands gently over her, pray-ing for no broken bones, no broken skin. "Talk to me. Are you hurt?"

She groaned and tried to sit up, but he placed a hand on her shoulder. "Just lie here for a minute," he told her.

"Macduff...where..." Tessa continued to try to catch her breath as she searched the track. "Is he okay?"

Fury bubbled within Grant. Was she seriously more wor-ried about this horse than her own welfare?

Because she wasn't going to relax until she knew about the animal, Grant glanced back and saw Cassie managing just fine, along with the new groom. They'd taken control of the horse and were leading him into the stables.

"He's fine," Grant told her. "Cassie has him."

Tessa's shoulders relaxed into the dirt and her eyes closed

as she exhaled a shallow breath. The color had left her face and her arm was draped across her ribs.

"I need to know what hurts, so I can tell the squad." He pulled out his phone and barely hit the 9 before she put her hand over his.

"No, I'm fine." Her eyes locked on to his. "Don't fuss with calling anyone."

"Like hell I'm not, Tessa."

Bad memories played through his mind like a horror movie...only it had been real life. Internal injuries were by far even more terrifying. He'd done a somewhat good job of keeping these two worlds—caring for Tessa, and her lifestyle—apart. But the two had just collided and blown up in his face.

"You're white as a ghost, Grant. Are you okay?"

He ran a hand down his face and nodded. "I'm fine. But you're going to get checked out. Internal injuries may not make their appearance known until it's too late."

"Grant—"

"You can either ride in an ambulance or I'm taking you, but this is not up for debate."

Tessa flinched at his raised voice.

"Is she okay?" Cassie asked, squatting down next to them.

"She's stubborn," Grant hissed, coming to his feet. "Talk some sense into her while I call for the medics."

While he did so, he at least heard Cassie taking his side. No way in hell would he allow Tessa to ignore what had just happened. And knowing her, she'd probably get right back on the damn horse and go another round.

After his call was placed, he returned to Tessa, who was now sitting up with Cassie's arm supporting her.

"They're on their way," he told them.

"I hate to leave her, but I need to tell Nash she's going to the hospital, and I need to go find Dad."

"Who's Nash?" Grant asked.

"The new groom," Tessa told him. "Go, Cass, I'm fine."

Cassie shot Grant a look, but he nodded, giving her the

silent go-ahead. There was no way he would be leaving Tessa's side.

"I'm sure Dad will be at the hospital as soon as I let him know," Cassie said.

"That's fine. I've got my cell, so he can call me, too."

As soon as the squad arrived and loaded Tessa—carefully, as per Grant's demands—he went to get his rental car to follow. As much as he wanted to ride with her, he needed his vehicle, because when they left, he sure as hell would be the one bringing her back.

"This is all really silly," Tessa complained as Grant eased his car into the drive, passing beneath the arched sign for the estate. "I can stay at my house just fine, Slick."

"We already went over this. You can stay at your house with me or at my house with me. Since you only huffed when I gave you your options, I decided we'd stay here so your dad and sister are closer."

Tessa rolled her eyes as he parked in front of the cottage. "I only live one property over."

He turned, offered her that killer smile complete with dimples and said, "Yes, but there are several acres separating the two. Your father and I agreed this was best."

"My father probably has no clue you have the hots for his daughter, either," she mumbled.

Grant barked a laugh and came around to help her out. She wasn't some invalid. She'd fallen off Macduff because she'd not been paying attention, and the once-abused horse was still skittish.

Cassie had bought the horse from an auction, and they all knew he'd been mistreated. But Cassie was a softy for any animal, especially ones not properly cared for. Tessa was confident she could keep him under control…and she had, until she'd seen Grant walking toward the stables, phone to his ear and wearing the most brilliant smile. He'd stolen her breath, and she'd lost her concentration. Macduff was nervous, anyway, but the accident was totally her fault.

Grant slid his arm around her as she started to climb from the car. "Really, I can walk," she protested. "I won't fall over."

"The doctor said you had a concussion, and you admitted you were dizzy." He tightened his grip. "You're not going down on my watch."

Okay, so a bit of her was thrilled at the fact he wanted to care for her, but she seriously could've taken care of herself. Did he think she was sharing his bed tonight? Surely that wasn't a reason behind his insistence to keep her at his place.

Once inside the cottage, Grant gave her no option but to sit on the sofa with her feet propped up. Her protests were completely ignored as he removed her boots.

"Now, what can I get you to eat? You haven't had dinner."

Tessa hadn't given food a thought. "What do you have? Just something light. I'm still queasy."

"I'm pretty sure there are some cans of soup in the cabinet."

Laying her head against the back of the sofa, she nodded. "That will be fine. Any flavor, I'm not too picky."

Even as tired as she was, she couldn't close her eyes. Watching Grant bustle around the kitchen, getting her dinner ready, really hit her hard. Aaron had never taken this much care of her. He'd never tried to put her needs first. Of course, hindsight was a real eye-opener, because the man had been only out for himself to begin with.

But there was something special about Grant. He obviously loved his family, which was a huge indicator that he was a nurturer. The fact he was so easy to talk to also proved to her that he wasn't the self-centered city slicker she'd first thought him to be.

When he brought her dinner on a tray, Tessa smiled. "You're so good to me, Slick. I could get used to this."

He took a seat on the coffee table across from her and smiled. "I could get used to you lying on my couch watching me."

After taking a few mouthfuls of chicken soup, she glanced back over at him and sighed. His eyelids were heavy, his hair all messed from running his fingers through it. Normally he looked so polished, the picture of perfection. Now he looked... exhausted.

"I'm sorry, Grant."

"What for?"

"This. Being a burden, scaring you."

He blinked and eased forward, cupping her face with one strong, warm hand. "You could never be a burden to me, Tessa. If I didn't want you here I could've taken you to the main house, to Cassie's or back to your own home. I want you here so I can watch over you, and I want you here because something is building between us and I refuse to ignore it."

Inching forward, Grant placed his lips softly on hers. "As for scaring me, if you ever do that again I'm going to hack into your computer and delete all your saved spreadsheets."

Tessa laughed, reaching over to smack his shoulder. "You wouldn't dare."

He eased back with a half grin. "Maybe not, but when you fell...there are no words, but I'll never forget that feeling."

He glanced aside, almost as if he was trying to compose himself. Had he truly been that scared, that worried for her? This wasn't the first time she'd seen the stark fear in his eyes when it came to horses. That first day they'd met he'd acted concerned for her safety.

"Hey," she said, waiting for him to turn back to her. "I've been riding since I got out of diapers, Slick. That wasn't my first fall and it won't be my last. Yes, it sucks, but sometimes it just happens."

Raking a hand down his face, Grant sighed and came to his feet. "Why don't you finish your dinner, and I'll go find you some more comfortable clothes to sleep in."

"What about you?" she asked. "You haven't had dinner."

"Honestly, my nerves are shot. I couldn't eat if I wanted to."

With that revelation, he walked away. Obviously, her fall

had torn him up in ways she never would've imagined. When she'd been lying on the ground and he'd been at her side, his face had been so pale, his eyes so wide as he'd tried to take in her entire body at once, assessing the damage.

At the E.R., he'd been forceful and matter-of-fact with the staff, almost demanding that she stay overnight for observation. The doctor had assured Grant that since she'd never lost consciousness, she would be fine to go home as long as someone watched her.

So here she was, being watched by a man who made her tingle with a simple touch, who kissed her as if she was the only desirable woman in the world, and who had her rethinking her reasons for remaining innocent.

This should be an interesting night.

Ten

"Melanie!"

Fear consumed him, bile rose in his throat as the scene before him unfolded.

Screams filled the evening, the thundering of hooves seemed to be in surround sound, and all Grant could do was look on as his twin sister held on to the out-of-control mare.

Their parents and the trainer all shouted commands, running after them, but Grant, still atop his own horse, could only stare from behind.

He'd done this. All in the name of a joke and a dare, he'd put Melanie in danger.

The shrill sound coming from his sister jolted him out of his horrified, frozen state, and he kicked his mount into gear and charged after them. He had to do something, had to rectify this somehow. Fear fueled him, while adrenaline blocked out all the possibilities of what might happen if that animal threw her.

He leaned into his horse, kicking his flank once again to move faster.

But it was too late. Melanie's mare saw Grant's coming in fast, and bucked, sending Melanie off the back. She landed with a jarring, sickening thud.

As he jumped off his horse and his parents and the trainer gathered around, Grant knew things had gone from bad to worse and hell was opening up to swallow him.

His beautiful, talented, always smiling twin sister wasn't moving....

Grant jerked up in bed, the sheet twisted around his waist, sweat dampening his forehead, his chest.

Damn. That nightmare hadn't made an appearance in so long, and he could've gone the rest of his life without having that dream.

There wasn't a day that went by when he didn't relive that life-altering moment. But the dreams...they were all too real and obviously the penance for his sin.

Grant swung his feet over the side of the bed, yanking the sheet off. He needed fresh air, some water, and he should probably check on Tessa.

Tessa. No doubt the events of today had brought on the nightmare. Because he'd been just as terrified seeing Tessa on the out-of-control stallion and then her fall...

Raking a hand over his face, Grant came to his feet and padded to the kitchen, careful to be quiet as he crept past Tessa's door. He'd insisted she keep it open in case she needed to call him for anything. She'd fought him a little on the matter, but Grant had refused to back down.

After he grabbed a bottle of water from the fridge and took a long drink, he set it on the counter, walked toward the patio and opened the door, welcoming the crisp night air. The refreshing breeze cooled his heated skin and calmed him, but that damn nightmare and images of today still rolled over and over in his mind.

Nothing was as nauseating, as horrifying or as crippling as watching someone you cared for caught in a helpless situation, and knowing there wasn't a damn thing you could do about it.

But unlike Tessa's situation, Grant had caused his twin's. His beautiful sister could've been killed. Sometimes he wondered if death would've been better than being a paraplegic.

"You okay?"

He turned, finding Tessa standing in the shadows. His T-shirt hit her midthigh, leaving beautifully toned legs revealed.

"I'm fine," he answered, turning back to the starry night, silently willing her to go away.

He couldn't keep looking at her, not when his emotions were so high and his heart was still in his throat.

And not when he'd just admitted to himself he was starting to care for her more than he thought he would. There was no way he could keep all his emotions separated now. More penance for his sins.

"Sorry if I woke you," he told her. "I was going to check on you in a minute."

Bare feet padded along the hardwood floors, and Grant clenched his fists as Tessa came to stand beside him. Her sweet jasmine scent mixed with the cool night air and surrounded him.

He hated how vulnerable he was. Hated how his need for her consumed him.

Turn back. Turn back before I take what I want.

"Want to talk about it?" she asked, her soft voice washing over him.

Sparing her a glance, he shook his head. "You should be in bed."

"I feel fine," she insisted, reaching out a delicate hand to grip his bare biceps. "What's keeping you up?"

Songs of crickets flooded the night, and Grant couldn't find the words. Right now he couldn't even think, given his vortex of emotions. Her fall, her nearness...her virginity.

"I guess I'm just still keyed up after today's excitement."

"Is that why I heard you cry out in your sleep a few minutes ago?"

Grant jerked around, causing her hand to drop. When she said nothing more, only crossed her arms over her chest, he muttered a curse and raked his fingers through his hair.

"I used to have nightmares," he admitted, not going into further detail. "I had one tonight. It's no big deal."

Bright blue eyes studied him for a moment before she

spoke. "They must be a big deal if this is an ongoing thing, Grant. Have you talked to anybody about them?"

"Like a shrink?" He laughed. "No. I'm fine."

Her gaze slid over his bare chest, then back up. She might as well have touched him with her soft fingertips because the effect was the same. His body responded, and there was nothing he could do to stop the heavy dose of arousal that kicked into high gear...as if he needed his hormones to bump up a notch.

"You should get back to bed," he told her, silently begging her to get her barely covered butt out of here before he forgot how delicate and innocent she truly was.

If she only knew the control she held over him...

"I want to help you." Stepping forward, she slid that delicate hand back up his arm and over the curve of his bare shoulder. "You may not want to talk about the dream, but I can stay up with you so you're not alone."

Grant's control snapped as he grabbed Tessa's slender shoulders and backed her up two steps to the frame of the patio door. Her eyes widened as she peered up at him.

"It's best I'm alone right now," he growled. "I want things I shouldn't, and my mood isn't the best. Go to your room, Tessa."

Her eyes filled with tears as she brought up her hands to cup his face. "You don't scare me, Grant. Whatever you're dealing with, I can help."

"I may not scare you, but right now I sure as hell scare myself."

Closing the slim gap between them, Grant crushed her lips to his. Her soft hands slipped around to grip the back of his neck, her fingers threading through his hair.

Why didn't she listen? He wanted her, more than any other woman before. If she'd just gone back to her room... Granted, he'd given her about a minute's warning, but damn, she was here in his house and barely dressed in the middle of the night. And he had all these emotions whirling around. This was so much more than lust, and it was so much more than sex that he wanted from her.

But damn it, he couldn't let himself get too personally involved.

Grant tried to deepen the kiss, but she beat him to it. He wanted to apply more pressure, but again she was ahead of him.

Obviously, she wasn't scared of the desperation in his touch, and she sure as hell wasn't scared of the warning he'd issued to her.

On one hand he was thrilled she hadn't gone back to her room, but on the other he worried he wouldn't be able to stop. The need for her clawed at him, consumed him.

Tearing his mouth from hers, he kissed a path down her throat. Her body arched into his as she groaned, giving him another reason to progress. When his fingers found the hem of the T-shirt, he slid his hands up beneath the cotton, finding soft, smooth skin and satiny panties.

He dipped one fingertip inside the snug elastic, needing more, silently questioning where the boundaries were.

A soft cry came from her lips as Grant lifted his mouth away. Resting his forehead against hers, he ran his fingers over her, nearly falling to his knees when her hips bumped against his hand.

With that silent invitation, he eased into her warmth, taking every bit of passion she was allowing. The fine line of control had snapped the moment she'd come to him, wanting to save him from himself. He couldn't be saved, but he could give pleasure, and right now that's all he had in him.

"Grant."

Her whispered plea had him claiming her mouth once again as his hand continued to pleasure her. She gripped his shoulders and her body jerked.

"Let go, Tessa," he all but growled against her lips.

And as if she'd been holding on to that same thin line of

control, her body stilled against his and she cried out, her fingernails biting into the bare flesh of his shoulders.

With her head thrown back against the door frame, her eyes squeezed tight and her mouth parted, she looked every bit the vixen he knew he could uncover.

When he removed his hand and stepped closer to slide his arms around her, he felt Tessa's entire body tremble, out of arousal or fear, he wasn't sure. She was an innocent, and he had her backed against a door frame like a horny teen who couldn't control himself. And he'd just taken a portion of her passion and used it, technically, to make himself feel better. She'd gotten too close to his hidden shame, and he'd opted to turn the tables, so to speak, and take what he wanted. Okay, not all he wanted, but enough that he knew he was a jerk.

So he stepped back.

Panting, her lips still moist and swollen from his touch, Tessa didn't look like a virgin, and he wanted her even more. Wanted her in his bed, spread all around him, so he could show her just how good they'd be together. But he also had to be realistic and not just a selfish ass.

"Go back to bed."

"Grant." She started to reach for him and he stepped back again, ignoring the flash of hurt in her eyes.

"Go, Tessa, before I ignore your innocence and take what I truly want."

A lone tear slid down her cheek as she blinked, then turned and walked quietly back to the guest room. Grant groaned and leaned against the door frame.

That damn tear was like a knife straight to his heart. He hadn't meant to hurt her, but if he'd taken what she was offering, she'd be even more hurt in the long run.

A woman like Tessa wanted more out of a man than just a fling. She wanted marriage, a family. And he wanted those things, too, but not in this world she lived in.

He'd kept the hurt and guilt in a separate compartment in

his heart for so long, but being around Tessa allowed each and every emotion to flood to the surface.

He truly thought he could keep his mind focused on work, had convinced himself he was ready to take on a film that would make him face his demons.

But after today's events, he knew he'd only been lying to himself.

In a few months he'd be leaving, and as much as he wanted Tessa, he knew even if they came to mean more to each other, neither of them would give up the life they so loved.

So he needed to keep his damn hands and lips off her, because she was getting harder and harder to resist. No matter how much he was coming to care for her, giving up what he'd worked for wasn't an option. He wouldn't give up his life in L.A. He'd worked too hard for his career.

Besides, he had run fast and far from the world of horses years ago.

Filming that world was one thing, but living in it would be pure hell. Especially now that he knew exactly what it felt like to have Tessa come apart.

Grant clenched his hand and slammed it against the doorjamb. How the hell did he undo that mental image? How did he expect to work with her and not want her even more?

When Grant woke the next morning, Tessa was gone and there was no sign she'd ever been there. Nothing less than what he deserved after his adolescent behavior.

He walked by her room, noting the perfectly made bed. Everything was back to the way it had been before she'd spent the night.

Grant walked into the room and spotted the T-shirt she'd slept in. It was neatly folded and lying atop the antique trunk at the end of the bed.

And because he was all alone, he lifted the garment to his face and inhaled her sweet scent.

He'd had his hands on her last night, had her trembling beneath him. She could've been his in every way.

But at what cost?

That damn clause prevented him from getting too involved, though he'd probably already crossed that line when he'd been feeling her bare chest and had slipped his hand inside her damp panties. But he knew Tessa would keep their secret rendezvous to herself.

Clause aside, if he'd slept with her, she would've regretted it, and the last thing he wanted her to see when she looked at him was regret. Hurt he could handle, regret...not so much.

He was still going to be leaving, and she deserved so much more than sex from a man who was only passing through.

Today he'd be talking with Damon and Cassie. Thankfully, he could avoid Tessa, and they both could take time to figure out what the hell was going on between them.

Lust, yes. Desire, most definitely. But was there more, only he couldn't put a definite name on it? The thought worried him, because he had a feeling he could want more with her, but couldn't let himself face all the pain and regret he'd fought so hard to keep away. And he couldn't risk getting back into a lifestyle he'd run so fast and far from.

There was a reason he hadn't visited his sister and saw his parents only when they came to him. He just couldn't tackle all the crippling emotions that always seemed to chase him.

Grant made his way to the main house and entered through the back door. After he'd been here for over a week, Damon had insisted Grant quit knocking and just walk in.

When he stepped into the kitchen, the sweet aroma of cinnamon rolls assaulted him. A beautiful, middle-aged woman with a cap of short silver hair was bustling around the room and humming. Grant cleared his throat so he didn't scare her.

She turned and smiled. "Good morning, Mr. Carter."

"Morning," he replied. "I'm supposed to meet Damon."

"Oh, he'll be down shortly." She picked up the plate of

gooey rolls and extended it toward him over top the granite island. "Fresh rolls from the oven. Would you like one?"

"I can't turn down anything that smells this good," he told her, reaching for a warm pastry.

"I'm Linda, by the way." She pulled out a small saucer and set it in front of him, along with a napkin. "Coffee?"

"Please. Black."

Soon he was in breakfast heaven. Homemade cinnamon rolls and coffee. He could so get used to this film set. Some he'd worked on had been out in the desert; a few had been in a jungle with no indoor plumbing. But this estate? Yeah, Grant could get used to these amenities…and he wasn't just thinking of the food.

"I'm happy to see someone sit and actually enjoy my cooking while it's hot," Linda told him. "Cassie rarely shows up because she's busy with Emily, and Tessa is too worried about keeping her weight as a jockey. Damon usually eats, but it's grabbing and heading out the door."

"And do you cook every morning, anyway?" Grant asked, sipping the steaming coffee.

"Every morning without fail. One of these days the family may decide to all come in and actually use that dining room." She smiled. "They're just too busy, if you ask me."

"Well, I have good news. Next week more of my crew will be arriving. You're in luck. They like to eat."

Linda laughed. "Well, then. Looks like I need to make a trip to the store and throw together some menus."

Grant polished off the roll and eased back in his chair, in no hurry to leave his present company. He had a feeling this woman might know things about this family that many others didn't.

"How long have you worked here?" he asked.

Linda placed her palms on the edge of the island. "This summer will be fifteen years."

Perfect.

"So you knew the late Mrs. Barrington?"

Linda nodded. "I did. She was a beautiful woman. Her girls most definitely take after her. That vibrant red hair, those bright blue eyes. A rare mix, but the Barrington women have a special mark of beauty."

"Was there ever any rivalry between Tessa and Cassie? Cassie seems very content to stay behind the scenes and be the trainer. Has that always been the case?"

"Cassie has always been a bit shy, but she'd do anything for anyone and sacrifice her own happiness to make others happy." Linda paused before going on. "I dare to say that's how she ended up with Emily's father, that arrogant prick. Pardon my language."

Grant smiled. "I'm getting a vibe that Cassie's ex-husband isn't liked around here very much."

"He's not liked at all. How could you leave a woman when she's just delivered your child? I ask you. He's no man, he's a selfish coward."

"I completely agree," Grant replied. "What about Tessa? What can you tell me about her?"

Linda smiled again, her eyes softening. "Sweet Tessa. She wants to be the best at everything, and she'll push herself until she becomes that way. I've never seen anyone more in competition with themselves than she is. To be honest, after her mama died, she completely submersed herself in the horses. She loved them before and competed heavily, but she had a life. Now she's in those stables all day and sometimes all night."

Not last night. Last night she'd been trembling beneath his hands, silently begging for things she couldn't possibly be ready for.

"I've heard her ex isn't too popular around here, either," Grant said, mentally moving on from last night's interludes.

Linda rolled her eyes and grabbed a pot holder as she made her way to the stove built into the wall. "That man wanted Tessa for two reasons—her name and her money. And then..."

Grant waited while she pulled another pan from the oven,

but when she didn't continue he rested his elbows on the counter and asked, "Then what?"

Shaking her head, Linda turned back toward him. "I'd best not say. You'll have to talk to Tessa."

"Did she love him?"

The woman smiled, cocked her head to the side. "I'm thinking I like where this line of questioning is going."

"It's all pertinent to the film."

She laughed. "That may be, but it's also important to you on a personal level, yes?"

"I'm not here for personal reasons," he replied.

No matter what was or wasn't happening between him and Tessa, he couldn't let anything slip. That clause hung over his head, and if he and Tessa decided to...whatever, then that would be in private and kept between them. Period. He had no other option if he wanted to take his career to the next level. And he needed this film and Russo Entertainment to get him there.

Some might say advancing his career was just another leg of this race he ran to stay as far away from his family and past life as possible. Grant liked to believe he was just securing his future.

"Grant."

He turned and came to his feet when Tessa's father stepped into the room. "Morning, Damon."

"Hope you weren't waiting too long."

"Not at all," Grant replied. "A cinnamon roll, coffee and wonderful company is never a bad thing."

Damon smiled and reached for a roll. "Linda's specialty. She's a whiz in the kitchen."

"Not that anyone in this family sticks around long enough to really enjoy my talents," she muttered with a slight grin.

"Are you ready to get started?" Damon asked. "I've arranged a tee time for ten o'clock."

"We're golfing?" Grant asked.

"I am. You can play caddie if you want."

Grant laughed. "I suck at golf, but let me run to the cottage and change, and I'll be back."

"I'll be here."

Grant rushed back to his house, barely glancing toward the stables, because he feared he'd see Tessa and that hurt in her eyes again. Female laughter rippled from the open doors and his heart flipped. She was in there with her sister, and they were fine. She probably hadn't given him another thought.

So while he was on the golf course with her father today, Grant would try his damnedest to not let her consume his every single thought.

Eleven

Tessa ignored the buzzing of her phone and pulled Don Pedro out of his stall. No way in hell was she answering, or even acknowledging another text from Aaron. What the hell was he thinking, texting her? He'd also called, but thankfully, she'd missed that and he hadn't left a voice mail.

Stupid jerk. Did he honestly think she'd want to have any contact with him after what he'd put her through?

She had the Arkansas Derby in a few days, and she had to qualify to move on to Kentucky. And she would qualify, as soon as she got distractions out of her life. Aaron would not be a distraction because she refused to allow him the mind space.

But there was another man, a more dangerous man, consuming her thoughts. Even though she'd tried all morning, she couldn't exorcise him from her mind.

Unfortunately she could still feel Grant's hands on her body, his lips on hers, the strength of him pressing her against the door. The way he'd forced her to relinquish control and completely come apart.

She had so many emotions swirling around in her, she didn't know where to put them all. On one hand she wanted more. She wanted to know how else Grant and she could pleasure each other, because she had a feeling she'd gotten only a meager sampling.

On the other hand she was embarrassed for her actions. She'd come to console him, and ended up practically clawing him and writhing in his arms.

And she was still tingling from the experience.

Now he wasn't just in all her thoughts, he was nowhere near her and still causing goose bumps to pop up.

"Everything okay?" Cassie asked, stepping into the stable from the ring. "You seem distracted."

"Aaron has been texting me."

No way could Tessa explain what she'd experienced last night...or hadn't experienced, since Grant put on the brakes. She'd wanted him, would've probably given in to her desires, but he'd given her an orgasm and sent her back to bed. What was that? The adult equivalent to milk and cookies? Why did he call the shots?

"What does he want?" Cassie asked, sliding her hands into her pockets.

Pulling herself back to the present, Tessa shrugged. "I have no idea. He's just asked if we can talk. I refuse to answer him."

"Jerk," Cassie muttered. "Well, we need to get going, because I'm supposed to meet with Grant this afternoon."

Tessa stilled. "What for?"

"He wanted to interview me and ask questions about my perspective regarding the movie. He's meeting with Dad this morning."

Tessa's grip on the reins tightened. She wondered what he thought about discovering her gone this morning. There was no way she could wake up and see his face, not after their raw, emotional—and physical—connection last night.

"Well, this is interesting," her sister said, a smile spreading across her face. "Has a certain producer caught your eye?"

Tessa laughed. "More like I've caught his."

"Even better," Cassie squealed, clasping her hands together. "You can't keep things like this from me."

Leading Don Pedro toward the ring, Tessa fell into step beside her. "I don't even know what there is to tell," she began. "He's made it clear he's attracted to me, but I don't have time for this, and we're so different.... I can't even name all the reasons."

"What's the main one?"

Tessa squinted against the bright spring sun. "His life is in the city. He's not a dirt-and-boots type of man."

"So? A sexy guy like Grant can be anything he wants. What else bothers you?"

"Our age. He's ten years older than me."

Cassie sighed. "You mean he's experienced?"

"Well, there's that, but he's just... I don't know. Out of my league."

Cassie gripped her arm and shook her. "Don't ever say things like that. Nobody is out of your league. If Grant is interested, why not see what happens? Age won't matter, and as far as him being a city boy, that's just geography. Unless you're not interested in him."

"I'd have to be dead not to notice him on a physical level, but when he kisses me—"

"Wait," Cassie interrupted, holding up her hand. "Kisses? As in plural? Why didn't you start there when I asked about him? Why start with all that's wrong instead of what's putting that dreamy smile on your face?"

"Because I'm scared," Tessa said honestly. "I want him too much and I just... I'm afraid to give in."

"Mama made us promise to hold out for love. I truly loved Em's dad, even though he didn't love me. I still do in some ways, even though he's gone." Cassie shook her head and smiled. "I've never seen you even question putting aside your fears for a man. That should tell you something, Tess."

Nodding, she returned her sister's grin. "I know. But I need time to think, and I can't do that and work on qualifying, too. So, let's get our day started."

"Fine, but this conversation is far from over."

Tessa laughed. "I had a feeling you'd say that."

Grant's meeting with Damon was insightful. They'd talked quite a bit already, but today Grant was able to get more personal, detailed information from the man. They'd gone over the script with a finer lens, as well.

He wanted Damon to have a hands-on experience. As co-producer, Grant wished to showcase not only the racing legend, but the man behind the Barrington dynasty.

And now Grant was headed to Cassie's cottage to talk to the shiest Barrington sister. He was very interested in getting her angle on being not only Damon's daughter and growing up with a famous father, but also as a trainer for the mogul.

Grant had barely knocked on Cassie's door before she answered it. "Hey, come on in."

He stepped over the threshold, taking in the spacious cottage that mimicked his. Of course, his wasn't littered with a Pack 'N Play, a high chair and various kid toys.

"Emily is lying down for her afternoon nap," she told him, closing the door behind him. "We should have a few uninterrupted hours."

She gestured for him to have a seat on the floral sofa. "Can I get you a drink?"

"I'm good, thanks."

Cassie took a seat at the other end of the couch. With a sigh, she propped her feet on the coffee table and offered him a smile. "I'm really excited about this film, Grant."

Easing into the cushions, he nodded. "I'm pretty anxious to get things going. Once my crew arrives, this place won't be the same for a few months."

Cassie shrugged. "It's the busiest time of the year for us, but we'll be here and gone with the upcoming races. So at times we'll all be tripping over each other and other times you'll have the place to yourself."

"I promise we will all work around your and Tessa's training. It was written into the contract, but I wanted you to hear it from me as well, so you didn't worry."

"I appreciate that." She eased an arm along the back of the couch and pinned him with her blue eyes. "Should we talk about you and my sister now or after you interview me for the film?"

Grant paused for a second, because not many things in this life surprised him, but then he laughed. "And what is it you'd like to know that she hasn't already told you?"

"I'd like to know if you're toying with her or if you're genuinely interested."

"Anything we have going on is really between Tessa and myself," he told her.

"Of course it is, but you need to understand who you're dealing with." Cassie slid her hair behind her ear and paused, as if to choose the right words. "Tessa has never made time for herself for anything. Dating especially. She's gone on dates, don't get me wrong, but she never dates for any length of time because the guys normally can't handle her love and dedication to her career."

Love and dedication to a career? She was speaking his language.

"She's had one very serious relationship and that ended recently," Cassie went on. "I won't get into details, because she'd kill me, but he used her. He'd put a ring on her finger and taken that as his green light to make her his mat to walk on."

Grant wouldn't mind meeting this jerk. Perhaps meeting him with a swift punch to the face.

"She's got major trust issues," Cassie told him. "Not only that, he was a big-time city slicker. So if you're seriously pursuing her, you have your work cut out for you."

"There's a clause in my contract that prevents me from fraternizing with crew members on location," he informed her. "And technically, Tessa would fall into that category, since we're working with her. So everything you think you know needs to be kept to yourself."

Cassie nodded. "Understood. But keep in mind, my sister doesn't deserve to be kept a secret, or only brought out when it's convenient for you."

"Are you warning me away?" he asked, knowing every

word she said was true. He just hated how she painted the accurate picture.

She tilted her head. "Not at all. I actually think Tessa needs a little distraction in her life. She needs to have fun, especially with this being the most stressful time for her. I just wanted you to be aware of how fragile she is, even though she tries to put up this tough persona."

He had a quick flash of Tessa being thrown from the horse, of trembling beneath his touch....

"I'm aware of how fragile she is," he said. "And I'm not backing down."

Cassie's smile widened. "Good. Now, what do you want to ask me about my childhood and my father?"

Twelve

"You can do this, baby girl."

Tessa stared down at her father, who patted her leg. The Arkansas Derby was about to start, and this intensity just beforehand was the moment she loved. That feeling before every race. The thrill of nerves swirling through her belly, the cheering crowd, the anticipation of thundering hooves against the hard dirt.

God, she loved her job.

"This is a cakewalk for you, Tess," her sister said. "You ready?"

Tessa nodded. "Let's do this."

Cassie led Don Pedro, and Damon walked by her side. Tessa knew Grant was around, but thankfully, he'd made himself scarce since the incident in the guesthouse a few days ago.

Perhaps he'd decided she wasn't worth the trouble. If that was the case, fine. At least she knew up front and not after her heart got too involved. But she had a feeling he was giving her room to come to grips with what had happened…or he was battling his own issues. Either way, Tessa was pleased with the space he'd given her.

The sun was bright in the sky, promising a beautiful day, and Tessa couldn't wait to celebrate. That attitude wasn't cocky, just positive thinking, which she'd learned to do long ago in this business.

A trail of riders made their way to the starting gate. A variety of colors from the jockeys' shirts and horse blankets added another layer of beauty to the sport. There wasn't one aspect of racing that Tessa didn't love, didn't embrace.

Her own light blue shirt with a bright green star and a diagonal white stripe across her torso and one sleeve had been her mother's design, and Tessa wore the jersey proudly with each race, feeling as if her mother was right there with her every time.

Once she and Don Pedro were in position, Damon and Cassie left her and Tessa took in a deep breath. All the training, all the countless hours always came down to just a few precious minutes.

She leaned down, patting her Thoroughbred's neck, and whispered, "We've got this, don't we, Don Pedro?"

In no time the signal was issued and Tessa readied herself for the gate to move, allowing her the freedom she needed to take a qualifying position.

Adrenaline pumped through her veins, and she gripped the reins, ready to take the first step in making her mark as another Barrington champion.

Grant couldn't help but cheer when the official results came in and Tessa qualified. She not only qualified, she came in first. Damn, but she was impressive to watch on that track.

He'd never been so nervous in all his life as he was in those moments before the gate lifted. Now he wanted to go to her, wanted to congratulate her. But he wouldn't be able to resist hugging her, kissing her.

He had to keep himself in check, though. Congratulations were one thing, but anything else in public could cost him everything.

Grant made his way to the stable, only to find Tessa surrounded by reporters and family. Slipping out his notepad and pen, he started scribbling. He'd been taking notes the entire day, on everything from the camaraderie of the jockeys to the excitement in the stands.

Tessa pulled off her matching blue helmet and wiped her

forehead as she smiled for one of the cameras. She was stunning. Her beauty radiated through her smile, and her love of the horses, of the sport, came shining through in ways words never could express.

Grant moved away, knowing anything he wanted to say to Tessa could wait until they were alone. As he turned to make his way back through the crowd, his phone rang.

Moving over to the far side, where there was less commotion, or as little as he could get, considering he was near the grandstands, he pulled his cell from his dress pants and glanced at the caller ID before answering.

"Hey, Dad."

"Grant," his father's voice boomed. "Haven't heard from you for a few weeks. How are things going?"

"Really well." He continued to move away from the crowd, heading toward the end of the stands. "I'm actually at a race right now."

"Oh, damn. I'm sorry, son. I never know when it's a good time to call."

"No problem. If I can't talk, I just won't answer. Is everything okay?"

"Fine." His father sighed. "To be honest, your mother is worried about you."

Grant turned his back to the sun and slid his free hand into his pants pocket. "Dad—"

"Now just listen," he interrupted. "I know you're going to say you're fine. I know you'll tell me there's nothing to worry about, but that's why I'm calling and not your mother. I'll tell her anything to give her peace of mind, but I want you to be truthful with me. Is this project harder than you thought?"

"The film itself won't start for another two weeks, so it's been pretty easy so far."

"You know I'm not talking about the actual film, son. How are you holding up working around the horses?"

Yeah, unfortunately Grant knew exactly what his father

had been referring to, but he'd tried to dodge it...just as he'd been dodging this topic for years.

"Honestly, it's hard, but not unbearable."

"Do you think you'll be able to stick it out?"

For the chance at starting his own production company? Hell yeah, he'd stick it out. Besides, this was the biggest film he'd ever worked on, and there was no way he'd let some minor insecurity form a roadblock on his path to being even more successful.

He'd originally taken on this film because so many key players were involved, and he wanted every layer of career achievement possible.

But he hadn't planned on Tessa. Hadn't expected to be blindsided by a feisty, yet innocent vixen who made him face his fears...and his feelings.

"I'll be fine," he told his dad. "So now you can tell Mom I am doing great and you won't be lying."

"When do you think we'll be able to see you?"

Grant smiled at an elderly couple that walked by. "I'm not sure. I'll be on location for a couple of months at least. I may be able to take a brief break right after that."

"Well, there's another reason for my call."

Grant knew it. He'd been waiting on this "other reason." Spotting a bench along a stone retaining wall, he made his way over and took a seat. He had a sinking feeling he'd need to be sitting when his father asked the next question.

"Since you're moving on and making progress," his dad continued, "your mother and I would like it if you would come visit when you're done filming. Melanie would like to see you."

Grant closed his eyes, waiting for that stab of guilt and angst that always accompanied his sister's name. He knew Melanie had asked to see him over the years, but he just couldn't. And he wouldn't put her through trying to be kind to him. How the hell could she even stand to say his name, let alone be in the same room with him? He'd nearly killed her...

and from the way she was living, he might as well have. He'd murdered her dreams, her promising future.

"I don't think that's a good idea, Dad."

His father sighed. "You can't avoid her forever, and you can't avoid the issue."

Oh, he could, and he had been for several years. Grant believed he was doing the best thing, letting his sister live without seeing him and being reminded of how he'd stolen the life she'd so loved.

In all honesty he wanted to see her. As twins, they shared a special bond. But he worried that she'd only be reminded of how he'd physically destroyed her.

Even though he hadn't seen her, he always asked about her, and never missed sending her a Christmas or birthday present.

Wow. What a coward's way out.

But in some ironic, twisted way, he was making this film as a tribute to her. A small gesture, considering, but he couldn't turn back time and reverse the damage he'd done.

"When I'm done filming, I'll fly you and Mom out to see me," he offered.

"We always come to you," his father said. "And not that we don't love seeing where you live and work, but you need to come home, son. It's been long enough."

No, it hadn't. Because Grant knew if he went back home and saw the stables, saw the old farmhouse, saw Melanie, he'd be imprisoned by that damn nightmare he'd worked like hell to stay out of.

He'd actually hoped taking on this film would help him conquer those demons once and for all. Conquer them so much that he could return home on his own terms, without the begging and pleading from his parents.

"Listen, Dad, I'll call you in a few days. Tell Mom I'm fine and I'd love to see you in L.A. when I'm done filming."

He extended his love and disconnected before his father's stern tone could kick in. Even though Grant was an adult, he still respected his parents and didn't want to disappoint them, but he couldn't go home.

It had taken him a good amount of time to be able to face even them, let alone his twin sister.

He'd left home only months after the accident and hadn't looked back since. He'd needed the polar opposite of that small farm community he'd grown up in. L.A. was as far away and as opposite as he could get.

So, no, when this film wrapped up, he would not be returning to Kentucky to his hometown.

Late that evening, when Grant knew everyone was either asleep or in for the night, he sneaked down the hall of the hotel to Tessa's room and tapped lightly.

He hadn't seen her alone since the night at his cottage. He missed her, missed talking to her.

How had something as common as sexual attraction turned into so much more?

The hotel door cracked slightly as she peered out, but when she recognized him, she pulled it open farther.

"Grant. What are you doing here?"

He took in her hair, slicked back into a low bun, but it was wet, so he knew she'd showered. The leggings and long-sleeved T-shirt she'd donned fit her petite, curvy body beautifully. The woman was never rumpled or disheveled. Ever.

"Can I come in?"

Without a word, she stepped back. To torture himself or to give her something to think about, he brushed against her on his way through the door, and appreciated the swift intake of breath she rewarded him with.

He'd been wandering around for most of the evening. He'd had dinner alone, looking over fresh notes about the race, the atmosphere, comparing them to old ones, emailing Bronson and Anthony. And then he'd been stewing over his father's call.

But he hadn't seen Tessa for...too long.

"You did amazing today," he told her, raking his eyes over her.

She closed the door, leaned back against it and smiled. "Thank you. It's a relief to have today over with, but now the work and pressure really begin. But this is the part I love. The buildup, the anticipation."

"Take this win and leave the rest for tomorrow," he told her.

He glanced around the neat space, noting the perfectly made king-size bed, the single suitcase on the stand.

"I didn't want to interrupt after the race. You had quite the press surrounding you." Her fresh-from-the-shower scent and those hip-hugging leggings were killing him. "I had to tell you congratulations."

Tessa's smile widened. "Thanks. That means a lot to me."

Pushing away from the door, she moved through an open doorway to a small living area. When she sank onto the floral sofa, she gestured toward the other end. "Have a seat."

He sat down on the edge of the couch, rested his elbows on his knees and leaned forward. "So, we go back to Stony Ridge tomorrow?"

"Yeah. More training awaits," she told him, tucking a bare foot up onto the couch. "Did you get more useful information today?"

"I did. I've touched base with Bronson and Anthony, and we're excited for next week, when they arrive."

Tessa stared at him, her gaze never wavering from his. "Want to tell me what's wrong? I know you came to congratulate me, but there's more."

How did she know? She barely knew him, and here she was, so in tune with his emotions, his body language. They were all alone, yet instead of any seducing or flirting, she'd picked up on his emotional state. What was he, a damn woman?

She'd gotten so far beneath his skin, he couldn't hide anything from her. Especially after she'd witnessed his raw emotions the other night.

"Long day," he told her. "I didn't mean to interrupt you

if you were getting ready for bed. I just didn't want to come by earlier when you were busy, and then I was sidetracked."

By the haunting words of my father's call, and so many damn emotions.

"You've avoided me," she told him. "For two days, you've talked to everyone but me."

"I'm working," he retorted, even though he knew where she was going with this. So he beat her to it. "Besides, you were gone the other morning when I got up, so I assumed you were uncomfortable. I wanted to give you space."

"You were angry." Tessa traced her finger over a small pink flower on the cushion and shrugged. "Seemed like you were hiding."

Angry, no. Fighting to earn her trust before taking things to the next level, yes. He'd never worried about getting to know a woman, learning all about her and actually caring for her before taking her to bed. Tessa had woken something in him, something even more primal.

"I don't hide from anything," he protested. "Especially a woman."

Her eyes came up and met his. "No? You've made a point to be in my business every day for five days, and the last two you vanish."

Grant gritted his teeth. "I was working."

"Me, too. So, do you want to talk about it?"

"What?"

She flattened her hand, smacking the cushion between them. "You have nightmares you refuse to face. Or we could discuss the fact that had you not stopped the other night, I would've given myself to you."

Silence settled between them, joining the already crackling sexual tension.

Her eyes narrowed. "Pick one."

Grant came to his feet, resting his hands on his hips. "Fine. Why were you ready to throw away your virginity on me the other night? You've held on to it this long, why not wait for someone who might actually stick around? Someone who is more compatible with you? Because, as you've established, we're too different."

For the first time since he'd stepped foot inside her room, he saw doubt flash across her face. Good. He wanted to make her think, make her really want him. Because he wanted her with a force he could barely control.

"We are different, Slick." Her blue eyes traveled up the length of him as she tilted her head and smirked. "And maybe you were right, stopping the other night."

"I was." Hard as it had been to put the brakes on, he'd known the decision was the right one, and he was the only one who'd been thinking beyond that point. But they would get there...when they were both ready.

Tessa came to her feet, crossed her arms over her chest and sighed. "I know we're different. I know all the reasons we shouldn't be together intimately, but there's a part of me that doesn't care. A part of me that just wants to let you do anything you want."

Grant had to really fight himself to stand still, to let her speak. But her words—her honest, raw words—were killing him.

"You do things to me," she went on. "The way I feel when I'm with you is...different. That may only be one-sided, but I'm finding the attraction harder and harder to fight."

No, this spark of something beyond physical was most definitely not one-sided. He'd found it harder than hell to stay away from her for two days, while trying to focus on the job.

"Why are you fighting it?" he asked.

"Because...well, what if I'm a disappointment to you? What if I'm disappointed myself in all of it? I mean, I've gone this long, and if I give in, what if I'm let down?"

Grant's control snapped as he snaked an arm around her waist and pulled her flush against his chest. Her hands came up to his shoulders as she caught herself.

With his lips a breath away from hers, he whispered, "I

guarantee when I get you in my bed, nobody will be disappointed, Tessa."

Her eyes widened. "When? You mean, you don't plan on stopping again?"

"I'm not taking you here," he told her. "I want you to be trembling with want. I want you to think about me, about us, when you're training, and I want your fantasies to override anything else."

"Why?" she whispered.

He nipped at her lips. "Because you're so self-contained, and I can't wait to see you out of control and knowing I caused it."

Her fingertips curled into his shoulders as he slid his mouth over hers. The brief, powerful kiss nearly had him dropping to his knees before her. But he had to remain in control here, because he was damn determined to get her to loosen up.

He tore his mouth from hers and stepped back. "Lock that door behind me, Country, and I'll see you back at Stony Ridge."

Once again, he left her when they both were nearly shaking with desire. But he wanted more than lust, more than just sex. And damned if that didn't scare the hell out of him.

Thirteen

Things were starting to progress at Stony Ridge. Trailers were set up for the actors and other producers and directors, who should be arriving in just a few days. This film was about to get under way, and for once Tessa was glad.

Now maybe Grant would have other things to do besides tempt her, tease her, then walk away. How dare he do that to her twice? What game was he playing?

She might be a virgin, but she wasn't that naive. He wanted her, yet he kept denying himself. Did he think he was being gallant? Chivalrous? Well, in her opinion he was being a player, and she would put a stop to that as soon as her training for the day was over.

She'd had enough of being pulled around. And honestly, she cared for him and knew he cared for her, or he would've already taken her or moved on. Grant had self-control, and he was holding on to every last shred for her.

Well, enough was enough. Tessa wanted him, and she would be the one to decide what was best for her body…not him.

She leaned down, patted Don Pedro and set out at a trot. Today she'd keep it easy, especially since Cassie had to take Emily to the doctor for shots.

"Care if I ride with you?"

Tessa turned to see her father coming from the stables, leading Cassie's newest problem child, Macduff.

"Not at all. You sure you want to get on him?"

Damon shrugged. "He'll be fine. I'm bigger than you, so you were easier to buck. And Cassie's been working with him."

Tessa nodded. "Then saddle up and let's go."

She waited, actually finding herself eager to ride with her father. So much in life got in the way of their time together. Between her training and preparing for the movie, Tessa figured this would be the last time for quite a while that they would have alone, with no added pressure.

She gripped the reins and fell in behind her dad. When he set out toward the back of the estate, she kicked her horse into gear and eased up beside him. She knew exactly where he was heading.

The early-morning sun beat down, promising another beautiful, yet unpredictable spring day. As always, she'd checked the forecast when she'd woken, and seen possible thunderstorms later in the afternoon.

"Won't be long, this place will be overrun with famous actors and the threat of paparazzi," her dad told her as he took in the new on-site trailers.

"I hope whatever security they have will be able to keep the crazies away." Tessa hated the thought of strangers around her horses. "I just hope they respect my privacy."

Damon laughed. "You may find you like the behind-the-scenes view. If not, you can always hide over at your house. No one will come there."

"Not unless it's reporters or crazed fans," she muttered as they passed the last of the trailers.

Damon laughed. "We have security for your property, too."

Tessa smiled, but her eyes were on the man talking to some workers who'd brought the trailers. Grant had on well-worn jeans, aviator sunglasses and a black shirt with the sleeves rolled up his muscular forearms. He might be trying to look as if he belonged in the country, but the man was still polished, still citified and damn sexy. Even his sporty rental car stood out next to the full-size trucks on the estate.

"Your producer is working hard to make sure everything is perfect for his crew," her father commented as they neared the pond.

"He's not my producer," she retorted.

Damon pulled back on his reins at the edge of the water and glanced over. "Honey, I know I'm an old man, and your father to boot, but anyone can see the way you look at him. And, more importantly, the way he looks at you."

Tessa groaned. She did not want to be discussing this with her dad. Cassie was about the only person Tessa ever confided her secrets to. Maybe if their mother had lived...

"I miss her, too," he told her in a low voice. "I know you miss her, especially now. I can tell you're confused, but if you want advice, I'd be happy to give it."

Tessa laughed. "I'm not discussing the birds and the bees with you."

Damon's own robust laughter rippled through the air. "Please, I don't plan on getting that in-depth here. I was talking more about your heart, Tessa."

When she glanced over to him, she saw he was serious. He wanted to offer his thoughts from a parenting standpoint. Considering he was the only parent she had, she valued his opinion and the special bond they had.

"What about it?" she asked, almost afraid of his response.

"Risks have to happen. If you want anything out of life, you have to take a risk. Standing on the sideline, watching as chances go by, will only leave you with regrets."

She swallowed and looked back out onto the glistening pond.

"You take a risk every time you compete," he went on. "You take a risk of getting hurt, of hurting someone else or your horse."

Tessa whipped her head back around. "I never even consider that a possibility."

His smiled warmed her. "Because you've learned to take the risk and lead by faith. You let your heart guide you each time you get on that horse and head toward the finish line. Love is no different."

"I never said anything about love." Even to her, the defense sounded weak. "He just...he confuses me."

"Your mother used to confuse the hell out of me," Damon said with a soft chuckle. "I started asking her out when she was sixteen, and she didn't say yes until she was eighteen. I knew she was the one, but I was older than her, and to be honest, I think that scared her. In some crazy way, she worried she wouldn't measure up to standards I'd set for the woman I wanted."

Tessa swallowed, unable to admit that was one of her main fears. Was it that easy to just let go?

"What worries you about Grant?"

With a shrug, she pulled on the reins when Don Pedro started to shift. "We're so different, Dad. He's not a country boy, but practically drips big city."

"And?"

"What do you mean, and? I hate the city. That was one of the reasons I broke it off with Aaron."

Her father's face turned to stone. "That man isn't even worthy of mentioning, and he is nothing like Grant. Aaron didn't care about you. If he'd looked at you even remotely the way Grant does, then things may have been different. But Aaron was using you and trying to steer you away from your career. Has Grant done any of those things?"

Tessa shook her head and sighed. "He's amazing."

"Well, you're an adult and you make your own decisions, but please, don't get so caught up in racing and this image of a perfect world you've built for yourself that you don't stop to take a risk...and enjoy the benefits."

Tessa closed her eyes, relishing the soft breeze, wondering what risk she should be taking. Maybe admit to Grant that she had developed feelings for him? Go to his cottage tonight and seduce him?

She nearly laughed. She wouldn't know the first thing about seducing a man, and certainly not one as sexy as Grant Carter.

But one thing was for sure. She was done waiting and playing his game.

Grant was completely worn-out. There had been a mixup with the number of trailers and they were still one short, but after some calls he'd gotten everything straightened out.

He'd sent a text to his coproducers, informing them they were good to go whenever they wanted to come. He figured they'd arrive earlier than stars Max Ford and Lily Beaumont.

The two headliners of the film were going to help him catapult to a whole new level, and Grant could hardly contain himself at the thought of his own production company. Marty had sent an email outlining the prospect, and Grant was glad no one had been around to see him read it, because he'd been smiling like a kid with a new puppy. And he may have read it through twice. Okay, three times.

He had just unbuttoned his shirt and pulled it from his jeans when someone knocked on his door.

Please, don't let it be another issue with the trailers.

When he jerked open the door, Tessa stood there, her hair flying loose around her shoulders. A fitted tank, with a long-sleeved plaid shirt over top, unbuttoned, showcased her flat stomach. Her jeans hugged her hips, and the punch of lust to his gut nearly made his knees give out.

She'd never looked this…relaxed. Seeing that massive amount of red hair dancing about in the wind, he nearly groaned, because he could practically feel it sliding along his bare body.

Which meant she couldn't come inside. The emotional impact she kept hitting him with was targeting closer and closer to his heart.

Grant stepped out onto the porch, pulling the door shut behind him.

"I'm sorry," she told him. "Is this a bad time?"

Her eyes raked over his bare chest and Grant clenched his fists. "No."

Those bright blue eyes darted around, as if she was suddenly insecure about something...or was reconsidering coming here.

"Everything okay?" he asked.

With a sigh, she shook her head. "Actually, no. I can't handle this tension between us anymore."

Damn. She was about to get aggressive, and he wasn't sure he could turn her down if she started showing signs of power and control. He'd witnessed this only in her schedules, never with attraction. And damn if that wasn't a whole new level of sexy. He was already turned on as it was, and his zipper was growing exceedingly tighter.

Taking her hand, he led her off the porch.

"Where are we going?" she asked.

He kept walking, heading toward the back of the estate, away from his cottage and the closest bed. Although he was about to his breaking point, so even the grass was looking pretty inviting right about now.

"Let's go for a walk," he told her. "Things are about to get crazy around here, and maybe I want to just do nothing. Not work and not talk about us. Maybe I just want to walk and hold your hand."

Tessa groaned. "It's going to storm soon," she told him. "And I need to talk about us. I need to know where I stand with you."

Grant kept walking, knowing his silence was driving her insane. But honestly, he had no clue what to say to her. He wanted her, plain and simple, but he really didn't think she was ready, and the last thing he wanted for her was regrets. He wanted so, so much more. But since he couldn't identify those wants, how could he express them to her? Life had been much simpler when this was only sexual attraction.

Tessa's delicate hand remained in his as they walked through the pasture. In the near distance, frogs croaked from the pond. Grant was starting to really settle in here, but he knew in his heart he couldn't get too attached to this place... this woman.

But that didn't stop him from wanting her, from aching for her and waking every night fantasizing about her.

"If you've decided I'm not worth your time, I get that," she finally said.

Grant smiled. He'd known she wouldn't be able to just relax and take a walk. He remained silent, because he also knew she wasn't finished saying whatever was on her mind that had caused her to show up at his cottage.

"I mean, you've had enough time to think about this, and knowing how different we are and how...inexperienced I am, I can totally see why you would want to keep your distance. But what I don't understand is why you kiss me, why you say you want me, yet do nothing about it."

The first fat drops of rain started and he jerked her to a halt, turning her to face him.

"I do nothing about it, Tessa, because I'm filled with nothing but lust. That's not what you need. You need gentle, and I can't guarantee that, either. I want you on a level I've never known. You drive me crazy with an ache that threatens to overtake me."

The skies cut lose as he thrust his hands into her hair and captured her lips. His tongue invaded her mouth, taking her, pleading for her to take him. She gripped his shoulders as the cool drops soaked them. But nothing could make him pull away from her. He'd come to the point where he craved her taste, needed her touch. What the hell would happen if he got her naked, lying against his body?

When she pulled back, glancing up at him with droplets dripping from her lashes, he groaned and took her mouth again. His hands traveled down to her abdomen and gripped the hem of her tank, tugging it up. He needed more...needed whatever she was willing to give. And when this was over, he'd have to be satisfied with what he got.

Tessa's body arched into his, her hips grinding against his erection. He encircled her bare waist with his hands, allowing his pinky fingers to dip below the edge of her jeans.

Never in his life had he craved a woman as he did Tessa. And seeing as how this was new ground for him, he was terrified he'd hurt her.

A clap of thunder tore them apart as lightning lit up the darkening sky. Tessa grabbed his hand, pulling him toward the pond. She was running and laughing as the rain continued to drench them. Even with her hair and clothing plastered to her body, she was stunning as she guided him through the storm.

They circled the pond, and Grant knew exactly where they were seeking shelter: the old cabin nestled in a grove of trees. Tessa led him onto the porch as another thunder and lightning combination filled the evening.

Panting, she leaned against the post and smiled up at him. But as he moved closer, her eyes widened, her smiled faded. He was losing control, and he wondered if he'd ever had it where she was concerned.

"Tessa—"

She covered his lips with one slender fingertip. "Please. Don't stop this again, Grant. I need you. I need this."

He was lost. No way could he say no to her.

This beautiful, precious woman was offering something so rare and special. He wanted to be the one to show her all about passion and desire. He wanted to be everything to her... but all he could be was her lover. No more.

"I can't deny you," he told her, pushing strands of clingy red hair away from her face. "I don't know why I tried. But I admit...I'm scared."

"Of what?"

"This. You. Your first time shouldn't be in a shack in a thunderstorm."

"This shack holds special memories for me. I used to dream here as a little girl. I would daydream about horses and Prince Charming." Tessa reached up, sliding her body against his as she circled his neck with her arms. "My first time can be anywhere, as long as it's with you."

He dropped his forehead to hers and whispered, "This may as well be my first time, as nervous as I am right now."

Tessa nipped at his lips. "Then let's get inside and fumble through this together."

Fourteen

Tessa couldn't believe she was doing this.

The old key was hidden above the door frame just like always, and as soon as she opened the door and replaced the key, she reached back for Grant's hand and led him inside.

He closed the door and she turned to him, nearly laughing at the pained expression on his face. He was so utterly beautiful and he was worried…for her. Her heart tripped in her chest and fell. That was it. She'd gone and fallen in love with this man she'd sworn to stay away from, the city slicker who'd invaded her privacy with not much more than a wink and a smile.

"Don't worry about me," she told him. "Do whatever you like."

Grant shook his head. "Funny thing. I don't know what I like anymore. This is all new with you and I want…I want this to be good. But I'm barely hanging on here, Tess."

She smiled, loving that she had this control over such a powerful man. Obviously, she was going to have to take the initiative or they'd be dancing around this sexual tension come Christmas.

With her eyes locked on to his, she peeled off her plaid shirt and let it fall to the ground with a noisy, wet smack. She toed off her boots and tried as gracefully as possible to shimmy out of her wet jeans. Although *shimmy* wasn't the right word— she more or less hopped and grunted until she was finally free. Not the sex appeal she'd been hoping for, but when she glanced at him again, his eyes were on her legs, her nearly transparent tank and her erect nipples. His gaze consumed her, burning her skin.

Praying for courage, Tessa reached for the hem and pulled the tank over her head, tossing it aside and leaving her in her very wet, lacy white thong and matching bra.

"I may have planned a little seduction at your cottage," she admitted, resisting the urge to cross her arms over her chest. "But when you opened the door, I kind of chickened out."

Grant continued to give her a visual sampling, and she wished he'd say something, do something. Her body was trembling with need and an ache she'd never known.

She'd been aroused before, plenty of times, but this time was so different. She feared she'd explode before he ever got his clothes off.

"Slick, if you don't say something, I'm going to have to wrestle myself back into those wet jeans."

He swallowed and took a step forward. "You're beautiful, Tessa. I wish I could go slow, but I'm afraid the second I get my hands on you I'm going to snap."

Feeling suddenly even more powerful, she propped her hands on her hips, proud of the way her chest jutted out. "I'm not glass, Slick. Let's see what you've got."

With a smirk, Grant started undressing at lightning speed, and it was Tessa's turn to stare. Thunder and lightning continued outside, and she had never been more excited to be stranded in the middle of a thunderstorm.

Once he was completely naked, Tessa couldn't keep from gaping. Of course she'd seen a naked man, but had never been with one.

"I'm not sure if I should feel self-conscious or if my ego just got boosted," he told her. "But the way you're looking at me isn't helping my control."

"Maybe I don't want you controlled," she whispered. "Maybe I want you not to hold back, but just take me."

She was playing with fire, and she totally knew it. But she'd waited her whole life for this moment, and she didn't want it to be perfect, to be slow and sensual. She didn't want him to think or analyze. She wanted action, wanted him without worry or rules or restrictions.

Tessa had nothing to compare this moment to, but if she was letting her emotions guide her? Yeah, they were out of control, and there was nothing more she wanted than to be... taken.

Grant moved forward, like a stalker to his prey. Shivers raced one after another through her body. Anticipation and arousal consumed her.

"Last chance, Country. You sure you want me...reckless?"

Tessa couldn't stand not having contact another second. She slid her hands up his damp, bare chest. "I wouldn't have you any other way."

Grant's arms wrapped around her waist, pulled her flush against his taut body, until every single point from her knees to her chest was touching him.

And then his lips were on her. Not on her mouth, but on her neck, trailing down to her breasts. He arched her backward, causing her to grip tight to his bare shoulders.

His assault wasn't unexpected; he'd warned her, after all. But what she hadn't anticipated was how she'd feel, how her body would respond...how the thrill of being taken, consumed, would override any euphoria she'd ever experienced.

Grant cupped her bottom, lifting her against him. He walked toward the old, sheet-covered chaise in the corner of the room and laid her there, his body coming down to cover hers.

The weight of him, the strength of him was so new, yet so welcoming. Instinct had her spreading her legs, allowing him to settle between them.

Grant's hands roamed down the dip in her waist and over her hips. "I want to touch you everywhere, Tessa. But right now, I can hardly wait to be inside you."

Reaching up to stroke the wet hair falling across his forehead, she smiled. "We both want the same thing, then."

"As much as I'm barely holding on here, I have to make sure you're ready."

Her skin tingled, her body ached and she was damn near quivering. If she was any more ready, she could finish this job alone.

Grant eased back, sliding a hand between them to find where she ached most for him. Just that one, simple touch had her hips lifting, her hands gripping his biceps.

"You're so beautiful," he murmured as he stroked her. "So responsive."

Tessa closed her eyes, allowing him to take over, and relishing the moment. As much as she wanted to move faster, she didn't want him to stop whatever his talented hands were doing.

Grant wanted to slide into her, but he couldn't stop pleasuring her with his hand. He wanted this to be solely about her. Her head thrown back, her eyes closed and her panting all brought pleasure to him.

And that right there told him just how special she was. He'd never been a selfish lover, but he'd also never taken the time to pleasure a woman and just watch her, ignoring his own wants, needs.

"Grant, please…"

Yeah, he couldn't deny her, not when she was already begging.

Grant eased back farther as realization dawned on him. "I don't have protection, Tess."

A sweet smile spread across her face. "You're lucky I was coming to seduce you. I have a condom in my jeans."

He shot off her and went in search of her wet jeans.

"Front pocket," she said, laughing.

Grant searched there, pulled it out and ripped it open. Once he was covered, he settled back over her.

When he leaned down to take her lips, Tessa wrapped her legs around his waist. Thunder rumbled so hard, so loud, the windows in the cabin rattled.

As she opened her body, her mouth to him, Grant tried to ignore that tug on his heart. He couldn't get too immersed in this, couldn't invest his emotions. Tessa had come to him, so he wasn't taking anything she wasn't willing to give. They both knew where the other stood. But right now, he didn't care about tomorrow, the film or what was going to happen after the project wrapped up.

All he cared about was Tessa.

With as much ease as he could manage, Grant slid into her, pausing when she gasped for breath.

He tore his mouth from hers. "You okay?"

She nodded, tilting her hips. "Don't stop."

Gritting his teeth, Grant complied. Never before had he been in this position, and he wasn't sure what to do, how to make this perfect for her.

But when Tessa ran her hands over his shoulders, threaded her fingers through his damp hair and started moving those hips, he knew she was needing more than him fumbling his way through this. Who was the virgin here? He was so damn nervous, but Tessa's sweet sighs and pants told him she was more than aroused.

Resting on his forearms, Grant leaned down, capturing her lips as their pace picked up a rhythm that was going to have him out of control in no time.

When her body quickened, he tore his mouth from hers, needing to watch her face. He wasn't disappointed as her muscles clenched, her mouth dropped open, her eyes squeezed shut and she let out the sweetest moan he'd ever heard.

All that wild, red hair spread out around her as she came undone, bowing her back. And that's all it took for Grant to follow her over the edge.

* * *

Tessa was…well…speechless.

How had she missed this experience all these years? She'd put her career, her horses and organized lifestyle all before her own needs. And now that those needs had been met, she would never let them go neglected again.

"I can practically hear you thinking," Grant told her, stroking his hand over her bare arm.

He lay on the chaise, Tessa atop him, their arms and legs tangled, and she had zero desire for this storm to pass. This moment in time was one of the few she wanted to freeze. She wanted to lock this moment in her heart, to hold it tight, because right now, in Grant's strong arms, she felt everything in the entire world was absolutely perfect.

"You're not having regrets, are you?"

Tessa smiled against his chest. "Never. Just enjoying us."

Those stroking fingertips sent shivers over her body. Every touch from this man reached something so deep within her, she feared she'd be ruined for anyone else.

"I've never appreciated being stranded in a thunderstorm," he told her. "But I have to say, this definitely has its perks."

Tessa laughed, making a fist on his chest and propping her chin on top. "I never thought of storms as romantic before, but now I won't see them as any other way."

"I've worked on scenes set in thunderstorms. They're not near as fun as this."

The sun had set, so only occasional flashes of lightning illuminated the cabin, allowing her to get brief glimpses of Grant's killer smile amid dark stubble.

"We can try to make it back," she offered. "I mean, I don't want you to feel like you're stuck."

"I have a beautiful naked woman on top of me. I assure you, even if the weather was sunny and perfect, I'd be in no hurry to leave." He gripped her hips, turning them to align with his. "I don't feel stuck. Lucky, satisfied and relaxed, but not stuck."

Tessa flattened her palm against his strong chest. "I'm glad I waited. I'm glad we met, even if I wasn't a fan of this film."

Grant chuckled. "And how do you feel about the film now?"

"I believe you'll do the best job portraying my family in a positive light. That's what I was most worried about."

When she rested her head against his chest again, Grant's hands slid through her hair, moving it off her back so he could stroke those fingertips up and down again.

"What else worries you?" he asked.

She laughed. "About the film or life in general?"

"You have that many worries, huh?" He kissed her forehead and nudged her legs apart until she straddled him again. "Maybe I should just take your mind off all of them for a while."

She jerked up. "Again? I mean, already? Aren't you...you know, done?"

Grant's rich laughter made her feel like an idiot.

"Hey, cut me some slack, Slick. I'm new here."

His hands encircled her waist. "Oh, you're not new anymore. You're experienced, and now I want you to take complete control. Do what you want."

Her mind raced. Other than what she'd read in books, she really had no idea what to do, because she'd never experienced anything firsthand.

"I only brought one condom," she told him as another bolt of lightning lit up the sky, slashing through the windows. "I wasn't expecting..."

"I've never had sex without protection," he told her. "My last physical was only a couple months ago and I was clean. But it's your call. I'll only do what you're comfortable with."

Tessa bit her lip, wondering what she should do. Her body told her one thing, her mind told her another.

"Well, I know I'm clean, and I've been on birth control for other health reasons."

He tipped his hips slightly and slid his hands up to cup her breasts.

"You're not playing fair," she told him.

"Oh, baby. I'm not playing. I'm taking this very, very seriously."

He wanted her to take control? Fine.

Tessa sank down on him in one slow, easy glide. She smiled as he groaned. More than likely he thought she was being torturous, but in all honesty she wanted to make sure she wasn't too sore. But, hey, if he thought that was sexy...

"Tessa," he all but growled. "Honey, you're killing me."

The endearments he tossed about warmed her. She kept telling herself not to read anything into them, but keeping an emotional distance was downright impossible.

Tessa blocked out any negative thoughts, because right now, she intended to show this city slicker just how country girls liked to be in control.

Fifteen

Tessa jerked with a start, wondering what had actually woken her up. Beneath her, spread out on the chaise, Grant groaned and twitched.

Arms and legs tangled, Tessa tried to sit up, but Grant's hands gripped her shoulders.

"Melanie, stop!" he yelled.

Tessa froze. Melanie? Whoever this woman was, she was causing him nightmares. *Please, don't be a girlfriend. Or worse...a wife.*

"Grant." Tessa tried to break from his hold as she patted the side of his face. "Grant, wake up."

The storm wasn't as violent as earlier, but growls of thunder still filled the night. The occasional lightning was the only thing cutting through the darkness of the cabin.

"I'm so sorry," he cried.

Tessa couldn't stand the anguish ripping from him. So she did the only thing she could think of: she slapped him, hard.

Grant stilled and his eyes flew open. For a moment she couldn't tell if he was truly awake, angry or still living the nightmare.

"Tessa?"

Still naked from lovemaking, she crossed her arms over her chest and eased back. "I'm sorry. I didn't mean to hurt you, but you were having a bad dream."

Grant ran a hand over his face and sighed. "Sorry I woke you."

"Seeing as how this is the second time you've woken me with a nightmare, and this time you yelled out another woman's name, care to tell me what's going on?" she asked, trying to remain calm.

Just because he'd done so didn't mean anything. He was obviously hurting, and Tessa wasn't naive enough to believe he hadn't been with other women before her.

But the fact he'd shouted it out while lying beneath her naked did warrant an explanation, in her opinion.

"Who's Melanie?" she asked, when he still didn't answer.

Grant shifted, obviously trying to get up, so Tessa came to her feet. Apparently the sexy moment was over. In the dark, broken by random flashes of lightning, she scrambled to find her clothes and get into them while Grant did the same.

"Melanie is my sister," he told her after several minutes of silence. "She's my twin."

A wave of relief washed over Tessa. Okay, so she wasn't dealing with the proverbial "other woman."

"Why do you have nightmares about her?"

Grant finished putting on his clothes and walked over to the door, opening it to look out onto the dark night. "Just something that happened in my past. Nothing that has to do with you."

She'd be lying if she didn't admit, at least to herself, that his comment hurt. Why wouldn't he open up to her? Was he that protective of his sister? Something had happened, and from the way his nightmares seemed to consume him, Tessa had a feeling whatever had gone on in his past was extremely traumatic.

"It's pretty dark out," she said, trying to change the subject and not be a clingy woman demanding to know what he was thinking. "We can try to go back, but I don't have a flashlight."

When she stepped up beside him, he wrapped his arm around her waist, tucking her against his side. "You're in such a hurry to leave. I'm going to start thinking you don't like my company."

"Oh, I thoroughly enjoyed your company," she said with a laugh, trying to lighten the intense moment. "I'm just not sure how comfortable either of us will be with nowhere to sleep tonight."

"I was fine with you lying on me. Of course, I'd recommend you lose those clothes you just put on."

Tessa swatted his flat abs. "You have a one-track mind now that I've let you have your wicked way with me."

"Oh, I had a one-track mind all along. I can just be more vocal about it now without offending you."

They listened to the rain, watching as the storm rolled through the night. Tessa would never look at this cabin the same again. This place had a special new meaning to her now. And a whole new meaning to her dreams.

"I hate to bring this up, but no one can find us here," he told her. "I can't let it out that we're sleeping together."

And if the secret nightmares hadn't caused enough hurt, this cold realistic fact sure did. She'd known there was a clause in his contract; he'd mentioned it before. But she hadn't thought it would be an issue. And now that they'd been intimate, she hadn't thought about lying or hiding it.

"I don't mean to make you upset," he added, obviously picking up on her thoughts. "I just can't afford to risk my career."

Wrapping her arm around his waist, she squeezed him tight. "I wouldn't do anything to damage your career. Besides, I don't expect you to keep sneaking out to sleep with me."

Grant turned, taking her by the shoulders and pinning her against the edge of the door. "Well, I expect more than just this, Tessa. Because I can't see you in public doesn't mean I can't come to your house every night, slide into your bed and pleasure you over and over. I've not even begun to explore you, and I'll be damned if another man is going to show you all there is to intimacy."

His matter-of-fact tone thrilled her.

"What if you get caught?" she asked. "Your crew will be

arriving in two days, and security will be tight around my premises and Stony Ridge. Do you plan on teleporting into my bedroom?"

He tipped his hips against hers. "Baby, I'll make it happen, if that's what you want."

Grant nipped at her lips, slid his hands through her hair to tilt her head, allowing him better access.

"Tell me that's what you want," he murmured against her lips. "Say it, Tessa."

God help her, she was drowning, and she had no one to blame but herself. She'd gotten this ball rolling when she'd set out to seduce him earlier, and now she was paying the price.

"Yes," she told him, gripping his hard biceps as his mouth traveled down her neck. "I want you no matter how we have to sneak."

This whole sneaking, lying and hiding scenario went against everything she knew. Her life consisted of schedules, organization and training, but she had a feeling she was going to love this new Tessa that Grant had uncovered.

The idea of sneaking around added an element of excitement and power. She would still have control over the when and where.

The only problem? What would this new Tessa do when the time came for Grant to leave? Because he'd still never said anything about staying.

"Looks like everything is ready to go," said Anthony Price as he admired the trailers and the equipment set up outside the stables. "I'm impressed there were no glitches. There's always a setback."

Bronson laughed. "There's a setback when *you're* in charge. I completely trusted Grant to take care of things."

Grant knew these half brothers felt a sibling rivalry. Of course, it wasn't that long ago that the two had been heated enemies. Then the secret, decades old, revealed the two were indeed both sons of Hollywood's most recognized icon, Olivia Dane.

"I had a few very minor hiccups, but managed to smooth them over before you both arrived," Grant admitted. "I would like to try to get the stable scenes shot either first or last. With Tessa and Cassie training for the Kentucky Derby, we really can't be in their way."

"I agree. We can shoot those first." Bronson looked through the folder he held, shuffling papers. "I'm intrigued about that cabin that's back on the property. I'd like to see it. Not that I don't trust your judgment, I just want to get a feel for it."

Grant smiled. Oh, he'd gotten his own feel for the cottage. And he wouldn't be able to keep a straight face while they were filming any scenes down there.

Not only had he violated the contract by getting involved with someone on the set, he had done the deed on the set itself.

"Max should be arriving tomorrow," Bronson said. "I'd like to get his take on things, as well. We just wrapped up a film together a few months ago, and he added some great insight."

"I worked with Max a few times," Grant replied. "He's one of the best actors I've ever been involved with, and Lily is such a sweetheart, I know this is going to be a major success."

"I agree," Anthony interjected. "I'd like to check out the grounds before everyone arrives, though."

Grant motioned toward the expansive stables. "Right this way."

As the three headed across the wide drive, Tessa flew by on Don Pedro and rounded the corner in the track. Grant couldn't help that his eyes followed, couldn't help his gut clenching at the sight of her as memories of a few nights ago stirred. Memories of a wild thunderstorm, when she'd abandoned everything she'd known. Every fear, every worry and every part of her she'd handed over to him with a trust that still made his knees weak.

"Damn."

Grant turned at the soft curse from Bronson, and found the brothers staring back at him.

"Tell me you didn't," Anthony said.

Grant shrugged. "What?"

"The beauty that just went by on the track," Bronson chimed in. "And I'm not talking about the Thoroughbred."

Grant took another step, hoping the guys would follow and he could face forward without looking them in the eye. "We've spent a good bit of time together. She's my go-to girl for questions and the tours."

"As long as you don't go to her for anything else," Bronson muttered as they neared the open door of the stable. "Marty will have your butt if you pull another stunt like you did with the makeup artist."

Grant laughed. Yeah, he'd never live down the whole makeup artist debacle. "I assure you, I'm not revisiting that time," he stated.

As they passed through the stalls, Grant noted Nash cleaning out Don Pedro's stall, and wondered if Tessa was still having reservations about the scruffy-looking man. To Grant he just seemed like a hard worker. Maybe a bit mysterious, with that long hair and scruffy beard, but he wasn't dirty, he kept to himself and worked harder than anyone else Grant had seen here.

So far Grant's investigator had turned up nothing. Apparently the new groom was just quiet.

He didn't even lift his head when the three men passed by. No, Grant didn't believe the stranger was out to sabotage the Barringtons or the upcoming race.

When Tessa sped by once more, visible through the stable doorway, Grant made a point to keep walking, keep his mouth shut and show no emotion. Damn, this fling might be harder to keep secret than he'd thought.

When they stepped out into the afternoon sunshine, Cassie greeted them.

"Hi, guys." She walked over, all smiles, and extended her

hand. "I'm Cassie Barrington. You must be Bronson and Anthony. We're so excited to have you here."

The brothers shook her hand and offered pleasantries.

"Tessa is just about finished," Cassie commented. "She's been pushing herself today, so I'm making her stop after this set."

Grant grunted. "Is today different from any other day with her self-discipline?"

Cassie laughed, holding her hand up to shield the sun from her eyes. "Not really, but something has been up with her the past two days. Can't figure out what."

Grant knew exactly what had been up with her the past two days. But he totally ignored the questioning looks from Bronson and Anthony. No way in hell was he even mentioning Tessa's name in anything other than a professional way.

The slightest slipup could cost him not only this film, but a future with his own production company.

After being intimate with Tessa, he couldn't help but look at everything from a whole new perspective.

No, he didn't want to lose this film or his credibility. But, more importantly, he didn't want to lose his family. Tessa had helped him see that.

And at some point, he'd have to tackle that heavy burden he'd carried for so long.

"Cassie, if you don't mind introducing Tessa to Anthony and Bronson, I'd appreciate it." God, he was a coward. "I have a phone call I just remembered. Also, your dad wasn't home, so when he gets here could you do those introductions, as well?"

"I'd love to," Cassie replied, oblivious to any turmoil within him. "Do what you need to. Tessa and I can take things from here."

As Grant walked away, he heard Anthony mention the pond and the old cabin. Yeah, Grant couldn't be part of that. One step near that old shack with Tessa around and everyone on set would know. He had never had a problem holding his emotions in check before, but something had stirred in his heart when he'd taken Tessa to bed. Something deep within him had awakened, and he worried that whatever it was would get him into trouble before all was said and done.

Sixteen

Tessa hated that she stared at the clock. Hated that her ex had left two more voice mails today pleading for her to call.

But most of all she hated that she was angry when each hour ticked by and Grant didn't show.

In the past two days, he'd barely been a blip on her radar. Today Anthony and Bronson had arrived, and Cassie had been the one to introduce them.

Her father had immediately swept the young Hollywood hotshots away, and Tessa had no doubt Damon had filled their heads with stories of the past. Stories from the family, from the racing seasons and his victories. The man was proud of all he'd accomplished, as well he should be. He'd not only won the Triple Crown, he'd raised two daughters and kept the family business close. No outside trainers, no outside jockeys. Stony Ridge was definitely a family affair, and definitely unique. Which was what made the Barrington legacy so special and film-worthy.

Tessa had just gotten into her cami and panty set and pulled her comforter back when something pecked on her second-story bedroom window. She crossed the room and eased the curtain aside to see Grant below, tossing pieces of mulch from her landscaping.

Tessa unlocked the window and slid it up. "What are you doing? I have a front and back door, you know."

"Well, I thought you would think this was romantic," he called up to her. "I needed pebbles, but all you had was bark.

Had to make do. But at least it all fell back to where it belongs. You should appreciate that, seeing as how you like organization."

Tessa laughed, rolling her eyes. "I'll go unlock the back door."

A shiver of excitement swept through her. Even though he'd seen every inch of her, she still snagged the short cotton robe off the end of her bed. Belting it as she bounded down the steps, she couldn't help but grin. Grant was nothing if not original.

When she unlocked the door and eased it open, he stepped right in and looked down at her with a wide smile. Only a small accent light in the corner of her kitchen lit up the space.

Tessa didn't usually have men in her house, so the overpowering presence of Grant excited her.

"It's late," she told him. "I was just about to go to bed."

"Sounds like perfect timing on my part."

When she started to turn away, he snagged her wrist, pulled her up against his broad chest and tipped her face back so that she looked him in the eye. "I've missed you," he murmured, a second before his mouth came down to claim hers.

His hands plunged into her hair as he tilted her head. Tessa had no choice but to wrap her arms around his neck and give back. She'd known him only a month, but she already knew the way he tasted, the way he held her so tightly, the way he kissed with passion and power. And she knew that, in those few days she hadn't been with him, she'd missed him.

How the hell would she cope when he left for good?

Grant eased back. "You have no idea how hard it's been for me to keep my distance."

Tessa pulled from his arms and headed out of the kitchen. "Not too hard. You've managed to not even speak to me. Pretty sneaky, having my sister do the introductions."

Footsteps hurried behind her and an arm snaked around her waist, lifting her off the ground. Not that she'd complain about the hard chest she'd fallen back into.

"I couldn't be near you," he all but growled in her ear. "It would take only one look and Bronson and Anthony would know. I can't hide how I feel about you, Tessa. I'm not the actor here."

Smiling into the dark, she clasped her hands over his. "Why don't you come upstairs and show me how you feel? There's no hiding in this house."

Grant swept her up and hooked an arm beneath her knees as he started for the staircase. "I've always wanted to carry a woman up the stairs and into her bed."

Tessa nibbled on his neck, inhaling the fresh aftershave she'd come to crave. "I'm glad I'm your first in something. Levels the playing field somewhat."

He stopped at the landing and looked into her eyes. "Honey, you're a first for me in so many ways."

Tessa wished there was better light, because she wanted to read his expression more clearly. Unfortunately, her bedroom was at the end of the hall and the glow spilling into the hallway a faint one.

"I hope you know I plan on staying awhile," he told her as he strode toward the room.

"I'd like to see you leave," she joked. "I admit I feel a little naughty being so secretive. I only hope no one noticed you sneaking over here."

"Glad I could bring out your inner vixen," he said with a loud smack on her lips. "And I doubt anyone saw me. I dressed in black and I walked."

Tessa jerked back. "You walked?"

Setting her feet on the floor, Grant aligned her body with his. "Yeah. I didn't want to risk anyone seeing my rental car pull in here, and walking makes it easier to dodge security, even though they're not that thick right now, and I actually think there's only one guard on duty tonight."

Tessa framed his stubbled face with her hands. God, she loved the feel of those whiskers beneath her palms. And dressed all in black? This man was the epitome of sexy.

"You went to a lot of trouble to be here," she told him, placing a quick kiss on his lips, then easing back. "I better make it worth your while."

Grant's eyes widened and his nostrils flared as she loosened the belt on her robe and sent the garment fluttering to the floor. She didn't have on the sexiest of pajamas, but this was Tessa. Cotton, simple, natural.

Of course, she'd be naked in seconds anyway, so what did it matter?

"You going to stare all night or start peeling out of your burglar gear?"

His lips tipped in a grin. "You have a smart mouth."

"Of course I do. That's one of my most redeeming qualities."

Grant pulled his long-sleeved T-shirt over his head and tossed it aside. Those glorious muscles, a sprinkling of chest hair and 100 percent raw male stared back at her. And as much as Tessa would love to stand and stare at him all night, she wanted to touch him even more. Wanted to explore him and take her time now that they were on her turf.

She already knew each time being with Grant would make it harder to let him go in the end…and harder to hide her feelings when they were in public.

But he'd shown her a new side of love, without using the words. And for now, she'd embrace the moment.

Tessa put Oliver in the stall and was surprised to see Max Ford already on the set so early. He must've really wanted to be here at the start of the day.

In the two weeks Grant had been sneaking into her bed, they'd gotten closer and developed a routine. But he always crept back out before sunup. She knew he would; he'd told her as much up front. But that didn't stop the thread of hurt that went through her each day she woke up alone.

Somehow the fact that he came and went during the night lessened their relationship. Tessa knew they had something special, but after the past two weeks she felt she was nothing more than a booty call.

At first the sneaking had been fun and flirty, but as the days went on she felt it only cheapened the moments they shared.

After brushing down Oliver, she went to get some feed, but as she turned a corner she hit the hard chest of Nash.

"Excuse me," he said, his voice low.

Tessa stepped back, still leery of the quiet man. "It's okay. I should look where I'm going."

"My fault." He made no motion to move, but propped his hands on his hips. "Lots of action going on today already."

"Yes," she agreed, surprised he'd said more than two words to her. "I imagine it will only get crazier in the coming days. Max is here now, and Lily is due to arrive tomorrow."

"Max Ford is playing your father, right?" the groom asked.

Tessa nodded as she studied him. His beard didn't seem to fit the man. His eyes were bright blue, almost as bright as hers. His hair was a bit long, falling over his ears and collar, but his hands looked very well groomed. Odd how some parts of him appeared flawless and other parts downright unkempt.

"Lily will be playing my mother," Tessa told him.

He seemed to process that as he shifted his feet on the straw-covered floor. "And will this film start before your parents were married?"

"I think so."

"They're covering your dad's personal life as well as his career?"

Tessa had no clue what this line of questioning had to do with anything, but she replied, "Yes. It's all pretty much set around my dad. The rest of the family will be secondary characters, I suppose. We're not nearly as exciting as him, anyway," she said, trying to joke. Only Nash wasn't smiling.

"I need to get some feed," she told him as she maneuvered around him. "Sorry I ran into you."

Before he could ask another bizarre question about the film, she headed down the aisle. At first she'd been skeptical, but Grant hadn't uncovered anything, and Nash's background check had been spotless. So far he'd been a hard worker. Quiet, mysterious, today a bit nosy, but he'd been gentle when caring for the animals and he'd never given any reason to believe he was out to harm anybody.

But Tessa still had that uneasy feeling.

After she'd fed all the horses, her own stomach growled. A few days ago she could've asked Grant to join her for some lunch, but not today. Their time for being out in the open was over…at least until the film wrapped up. But what then? Once the movie was done Grant would return to L.A. and Tessa would remain right here.

This path they'd started down was not going to lead them to a happy place, and she really wished she'd listened to herself in the beginning. But in all honesty, she would've still taken this road with Grant. There was something unique and different about him. He made her feel special, hadn't made her feel as if her morals and her choices were ridiculous. He'd actually respected her more for her decisions in life.

And that's how she knew this was the man her mother had told her to look for. One who didn't laugh at her for her thoughts, dreams or goals. One who encouraged her, cherished her and lifted her up. Who cared for her even after she'd shared her morals and her reasoning.

Tessa stopped just outside the stables and watched as four beautiful males stood in a serious-looking meeting. Grant drew her gaze, but Bronson, Anthony and Max were very nice to look at, as well. They were all happily married, and Tessa wondered how they made that work, as all three men had demanding jobs. From what Tessa had heard, Max was a newlywed and his wife was from the East Coast.

Tessa rolled her eyes. What on earth was she doing, thinking about marriage and long-distance relationships? She and Grant had never discussed anything beyond the filming.

Added to that, she had a race to prepare for. She didn't have time to choose monogrammed towels for nuptials that were taking place only in her head.

When she marched in the back door, Linda was pouring a glass of sweet tea. With a smile, she slid it across the island to Tessa.

"I saw you coming," the elderly woman said. "You looked like you could cool off. I know just from standing in here, looking at the fine man scenery, how heated I was getting."

Tessa laughed. "You're rotten, Linda."

"I'm old, honey. Not dead. And those four men out there are going to have all the women in town begging to be extras on the set."

Tessa took a long, refreshing drink. "Good thing we have added security. Besides, three of those four are married."

"Might as well be all of them," Linda muttered.

Tessa's glass clunked back down on the smooth granite surface. "Don't be shy now. Say what's on your mind."

With a shrug, Linda rested her hands on the edge of the counter. "Just saying the way that man looks at you, he won't care about no other woman sniffing around."

The nerves in Tessa's belly fluttered. How did he look at her? Was it just lustful or was there more? She wanted to know, wanted to sit and gossip, but where would that get her? If she was destined for heartache at the end of this film, there was no point in getting her hopes up now.

"Don't frown, Tessa," Linda told her with a smile. "I know you well enough to know you're already calculating how much time you have left with your man. But trust me, love works in its own way. People don't trust that sometimes. Just step back and let your hearts figure out what's best."

Tessa shook her head. "Oh, there's no love. We just..."

Linda's brows rose as her grin spread. "I know what you're just doing, and I'm so happy for you. Your mama would love Mr. Carter."

Sliding her fingertip over the condensation on her glass, Tessa tried not to let the burn in her eyes turn into full-fledged tears. There wasn't a doubt in her mind that her mother would love Grant. What wasn't to love?

"You borrow trouble," Linda went on. "Enjoy yourself. You're only young once, honey. Trust me when I say this will all work out."

Tessa reached across the counter and squeezed Linda's hand. "I'm so glad I have you."

"The feeling is mutual. I love you and Cassie like you're my own girls. I'm always here anytime you need me."

"I know you are. That means so much to me." She paused, then added, "But you need to know that whatever you think about Grant and me, you can't repeat it. He could lose this film if anyone finds out."

Linda straightened. "I've seen things, heard things in my years here that would curl the hair on your head. I've kept secrets and will take them to my grave. I won't utter a word about your man."

Tessa wondered what secrets the woman held on to. Secrets made Tessa nervous, but she knew there was no way Linda would budge.

One good thing, at least no one would discover Tessa and Grant's affair. She hoped.

Seventeen

"I hate her already."

Cassie laughed. "That's because she's stunning, rich and nice. Let's tie her up by her perfectly polished toes."

Tessa eyed Lily Beaumont, Southern beauty and female lead, as Bronson and Anthony showed her around the property and pointed out her trailer.

Cassie and Tessa had been trying to work, but they were just as starstruck as everyone else. The film star's beauty and that Southern accent had all the men at Stony Acres ogling the Hollywood sweetheart.

"It's hard to hate someone when they're beautiful and sweet," Tessa sighed. "I really want to, though. I mean, she's not even fat. Is she perfect everywhere?"

"Maybe she has a third nipple."

Cassie laughed at her own joke as Tessa slung her arms over a fence post. If she was honest with herself, it wasn't Lily's beauty that bothered her so much…it was how Grant would react to it.

The man lived in the land of perfection, worked with gorgeous women all the time. And Tessa had seen Lily in movies before, but in person…she was beyond stunning.

"Regardless of our green-eyed monster rearing its ugly head," Cassie said, leaning in next to her on the fence, "Lily is the perfect person to play the younger version of Mom."

Tessa smiled. "She really is. Mom's beauty was flawless,

she had that accent and such delicate mannerisms. Lily may not have to do much acting at all."

"We better get back to work." Her sister patted her arm. "Once our jealousy for her perfect figure and her ability to look beautiful after flying across the country subsides, we'll go introduce ourselves."

Tessa started to turn when she spotted her father coming from the house. "Looks like Dad is already beating us. I wonder what he thinks of her playing Mom."

"He okayed it. That was one stipulation for him agreeing to the film," Cassie informed her. "He wanted to have final say so over who portrayed him and Mom."

Tessa turned her gaze to her sister. "I didn't know that. I'm glad. I think Max and Lily will be perfect."

While Tessa had hated the thought of this film in the beginning, now she was growing more and more anxious to see the finished product. After getting to know Grant, seeing how much care he was taking with her family's legacy and portraying everything just so, she realized this film would be a beautiful tribute to her parents.

Cassie's arm came around to settle on Tessa's shoulders. "This is going to be hard for us. Seeing how Mom and Dad fell in love, married, raised a family…"

"…and when she died," Tessa finished, around the lump in her throat. "Yeah, it will be hard, but I'm sure Dad will need us to be strong. This film is a good thing. Our family has worked hard for where we are, and I'm glad Hollywood took notice of it."

"Speaking of working hard, let's get to it, sis."

Tessa looped her arm around her sister's waist and they turned from the fence, heading back to the stable. As they held on to each other, Tessa knew they'd be doing a lot of leaning on the other for support during this time. As exciting as it was to have Hollywood's hottest actors and producers making this film, the reality was that their family had real emotions and would forever have that void that only Rose Barrington had filled.

Grant hadn't seen Tessa in two days. He'd barely seen her flash by in the ring. He'd put in long nights, sometimes all night, as some scenes needed to be shot late and the lighting with the moon and such had to be exactly right.

He worried that she'd been in her house, in her spacious bed, waiting for him. And as much as he ached to sneak back over there, he hadn't been able to catch a break.

On the mornings when she'd come over to the estate, he'd been heading into the cottage to catch a few hours' sleep before going at it again.

She hadn't approached him, hadn't even glanced his way.

So, being the smart man that he was, he knew she was either trying to hide their relationship, was pissed or was worried about training. He'd venture to say all of the above.

Lily had told him how wonderful the Barrington ladies were and how much Tessa looked like her mother. Grant had merely nodded, because he seriously feared if he opened his mouth and started discussing Tessa with anyone on the set, all his emotions would show.

But a second day of not seeing Tessa was killing him. In two more days the crew was taking a three-day break. It had been scheduled in advance, and Grant knew exactly what he would do with that time off.

He needed to be with Tessa for more than just sex. He needed to show her how important she was to him.

After he made a few calls, he headed back to the pond, where today's sequence would be filmed. A simple picnic with Max and Lily...aka Damon and Rose.

Watching them fall in love through the camera was magical. Everything about this film so far gave him goose bumps, and that rarely happened on the set. Perhaps he was so emotionally involved with the family, he automatically felt a strong bond with the backstory of the characters.

But as he watched on the screen for the first kiss, Grant didn't see Max and Lily, or even Damon and Rose. He saw himself and Tessa.

Had he fallen for her? How the hell did that happen? He'd warned himself not to get in too deep with her, but now that he'd admitted to himself how he felt, he knew more than ever he had a past he needed to face. If he didn't, there would be no chance of a future.

Grant had every intention of settling down, of falling in love. He wanted a marriage like his parents had, like the Barringtons had.

And Tessa might have a list of reasons as to why they didn't belong together, but he was about to show her all the reasons they did.

If Grant wanted to catch Tessa, he knew he'd have to beat her to the stables and talk to her before she started her training. Thankfully, he'd gotten to bed around one in the morning, as opposed to being up all night. After a few hours of sleep, he was ready to talk to her and drop a hint of his surprise.

Grant pulled his barn jacket tighter around his chest as the cool early-morning air sliced through him. As soon as the low-hanging fog wore off, however, the day promised to be beautiful.

The fresh smell of straw and horses hit him before he entered the stable. While he was getting more used to the atmosphere, he still wasn't fully comfortable.

Oliver bobbed his head over the door of his stall, almost as if looking for him. "Hey, buddy," Grant said.

There, talking to the horse was a major step. Touching and, heaven forbid, riding were still off-limits.

He moved farther into the stables, nearly jumping out of his skin when Macduff started causing a ruckus, stamping his hooves and bucking.

That one would need a lot of work and loving care, but he had confidence in Cassie. From what he'd seen of her as a sister, daughter and mother, she was gentle and nurturing. Just what that hellion needed.

As he passed by Macduff, very cautiously, Grant eased over to the other side of the aisle...and tripped. Once he'd regained his footing, he turned back to see what he'd fallen over.

And saw a foot sticking out of the open stall.

Tessa was lying amid the hay, a plaid blanket wrapped around her, straw in her hair and the most peaceful look on her face.

Moving into the stall, Grant squatted down beside the sleeping beauty and pushed a strand of crimson hair from her silky cheek. She stirred, but remained asleep, a small smile lighting up her face.

Even in sleep she stole his breath. Given this reckless manner in which he'd found her, Grant couldn't help but smile himself. Miss In Control At All Times looked as if she'd spent the night rolling around in the stall.

Which conjured up another image, of both of them in the stall. A bit itchy and uncomfortable, but he'd take Tessa any way and anywhere he could. His attraction and need for her knew no bounds.

"Hey, Country." He cupped her shoulder and squeezed. "You're sleeping the day away."

Watching her lids flutter as she came awake only added to that zing in his heart. Damn it. Zing? He was totally gone where she was concerned, if he was thinking of words like *zing*.

But there was nothing about her he didn't find appealing. Now what would she have to say about that, once he decided to tell her how he truly felt?

"Grant." She sat up, smiled and wiped straw and hair from her face. "What are you doing here? Did you work all night again?"

"We wrapped up around one or so." Because he wanted,

needed to touch her, he plucked straw from her flannel shirt. "What are you doing, sleeping with the horses?"

"Keeping an eye on them."

She came to her feet and promptly started folding her blanket. Grant stood as well, crossing his arms over his chest.

"What on earth are you watching them for?" he asked.

"Macduff wasn't acting right, and Nash offered to stay, but I sent him on home."

"Is Macduff okay?"

She stacked the blanket on a tack box in the corner and turned back to offer a smile. "I think he's still adjusting. If he keeps acting off, not eating and being pouty, I'll have Cassie call the vet."

With her hair in disarray, her shirt untucked and rumpled, Grant found himself liking this morning Tessa.

"Oh, no," she said, holding her hands up. "You've got that look."

He stepped forward. "What look is that?"

"You know."

Grant smiled, closing the gap between them. "I do know, but you don't seem to be putting up much of a fight."

Her eyes darted around as she backed into the corner.

"Nowhere to go," he whispered as he reached her. "And we're all alone."

He placed a hand on either side of her face, caging her in between his body and the wall. Her eyes widened and arousal shot through them as she stared back. That unpainted mouth beckoned him...and who was he to refuse.

Softly, slowly, Grant claimed her lips. Tessa's body arched into his as she opened for him. He could completely drown in her love. That may be his ego, and his hope, talking, but Grant had a gut feeling that what they'd formed here was indeed love. He knew she felt it as well, but saying the words aloud needed to come at the right time.

And he couldn't fully give himself until he confronted his family and his past.

He nipped at her lips and lifted his head, pleased to see her swollen mouth and closed lids.

"I had a reason for coming in here," he murmured. "But you make me lose my train of thought."

Tessa looked up at him. "You mean preying on a sleeping woman wasn't your goal?"

"No, just an added perk." He rested his hands on her shoulders, loving the feel of her delicate body beneath them. "I have a three-day break coming up."

"Really? And I suppose you have plans in mind?"

Did he ever. "We have plans," he corrected. "I've even discussed things with Cassie, and she thinks it's a great idea for you to take some time off."

Tessa broke free of his hold and stepped around him. "Wait a minute. I can't take three days off. I'm training."

He turned to face her, ready to defend his case, because he knew this argument was coming. "You've been training and living in the stables your entire life, Tessa. Let's be honest, all you've done is work. You deserve a break."

With jerky, frantic motions she started pulling her hair back into a low ponytail, then tugged a band from her wrist to secure it.

"I can't just leave. I have a schedule, Slick. I need to stick to it. My horses need to be exercised daily."

"And Cassie has already said she'd be more than happy to do that."

Tessa crossed her arms, chewed on her lip, and Grant knew she was thinking of another reason. Was she worried about spending so much time alone with him? The getaway certainly added a whole new layer to their relationship.

He merely kept his mouth shut and waited, because for every argument she had, he had a response. He would be taking her away from here even if he had to throw her over his shoulder and manhandle her out.

"I'm not comfortable leaving Nash, with him being so new."

Grant laughed. "He's your father's employee. I'm sure your

dad has control over his own worker. Besides, he's been here long enough to know what to do for a couple days."

"What about the clause? Now Cassie knows we're…"

Still smiling, Grant shrugged. "She's your sister. I was aware she already knew, and I know she won't tell anybody. I trust her, and I needed someone to help me get all this arranged, anyway."

Tessa sighed, glancing up to the ceiling and shaking her head. "Why am I even considering this?"

Grant eased forward, knowing he had her, but going in for the kill, anyway. "Because you want to." He slipped his arms around her waist and pulled her flush against him. "Because you know you need the break and because you want my body."

"Well, that's a little TMI for this early in the morning."

Both Grant and Tessa turned to see Cassie smiling at them.

"Sorry to interrupt," she said. "Just thought I was coming to work."

Tessa laughed. "Don't mind him. He's got a one-track mind."

Grant's cell chimed from his pocket. Stepping back from Tessa, he pulled it out and sighed. "I have to take this," he told her. "We'll talk later."

As much as he hated leaving without her definite answer, even though he knew she'd go, he had to take the call. Max Ford's agent was on the phone and the man was not known for his patience, so keeping him waiting was not smart.

After Grant stepped outside and took the call, he sent off some texts to Tessa, letting her know when to be ready, when he'd pick her up and what to pack. The packing thing was easy, considering he had that detail planned, as well.

He could hardly wait to wrap up today's shoot, because for the next three glorious days, Tessa Barrington would be his, and she was going to find out just how important she'd become to him.

Eighteen

Seriously?

Tessa eyed the private jet as she stepped from Grant's rental car. "You've got to be kidding me," she said, glaring at him over her shoulder.

"What?" He closed his car door and rounded the hood to take hold of her arm. "We're getting away. How else do you think we'll get there?"

"I assumed we'd drive somewhere, but seeing as how I don't even know where you're taking me, I really hadn't thought about a plane."

Grant chuckled. "If it takes more than a couple hours by car, I always fly."

And in her world she flew as little as possible, seeing as how she loved the open road, loved seeing new places, meeting new people. Most often when she traveled, though, it was with horses and not a powerful, sexy man.

Just another difference between them. His jet practically screamed business mogul. Being showered with luxurious gifts was new...and another reminder of how different they were. Not that her family couldn't afford such things; they just didn't focus on flashy trips or material objects.

Of course, her father had a jet, but Tessa rarely used it. When did she have time to travel other than going from race to race?

"So where are we heading?" she asked as Grant led her toward the steps of the plane.

"I believe you mentioned something about never having a prom."

Tessa halted in her tracks. "I'm almost afraid to ask what you're talking about."

Squeezing her arm, Grant urged her on up. "Consider this the limo to pick you up."

Glancing back over her shoulder as she climbed the steps, Tessa smiled. "I only have this small bag, no room for a formal."

"I've taken care of everything, as any good prom date would."

Tessa's belly did a flip. The man literally thought of everything. But she wondered just what would be waiting for her once they got to...wherever it was they were going.

"Good evening, Miss Barrington," the pilot said as she stepped on board.

She smiled. "Good evening."

Tessa moved inside the luxurious cabin. Behind her, Grant chatted with his pilot for a bit before he joined her. Tessa was still standing in amazement, studying the openness of the plane.

In the far back was an L-shaped sofa, while off to the other side were two club-style chairs and a flat-screen television. Another small seating area was directly in front of her, and there was a door in the back, no doubt leading to a bedroom.

"Wow, this is impressive, Slick." She moved over to the sofa and sank onto the corner cushions. "Now I know why you fly everywhere."

Grant laughed and took a seat in a club chair. "You'll have to come over here to buckle up, babe."

Tessa moved to the other seat and fastened her belt. In no time they were taxiing down the runway and soaring into the sky. She loved watching out the window, loved seeing just how small everything got in seconds.

"How can you drive everywhere, when it's clear from the way your face lights up, looking out the window, that you love to fly?" he asked beside her.

Tessa shrugged, keeping her gaze on the ground below. "I love the adventure of a road trip. In a plane it's all over so fast. Besides, I like to travel with my horse."

Grant reached out, taking her hand in his and stroking his thumb along her palm. Part of her wanted to read more into this trip, but the other part, the realistic part, kept her grounded.

He was just taking her off somewhere so they didn't have to sneak. Being away from the film, away from where the paparazzi were camping out, would be easier. She actually appreciated how much he'd gone through to get them out. He'd talked to Cassie to clear the schedule.

The old Tessa would've been angry at him for going behind her back. But the new Tessa, the one who had fallen for this Hollywood hotshot, was flattered.

"When will you tell me where we're going?" she asked.

Grant shrugged. "It's nothing too exciting. Just a little cabin in the woods in Colorado. I own a good portion of the area, so we'll have complete privacy."

She eyed him, quirking a brow. "Define 'a good portion.'"

"The mountain. I own the entire mountain."

Of course he did. Why buy the house when you can buy the mountain? Silly of her to think differently. Granted, she and her family had money, but they didn't think in terms of mountain buying.

Right now all she wanted to do was enjoy these next three days. Anything that came after that would just have to wait.

For once in her life she wasn't looking at a spreadsheet, wasn't going by a schedule and wasn't worried about training.

Whatever Grant had planned was fine with her, because he'd shown her he was more than capable of making her forget her surroundings. Now she couldn't wait until he showed her again.

And she fully intended to enjoy this little fantasy while it lasted.

* * *

Little cabin?

Tessa laughed as they parked in front of the "cabin."

"I believe you referred to this as little."

Grant nodded. "It is, compared to the home I have in L.A."

She rolled her eyes and exited the car. The two-story log home was built in a rustic style, but with a wide porch stretching across the front and a rather large second-floor balcony with three sets of double doors leading out onto it, Tessa had a feeling this home was easily five thousand square feet.

"Did you have this built?" she asked.

He pulled their two pieces of luggage from the trunk and headed toward the front door. "Yes. I wanted someplace I could escape to between films. I have a condo in Hawaii, but I've always loved the mountains. There's something so peaceful about being up here with the fresh air, the quietness. I rarely get up here, but it's so worth it when I do."

So he liked the country. Okay. Maybe they weren't so different, after all.

Grant unlocked the door and gestured for her to enter ahead of him. If she thought the outside was impressive, the inside was spectacular. The floor plan was completely open, with a large sunken living area. Windows covered the entire back wall and overlooked the city below. *Breathtaking* wasn't the right word to describe it.

"I'd live here if I were you," she told him, making her way to the picturesque windows. "How do you ever leave?"

"Well, when work calls, I have no choice."

Tessa turned back to him and raised a brow. "I'm ready to sell my house and live here. Do you rent rooms out?"

Laughing, Grant crossed the spacious living area and came to stand beside her. "You should see this in the fall when all the leaves have turned. Or in the winter with all the snow. It's almost magical."

Tessa wanted nothing more than to still be around during those seasons, yet realistically, that probably wasn't going to happen. But her imagination was pretty good, and she could practically see the assortment of colors on the trees in September, the pristine white branches in January.

This cabin wasn't just magical, it was romantic.

Tessa turned, slid her arms around Grant's waist and rested her head against his chest. "Thank you so much for bringing me here. Had I known how amazing this was, I wouldn't have argued."

He wrapped his arms around her, stroking her back. "It's okay. I knew you'd see the error of your ways once you arrived."

Tessa swatted his shoulder and laughed.

"You haven't even seen the best part yet," he told her, easing back to look into her eyes. "There's a surprise in the master suite for you."

Tessa couldn't stop her eyes from roaming over his body.

"Not that," he told her with a smile. "I have something for you. You can go look now or later."

"Well, considering it's about nine o'clock, I have a feeling that we'll be otherwise occupied, later...."

He nipped at her jawline, traveled toward her ear. "You do have the best ideas," he whispered against her skin. "But I assure you, there's plenty of time for you to have your way with me."

Tessa couldn't help but laugh again. "You're always so eager to offer your services. But I'm selfish, and I want my surprise."

Grant's cell rang, cutting into the moment. When he groaned, Tessa stepped back, disappointment spreading through her. Of course these three days wouldn't go uninterrupted. He hadn't said he'd stop working, just that they were going to get away.

Well, they were away...with phones.

Could anybody truly get away anymore? There were far too many ways to access someone, and unless there was an emergency, Tessa honestly didn't want to be bothered. Once she'd warmed up to the idea of going away, she'd wanted Grant all to herself with no outside matters interrupting them.

Silly of her to assume that's what he'd want.

Perhaps he wasn't as emotionally invested as she'd first thought.

"Sorry about that," he told her, pulling his phone from his pocket. When he glanced at the screen, he sighed. "I have to take this. The master suite is upstairs, at the end of the hall."

While Tessa was excited to see her present, she would rather do so with him and not have to share his attention with callers.

God, that sounded whiny. He'd taken her away on a private jet, to a cabin and mountain that he freakin' owned, and she was throwing a pity party in her head. Yeah, that was wrong. But she'd truly thought they were on the same page. Truly thought this trip was about taking their relationship to another level.

Apparently, she shouldn't assume.

After her mental lecture, Tessa headed upstairs. The wide hallway led straight toward a giant bed. The entire second floor was a giant master suite.

Seriously, she really wanted to live here. Could all her horses come? A stable would have to be built and…

Tessa shook her head. This was fantasy. She wasn't living here, she was briefly vacationing. After three days she'd be back to reality and Grant would resume his grueling schedule and traveling, as well. They were shooting at the estate, but they also planned on being at the main race, to capture the pure essence of the industry and her father's legacy.

Her cell vibrated in her pocket, but when she pulled it out and saw a text from Aaron, she cringed.

Stop avoiding me. I said I was sorry. I need to see you.

Tessa shoved the phone back into her pocket. As always, she didn't reply, and she certainly wasn't going to start now, when she was ready to enjoy a few days with Grant. No way was Aaron and his persistent texts ruining her weekend. She refused to allow anything to interrupt her and Grant's special getaway.

As she stepped into the massive bedroom, all done up in creams and soft earth tones, she turned, taking in the natural beauty of the exposed beams in the ceiling and on the walls, the wide windows offering more spectacular views of the mountains.

And there, hanging on the closet door, was a large white garment bag with a paper pinned to the front, with her name on it.

As she crossed the room, Tessa's mind ran wild. What on earth could he possibly be thinking?

She unzipped the bag, exposing the most exquisite gown she'd ever seen. Long, strapless, sapphire-blue, of flowing chiffon material... Tessa slid her fingertips over the delicate fabric before taking it from the bag. Did he intend for her to wear this? Obviously, but now?

Why not? The dress was beautiful and the thought of playing dress-up totally appealed to her. When did she ever get out of her riding boots and flannel? Dressing up to her was wearing her riding attire during races, because of the silky material and the bright colors.

Quickly, Tessa shed her clothes, folded them and laid them on the old trunk at the foot of the bed, then donned the gown. The side zipper went up perfectly, almost as if this dress was tailor-made for her.

As she looked in the mirror, she saw that the dress matched her eyes. And with her red hair spilling over her shoulders, for once in her life Tessa felt beautiful.

She swallowed the sting of tears as she reminded herself this was still a fantasy. But she would live it happily these next three days...which would have to last her a lifetime.

Nineteen

Grant had changed into his black dress pants and a black shirt. That was as far as he was willing to go for this prom. Besides, the attire didn't matter, it was the memories.

He'd finished his phone call with his mother and had changed as fast as he could in the downstairs bedroom. His clothes had been packed. He'd called in favors all over the place to get deliveries made to the house on short notice, and he'd paid a hefty price.

Tessa stood at the top of the stairs with her crimson hair floating around her shoulders. The strapless blue dress flowed over her petite frame and made her eyes even more vibrant.

And suddenly the amount he'd spent meant absolutely nothing. He'd double it in a heartbeat to see Tessa looking so stunning, so sexy and so his for the next three days.

"I have no idea what you've got planned," she said as she started her descent. "But I'm in love with this dress."

Grant laughed, holding out his hand to take hers as she reached the base of the steps. "I'm loving how you look in that dress. You can thank Victoria Dane Alexander for that dress."

Tessa's eyes widened. "The famous designer?"

"She's the sister of Anthony Price and Bronson Dane. I called in a favor, and she happened to have several designs on hand for last-minute calls such as mine. She was more than happy to ship this once Cassie informed me of your size."

Tessa's eyes watered. "You must've had this planned, but you asked me just this morning."

Grant shrugged. "I knew I'd get you away from that stable one way or another, even if I had to drag you."

"You're amazing, Grant. I can't believe you just snap your fingers and people do what you want."

He laughed, escorting her toward the patio doors. "It's not quite that easy, but it does help to know the right people, have money and an ambition."

Turning to face her before he led her outside, Grant smoothed his palms over her bare shoulders, down her arms, and grabbed hold of her hands. "Are you ready for prom night?" he asked.

Tessa blinked, her mouth wide, then she smiled. "You're kidding."

"Not at all. It's a shame you never had one, so I re-created it...in a way."

She laughed. "This is by far a step above a high school prom, Slick. You flew me here in a private jet, and we're on a mountain you own. Oh, and you provided a dress from one of the top designers in the world, who happens to be married to a prince. Did I leave anything out?"

He pushed the glass double doors open and led her out onto the wide balcony. "Actually, yes." Thank God the flowers were in place—that hefty tab was worth it, as well. Grant picked up a small bundle of red roses from one of the stone posts. "Your flowers."

"Great, now my mascara is going to run," she said, dabbing at her eyes. "This is why I never wear makeup."

Grant swiped his thumb beneath one leaky eye. "You're beautiful with or without, Tessa."

She held the bundle to her face, closed her eyes and inhaled. When she focused back on him, a radiant smile lit up her entire face.

"Is it pathetic to admit a man has never gotten me flowers before?" she asked. "I mean, I've had flowers presented to me at races, but from a man who..."

He slid his thumb along her jawline. "Who what? Cares for you? Finds you intriguing, mesmerizing, sexy?"

"Yes," she whispered.

Grant cupped her face and nipped at her glossy lips. "You don't know how glad I am to be your first...again."

Tessa's body trembled against his. "You're spoiling me, Slick. I'm not sure I'll be able to let you go once the film is done. I'm loving this fantasy getaway."

He wasn't ready to think that far ahead, wasn't ready to discuss the future and certainly wasn't ready to let her go.

Yes, he wanted her for longer than the filming, but he could make no promises...yet. First he had to fully seduce her. He'd already seduced her body; now it was time to seduce her heart. He also had to return home...soon. Which was what the call from his mom had been about.

"I'm sorry," Tessa told him, shaking her head. "I didn't mean to make you uncomfortable when I said that."

Had she taken his silence as an indicator that he was uncomfortable? She couldn't be further from the truth. But right now was all about her, and he wanted Tessa to see just how much he cared for her. Just how far he'd go to see her smile, to take a break and enjoy life...with him.

Grant stepped away, went over to the outdoor entertainment area and turned on the music. When he glanced back at Tessa, she burst out laughing.

"You're kidding, right?" she asked.

"All the music from tonight is from your senior year," he told her, as a familiar tune filled the night. "What else would I play for your prom?"

"Well, at least it's not oldies from *your* prom," she joked.

Grant plucked the flowers from her hands, set them aside on the table and jerked her into his arms. "Now you're fighting dirty. You calling me old?"

She shrugged, sliding her hands up his chest, over his shoulders and into his hair. "Not if you think you can keep up with me."

Grant's body heated as he pulled her flush against him. "Oh, baby, why don't you try to keep up with me?"

"With pleasure."

She pressed closer and opened her mouth to his. Grant splayed his hands across her back, loving the bare skin he encountered, but loving how she shivered in his arms even more. He caused that. He knew just how to hold her, how to kiss her, how to make love to her. There was no other man on earth who could say that.

Grant might have power, but this petite sprite held all the control where he was concerned...and that was even more of a turn-on.

Tessa's breasts pressed against his chest as the upbeat song ended and a slower one began. Still gliding his mouth over hers, he began to sway. Dancing with Tessa wasn't something he'd ever thought of doing before she'd mentioned the prom, but he was so glad he'd come up with this somewhat silly plan.

Any reason to have her in his arms was good enough for him, and if they had to fly a few hours to get away, to make her feel special, it was all worth it.

He was merely laying the groundwork for his future—hopefully, with her.

Tessa eased back, her hands playing with the ends of his hair, her body still pressed against his. "I can't believe you went through all of this for me."

"Why can't you believe it?" he asked.

She shrugged. "Dinner and a movie is one thing. Flying to a private mountain to dance under the stars is another."

"You deserve this and so much more," he told her.

"I hate sneaking because of the film," she told him, going for honesty. "But if this is your idea of being sneaky, I'm completely behind it."

"Stick with me, babe. No one will catch us, and you'll have the time of your life."

"I just…"

Looking into those bright blue eyes, Grant waited, but she

shook her head and rested it against his shoulder. He wanted to know what was on her mind—not just now, but all the time. Hadn't they passed the point of keeping things locked inside? Not that he had any room to judge.

When Tessa shivered against him, he looked down. "I guess I was too busy planning the prom to take into consideration the weather with that dress."

She wrapped her arms around his waist and moved her head to rest against his chest. "You'll have to get creative to keep me warm."

She was killing him. In that dress, with her sexy words and her somewhat still innocent ways, Tessa Barrington was surely going to be the death of him.

But this trip was about laying it all on the line. Coming clean about where he stood with his feelings, what he wanted from her, and finding out what she was willing to sacrifice to be with him.

Could the man be more perfect? How in the world would she ever be able to say goodbye to him, let alone date anyone else?

But she wanted to concentrate on now. Her whole life she'd planned ahead, unable to truly enjoy the moment.

And if there was ever a moment to enjoy, this was it. Standing in Grant's arms, dancing beneath a starry sky while he did his best to re-create an event in her life she'd missed.

Yeah, a little chilly air wasn't going to ruin things for her.

But a part of her knew they were still sneaking—now just on a grander scale.

Obviously, this level of sneaking was meant to impress her…and it did. But it also drove home the point that he was not taking their relationship beyond intimacy of the body—forget intimacy of the heart.

"I'm having a hard time keeping my hands off you," he whispered in her ear. "With your body against mine, the way you look in that dress. I've had you, but I can't stop wanting you."

Tessa smiled into his chest. His raw words shot straight to her heart. She loved this man. Loved him for his passion for life, loved him for the reckless way he made quick decisions, and loved him for the way he maneuvered so much to give her a few days of absolute bliss and peace.

The man was completely unselfish, and right now she held all the power.

No matter what the future held for them—whether as a couple or apart—they were together now. And this was a fantasy night he'd staged just for her.

Mustering up a bit of courage, Tessa took a step back from his arms, reached for the hidden side zipper and eased it down until the dress fell to a puddle at her feet.

Grant's eyes slid down her body, sending even more chills racing over her bare skin.

"I do like an aggressive woman."

That was good, because she liked that look in his eyes. "I always feel beautiful around you. Like I'm the only woman in the world."

Grant reached for her, sliding his hands around her waist and pulling her against him. "You're the only woman in my world."

Before she could question exactly what he meant by that, Tessa was swept into a fantasy come to life as Grant laid her down on the cushioned chaise and made love to her beneath the stars.

Twenty

Tessa rolled over in bed, finding the other side completely empty. Darkness enveloped the room, and she glanced at the clock on the nightstand. Nearly one in the morning.

Where was Grant?

Grabbing the throw that was folded at the bottom of the bed, Tessa wrapped it around herself and padded carefully through the spacious master suite. The double doors on the far wall were cracked, and when she peeked through, she saw Grant standing against the railing, the full moon casting him in a soft glow.

Easing one of the doors open, she made her way out into the cool night, then stopped. What if he wanted to be alone? Maybe he'd come out here to think? Just because they shared a bed didn't mean she had the right to invade his privacy.

She'd barely turned to go back inside when his voice cut through the night.

"Stay."

Tessa froze. When he didn't turn, didn't say anything else, she adjusted the throw around her and walked toward him. Pressing her back to the rail, she settled next to him. But when she looked up at him and saw anguish in those once-sultry eyes, worry consumed her.

"You had another nightmare?" she asked.

Grant's eyes remained fixed on something in the distance, almost as if he was watching whatever nightmare that plagued him unfold. Tessa didn't say another word. He'd told her to stay. Maybe he didn't want to talk, but he obviously didn't want to be alone. That in and of itself was a huge step up from his last nightmare.

"My sister is paralyzed from the waist down because of me."

That statement, in his rough, throaty tone, had Tessa locking her eyes on his, waiting for him to elaborate.

"We used to take riding lessons," he went on, still staring out into the night, as if he was talking to himself. "Melanie loved horses. As a little girl she would wear cowgirl boots with everything, even her nightgown. She loved everything about horses.

"We took lessons, and we were pretty damn good. I ended up quitting because of sports and girls, but Melanie kept at it. I supported her, and she always came to all my games. We were just...there for each other, you know?"

From Tessa's angle she could see moisture gathering in his eyes. Her heart ached for him, for the battle he'd fought with himself and for the demons he'd carried for so long.

"One day I went with her to the barn. We lived in Kentucky and had several acres. Nothing major, but enough for a barn and a couple horses. We'd just graduated the week before, and she would be off to college in the fall for equine studies. I was ready to move to L.A. and hit film school."

Grant gripped the rail, dropped his head forward and sighed. "I ruined her life, Tessa. I made her race me, knowing the horse she was on was new, knowing it was skittish and rebellious.

"My horse spooked hers when I came up behind them, and the thing took off. Melanie started screaming, calling out commands, but the stallion kept going. I can't...I can't get that image out of my brain."

He lifted his head, turned his face toward hers, and Tessa couldn't help but reach for him. She rested a hand on his bare arm and waited for him to go on.

"When I kicked my horse to go faster, that scared hers even more and he bucked. She fell off the back and…"

His eyes closed, as if he was trying to block out the memory. A moment later he drew in a deep breath and focused his gaze back on hers.

"I don't know what I thought I could do, but I just wanted to get up beside her, to help somehow. But I ended up doing so much more harm than good.

"Now you know why I'm so leery at the stables, why I freaked out when you fell. I couldn't live through that again, Tessa."

"What does your sister think of you working on this film?" she asked.

Grant shrugged. "I haven't talked to her since I left for film school. After the accident, she had surgeries and therapy, but the doctors told us the chance of her walking or using her legs again were slim to none. After a couple months, I couldn't handle it anymore. I couldn't look at her because guilt would eat at me. She should hate me, should curse me every day of her life. I stole everything from her, Tessa."

Tessa's heart broke for this man. "Don't you think you hurt her even more by shutting her out? She's your twin, right? I'm sure you two shared a special bond before the accident. You think because she is in a wheelchair that she doesn't love you?"

"She shouldn't."

Grant stepped away and turned his back on Tessa. Oh, hell no. He wasn't shutting her out, too. Not after this revelation. Not when his hurt was threatening to become a wedge between them.

"You're not a one-man show, Grant. You don't need to tackle everything alone. Talk to me. You opened up to me for a reason. Let me help."

He whirled on her, arms flying. "Help? What can you help do, Tessa? I ruined her life. And I'm telling you because I want you to know the real me. The uglier side, the damaged side. I want you to see that I have issues, I have fears, and they all stem from the world you live in. I've been able to keep my distance for the most part, but the more involved with you I get, the more immersed in that world I find myself. I'm terrified. The more I'm with you, the harder it is to keep my emotions under control."

His last two words were whispered, and the weight of his statement crushed her. He was right. Horses, racing, fast speeds were all part of her world...the only world she knew and a world he wanted no part of. And another reason he'd chosen to be so secretive. Coming out in the open about his feelings would only make him force things he just didn't know if he could face.

"Accidents happen, Grant," she assured him. "People can be injured anytime, anywhere. I could be put in a wheelchair by falling down steps or being in a car accident. Don't let that fear control you. Don't you think it's held on to your life long enough?"

"But I caused this accident and the result is crippling." His eyes sought hers as he raked a hand over his messed hair. "I needed you to know. I couldn't keep this inside anymore... not with you."

"Why now? Why let me in now?"

He closed the space between them, lifting his palms against her cheeks and framing her face. "Because I'm falling in love with you, Tessa."

Her heart caught in her throat. "You're... Are you serious?"

A ghost of a smile danced across his face. "I am. But I need you to know why I worry. Your world revolves around this lifestyle that threatens to consume me at times."

"I don't think you'd be as stressed and controlled by this fear if you'd talk to your sister," Tessa told him, reaching up to hold on to his wrists. "What do your parents say?"

"They're always trying to get me to come home. I've been able to avoid it over the years by flying them out to see me. I just don't know that I can face Melanie."

"Maybe we could face her together?"

Grant's eyes widened. "No. I'm not putting this on you."

"You didn't put this on me," she countered with a smile. "Maybe I want to help, because I've fallen in love with you, too."

He nipped at her lips once more. "I know. I knew when you came to my cottage, ready to seduce me. I knew you'd never give yourself to someone you didn't love."

"I did love you then," she admitted. "I had barely admitted it to myself. I actually kept trying to deny it, but there's no fighting such a strong emotion. I never had a clue love could be so all-encompassing."

Worry lines settled between his brows. "How will this work? I mean, I still can't publicly be with you until this film is over. I live in L.A. and you live in Virginia."

Tessa nodded. "There's a lot against us. We'll just have to find a way."

Grant wrapped his arms around her, pulled her close. Inhaling his warm, masculine scent, Tessa tried to relax. They had to make this work. She'd given up too much of herself to accept anything less.

"Don't worry, Tessa," he whispered. "No matter what I have to do, we will find a way."

She clung to the man, the promise, and the hope for their future. Because she'd never fully loved like this before, and this unchartered territory scared her to death.

As much as Tessa hated to have the magical weekend come to an end, she knew it was time for them both to get back to work. After all, the sooner Grant wrapped up the film, the sooner they could go public with their relationship.

She loved that term in regards to what she and Grant had. For the first time in her life, she truly felt she was on the right path with the right man. And she couldn't help but think her mother was smiling down on her with approval. Tessa only wished her mom was here in person to share in their happiness.

"Will we be able to visit your mountain again?" Tessa asked as Grant escorted her to the awaiting car, driven by their one and only accomplice, Cassie.

Tessa had simply told her father she was taking a couple days off to go visit a friend. Damon Barrington was a smart man and more than likely knew what was up, but he didn't say a word.

"Anytime, babe."

"Well, looks like the getaway agreed with you two," Cassie told them. "I'm glad you're back, though."

"Something wrong?" Tessa asked, as Grant put their bags in the trunk.

Her sister's eyes were shielded by her sunglasses, so Tessa couldn't get a feel for what was going on. The wind on the tarmac whipped Cassie's red hair about her shoulders.

"Aaron called me while you were gone."

Tessa froze.

"The ex?" Grant asked, placing his hand on the small of Tessa's back as if to stake his claim.

Cassie nodded, reaching back to control her hair in the strong breeze. "He informed me you've been ignoring his calls. I told him you were busy working, and I may have..."

"What?" Tessa asked.

"I may have said you were seeing someone."

Grant swore, and Tessa groaned. "Oh, Cass."

"Wait," Grant said after a moment. "Did you tell him my name?"

Cassie shook her head. "No. I've not told anybody. I just said that so he'd know you've moved on."

Grant rubbed his hand along Tessa's back. "It's okay, then. As long as he doesn't know who, I'm safe, and hopefully, he'll see she's not available."

Tessa jerked on the car handle. "I wasn't available to that jerk even before you came along, Slick. He had his chance, and forgiveness is not an option."

Grant smacked a kiss on her lips. "Hopefully, he's done calling."

While Cassie got into the driver's seat, Tessa settled in the back next to Grant. These were their last few moments of freedom before he headed back to working on the film. He'd still come to her house, but she absolutely couldn't wait to be his, in public, without the sneaking around. Although sneaking did have a certain naughty appeal.

"I want to be able to see all hands at all times back there," Cassie called back as she pulled out onto the main road. "I don't play chauffeur to just anybody."

"We appreciate all you've done," Grant said, draping an arm around Tessa's shoulders.

"I'm just glad my sister is happy."

They chatted about the upcoming race in Louisville and strategy. Tessa couldn't wait to get to the race, couldn't wait to see that blanket of roses draped across Don Pedro. He deserved the win for all his hard work, too.

"I love the Shakespearean names, by the way," Grant interjected at one point.

She caught her sister's eye in the rearview mirror. "Well, we have a little difference of opinion when it comes to their names," Tessa stated. "She's more pessimistic than I am. Mine are Don Pedro and Oliver, but Cassie's newest rescue is Macduff."

From the front seat Cassie laughed. "He may be the hero in *Macbeth,* but he's a killer in the end."

Grant chuckled. "So Tessa is the romantic and you're the more...cynical sister?"

"I prefer to think realistic," Cassie said, throwing a smile over her shoulder.

Tessa knew Cass had had a bad time after her ex left, so she could hardly fault her for being so bitter. Poor Macduff, he'd just have to live with the name.

Cassie dropped Tessa off first, so Grant could properly kiss her goodbye without prying eyes.

"See you in my room tonight," she murmured against his lips.

"Leave the back door unlocked for me," he told her as he pulled her bag from the trunk.

After grabbing the suitcase and waving them off, Tessa drew her keys from her purse and let herself into her house, smiling as she closed the door behind her.

"When you move on, you really move on."

She jerked around, heart pounding, to find Aaron comfortable as you please in her living room, sprawled out on her sofa.

"What are you doing here?" she exclaimed, remaining by the door, trying to order her heart rate to calm. The unexpected visitor had scared her to death.

Rising to his feet, Aaron crossed the floor and narrowed the gap between them. At one time she would've been excited to see him. At one time she'd thought herself in love and ready to accept his ring.

Right now all she felt was anger and a sense of being violated. He'd already tried to use her, and spread rumors of cheating and using illegal drugs for her horses, a fact that was quickly disputed. Did he honestly believe she'd invite him into her home?

"How did you get in here?" she asked.

"I came to see you," he told her, as if this was a perfectly normal visit. "You wouldn't return my texts or calls. Cassie was of no help when I talked to her the other day, and I wasn't able to get away from the city until now. She told me you'd moved on, but I knew once I came back and explained how wrong I was, and how sorry I am for hurting you, you'd see that we belong together."

Tessa laughed, crossing her arms over her chest. "Seeing you only makes me hate you more for how you treated me. How the hell did you get in?"

"The spare key you have hidden outside."

She made a mental note to move the thing the second he

was gone. Never in her wildest dreams would she have thought he'd use it.

"Get out, Aaron," she told him with a sigh. "You wasted your time coming here."

"Because you were locking lips with the famous Grant Carter?"

Damn it. He couldn't know that. Of all people, he would use that against her, for no other reason than spite.

"Anything in my life, personal or otherwise, is absolutely none of your business. Now get out or I'll call the cops and have you arrested for trespassing."

His hand came up and caressed her cheek. Tessa stepped back and swatted it away. "Don't," she told him in her lowest tone.

"I made a mistake, Tessa. I know I used you, I know I hurt you, but I want to make this work."

Resisting the urge to roll her eyes, she shook her head and jerked her front door open. "There is no 'this' to work on. You treated me badly, I dumped you, it's over. Now, I have work to do."

Before she could react, Aaron reached out, wrapped his hand around her arm and jerked her toward his chest.

"You seriously think I'll just walk out of here? We belong together, Tessa."

She was too angry to be scared of his strong grip, of his harsh tone. "Get your hand off me."

"Was I not good enough for the almighty Barrington princess? You claimed you hated city life when I tried to get you to move. What do you think that hotshot will do, huh? Do you think he'll move here and settle in the country with you?"

Tessa said nothing as she tried to break his strong grasp.

"He has a reputation, you know," Aaron went on. "He's a player, Tessa."

"At least he doesn't manhandle me."

Aaron gave her arm a good squeeze as he shoved her away. "You'll regret leaving me. That's a promise."

When he walked out the door, Tessa's level of fear spiked. She didn't take well to threats, especially just before her biggest season.

What had he wanted from her? Did he not get the message the first time, when she'd told him she never wanted to see him again?

He'd been with her for her family's name, for their wealth. She'd been gullible once, and she sure as hell wasn't going to be that way again.

No matter what Grant's reputation was in the past, Tessa knew better now. He'd told her he loved her, and she fully believed him.

Rubbing the tender skin on her arm, where bruises were already forming, Tessa closed the front door and locked it. A car flashed by the side window and sped down her driveway. Obviously, he'd parked behind the garage, where she couldn't see it. Jerk.

Nothing could get in the way of her racing season or her new relationship with Grant.

But he needed to know about this unexpected visit. If Aaron let this secret slip, it could destroy Grant's future, damage his career.

She needed to focus solely on the race, but right now she had to shift focus to Grant and keeping him safe.

Twenty-One

Grant turned the knob on the back door, surprised to find it locked. He knew it was later than usual, but he'd promised he'd come over. Had she gone to bed? Surely she wouldn't just forget.

Just as he was pulling his cell phone out to call her, Tessa flipped on the kitchen light and came rushing to the door to unlock it.

"Sorry. I was trying to watch for you, but with your black ninja gear it was kind of hard to see."

"I assumed it would be unlocked," he told her as he came in and shut the door behind him.

"I prefer it to stay locked while the movie is being filmed. Never know what crazies will go traipsing around."

When she crossed her arms over her chest and glanced around the room, Grant stepped forward. "Hey, what's wrong?"

Meeting his gaze and attempting—and failing—to smile, she shrugged. "Just trying to stay cautious."

He rested his hands on her slender shoulders. "I live in a land where people get paid to lie. You, my darling, are terrible at it. Now, what's going on?"

"Aaron was inside my house when Cassie dropped me off."

"What? Why didn't you call me right then?"

Tessa shrugged. "Honestly, I was trying to figure out how to protect you. I didn't want you rushing over here. What if he stayed behind? What if he was waiting for you? He could've snapped pictures and held them over you for blackmail, or he could've started an altercation. I couldn't chance it."

"I don't give a damn about me, Tessa. You're obviously shaken up. I should've been here." Rage boiled within Grant at some bastard who thought it was okay to toy with her. "What the hell was he doing in your house?"

"He apparently used the hidden key, which I have since removed."

She stepped away from Grant and started toward the living room. After turning on the lamp on the end table, she took a seat in the corner of the floral sofa. When she crossed her arms around her waist and stared up at him, Grant settled directly in front of her on the squat coffee table.

"What did he say?" he asked, trying to keep his anger under control, when in reality he was ready to punch this Aaron jerk in the face.

"Just that he wanted me back, that he made a mistake." Tessa's eyes met his. "He also saw us kissing."

Grant cursed, raking a hand over his head. "Well, we can't change that now. If he says anything we can just call him a jealous ex who didn't like a Hollywood type staying here."

"I'm sorry," she told him. "I don't want to come between you and this film. I just wanted to make sure he was gone, and I knew you'd be discreet coming out tonight."

Grant reached for her hands. "Nothing will come between me and the film...or me and you."

He would go to Bronson and Anthony and just explain, he decided. At this point, he needed to tell them, because he was falling deeper and deeper in love with Tessa and couldn't avoid the truth any longer.

Besides, he wanted to stop hiding. It wasn't fair to the relationship they'd developed, and it wasn't fair to her. What they had was special and couldn't be kept behind closed doors.

Glancing down at their joined hands, Grant zeroed in on the bruises on her forearm.

"What the hell is this?" he asked, gently stroking her skin. His eyes came back up to hers. "Tessa?"

"Aaron was pretty upset when I refused him and demanded he leave. Nothing I couldn't take care of."

Grant came to his feet. "He assaulted you."

Tessa leaned her head back on the sofa and laughed. Actually laughed, while he was fuming with rage.

"He didn't assault me," she corrected. "He grabbed me, I threatened to call the cops, he left. End of story."

"This is not something to blow off." Grant sank onto the cushion next to her. With a sigh, he reached up to stroke her cheek. "Why do I find your independence so appealing?"

Shrugging, she smiled and nestled her face against his palm. "Same reason I find your arrogance and white knight routine appealing."

"I wish you would've called me. I'd gladly accept an altercation and an opportunity to punch him in his face."

"I was fine. Besides, you'd just been here and I knew you needed to talk to Bronson and Anthony about the film. You coming right back would only confirm Aaron's allegations. Right now he has no proof and just sounds like a jealous ex."

"Nothing is more important than you, Tessa." Grant cupped his other hand over her cheek and forced her to look him in the eye. "Nothing."

"I'm fine," she repeated.

"I hate seeing you hurt, knowing some bastard put his hands on you."

"He's not coming back, and if he tries to blackmail me, we'll face this together."

Grant shook his head. "Yes, we will. But I worry—"

She placed a fingertip over his lips as her gaze held his. Their conversation from a few nights ago kept replaying in his mind, and she knew exactly what he was thinking.

"Slick, you can't keep me down. I know you are scared of the horses, I know me riding them bothers you, but it's who I am. I might get hurt, but I'll get over it and move on. And I hope I do all of that with you." Her other hand slid up his chest and around his neck. "Now are we going to talk all night or are you going to take me to bed?"

Grant laughed. "I've created a monster."

"And you love every minute of it."

True. He did. But if he ever got a hold of this Aaron jerk, he'd pummel his face for the marks he'd put on Tessa. No man should ever lay his hands on a woman in such a manner.

And Grant might just have to look the guy up to remind him of that.

The Kentucky Derby was the most prestigious horse race known to man—and there was so much more to it than over-size hats and mint juleps. The buildup, the anticipation, the glamour all centered around a few short moments on the track and a lifetime of praise for one lucky winner.

And Tessa was going to be that winner. She'd trained her whole life for this. Waited to follow in her father's footsteps, knowing she'd be the first female jockey to win.

Nerves danced in her belly. She knew Grant and his crew were here taping, but she didn't have time to worry about their job...she had her own job to do.

Once the race was over, she'd see Grant—hopefully in the winner's circle. So far Aaron had kept away, and hopefully, he would stay that way. Right now, she didn't have space in her mind for him.

"You've got this," Cassie said, holding on to the lead line and taking Don Pedro toward the gates. "It's a beautiful day for a race."

Tessa glanced over to the beautiful women in their delicate, colorful hats, the men in pale suits. The laughter, the drinking, the betting—she loved the whole ambience. There was something magical about the Derby and she wanted to take a piece of that magic home with her—the same way her father had done.

"I'm proud of my girls." Damon walked on the other side

of the horse and escorted them to the gate. "Both of you have done me proud no matter how today turns out. Your mother would be proud, too."

Tessa didn't want to get choked up, didn't want to even think of the fact that her mother wasn't here to share in this monumental moment.

Eyes straight ahead, Tessa focused on the beauty of the sunshine, the soft gentle breeze. Seriously, the day couldn't be more perfect.

As she lined up amid the other jockeys, she didn't speak and barely threw a smile to those on either side of her. While the horse racing industry was a close-knit community, Tessa had never been one to be too chummy just before a race. Everyone had their own little quirks, and hers was that she got into the zone by focusing and having chitchats with herself in peace and quiet.

The crowd cheered, creating a roar over the entire track. Nothing mattered but the end.

Tessa gripped the reins with one hand and reached down to pat Don Pedro with the other. It was showtime.

Tessa and Don Pedro were immediately swallowed up by press, cameras and family in the winner's circle. Grant wanted to go to her, tell her that he'd decided to come clean with Bronson and Anthony. He wanted her to know that she came first in his life.

But he remained where he was near the grandstands. He wanted to talk to her in private, wanted to be able to have her undivided attention and let her know that she was the most important part of his life.

He also wanted to get to Bronson and Anthony soon, because he didn't want them hearing it from an outside source.

No way in hell would he let Aaron get any pleasure from grade-school-level tattling.

Grant hated lying, and he thought for sure Anthony and Bronson would understand. But they'd have to tell Marty, and he wasn't so understanding.

Hours later, when Tessa was back in her Louisville home, because most jockeys and owners kept a place in the area, Grant knocked on her door, ready to come clean, to tell her what he'd decided. Excitement and nervousness flooded him.

When she opened her door, her red hair was down, free from the tight bun she'd had it in while racing. Her face was void of any makeup and she'd put on an oversize denim shirt and black leggings.

"Grant." She crossed her arms over her chest. "I thought I would've seen you after the race."

Yeah, he knew she'd be upset about that, but he honestly couldn't go to her just then. He'd needed to be alone with her, to tell her what had transpired while she'd been fulfilling her dreams. He had some dreams of his own...and every single one of them included her.

"I couldn't get down to you." Mentally, he hadn't been able to, he added silently as he stepped over the threshold. "We need to talk."

Her eyes widened, but she nodded as she moved toward the open living room. When she picked up a large bag of ice and eased down onto the sofa, Grant eyed her.

"What happened?"

She lifted her shirt and shifted the ice pack beneath it, wincing as she did. "I was careless."

That sliver of fear slid through him, gliding right over the excitement he'd felt only seconds ago.

"What happened?" he repeated.

Settling back against the cushions, Tessa closed her eyes and sighed. "We were in the barns, and Nash was brushing Don Pedro. I stepped behind another horse and got kicked. Rookie mistake, but my mind was elsewhere."

Grant rested his hip on the edge of the couch and started unbuttoning her shirt from the bottom. "Let me see."

"It's not a big deal, Grant."

Ignoring her protest, he got four buttons undone and slid the material aside before removing the ice pack.

The giant bruise covered her entire side, and it sickened him to see her delicate skin so marred. But so much more could've happened to her. There was no guarantee that because she was a professional she was exempt from injuries.

"Tell me you went to the hospital to have this checked out," he exclaimed, eyeing her.

"Gee, thanks for the congratulations on my win, Slick."

He met her gaze, knowing her victory was the most important moment of her life so far. "I've never been more proud. We got some good shots of you, by the way."

"Really?" she asked, her smile beaming. "That's awesome."

"Now, please tell me you had this looked at."

Rolling her eyes, she nodded. "The on-site doctor actually had a portable X-ray machine. I have two cracked ribs, but I'm fine."

Cracked ribs? The countless possibilities of what could've happened filled his mind and made his stomach clench.

"Fine?" Grant sighed, gently replacing the ice and leaving her shirt undone. "This isn't fine, Tessa. That careless mistake could've cost you more than just a few cracked ribs."

Brows drawn together, she stared up at him. "What is wrong with you? I said I'm fine. They will heal."

He got to his feet, paced the spacious living area, trying to find the words. He'd had his mind made up when he'd come. He was ready to drop the film for her, ready to give this a try, but how could he when she reminded him of that painful time in his past? How could he be with her knowing she lived the life that had crippled his sister and held a choke hold on him, as well?

Damn it. He hated how quickly he could be reduced to

being so vulnerable where Tessa was concerned. Tears burned his eyes and he gave himself a minute before he spoke.

"I can't do this anymore," he whispered as he turned back to look at her. "*We* can't do this anymore."

She tried to straighten up, but cried out in pain and held her side. "Don't do this to me."

When he started to step forward to help her, she shot daggers at him with her eyes, so he stopped. "Don't...not if you're ending things."

"I can't handle this, seeing you hurt, knowing at any time you could be paralyzed, too."

"We've been over this," she cried. "I thought we'd moved past all of this fear you had. Did you even call your sister like I asked you to?"

Grant shook his head, cursing the tears still threatening to consume him. "I will. I swear. I'm just... I can't go all-in yet with you. I love you, but..."

With careful movements, Tessa rose to her feet and clutched her shirt around her torso. "You're a coward, Grant Carter. You can't take on a relationship with me until you tackle the relationship with your sister. And I don't want a man in my life who can't live with me the way I am."

Grant didn't blame her for being angry, Hell, he was angry with himself. This wasn't what he'd planned to tell her when he arrived, but once he'd seen her hurt, that torrent of fear had rushed through him again and he realized he couldn't live his life always worried.

Tears gathered in Tessa's eyes, but she lifted her chin and narrowed her gaze. "You have no idea what I would give up for you. I'd give up everything this second if I knew you were ready, because I believe in us. I believe in you. But you have to face Melanie."

Grant stepped forward, stopping when she held up her hand. "No. I don't want to hear it. You obviously already made your choice."

Swallowing back emotions, he shoved his hands into his

pockets. "I can't be anything to you with how my life is right now, Tessa."

"You can't be anything to me until you decide that what we have is more powerful than your fear."

She turned to walk from the room, throwing a glance over her shoulder. "Lock the door on your way out."

And she was gone. The hurt in her voice, the unshed tears… he'd caused all that.

It was time to talk to Melanie, put this nightmare from his past to rest one way or another.

He'd lost his sister years ago, and now he'd lost the woman he loved and wanted to spend his life with.

Tessa was right. He'd been a coward, but no more. It was time to face those demons that had chased away everything good in his life.

Twenty-Two

He'd come too far to back out now. And after years of avoiding this confrontation, Grant knew there was nowhere else to hide. He'd tried traveling, he'd tried drowning himself in work and he'd tried avoiding the topic altogether.

But the fact of the matter remained that years of fear and nightmares had led him right back to where he'd begun, in a small town in Kentucky. And now he stood on the stoop of his sister's small, one-story cottage.

His parents knew he was in town, but he'd assured them he wanted to talk to Melanie alone. God, how he wished Tessa were with him now. She was so courageous, so strong. He needed to draw from that strength. But she was in his heart, and she'd made him face this moment, made him realize that nothing in his life would truly be right, and that he couldn't move on without finally letting go of the guilt.

And there was only one way to do that. First, he'd settle his past, then he'd try to win back his future.

Before he could press his finger to the bell, the wide front door opened and Grant's whole world stilled.

"Were you going to knock or had you changed your mind?"

Melanie sat in her wheelchair, her long dark hair spilling over one shoulder, her legs so thin. But it was her face that shocked him the most. She was smiling…at him.

"Grant?" Her eyes sought his. "Are you coming in?"

Swallowing, he merely nodded. God, what an idiot. He

couldn't even speak as he stepped over the threshold. She'd eased back, and once he was in she closed the door.

He took in the open floor plan, the spacious layout and sparse furniture. Perfect for getting around in a wheelchair.

"Dad told me you were coming," she said, her voice sounding just as unsure as he felt. "Do you want to come into the living room?"

When he turned to look at her, damned if his whole heart didn't clench. That questioning expression on her face only added to the guilt he felt, the shame he was here to finally admit.

"If my being here is too hard, I'll go." He shoved his hands into his pockets, waiting to follow her lead. The last thing he wanted was to make her even more uncomfortable. "I just… God, Mel…"

She bit her lower lip and nodded. "I want you to stay. I miss my baby brother."

The childhood joke had him smiling. "You're only older by twelve minutes."

Shrugging, she wheeled past him and into the living room. Following her, he ran through his head all he wanted to say. As if years of torment and grief could be summed up in a few moments. As if any words would rectify this situation he'd caused.

When she stopped next to the couch, he took a seat beside her. He'd barely settled when she reached over and grasped his hand.

And just like that, something inside him burst. Emotions over a decade old poured out of him, and he wasn't the least bit ashamed that he sat there crying like a baby.

"Mel, I can't even begin…"

He held her hand to his mouth, pressed a kiss on her knuckles. Tears streamed from his eyes as she brought her other hand up and cupped his cheek.

"Grant, it's okay. I'm fine."

She was coming to his defense, trying to minimize the severity of this situation, this life he'd caused her. Hell no.

"Don't," he told her, gripping both her hands in his as he wiped his damp face on his shoulder. "Don't defend me. I deserve nothing but anger from you. I honestly can't take it if you're going to pretend life is just fine. I stole everything from you, Mel. I robbed your life of all the dreams you had."

She shook her head and offered him that sweet smile he'd sworn he'd never see again. "You stole absolutely nothing. I had a rough time at first, obviously adjusting, but I love my life, Grant. Do I wish I could walk? Of course, but I'm doing so much with my life, I can't be sorry I'm in this wheelchair."

Grant slid off the couch, crouched down at her feet, still clutching her hands. "I want to fix this. I'm used to getting what I want, used to having all I wish for. But I can't undo this, Mel. It eats at me. I've struggled with what I've done, struggled with losing you. But every time I think of all that, I realize what you lost."

Tears welled up in her eyes. "Being in a wheelchair is nothing compared to losing my brother. Nothing, Grant. I never blamed you. I ached for you, for the guilt I knew you'd taken upon yourself, for the fear that made you run."

He dropped his head to their joined hands. "I'm done running, Mel. I don't deserve to be asking to be part of your life again, but I want to be. Is there any way we can try? Is there anything I can do?

He closed his eyes, silently pleading for her to love him, though he deserved to be kicked out of her home, her life.

Instead of harsh words, she kissed the top of his head. "I've waited years for you to come back to me."

Lifting his gaze to hers, Grant felt the weight of guilt and crippling fear ease from his body. "I love you, Melanie."

"I know you do," she told him with that sweet smile. "And if you ever run from me again, I'll hunt you down."

Laughing, Grant came to his feet, kissed her hands and sat back on the couch.

"Now, tell me about this film you're working on." She held up a palm before he could say anything. "But first, tell me about the woman. I know there's a woman involved, or you wouldn't have stayed on the set this long, with all the horses there."

Laughing, Grant began to explain Tessa, explain how he'd messed things up with her, but planned on making them right.

"Sounds like someone I'd love to meet."

"I can't wait for you to meet her," he told his twin. "You'll love her."

As he started to explain the film, Melanie's eyes welled up with tears, but she smiled the entire time. And Grant knew he'd won back a place in his sister's heart. Of course, he had a feeling she'd been holding his spot for a long time.

In the days since coming back to Stony Ridge, Tessa hadn't seen Grant. Hadn't seen movement around his cottage, hadn't seen that flashy sports car…nothing.

She should've known when he hadn't come down to the winner's circle after the biggest race of her life that his priorities were film first, her second.

The hurt sliced deep, but there wasn't much she could do about it. No way could she fight against the heavy weight that lived inside Grant's heart.

Trying to focus on her life without him, she shoved her hair over her shoulders and headed toward the main house.

The scene today would be shot in the living room, so Tessa made a point to get there early so she could talk to Bronson or Anthony. Not that she cared where Grant was; she was just curious. That's all.

As she entered the back door, Linda was taking freshly baked bread from the oven. Tessa inhaled the tantalizing aroma. "You could tempt a saint with your baking," she told her.

"I keep thinking that man of yours will come in, but I haven't seen him since before you all left for the derby."

Tessa shrugged. No way was she commenting on the "man of yours" part, or the fact that he'd been absent around here.

"Has Bronson or Anthony come through yet?"

"I believe Damon was talking with Bronson in the living room. They've arranged all the furniture and even brought in some new pieces for the shoot today."

Tessa had to admit this was pretty cool. As much as she'd hated the film at the beginning of the process, she kind of liked the crew that had been here.

"Care for some bread? Better get it before the guys come in," Linda told her, setting the bread on the cooling rack. "I swear, this bunch likes to eat. Makes me so happy."

Tessa laughed. "Maybe later. I really need to speak to someone first."

Sure enough, Bronson was in the living room, but her father was nowhere in sight. Perfect. She certainly didn't want to discuss Grant around her dad.

"Bronson," she said, stepping over the lighting cords. "Do you have a minute?"

He turned from setting up a camera and offered her a killer smile. "Of course. What can I do for you?"

"Is Grant going to be on set today?"

Yeah, just come out and ask. No leading into that. She may as well stamp Pathetic on her forehead.

Bronson's brows drew together. "You hadn't heard?"

"What?" she asked, fearful of what was coming next.

"I assumed everyone knew, but Grant quit."

Tessa's breath caught in her throat. "Quit? How can he quit?"

With a sigh, Bronson rested his hands on his hips. "I really hate getting in the middle of things, but I work with celebrities, so that's virtually impossible. Grant resigned his position because of the clause he violated."

Tessa's mind ran all over the place. They knew about her and Grant? Was he forced to quit?

"I can't say that I blame him," Bronson went on. "He's in love with you, you know."

Tessa nodded. "I know, but we aren't together anymore. In Louisville we…"

"That's strange." Bronson rested a hip on the edge of the new prop sofa. "He came back the day after the race, spoke with me and Anthony, got Marty Russo on the phone and resigned, stating he'd violated the conduct code."

"You mean, you didn't hear it from someone else?" she asked.

"Actually, I already had an idea something was going on between the two of you. Someone named Aaron Souders left a message with my assistant, stating he had some news about Grant he was going to take to the press, but Grant is the one who told me."

Tessa rested her hand on the end table, trying to take in Grant's actions. What was he doing, giving up all his dreams like this? How could he just drop the one movie he'd been waiting to make?

"Marty was pretty disappointed, especially with Grant so close to getting his own production company."

Tessa jerked her attention to Bronson. "His own company?"

The producer's dark eyes widened. "I see you didn't know about that. Grant was offered his own company under Russo Entertainment once this film wrapped up. I'm not sure if Marty will still offer that to him now that he's quit."

Tessa wrapped her arms around her waist. Questions, nerves, confusion all consumed her.

"Where's Grant now?"

Bronson shrugged. "He mentioned going home, said he had a past to face. After that I don't know where's he's going. I do know that Anthony and I are meeting with Marty, though. There's no way we can't stand up for Grant, when he's the best guy we've ever worked with on set and we need him."

Facing his past? Her heart clenched. Could he truly be ready to work through the nightmares and move forward?

"But what about the clause?" she asked.

Bronson smiled. "I'm pretty sure that was for the old, care-free Grant. The new Grant has eyes for only one woman now."

Tessa had an idea, but she needed help, and Bronson was just the man for the job. If Grant was strong enough to put his heart on the line and go home, then she was certainly strong enough to put her own heart on the line and go after her future.

"Call Grant," she told him.

Grant couldn't believe he was back on the set. So much had happened in the past two weeks. He'd spent a good portion of that time with his sister and his parents, falling back into old patterns and reconnecting those bonds he'd thought for sure he'd severed. But they'd welcomed him with open arms, and he promised to bring Tessa once racing season was over.

But then he was doubly shocked when Marty called and asked him to return to the set. Apparently, Bronson and Anthony had come to his defense and informed Marty that Grant was in love with the woman he "broke the clause" with, and now Grant was needed back at Stony Ridge.

But being there was hard. Everywhere he looked he saw Tessa. Glancing at the stables, he could practically see her stalking through with her tattered boots and hip-hugging jeans. At his cottage he saw her when she'd spent the night, all virginal in his T-shirt, her hair spilling over her shoulders.

Today, though, would be a true test of his will. They were shooting at the cabin on the back of the property, and Bronson had asked Grant to get there early to help set up the lighting.

Sure. No problem.

He'd planned on going to her now that he was back, but he'd wanted to do it in his own time. He had hoped for something more romantic than a scene with everyone standing around as spectators to the life he'd derailed, and was desperately trying to get back on track.

Grant headed out there on foot, needing the time to think. Of course, during his walk he thought back to the thunderstorm, when he and Tessa had come here…and she'd given herself to him for the first time.

Man, he missed her. He had to figure out a damn good way to let her know just how much he truly loved her, because he'd totally botched things up back in Louisville.

He remembered that the key was hidden above the lintel, but when he glanced up, he found the door already open a tad. Easing the creaking panel wider, Grant stopped in the doorway and stared at the most beautiful sight.

"I was hoping you'd show."

Tessa sat on the chaise where they'd made love. She was wearing the gown he'd purchased for her when they'd gone to Colorado, and she had the most beautiful smile on her face.

Realization dawned on him. "We're not filming here today."

"No, you're not."

Grant eased on in, closing the door behind him.

"I was going to make you grovel," she stated as she crossed one slender leg, shifting the side split of the dress to reveal skin all the way up to her hip. "But then I realized you'd already been through a lot, and so have I, and I'm done playing games."

He laughed. "And you're taking charge again."

"Of course. First, I know you went to see Melanie. How did that go?"

Grant slid his hands into his pockets, resisting the urge to cross the room, rip that dress off her and worry about talking later.

"Better than I'd ever hoped. She's amazing, and I cannot wait for you to meet her. She's come so far and actually works on a horse farm for handicapped children."

Tessa's smile widened. "I'm so happy you went to see her. I'm really proud of you. But now I want to move on to the nonsense of you quitting over the clàuse."

Grant shrugged. "I figured Aaron would no doubt tattle, so I beat him to the punch. I'm man enough to stand up for what I want, and admit when I do something wrong."

"And what do you want?" she asked, coming to her feet.

His heart picked up its pace as she crossed the small room. "I want everything."

"This film?"

"Yes."

She ran her hand up over his chest. "The production company you didn't tell me about?"

He swallowed. "Yes."

Her lips hovered just under his. "Me?" she whispered.

"God, yes."

No more playing around. Grant snaked his arm around her waist and closed the narrow gap between them as he slammed his mouth down onto hers.

That taste, that touch, the soft sighs…he'd missed them all. He'd ached for them while he and Tessa had been apart.

She wound her arms around his shoulders and flattened her chest against his. All too soon she lifted her head.

"Bronson claims if we marry the clause is void."

Grant smiled. "Is that so? And here I'd planned on asking you to marry me without even knowing about that little loophole."

Tessa stepped back, went over to the old end table and picked up a sheet of paper. "Actually, I have everything spelled out right here."

Looking down at all the colors and bold lettering, Grant laughed. "Another spreadsheet?"

"This one is much more enjoyable than the last one I gave you."

His eyes scanned the days, the hours. "You have me in all the slots, Country."

"That's right, Slick. You're all mine. So don't ever, ever think of leaving me again, because you know how I hate to redo my spreadsheets."

He tossed the paper aside, sending it fluttering to the floor. "You know what I hate? That fact that you have on too many clothes."

Yanking the side zipper, Grant helped her peel out of the dress, leaving her clad in absolutely nothing but a smile.

"So it looks like we need to marry so I can keep my job," he told her as he ran his hands up over her curves.

"I'll do anything to keep your reputation and career intact."

Smiling, he picked her up and laid her on the chaise. "I may also need to marry you because these last two weeks were pure hell, and I love you more than any film or any production company."

Delicate fingertips came up to trace his cheek. "I'm glad you were miserable, because you deserved it. Now you deserve to be rewarded for your good behavior."

Grant laughed as he started shedding his clothes. "I do love a woman in charge."

* * * * *

SINGLE MAN MEETS SINGLE MUM

JULES BENNETT

To Jill, Amy and Inez.
I love you three more than the frozen yogurt we devour.
Thanks for the road trip and all the laughs.
May we have many, many more!

One

Oomph!

Out of nowhere, Ian Shaffer had his arms full of woman. Curvy, petite woman. A mass of silky red hair half covered her face, and as she shoved the wayward strands back to look up, Ian was met with the most intriguing set of blue eyes he'd ever seen.

"You okay?" he asked, in no hurry to let her down.

He'd taken one step into the stables at Stony Ridge Acres and this beauty had literally fallen into his arms. Talk about perfect timing.

The delicate hand against his shoulder pushed gently, but he didn't budge. How could he, when all those curves felt perfect against his body and she was still trembling?

He may not know much about the horse industry, but women… Yeah, he knew women really well.

"Thank you for catching me."

Her low, husky voice washed over him, making him

even more thankful he'd come to this movie set to see to his client's needs in person…and to hopefully sign another actress to his growing roster of A-listers.

Most agents didn't visit movie sets as regularly as he did, but he sure as hell wasn't missing the opportunity to keep Max Ford happy and allow prospective client Lily Beaumont to witness just what a kick-ass, hands-on agent he was. Given his young age, the fact that he was known as a shark in the industry happened to be good for business.

Ian glanced to the ladder that stretched up into the loft of the spacious stables. His eyes narrowed in on the rung that hung vertically, the culprit of the lady's fall.

"Looks like your ladder needs repairing," he told her, looking back to those big, expressive blue eyes.

"I've been meaning to fix it," she told him, studying his face, his mouth. "You know, you can let me down now."

Yeah, he was probably freaking her out by keeping her in his clutches. But that didn't stop him from easing her down slowly, allowing her body to glide against his.

Hey, he may be there to concentrate on work, but that didn't mean he couldn't enjoy the samplings of a tempting woman when an opportunity presented itself.

Keeping his hand on her arm, Ian allowed his gaze to sweep down her body. He justified the touch by telling himself he was looking for signs of injury, but in all honesty, he simply wanted to get a better look. If this was what they called taking in the local scenery, then sign him up.

"Are you hurt anywhere?" he asked.

"Just my pride." Stepping back, forcing his hand to fall away, she brushed her fingers down her button-up plaid shirt. "I'm Cassie Barrington. And you are?"

He held out his hand. "Ian Shaffer. I'm Max Ford's agent."

And if all went well, he'd be signing Max's costar Lily,

too. There was no way he'd let her go to his rival agency without one hell of a fight first. And then maybe his very unimpressed father would see that Ian had become a success. He was a top agent in L.A. and not just hanging out at parties with women for a living. He'd become a powerful man in the industry.

Though the parties and women were a nice added bonus, Ian enjoyed stepping away from the glamour to be on set with his clients. And it was that extra touch that made him so successful. Between forging connections with producers and getting to know the writers and actors better, he could place his clients in the roles best suited to them.

The role Max was playing was perfect for him. The top actor was portraying the dynamic Damon Barrington, famous horse owner and former jockey. And for Ian, escaping L.A.'s hustle and bustle to spend time on a prestigious Virginia horse farm was a nice change of pace.

"Oh, Max mentioned you'd be coming. Sorry for falling on you." Her brows drew together as she gave him a quick assessment. "I didn't hurt you, did I?"

Ian shoved his hands into his pockets, offering her a smile. She could assess him anytime she wanted. "Not at all," he assured her. "I rather enjoyed the greeting."

Her chin tilted just enough to show defiance. "I don't make a habit of being clumsy…or throwing myself at men."

"That a fact?" he asked, trying not to laugh. "Such a shame."

"Do you make a habit of hitting on women?" she asked.

Unable to resist the gauntlet she'd thrown before him, Ian took a step forward, pleased when her eyes widened and she had to tip her head up to hold his gaze.

"Actually, no. But I'm making an exception in your case."

"Aren't I lucky?" Her tone told him she felt anything

but. "Max should be in his trailer. His name is on the outside, and I believe another trailer was recently brought in for you."

Apparently she was in a hurry for him to be on his way—which only made him want to stay longer. Finding someone who didn't care about his Hollywood status, someone who wasn't impressed with his power and money, was a refreshing change. The fact that someone was curvy, wore jeans as though they were made to mold those curves and had expressive baby blues was the icing on the proverbial cake.

"So you're the trainer and your sister is the famous jockey?" he asked, crossing his arms over his chest.

The warm late-spring sun beat against his back as it came through the wide doors of the stable. Summer blockbuster season was just around the corner and, hopefully, once the film wrapped and he'd signed Lily, his agency would still be on top. His ex-partner-turned-rival would no longer be an issue.

He'd started working for an agency right out of college, thanks to a referral from a professor he'd impressed, but some lucky breaks and smart business sense had had him quickly moving to open his own. Unfortunately, he'd taken on a partner who had stabbed him in the back and secretly wooed most of their clients in the hopes they'd work exclusively with him in a new venture.

For the sake of his pride, he had to win Lily over and get her under contract. But how could his mind be on business with this voluptuous distraction before him?

"You've done your homework," she commented. "I'm impressed you know about me and my sister and our different roles."

"I do my research. You could say I'm pretty hands-on as an agent."

"Apparently you're hands-on with everything."

Oh, that was such a loaded statement—one he wouldn't mind exploring if he had the time. His eyes held hers as he closed the gap between them. The pulse at the base of her throat quickened and her breath caught as she stared, unblinking, at him.

Damn work responsibilities. But surely a little flirting, hell, even a fling, would make this an even more riveting trip.

"Everything," he whispered. "Let me know if you ever want an experience."

When her gaze dropped to his mouth again, Ian resisted the urge to grab her, to taste her. There would be plenty of time for…anything she was willing to give. Besides, wasn't the chase half the fun?

"I think you know where my trailer is."

And because he'd probably crossed some sort of moral, ethical boundary, Ian turned and walked from the barn, leaving her with her mouth open.

Well, this was already the most exciting movie set he'd ever visited and he hadn't even seen his client yet.

Cassie tightened her grip on MacDuff's lead line. He was still new, still skittish, but she was working with him every single day and he was showing improvement. Every now and then he'd let her father, Damon Barrington, ride him, but he had a touch that every horse seemed to love.

At least MacDuff had quit trying to run from her. Now, if she could just get him to understand her silent commands that he had to mimic her pace and direction when they walked.

Her work with MacDuff and the other horses was just one of the many issues that had ended her marriage. Derek had wanted her to stop spending so much time with the "strays" she brought in. He'd insisted she stop trying to save every animal, especially when she'd become pregnant.

Cassie would never stop trying to save animals...especially since she hadn't been able to save her marriage. Her husband had obviously loved women and liquor more than her and their baby. His loss, but the pain still cut deep.

She focused on the line, holding it tight and trying to keep up with the routine because she was running a tad behind now.

Of course, she'd been thrown off her game already this morning after falling into the arms of that handsome, bedroom-eyed stranger. For a split second she'd wanted to revel in the strength with which he held her, but then reality had slapped her in the face, reminding her that she'd fallen for a smooth talker once. Married him, had his child and hadn't seen him since.

Well, except when he'd shown up for the divorce proceedings, mistress in tow. As if that busty bleach blonde would ever play stepmom to Cassie's precious baby. Hell. No.

Cassie swore she'd never let another man play her for a fool again, and she sure as hell wouldn't get swept away by another pretty smile and sultry touch.

Unfortunately, when she'd fallen into Ian's arms, she'd forgotten all about that speech she'd given herself when her husband had left. How could she have a coherent thought when such strong arms were holding her flush against a taut body? No woman would blame her for the lapse in judgment.

But no more. Cassie had her daughter to consider now.

With sweet Emily just turning one, Cassie knew she'd definitely gotten the best part of her marriage, and if Derek didn't want to see their baby, he was the one missing out.

So, no more sexy men who thought they were God's

magnificent gift to this world. Although Cassie had to admit, even if just to herself, that her insides had tingled at Ian's touch. He'd been so strong, had smelled so…manly and had looked in her eyes as if she truly was a beautiful, desirable woman.

She hadn't felt anything but frumpy and still a bit pudgy since having Emily. The extra weight that refused to go away coupled with her husband leaving her for another woman were damaging blows to her self-esteem. Yet, Ian had held her with ease, which wasn't helping her ignore the potency of the mesmerizing man.

Getting swept away by another handsome man with sultry eyes and a powerful presence wouldn't do her any good. She had to concentrate on helping her sister, Tessa, win her way to the Triple Crown. They'd worked side by side nearly their entire lives, always with the dream of being Triple Crown winners like their father. And here they were, about to make history, and Cassie couldn't be more excited.

When Cassie had been too far along with her pregnancy, her father had stepped up to train Tessa. This racing dynasty truly was a family affair.

One race down, two to go.

The fact that the Barrington estate had been turned into a film set was icing on the cake. A script surrounding her father's legacy, legendary racing and past winning streak had piqued the interest of Hollywood A-listers, and, suddenly, the horse farm was all abuzz with lighting, sound guys, extras and security.

Cassie actually loved seeing her father's life played out by Max Ford, the handsome, newly married actor. And playing the role of her late mother was beautiful Southern belle and it-girl Lily Beaumont. So far the two were doing an amazing job, and Cassie couldn't wait to see the final product.

To cap off the racing season, Cassie was moving full throttle toward opening her own riding school for handicapped children. Since having her own child, Cassie wanted to slow down, and she'd always had a soft spot for kids anyway...something she'd thought she and her ex had in common.

Launching the school would be one more step in the healing process. So now she just needed to keep saving up—she wouldn't dream of asking her father or anyone else for money—to get it off the ground.

"Daydreaming?"

Keeping a firm grip on the lead line, Cassie glanced over her shoulder to see Tessa moving toward her in slow, cautious steps. MacDuff really did get treated with kid gloves by everyone until he learned they were his friends.

"Maybe just a little," Cassie admitted, gently pulling MacDuff into a soft trot. "Give me just a few minutes and we'll get to work."

Tessa shoved her hands into the pockets of her jeans. "I'd rather hear what has my big sister so distracted this morning."

Cassie rolled her eyes at Tessa's smirk and quirked brow. She led MacDuff forward a few steps, stopped and moved back a few steps, pleased when the stallion kept up with her exact number and didn't try to fight her.

He was learning. Finally.

"I'm always amazed at how broken they seem to be," Tessa said softly. "You have this patience and gentleness. It's almost as if they know you're determined to help them."

"That's because I am." Cassie reached up to MacDuff's neck, offering him praise. "He's just misunderstood and nobody wanted to work properly with him."

"He was abused."

Cassie swallowed as she led MacDuff back to the stables. The thought of someone beating him because he hadn't had the right training sickened her. She'd known he'd been abused on some level, simply because of how he'd arrived all wide-eyed and nervous and then threw Tessa the first time she'd mounted him. But the second any horse, rescued or not, stepped onto Stony Ridge Acres, they were treated like royalty. No matter their heritage. Yes, they bred prizewinning horses and bought from a long lineage of winners, but it wasn't always about the win.... It was about the love and care of the animal. And since Stony Ridge was a massive farm, they could take in those strays Cassie had a soft spot for.

She'd always loved watching the trainers her father had for his horses. Years ago, female trainers had been frowned upon, but her father had insisted women were more gentle and less competitive by nature than men, thus producing better-tempered horses—and winners.

"You didn't happen to see a certain new hunk on the set this morning, did you?" Tessa asked as she pulled out the tack box and helped to brush MacDuff.

Cassie eyed her sister over the horse's back. "Aren't you engaged?"

"I'm not dead, Cass." Tessa brushed in large circular strokes. "I'll take your lack of answering to mean you did see him."

Saw him, fell into his arms, got lost in those sexy eyes that could make a woman forget she'd been burned...and maybe reveled in that powerful hold a tad too long.

"Even you have to admit he's one attractive man," Tessa went on.

"I can admit that, yes." Cassie switched from the curry-comb to the dandy brush. "I may have had an incident this morning involving that loose rung on the ladder to the loft and Mr. Shaffer."

Tessa stepped around MacDuff's head, dropped the brush into the tack box and crossed her arms over her chest. "Okay, spill it. You know his name and you said 'incident.' I want all the details."

Cassie laughed. "It's no big deal, Tess. I fell off the ladder. Ian happened to be there, and he caught me."

"Oh, so we've gone from Mr. Shaffer to Ian."

"He's Max's agent and apparently visits his clients' film sets. We exchanged names," Cassie defended herself. "Seemed like the thing to do since he was holding me."

"I love where this story is going." Tessa all but beamed as she clasped her hands together.

Laughing, Cassie tossed her brush aside, as well. "No story. That was pretty much it."

"Honey, you haven't even mentioned a man's name since *you know who* left and—" Tessa held up a hand when Cassie tried to intervene "—your face seemed to brighten up a bit when you said his name."

"It did not," Cassie protested.

Tessa's smile softened. "If you want to argue, that's fine. But he's hot, you finally showed a spark of life about a man and I'm clinging to hope that you haven't given up on finding love. Or, for heaven's sake, at least allowing yourself a fling."

Cassie rolled her eyes and patted MacDuff's side. "Just because this romance business is working for you doesn't mean it will for me. I tried that once—it didn't last. Besides, I have no time for love or even a date between training with you and Emily."

"There's always time. And, romance aside, have a good time. A little romp with a sexy stranger might be just what you need," Tessa said with a naughty smile. "Aren't you the one who forced me to take a few days off last month? You have to make time for yourself."

Cassie had conspired with Tessa's now fiancé, producer Grant Carter, to whisk Tessa away during her training and the filming of the movie. Grant had wanted to get Tessa far from the limelight, the stress and the demands of their busy schedules, and Cassie had been all too happy to help because her sister needed a break.

Tess had found the right man, but Cassie seriously doubted there was a "right man" for her. All she required was someone who loved her and didn't mind her smelling like horses more often than not, someone who would offer stability in her life, make her feel desirable and love her daughter. Was that too tall of an order?

"I'm not looking for a fling," Cassie insisted, even though she'd pretty much already envisioned a steamy affair with Ian.

Tessa raised a brow. "Maybe a fling is looking for you."

"I just met the man. I'm sure he's not going to be around me that much anyway, so there's very little chance of seduction. Sorry to burst your bubble."

"Maybe you should show Ian around the estate," Tessa suggested as she went to grab a blanket and saddle for her racing horse, Don Pedro.

Cassie sighed, closing the gate to MacDuff's stall. "I don't want to show him around. Max is his client—he can do it."

"Max is going to be busy filming the scene with Lily down by the pond. I want to make sure we're there to see that taping."

Cassie smiled and nodded in agreement. She loved watching the two actors get into character, loved watching her father's reaction to reliving his life through the eyes of a director, and there was no way she'd miss such a monumental scene. This was the scene where Max would propose to Lily. The replay of such a special moment in her parents' lives was something she had to witness.

"I'll make sure we're done here about the time shooting starts," Cassie assured her sister. "All the more reason I don't have time to show Ian around."

"Now, that's a shame."

Cassie and Tessa both turned to see the man in question. And just like with their earlier encounter, the mere sight of him caused a flutter to fill her belly. Of course, now she couldn't blame the sensation on the scare from the fall... only the scare from the enticing man.

"I'd like to have a look around the grounds if you have time," he said, looking directly into her eyes, seeming to not even notice Tessa.

Cassie settled her hands on her hips, cursing herself when his gaze followed her movements. Great, now she'd drawn his attention to her hips...not an area a woman wanted a man looking.

"I thought you went to see Max," Cassie said, refusing to acknowledge his request.

"I saw him for a brief moment to let him know I was here. He actually was talking with Grant and Lily."

Cassie cast a glance at her sister, whose face had split into a very wide grin. *Darn her.*

With a gracefulness that would've pleased their late mother, Tessa turned, extended her hand and smiled. "I'm Tessa Barrington, Cassie's sister. We're so glad to have you here at the farm."

Ian shook Tessa's hand as the two exchanged pleasantries. He finally settled his gaze back on Cassie. Did those eyes have some magical power? Seriously, why did she have to feel a jolt every single time he looked at her?

"Go ahead and show Ian around, Cassie. I'm fine here."

If Cassie could've reached out and strangled her sister

with the lead line she so would have, but then Ian would be a witness.

"It will have to be tomorrow or later this evening." No, she wasn't too busy right now, but she wouldn't allow Mr. Hollywood Hotshot to hold any control over her. "I'll come find you when I'm ready."

"Well, I'm going to walk Don Pedro out," Tessa said. "It was a pleasure to meet you, Ian. Cass, I'll see you later."

Great, now they were alone. Cassie would definitely kill her sister for that little stunt.

Ian stepped closer, and Cassie held her ground. This was her property and no matter how charming, how sexy and how...

Damn, he smelled good. She lost all train of thought; Ian's masculine scent was enough to render her mind blank. How long had it been since she'd been with a man, felt his touch?

Too long. So why did this man with an inflated ego turn her on? Could she not attract the right kind of guy just once?

"I can wait till tomorrow," he told her. His eyes searched her face as a hint of a smile played around her lips. "I'm a pretty patient man."

Placing a hand on his chest to stop him may have been a mistake. A jolt of awareness tingled up her arm. The strength, the chiseled pecs beneath her palm... Yeah, she was very aware of the sexiness that encompassed Ian Shaffer.

"I appreciate the fact you're taking the time to use your charm on me, but I'm too busy for games. Besides, I'm pretty sure I'm a lot older than you."

Ian shrugged. "Age hadn't entered my mind."

Cassie laughed. "I'm pretty sure I know what entered your mind."

He stepped forward again, giving her no choice but to

back up until the gate to a stall stopped her. Ian put one hand on either side of her head, blocking her.

"Then I'm sure you're aware I find you attractive." His eyes dropped to her mouth, then traveled back up. "I can't wait for that tour, Cassie."

He pushed off the stall and walked out of the stable. When was the last time a man had caught her attention, inspired her sexual desire so fast? The danger of falling into lust scared her to death.

But she had to be realistic. There was nothing special about her. And if she did allow herself to act on these very new, very powerful emotions, she highly doubted he'd remember her name in a few months.

No way could she succumb to his charms.

TWO

Cassie's parents had been married nearly twenty years when her mother was killed suddenly in a car accident. She'd always admired the love her parents had for each other, always wanted a marriage like that for herself.

Unfortunately, a happy, loving marriage wasn't in the cards for her. And hindsight was a harsh slap in the face because Cassie realized she'd probably married Derek too quickly.

She'd craved the love her parents had had and thought for sure Derek—the Barringtons' onetime groom—had the same outlook on marriage…. As in, it was long-term and between only two people.

How could she trust her feelings for a man again? Cassie swiped the tear from her cheek as she headed back toward the stable. The sun was slowly sinking behind the hills surrounding the estate. Spring was gradually turning into summer, giving the evenings just a bit more light.

The day's filming was complete and the scene she'd just witnessed had left her raw and hopeful all at the same time.

Max Ford and Lily Beaumont had beautifully reenacted Cassie's parents' proposal. Cassie had heard stories, had seen pictures of her parents' early love. But to witness that moment in person... Cassie had no words for how precious the experience had been.

She'd stood with Tessa off to the side, and even with the directors and producers stopping and starting and re-arranging in the middle of the scene, the moment had captured her heart.

Added to that, each time she'd glanced at Ian, his gaze had been on hers. He hadn't even bothered trying to hide the heat that lurked in those dark, heavy-lidded eyes. Thankfully, at one point he'd slid on his aviator shades, but his dominating presence still captured her attention...and her hormones.

There went those lustful emotions again. She couldn't afford to get swept away by a sexy body and killer smile. Lust was the evil that had overtaken her once before and look where that had gotten her. Oh, she didn't regret her marriage because she had Emily, but the pain from the rejection and having her love blatantly thrown back in her face was humiliating. Who wanted to be rejected?

Cassie reached the stable, intending to work with MacDuff again, but her eyes moved up to the rung of the ladder that still hung vertically.

She'd meant to mention the problem to Nash, the new groom, but between the emotional shoot and a certain hot agent plaguing her mind, she'd simply forgotten. Besides, he'd been so busy today cleaning out all the stalls, she really hated to add to his list.

Her father took pride in his stables, always making sure everything looked pristine and perfect. Cassie would bite the bullet and fix the ladder herself. At least working on something would keep her mind off Ian...hopefully. Her tendency to fix things and have everything in her life make sense would have to be satisfied with just this piece of wood for now. The Ian issue—and she feared he was fast becoming an issue—would have to wait.

She grabbed the hammer and several long nails from the toolbox in the equipment room. She shoved the nails in her back pocket and held on to the hammer as she climbed the ladder that stretched to the loft of the stable.

The setting sun cast a soft glow into the structure. Horses neighed, stomped hooves and rustled in their stalls. The sounds, the smells—none of it ever got old. Cassie loved her life here and she looked forward to bringing her daughter up in such a beautiful, serene environment.

During her four years of marriage, she'd been away from the estate. Even though she and Derek had lived only ten minutes away, it just wasn't the same as being on the grounds. Cassie loved living in the cottage, being with the horses and knowing her family was all right here helping with her emotional recovery.

With her tears mostly dry, Cassie sniffed. Crying had never been her thing. Anger fit more into her life, especially since she'd been abandoned only two months after giving birth. Tears hadn't brought her cheating husband back, not that she'd wanted him after the fact, and tears certainly weren't helping her raise her daughter or move on like the strong mother she needed to be.

Halfway up the ladder, she eyed the broken rung, then carefully slid it back into place. Widening her stance as far as she could to balance her body while holding the hammer, she reached around into her back pocket for a nail.

"I can help you with that."

Cassie glanced over her shoulder to see Ian at the base

of the ladder, his watchful gaze raking over her body. *Great.* She had red-rimmed eyes and a red-tipped nose, she was sure. She was not a pretty crier. She always got the snot-running, red-splotchy-face and puffy-eyes look.

Cassie slid a nail out and turned back around to place it against the wood. "I've got it, but thanks."

She knew he hadn't left, but Cassie didn't say anything else as she worked quickly and repaired the rung. With a hefty tug on the wood, she made sure it was securely in place before she started her descent. Just as she'd gotten to the last rung, Ian moved his hard body against hers, trapping her between the ladder and a most impressive chest. Her body was perfectly aligned with his, causing ripples of heat to slide through her. They were both fully dressed, but the sensations spiraling through her had never occurred before, even when she'd been completely naked with her ex.

Yeah, she was doomed where this sexy stranger was concerned.

Cassie swallowed, closed her eyes. Ian made her aware of just how feminine she was. When was the last time she'd felt desirable? Was it so wrong to want a man to find her attractive? After being married to someone who kept looking elsewhere for his desires to be fulfilled, Cassie knew she was probably grasping at any attention at this point.

She also knew she didn't care—not when his body was so hard, so perfectly perfect against hers. Not when his soft, warm breath tickled the side of her neck, and not when his masculine aroma enveloped her.

"What are you doing here?" she whispered.

Ian slid his arms up to align with hers, his hands covering hers on the wood. "I saw you walking this way. You looked upset."

No. He didn't care. He couldn't. Not this soon and not about her. Sexual desires were clouding his mind...and hers, too, apparently, because she was enjoying the heat of his body a little too much.

What man would follow a woman into a stable just because she looked upset? No. He'd followed her for one reason and one reason only. A reason she certainly didn't think she was ready for.

"I'm fine," she lied.

Ian nuzzled her hair. Oh…when he did that she forgot all arguments about why being attracted to someone so full of himself was wrong. Her mind completely voided out any pep talks she'd given in regard to steering clear of lustful feelings and attractive charmers.

"You're a very beautiful woman, Cassie." His soft voice slid over her body, reinforcing those tremors that were becoming the norm where he was concerned. "I tried to ignore this pull I have toward you, but it was damn hard when I saw you during the shoot. How do you do that to a guy?"

Um…she had no clue. Power over men had certainly never been something she'd mastered. If it had, she'd still be married.

"Ian, we just met and…"

He used one hand and slid the hammer from her grasp, letting it fall to the concrete floor with a loud thud.

"And I'm older than you," she continued. "I'm thirty-four. You can't even be thirty."

With an arm around her waist, he hauled her off the ladder and spun her around until she faced him—their mouths inches apart.

"I'm twenty-nine, and I assure you I'm old enough to not only know what I want, but to act on it."

His mouth came down on hers, hard, fast, hungry. Cassie didn't have time to think or refuse because her body was already melting into his.

The passion pouring from him stirred her desire even more as she gripped his thick biceps. Giving in to just a few seconds of bliss wouldn't hurt.

And when Ian's mouth traveled from her mouth down the column of her throat, Cassie tipped her head back as her breath caught. What was he doing to her? A full-on body attack. His mouth may be in one spot, but Cassie could feel every inch of her body tingling and wanting more.

Wait…this wasn't right. She couldn't do this.

Pushing him away, Cassie slid her hand up over the exposed skin peeking out of her shirt…the skin his mouth had just explored.

"Ian, I can't… We can't…" Words were useless because her mind was telling her one thing and her body was telling her another. "I just met you."

"You're attracted to me."

She couldn't deny the statement. "That doesn't mean I should act on it. I don't just go around kissing strangers."

"After you learned my name this morning, I was no longer a stranger."

Those dark eyes held her gaze. Even without a word the man exuded power, control. Derek had been so laid-back, so uncaring about everything that this was quite a change.

And Cassie would be lying if she didn't admit the fact that Ian was the polar opposite of her ex turned her on even more.

"You're only here for a short time," she went on, crossing her arms over her chest. "We can't just…you know."

"Have sex?" he asked, quirking a brow.

Oh, mercy. The words were now out, hovering in the air, and from the smirk on his face, she was the only one feeling awkward at this moment.

"Yes, that." *Dear Lord.* It wasn't as if she hadn't had

sex before; she'd had a baby, for crying out loud. But she couldn't discuss something like that with him. Now she felt foolish and juvenile. "Acting on sexual attraction isn't something I normally do."

That was an understatement, considering she'd had sex with one man and that had been her husband. What if she did throw caution to the wind? What if she had some sordid affair?

Seriously? Was she contemplating that? She was a mother—a mother to a little girl. What kind of example was she?

"You're thinking too hard." Ian started to step forward, but he stopped when Cassie held up a hand.

"Don't. I can't think when you're touching me."

"I'll take that as a compliment."

Cassie rolled her eyes. "You would."

"See? You know me already."

One of them had to think rationally. Apparently it would be her. She maneuvered around him toward the opening of the stable.

"You're going to have to keep your hands and your mouth to yourself."

Those tempting lips curved into a smile. "You're no fun."

"I don't have time for fun, Ian."

And more than likely he was the proverbial good time back in L.A. She could easily see him hopping from one party to the next, beautiful women draped over his arm, falling into his bed.

Cassie flicked the main switch to light up the pathways between the stalls. The brightness from the antique horseshoe-style chandeliers put a screeching halt to any romantic ambience that had been lurking in the darkening stable.

When she turned back around, Ian had his hands on his narrow hips, his focus still locked on her. There was a hunger in his eyes she'd never seen from any man before.

Without a word, he closed the gap between them. Cassie's heart had just started to settle, but now it picked back up again. She should've known better than to think the intense moment would pass.

Ian framed her face with his hands and brought his mouth to within a fraction of an inch of hers. "A woman who kisses, who responds to my touch without hesitation, has pent-up passion that needs to be released."

His lips barely brushed hers. "Come find me when you're ready."

Ian walked around her, leaving her still surrounded by that masculine scent, his arousing words and the tingling from his touch still on her lips.

She'd known the man twelve hours. There was no way she could handle him being on the grounds for two more months. She was a woman—a woman with needs.

And a part of her wondered just what would happen if she allowed herself to put those needs first for once.

Three

Two days had passed since she'd been up close and personal with Ian, but Cassie was more than aware of his quiet, yet dominating, presence on the estate. She'd seen him from a distance as he talked with Max. She'd found out she'd just missed him on the set of one scene she'd gone to watch, but she refused to admit she was wondering about his schedule, about when she'd see him again. Feel his body against hers.

She refused to fall for another man who set her hormones into overdrive, so where did that leave her? Considering a fling?

Groaning, she made her way from the stables to the main house. The sun was making its descent behind the mountains and Emily was at her weekly sleepover with Tessa and Grant. After witnessing the shooting of the engagement scene over the past couple of days, Cassie was feeling more and more nostalgic.

She missed her mother with each passing day; seeing Rose's life depicted in the film had Cassie wanting to feel closer to her. And with Emily away for the night, this was the perfect opportunity to reminisce and head up to the attic, where all her mother's things were stored.

Rose's unexpected death had shaken up the family in ways they'd never even imagined. As teen girls, Tessa and Cassie had really taken it hard, but they'd all been there for each other, forming an even stronger bond. But Cassie still ached for her mother's sweet smile, her encouraging words and her patient guidance.

Because right now she truly wanted a mother's advice. Ian had her completely tied in knots. When he'd left her in the stables two days ago, Cassie had never felt so torn, so conflicted in her life. And he hadn't approached her since. What was up with that? Had he changed his mind? Had he decided she wasn't worth the trouble?

Why was she even worried about this anyway? No doubt Ian was used to those flawless women who had been surgically perfected. More than likely Cassie's extra pounds and shapelier curves were not what Ian was looking for in a…fling? What was he doing exactly with his flirting? Where had he expected this to go?

Never mind. He'd thrown out the word *sex* like nothing. Cassie knew exactly where he was headed with his flirting.

Leaving the attic door propped open, Cassie headed up the narrow wooden staircase. At the top she flicked on the small light that was so soft, it really only set off a glow on one wall. But that was the wall where her mother's boxes were stacked.

In the silence of the evening, Cassie was all alone with her thoughts, her memories. She pulled the lid off the first bin and choked back tears.

How could anyone's life, especially that of her beautiful,

loving, vivacious mother, be condensed to a few boxes? All the memories, all the smiles, all the comfort Rose Barrington had offered to the world...all gone. Only tangible items remained stored neatly in plastic bins.

Cassie couldn't help but smile. Her very organized mother wouldn't have had it any other way.

After going through pictures from her parents' simple, elegant wedding day, Cassie knew the wedding dress was around. Tessa actually planned on wearing it for her upcoming vows, and Cassie couldn't wait to see her baby sister in their mother's gown. Just that image was enough to have her tearing up again.

This film was certainly wreaking havoc on her emotions, that was for sure.

Cassie kept searching through storage bins, looking for a box or a folded garment bag. Would the crew need to duplicate that dress for the wedding scene? More than likely they'd already researched pictures to find inspiration for the costumes, just as they had for the settings.

Cassie had been itching for a chance to look through the old photos again herself.

Moving from the bins, Cassie went and looked inside the narrow antique wardrobe, where she discovered a white garment bag. Slowly unzipping, so as not to tear the precious material inside, Cassie peeled back the bag and pulled out the classy gown she'd been hunting for.

The dress had been preserved so that the cream-colored material was still perfect. Tessa would be just as beautiful a bride as their mother had been.

Cassie had thought about wearing it for her own wedding, but her ex had insisted on getting married at the courthouse. She should've known then that he wasn't the one. Not that there was anything wrong with a small civil ceremony, but Derek had known she'd always wanted a wedding in the small church where her parents had married. She'd wanted the lacy gown, the rice in her hair as they ran to their awaiting car...the special wedding night.

None of those young-girl dreams had come true.

Unable to resist, Cassie stripped from her jeans, boots, button-up and bra and pulled on the strapless floor-length dress. A straight cut with lace overlay may be simple to some, but the design was perfect to Cassie.

Smoothing a hand down the snug bodice, Cassie went to the antique mirror in the corner. If she fell in love one day—real love this time—maybe she could wear it. Wouldn't that be a beautiful tradition? Rose, Tessa and Cassie all wearing the same gown. Perhaps if the material held up and the gown was well preserved again, little Emily would one day walk down the aisle wearing the dress her grandmother had.

If it weren't for baby weight, the frock would fit perfectly. Unfortunately, right now her boobs threatened to spill out the top and lace was definitely not a forgiving material, so her curves were very...prominent.

Behind her, the attic door clicked. Cassie turned, her hand to her beating heart as footsteps sounded up the stairs. No time to cover up all her goods, so she kept her hand in place over her generous cleavage.

"Hello?" she called.

Ian rounded the landing and froze. He took in her state of dress—or undress, really—of course zeroing in on where her hand had settled.

So much for her evening of reminiscing. Could fate be any more mocking? Dangling this sexy stranger in her face when she knew full well that nothing could or should happen?

"What are you doing?" she asked, keeping her hand in place and trying to remain calm. Kind of hard when she was on display and just the sight of the man had her heart accelerating.

"I wanted to apologize for the other day," he told her, coming up the last couple of steps. "I never force myself on a woman, and I didn't want you to have that impression of me. But if I'm going to be here any length of time, and I am, we need to clear the air."

Clear the air? Cassie sighed and prayed because she had a sinking feeling they may be there for a while.

"Well, now's the perfect time because if that door latched all the way, we're locked in here."

Ian drew his brows together. "Locked in?"

"The door locks from the outside. That's why I had left it standing open."

Pulling up the hem of the dress with one hand and trying to keep the bodice up with the other, she moved around him down the steps and tugged on the handle. She leaned her forehead against the door and groaned.

"I didn't know," he murmured behind her.

Cassie turned and looked up the steps to see Ian looking menacing and dangerous—in that sexy way only he could—standing at the top. His muscles filled out his long-sleeved T, those wide shoulders stretching the material, and his dark jeans fit his narrow hips beautifully.

She knew firsthand exactly how that body felt against hers. Knew just how well he could kiss a woman into forgetting her morals.

In a house this size, with only her father living here and his bedroom on the first floor, no one would hear them yell until morning, when they could open the small window and catch someone's attention.

Risking another full-body glance at Ian, Cassie knew she was in big, big trouble. Her attraction to him was the strongest she'd ever felt toward a man. But it wasn't so much the level of heat between them that scared her; it was the quick onset of it. It felt as if she had no control over her own reaction. She'd been helplessly drawn to this intriguing man. How could she trust her emotions right now? He was honestly the first man to find her desirable since her ex. Was he just a sexy diversion or were her feelings more in-depth than that?

Earlier tonight she'd flirted with the idea of a fling, but now the reality of being trapped with Ian made her heart flutter and nerves dance in her belly.

Her gaze met his. Crackling tension vibrated between them in the soft glow and the silence.

And Cassie had all night to decide what to do with all her attraction and the hungry look in Ian's eyes...

Ian stared down at Cassie, struck by those creamy exposed shoulders, that poured-on, vintage-style wedding gown molded to her sweet curves. From his vantage point, he could see even more of her very exposed breasts and most impressive cleavage—even though she was trying her hardest to keep gravity from taking over the top of that dress.

Mercy. Being straight in front of her had been torture, but this angle offered a much more interesting, gut-clenching view. Not that he was complaining.

Being stuck in an attic with Cassie would be no hardship because he'd caught a glimpse of the passion she held beneath her vulnerability. And there wasn't a doubt in his mind that her war with herself stemmed from some past hurt.

Cassie attempted to cross her arms over her breasts, which only tortured him further, because she failed to cover the goods and actually ended up offering him an even more enticing view. Was she doing this as punishment?

"Text Max and have him come to the main house and ring the doorbell. Dad won't be in bed yet."

Ian shook his head. "Sorry. I only came over to apologize to you, so I left my phone in my trailer to charge."

Groaning, Cassie tipped her head back against the door and closed her eyes. "This isn't happening to me," she muttered. "This cannot be happening."

Ian had to smile. Of all the scenarios he'd envisioned on his short walk from his trailer to the main house, he hadn't once thought of being stuck for hours with someone so sexy, so unexpected, and wearing a wedding dress to boot.

This couldn't have been scripted any worse...or better, depending on the point of view.

Cassie lifted the dress and stomped back up the steps, her shoulder slamming into him as she stormed by.

"Wipe that smirk off your face, Ian. Nothing about this is comical."

"Can't you call someone with your phone?" he asked, turning to face her.

Cassie propped her hands on her hips. "No. I came up here to be alone, to think."

Damn, she was even sexier when she was angry. But getting too wrapped up with Cassie Barrington was a dangerous move. She wasn't a fling type of girl and he'd pushed too hard in the stables. Had she given in to his blatant advances, he knew she would've regretted it later.

He needed to do the right thing and keep his hands off her. He was here for two main purposes: keep Max happy and sign Lily so she didn't go to his rival. Period.

But his hormones didn't get the memo, because the more he was around Cassie, the more alluring and sexy she became. Of course, now that he'd seen a sample, he had to admit, he wanted to see more. That dress... Yeah, she looked like a 1950s pinup. Sexy as hell, with all the right curves and none of that stick-thin, anorexic nonsense, and she was even hotter with a slight flush from anger.

For the past two days he'd seen her working with her sister, training the horses and driving him unbelievably mad with the way her lush body filled out a pair of jeans. He'd seriously had to get his damn hormones in check and then approach her with a much-needed apology for his Neanderthal tendencies.

But now that he was here, those hormones were front and center once again, overriding all common sense and rational thoughts.

"How did you know I was up here?" she asked. "I figured all the crew was either in their trailers or back at the hotel."

"I ran into Grant on my way to your cottage. He told me you were here. As I was coming in the back door, your cook, Linda, was going out for the night and she said you mentioned coming to the attic."

"You came all this way just to apologize? I'm sure you would've seen me tomorrow."

Ian shrugged, shoving his hands into his pockets. "True, but I knew too many people would be around tomorrow. I assumed you wouldn't want to discuss this in front of an audience. Besides, I think we need to address this spark between us and figure out what to do with it since I'll be here several weeks."

Cassie threw her hands in the air. "Could you at least turn around so I can put my clothes back on?"

His eyes traveled down her body, darting to the pile of clothes behind her, zeroing in on the leopard-print bra lying on top.

"Sure," he said, trying to get the visual of her in that leopard bra out of his mind before he went insane.

Fate may have landed him up here with the sassy, sexy

Ms. Barrington, and fate also provided a window directly in front of him, where he was afforded a glorious view of Cassie's reflection as she changed. Of course, that made him a bit of a jerk, but no man with air in his lungs would look away from that enticing view. This evening just kept getting better and better.

Cassie would probably die before she asked for help with the zipper, so he didn't offer. And she didn't have any trouble. As the dress slid down her body, Ian's knees nearly buckled.

Lush didn't even begin to describe her. Her full breasts, rounded belly and the slight flare of her hips were a lethal combination.

"As I was saying," he went on, cursing his voice when it cracked like that of an adolescent. "I realize that neither of us was prepared for the instant physical attraction—"

"You're delusional," she muttered as she tugged her jeans up over her hips and matching bikini panties.

"But just because I find you sexy as hell doesn't mean I can't control myself."

Her hands froze on her back as she fastened her bra. Apparently his words had struck a chord. She glanced up and caught his gaze in the reflection. Busted.

"Seriously?" she asked with a half laugh. "Why did you even turn around?"

"I didn't know the window was there." That was the truth.

"And you weren't going to say anything?"

Ian spun around—no point in being subtle now. "I'm a guy. What do you think?"

Rolling her eyes, Cassie shrugged into her shirt and buttoned it up with jerky, hurried motions.

Fighting the urge to cross the room and undress her again, Ian slid his hands into his pockets and met her gaze.

"You are stunning," he told her, suddenly feeling the need to drive that point home. "I'm not sure why that statement caught you off guard."

Most women in Hollywood would pause at such a comment, try to deny it in order to hear more pretty words in a vain attempt to boost their own egos, but Ian knew Cassie was different. She truly didn't believe she was beautiful, and he had a feeling all that insecurity circled back to whatever the basis was for her vulnerability.

Damn, he didn't have time to delve into distressed damsels. But there was a desire in him, something primal, almost possessive that made him want to dig deeper, to uncover more of Cassie Barrington. And not just physically.

That revelation alone scared the hell out of him.

"I don't need to be charmed, Ian." She propped her hands on her hips. "We're stuck up here and lying or trying to make me want you isn't going to work."

"I don't lie, Cassie." When she quirked a brow, he merely shrugged. "I find you sexy. Any man would be insane or blind not to."

Cassie shook her head. After zipping the dress into a white garment bag, she headed over to a storage box and popped off the lid. She flopped down on the floor, crossing her legs and offering him the view of her back.

He waited for her to say something, but she seemed to have dismissed him or was so wrapped up in the memories of the photos she was pulling out, she just didn't care that he was there.

"You ever look at a picture and remember that moment so well, you can actually feel it?" she asked, her soft voice carrying across the room.

Ian took that as his invitation to join her. He closed the distance between them, taking a seat directly beside her. Cassie held a picture. A young girl, he presumed it was her, sat atop a horse, and a dark-haired beauty, who he assumed was her mother, held the lead line.

"That was my first horse," she told him, her eyes still on the picture. "I'd always ridden with Dad and helped him around the stables, but this one was all mine. I'd picked him out at auction and Mom and Dad told me I had to care for him all by myself."

Ian looked at the image of a young Cassie. "How old were you?"

"Eight. But I knew as soon as I saw him that I'd want him. He was skittish and shied away from the men, but when I approached him, against my father's advice, he came right to me and actually nuzzled my neck."

Ian listened to her, refusing to let himself fall into her sea of emotions. He'd noticed her and Tessa holding hands at the shoot, tears swimming in both of their eyes.

"I've never ridden a horse," he admitted.

Cassie dropped the picture back into the bin and turned to stare at him. "Seriously? We'll have to rectify that while you're here."

Ian laughed. "I wasn't asking for an invitation. Just stating a fact."

She turned a bit more to face him, her thigh rubbing against his. Did she have a clue that she was playing with fire? She may be older than him, but something told him she wasn't necessarily more experienced.

Arrogance had him believing they weren't on a level playing field. He had plenty he wanted to show her.

"I love teaching people how to ride," she went on, oblivious to his thoughts. "It's such an exhilarating experience."

Cassie's wide smile lit up her entire face. The room had a soft glow from the single-bulb sconce on the wall and Ian could resist those full lips for only so long...especially now that he knew exactly how they tasted.

Without warning, he slid his hands through her hair and captured her lips. She opened freely, just like when they'd been in the stables.

Ian tipped her head, taking the kiss deeper. He wanted more, so much more. He wanted to feel her hands on him as he explored her mouth, relishing her taste, but she didn't touch him. Maybe she did know how to play this age-old game of catch and release.

Easing back, Ian took in her swollen lips, her heavy lids and flushed cheeks and smiled. "Actually, *that's* an exhilarating experience."

And God help them both because between the interlude in the stables and that kiss, he had the whole night to think about how this sexual chemistry would play out.

The real question was: Could he make it all night without finding out?

Four

Cassie jumped to her feet, instantly feeling the chill without Ian's powerful touch. The man was beyond potent and he damn well knew it.

"You seriously think because we're locked in here and we kissed a few times that I'll just have sex with you?" Cassie ran a shaky hand through her hair, cursing her nerves for overtaking her as fast as those heated kisses had. "I don't know what lifestyle you lead in L.A., but that's not how I work."

Ian stared up at her, desire still lurking in those dark-as-sin eyes. "Are you denying you were just as involved in those kisses as I was?"

"You had your hands all over me," she threw back. "Just because I like kissing doesn't mean I always use it as a stepping-stone for sex. I technically just met you, for crying out loud. I don't know anything about you."

Moving as slowly as a panther hunting its prey, Ian came

to his feet and crossed to her. "You know how quick you respond to my touch, you know how your heartbeat quickens when you wonder what my next move will be and you know you're fighting this pull between us."

Cassie raised a brow, trying for her best bored look. "That has nothing to do with Ian Shaffer. That's all chemistry."

"So you don't deny you want me?" he asked with a smirk.

Crossing her arms and taking a step back, Cassie narrowed her eyes. "Drop the ego down a notch. You just proved how very little we know about each other. You may sleep with virtual strangers, but I don't."

Ian laughed, throwing his arms in the air. "Okay. What do you want to know?"

"Are you married?"

Shock slid over his face. "Hell no. Never plan to be."

Commitment issues? Lovely. Hadn't she just gotten out of a relationship with a man of the same nature?

On the other hand, Ian wasn't cheating on a wife back in California. That was at least one mark in his favor. Okay, the toe-curling kisses were major positive points in his favor, but she'd never confess that out loud. And she wasn't actually looking to jump back into another relationship anyway.

"No girlfriend?" she asked.

"Would I be all over you if I did?"

Cassie shrugged. "Some guys wouldn't care."

That heated gaze glided over her and was just as effective as a lover's touch. Her body trembled.

"I'm not like a lot of other guys."

He was powerful, sexy and wanted in her pants. Yeah, he was just like some guys.

With a sigh, Cassie laughed. "I can't believe this," she

muttered more to herself than to Ian. "I'm actually playing twenty questions because I want to have sex."

"Sweetheart, I don't care a bit to answer a hundred questions if you're considering sex."

Lord have mercy, it was hot up there. Not just because of the ridiculous way her body responded to this charmer, but literally. The heat in the attic was stifling.

Cassie unbuttoned the top two buttons of her shirt, exposing her cleavage area, but she needed air. She rolled her sleeves up and caught Ian's eyes taking in her actions.

"Don't get excited there, hotshot. I'm just trying to cool off."

Sweat trickled between her shoulder blades and she so wished she'd at least pulled her hair up earlier. There had to be something up here. As she started to look around in boxes for a rubber band of any type, she tried not to think of Ian and if he had sweat on the taut muscles beneath his shirt.

Okay, that mental blocker was broken because all she could see was glistening bronzed skin. And while she hadn't seen him without a shirt, she had a very good imagination.

"Can I help you find something?" he asked.

Throwing a glance over her shoulder, she caught his smirk as he crossed his arms over his chest. "I just need something to pull my hair up. I'm sweating."

There, that should douse his oversexed status a little. What man found a sweaty woman attractive? And she was pretty sure her wavy red hair was starting to look like Bozo the Clown's after a motorcycle ride…sans helmet. She lifted the flap off a box in the far corner and shuffled things around in her hunt.

"So, why is an agent needed on a film set?" she asked,

truly wondering but also wanting to keep his mind on work—which was what he should be doing anyway.

"Max is one of my top clients." Ian unbuttoned his shirt halfway. "I often visit my clients on set to make sure they're taken care of. And with this being a very impressive script and plot, I knew I had to be here. I've actually blocked off a good bit of time to spend at Stony Ridge."

And wasn't that just the news she needed to hear? Mr. Tall, Dark and Tempting would be spending "a good bit of time" here. Just what her very inactive sexual life needed... temptation.

"Yes," she shouted as she grabbed a rubber band off a stack of school papers from her primary days.

"Max is a great guy, from what I've seen." After pulling her hair into a knot on top of her head, she turned to Ian. "He and Lily are doing an amazing job, too. Lily seems like a sweetheart."

Nodding his agreement, Ian rested a hip against an old dresser. "She's rare in the industry. L.A. hasn't jaded her or sucked the goodness out of her. She had a rough patch with a scandal at the start of her career, but she's overcome it. She's a rare gem."

"And I'm sure you've tried to get her into bed."

Rich laughter filled the space. The fact he was mocking her only ticked Cassie off more. But, if she were honest, she was ticked at herself for wanting him.

"I've never slept with Lily," he told her, a grin still spread across his handsome face. "I've never even tried to. I'm actually hoping to sign her to my agency. I respect my clients and they respect me. This business is too risky and too exposed for anything like that to remain a secret. There are no secrets in Hollywood."

"Is that all that's stopped you? The fact that people could find out?"

Ian straightened to his full height and took a step toward her. *Great.* She'd awoken the sex beast again.

"What stopped me," he said as he took slow steps toward her, "was the fact that, yes, she's beautiful, but I'm not attracted to her. Added to that, I want a professional relationship with her, not a sexual one. If I want a woman in my bed, she won't be on my client list. Plain and simple."

He'd come close enough that Cassie had to tip her head back. Thankfully, he hadn't touched her. Too much more touching—or, heaven forbid, kissing—and she feared her self-control would be totally shot.

Cassie swiped a hand over her damp neck. "Is everything a business strategy with you?"

"Not at all. Right now, I'm not thinking anything about business."

The way his eyes held hers, as if she was the only person that mattered right now, made her wonder...

She may be naive and she was certainly still recovering from Derek walking out on her, but what would a fling hurt? Tessa had even verbally expressed Cassie's thoughts on the matter. She'd married for "love," or so she'd thought. Hell, she'd even saved herself for marriage and look how that had turned out.

"I promise I won't ravage you if you'd like to take something off," he told her with a naughty grin. "I'm sure your shirt will be long enough to cover things if you need to get out of those jeans. If not, I've seen naked women before."

Yeah? Well, not *this* naked woman, and with that last bit of baby weight still hanging on for dear life, she most definitely wasn't comfortable enough with her body to flaunt it. Even if she did indulge in a fling with the sexy agent—and she couldn't believe she was seriously considering such a thing—she wasn't going to make the catch so easy for him. What fun would that be?

Deciding to teach him a lesson, Cassie reached up and patted the side of his face. "You're so sweet to sacrifice yourself that way."

Cassie knew her mother had a box of old clothes up here. Perhaps something could be used to cool her off and make Ian squirm just a bit more.

As she went toward the area with the clothing boxes, she opted to keep Ian talking.

"So, tell me more about Lily." Cassie pulled the lid off an oblong box and nearly wept with relief at the colorful summer dresses inside. "She's very striking and has a strong resemblance to my mother."

"When this film came across my desk, I knew I wanted Max to try for it and I was sincerely hoping they paired him with Lily. This role was made for her. She's already got that Southern-belle charm your mother had, according to everyone on set. Lily has the sweet little twang in her voice like all of you Barringtons do."

Cassie turned, clutching a simple strapless cotton dress to her chest. "I do not have a twang."

Ian quirked a brow. "It's actually even more prominent when you get ticked. Very cute and sexy."

Rolling her eyes, Cassie turned back to the box and placed the lid back on. "I'm going to change. Could you try not to stare at me through the reflection again?"

Ian shrugged one broad shoulder. "I promise."

Cassie waited for him to turn around or move, but he just sat there smiling. Damn that man. Now that she'd reminded him he'd seen her pretty much naked, Cassie had no doubt she'd just thrown gasoline on the fire.

"Aren't you going to turn around?" she finally asked.

"Oh, when you just said not to look at you through the reflection, I assumed you wanted to let me in on the full viewing."

"I didn't want to let you into this room...let alone treat you to a viewing."

Cassie resisted the urge to kiss that smirk off his face. He knew he was getting to her, and she wondered just how much longer she'd deny it to herself.

"I'll move, then," she told him, stomping to the other end of the attic behind a tall stack of boxes. "And don't you follow me."

"Wouldn't dream of it." He chuckled. "But you're just putting off the inevitable, you know."

She quickly wrestled out of her clothes and yanked the strapless dress up over her heated body. Her bare arms and legs cooled instantly.

"I'm not putting anything off," she informed him as she came back around the boxes. "I know your type, Ian. Sex shouldn't just be a way to pass the time. It should mean something, and the couple should have feelings for each other."

"Oh, I feel something for you. And I plan on making you feel something, too."

Why did her body have to respond to him? And why did she always have to be so goody-goody all the time?

She didn't even have the ability to make him squirm. No wonder her husband had left her for another woman.

"I'm not sure what put that look on your face, but I hope it wasn't me."

Cassie drew her attention back to Ian, who had now moved in closer and was very much in her personal space. His dark eyes stared at her mouth and Cassie really tried to remember why she was putting up such a fight.

Had her husband ever looked at her like this? As though he was so turned on that all that mattered was the two of them? Had he ever made her tingle like this or feel so feminine and sexy?

No to all the above.

Cassie swallowed. If she was really going to do this, she needed to be in control. She'd been dominated enough in her marriage and right now she wanted something totally different. She wanted sex and she wanted Ian.

Mustering up all her courage, Cassie looked up at him with a wide smile and said, "Strip."

Five

It wasn't often Ian was shocked—he did live in Hollywood, after all. But that one word that had just slid from Cassie's lips truly took his breath and left him utterly speechless.

"Excuse me?"

Raising a brow, she crossed her arms as if she dared him to refuse. "I said strip. You want this, fine. But on my terms."

"I don't do sex with rules."

Cassie shrugged. "I don't do flings, but here we both are, stepping outside of our comfort zones."

Damn, she was hot. He never would've guessed the shy, quiet sister had this vixen streak. Of course, she admitted she was stepping outside her comfort zone, so perhaps this was all new territory. He had to hand it to her—she was doing a spectacular job. But he couldn't let her have all the control.

Reaching behind his neck, Ian fisted his shirt and tugged it off, flinging it to the side. Hands on his hips, he offered a grin.

"Now you."

Cassie laughed. "You're not done yet."

"No, but I'm ahead of you." He met her gaze, the silent challenge thrown down between them. "I'm waiting."

Even though her eyes never left his, he didn't miss the way her hands shook as she reached beneath the dress and pulled her panties down her bare legs.

Just that simple piece of silk lying discarded at her feet had his pulse racing, his body responding.

She quirked a brow again, as if waiting for him to proceed.

Without hesitation he toed off his shoes and ripped off his socks. "Looks like you're down to only one garment now," he told her, taking in the strapless dress she'd donned.

And it was about to get a whole hell of a lot hotter in here.

She eyed the lamp across the room and started for it.

"No," he told her. "Leave it on."

Glancing over her shoulder, she met his stare. "Trust me when I say you'll want that off."

"And why is that?"

Turning fully to face him, she pointed to her body. "In case you haven't noticed, I'm not one of those Hollywood types who starve themselves for the sake of being ultra-thin."

Crossing the narrow space between them, Ian ran both his hands up her bare arms and tucked his fingers in the elastic of the top of the dress, causing her arms to fall to her side.

"Oh, I've noticed." He yanked the dress down until it

puddled at her feet, leaving her bare to him. "And that's precisely why I want that light on."

Her body trembled beneath his. No way did he want her questioning her gorgeous curves or the fact that he wanted the hell out of her.

Without a word he shucked off his pants and boxer briefs and tossed them aside.

Her eyes drank him in, causing the same effect as if she'd touched his entire body with her bare hands. Dying to touch her, to run his fingers along her curves, Ian snaked his arms around her waist and tugged her against him.

"As much as I want to explore that sexy body of yours, I'm hanging on by a thread here," he admitted as his mouth slammed down onto hers.

Cassie wrapped her arms around his neck. Their damp bodies molded together from torso to thigh, and she felt so perfect against him.

Perfect? No, she couldn't be perfect for him. Perfect for right now, which was all either of them was after.

They were simply taking advantage of the moment...of the sexual attraction that had enveloped them since she'd literally fallen into his arms only a few days ago.

Ian gripped her waist and lifted her.

"Ian, don't—"

"Shh," he whispered against her mouth. "I've got you."

Her lips curved into a smile. "What about a condom? Do you have that, too?"

Condom, yes. They needed a condom. His mind had been on the subtle moans escaping from her lips and getting those curves beneath his hands.

He eased her down his body and went to his jeans, where he pulled a condom from his wallet and in record time had it on.

When he turned back to her, he fully expected her to

have her arms wrapped around her waist, maybe even be biting her lip out of nerves. But what he saw was a secure woman, hands on her hips, head tilted and a naughty grin on her face.

"Your confidence is sexy," he told her as he came back to her.

"You make me feel sexy."

Yeah, she wasn't a Hollywood size zero. Cassie Barrington was more old-school Hollywood starlet. She was a natural, stunning, vibrant woman, and now that she'd agreed to leave the light on, he could fully appreciate the beauty she was.

And when she reached for him and nearly wrapped herself around him as she claimed his mouth, her sexy status soared even higher.

Damn, he wasn't going to make it through this night.

Ian backed her against the wall and lifted her once again. This time her legs went around his waist and he had no control. None. The second he'd shucked that dress off her he'd been holding on by that proverbial thin thread.

Ian took her, causing her body to bow back, and her head tilted, eyes closed as she groaned once again.

As their hips moved together, Ian took the opportunity to kiss his way across her shoulders and the column of her throat before taking her face between his palms and claiming her mouth.

Sweat slick between them, the air around them grew even hotter as Cassie gripped his bare shoulders. Her nails bit into his skin; her heels dug into his back.

He wouldn't have it any other way.

She tore her mouth from his. "Ian, I—"

Yeah, he knew. He was right there with her as her body stilled, trembled. Following her over the edge, watching her face as she succumbed to the passion was one of the most erotic moments of his life.

Her body slid down his and he was pretty sure she would've collapsed to the floor had he not been leaning against her. He needed to lean into her or he'd be a puddle, too.

And the night had just begun.

Cassie slid back into her dress, ignoring the panties. Why bother with modesty at this point?

She may not live in Hollywood, but she'd put on one hell of an acting display. Ian thought her confident? She'd played along simply because she secretly wanted to be that wanton, take-charge woman, that woman who claimed what she wanted. And if he thought she was so comfortable with her body in this situation, then who was she to tell him different?

She'd been meek in her marriage, not a sex goddess in any way. But the way Ian had looked at her, touched her, was nothing like she'd ever experienced.

How could a man she'd known only a handful of days provide so much self-assurance? He'd awakened something within her she hadn't even known existed.

Cassie was certainly not used to one-night stands or flings, but she couldn't regret what had just happened. A virtual stranger had just given her one of the greatest gifts…self-esteem. Not too long ago she'd thought she'd never have that back, but right now, with her body still tingling from his talented hands and lips, Cassie knew without a doubt that she was better than the husband who had left her for another woman.

She'd just scooped up her discarded panties from the floor when Ian placed his hands around her waist and tugged her back against his bare chest.

"How's that age thing now?" he asked, nipping her ear. "Any complaints about how young I am?"

Laughing, Cassie shook her head. "You certainly know what you're doing."

His lips trailed over her neck. "I'm not done, either."

Oh, mercy. Her entire body shivered as she let her head fall back against his shoulder, enjoying the kisses he sprinkled across her heated skin.

"I'm not sure why you put this dress back on," he told her between kisses. "It's so hot in here and all."

Yes, yes, it is.

Cassie turned in his arms, noticing he was still completely naked. Those ripped muscles beneath taut, tanned skin begged for her touch.

"I didn't get to appreciate all of this a moment ago, before you attacked me," she told him, trailing her fingertips along his biceps and across his pecs.

"Appreciate me all you want," he told her with a crooked grin. "But let it be known, I didn't attack. You ordered me to strip, so I believe you started this."

Cassie playfully smacked his chest. "Who started what? You were the one who propositioned me in the stables."

"How's a man supposed to react when a sexy woman falls into his arms?"

"Yes, naturally that's what most people would do," she said, rolling her eyes.

Ian reached down, cupped her backside and widened his sexy smile. "I'm glad this little incident happened with the lock."

Cassie had to admit she was, too. There was no way she would've been able to focus on work with all her emotions fluttering around inside her. Now hopefully she wouldn't have to worry about this overwhelming physical attraction to Ian. They'd had sex, gotten it out of their systems and could move on.

His body stirred against hers. Okay, maybe they hadn't gotten it out of their systems.

"We still have hours before anyone will find us." He started backing her up again. "I have so many ideas to fill the time."

The backs of Cassie's thighs hit the edge of an old table. Ian wasted no time hoisting her up onto the smooth wooden surface.

"Do you have more condoms?" she asked.

His heavy-lidded gaze combined with that Cheshire-cat smile had her quivering before he even spoke.

"I may be out of condoms, but not out of ways to pleasure you."

And when he proceeded to show her, Cassie was suddenly in no hurry for daylight to come.

Six

Unable to sleep for appreciating the feel of this sexy woman tangled all around him on the old chaise, Ian smoothed a hand down Cassie's bare back. Trailing down the dip in her waist, up over the curve of her hip had his body stirring again.

What on earth was he doing? Sex was one thing, but to lie awake most of the night rehashing it over and over in his head like some lovesick fool was, well…for fools. Not that he was any expert on relationships.

His mother was gearing up to divorce husband number four, no doubt with number five waiting in the wings, and his father… Ian sighed. His father probably wasn't even capable of love. Ian hadn't spoken to his father in years and rarely talked with his mother. He had nothing to say to either and it was obvious both of his parents were battling their own issues that didn't include him.

It shouldn't come as a surprise that Ian didn't do relationships.

He was great at his job, however, and what he wanted was to take his client roster to the next level. Lily Beaumont was the key.

Yet here he was, getting involved with Cassie Barrington. And, yes, they'd just had sex, but during the moments in between their intimacy, he'd gotten a brief glimpse of a playful, confident woman and he couldn't deny he liked what he saw.

The sound of a car door jarred him from his thoughts. He eased out from beneath Cassie's warm, lush body and moved over to the small window that faced the side of the house.

Tessa and Grant had arrived. He didn't know if he wanted to call for their attention or crawl back over to Cassie and give her a proper good-morning wake-up.

But their night was over, and he had responsibilities. He honestly had no clue how she'd react once she woke up. Would she regret what they'd done? Would she want more and expect some sort of relationship?

Ian gave the window a tug and it rose slowly with a groan.

"Hey," he yelled down. "Up here."

Tessa and Grant both looked around and Ian eased his arm out to wave. "We're locked in the attic," he called.

"Ian?" Grant shouted. "What on earth? We'll be right up."

Of course, now it dawned on him that both he and Cassie were as naked as the day they were born, and he turned around to see her already getting up. Shame that he hadn't ignored the rescue party and gone with his original idea of waking her, especially now that she was covering that made-for-sex body.

"Was that Tessa and Grant?" she asked, tugging on her jeans from the previous day.

"Uh-huh." He pulled on his own clothes, trying to keep his eyes off her as she wrestled into her bra.

Several moments later, the door below creaked open and Ian rushed over to the top of the stairs to see Tessa.

"We'll be right down," he told her, hoping to save Cassie some time to finish dressing.

He didn't know if she wanted it public knowledge that they'd slept together. This was all her call. He was much more comfortable with a fling than he figured she was. Plus this was her home, her family, and the last thing he wanted to do was put her in an awkward position.

"Who's up there with you?" Tessa asked, her brows drawn together.

"Your sister."

Tessa smiled. "Really? Well, we'll meet you all down in the kitchen. Take your time."

Once she walked away, Ian glanced up to Cassie, who was wearing a lovely shade of red over her neck and face.

"I tried," he defended, holding out his hands. "But I'd say your sister knows."

Cassie nodded. "That's okay. Tessa won't say anything."

Okay, maybe he hadn't wanted a relationship, but her statement hit a nerve. Seconds ago he'd thought he was fine with a fling and she wasn't, but perhaps he'd had that scenario backward.

"Is that what we're going to do? Keep this quiet?"

Smoothing her tousled hair away from her face, Cassie eyed him from across the room and sighed. "I don't know. This is all new to me. Can we just go downstairs and talk later?"

The voice of reason had him nodding. He didn't want to

analyze what had happened too much. They both needed to concentrate on their jobs. After all, he had a mission and she was in the middle of the biggest racing season of her life.

Cassie started to ease by him when he stepped in front of her, blocking her exit. Her eyes went wide, then dropped to his mouth. Why was he doing this?

Quit stalling and let her go.

But he needed one more taste before their night officially came to an end.

He shoved his hands into her hair, tilting her head as he closed the distance between them. "Before you go," he whispered as his mouth slid across hers.

She melted into him as she returned the kiss. Her hands gripped his wrists as he held on to her. As much as Ian wanted her naked once again, he knew that was not an option.

Easing back, he smiled when her eyes took a moment to open. He released her, and, without a word, she walked by him and down the stairs.

And like some nostalgic sap, he glanced around the attic and smiled. This was definitely his favorite place on the estate.

Ian met up with Cassie in the kitchen. As soon as he entered the open room, he took in several things at once.

Tessa and Grant were seated at the bar, where Linda was serving cinnamon rolls. Both Tessa and Grant were eyeing Ian with knowing grins on their faces.

But it was Cassie, yet again, who captured his attention.

The woman he'd spent the night with was currently squatting down in front of a little girl with soft blond curls. The little girl looked nothing like Cassie, but the interaction didn't lie. The way she clung to Cassie, Cassie's sweet smile and laughter as she kissed her—it all had a sickening feeling settling deep in his gut.

"And who's this?" he asked, hoping it was Linda's grandchild or something because he knew Tessa and Grant had no children.

Coming to her feet with the little girl wrapped in her arms, Cassie still wore that vibrant smile as she turned to face him. "This is my daughter, Emily."

All eyes were on Ian. Granted, they were watching him because of the unspoken fact that he and Cassie had spent the night together, but they couldn't know the turmoil that flooded him. Cassie had a child and hadn't told him.

Not that they'd played the getting-to-know-you game before they'd shed their clothes, but wasn't that something that would come up?

Cassie's smile faded as Ian remained silent. Her protective hands held Emily close to her chest.

"Why don't you have some breakfast?" Linda asked, breaking the silence.

His eyes darted to her, then back to Cassie, who still watched him with a questioning look. Tessa and Grant had yet to move as they also took in the unfolding scene.

"I have things to do," he said as he walked by Cassie, ignoring the hurt in her eyes, and out the back door.

He couldn't stay in there another second. Rage filled him at the idea that Cassie had kept such a vital part of her life a secret. Was she the mother who pawned her kid off on other people so she could go have a good time? She'd been so confident, so eager to please him last night. Perhaps he was just the latest in a long line of men she threaded into her web.

No, he hadn't wanted anything beyond sex. And he sure as hell didn't want to discover that the woman he'd spent the night with was manipulative and selfish, looking for attention…just like his mother.

Humiliation flooded her.

The look of utter shock layered with anger had consumed Ian when she'd announced Emily was her daughter.

"Cass?"

Swallowing the hurt, Cassie turned to see her sister watching her. Because this awkward moment didn't need any more fuel added to the fire, Cassie smiled.

"Thanks for watching her last night," Cassie said as she held Emily with one arm and grabbed the overnight bag off the counter. "I need to go change and then I'll meet you at the stables."

"Cassie." Tessa slid from the stool and crossed to her. "Don't do this."

"Do what?"

Blue eyes stared back at her and Cassie wanted nothing more than to sit and cry, but feeling sorry for herself wouldn't accomplish anything. She'd tried that when Derek had left her.

"I just want to go feed Emily and change." Cassie blinked back the burn of tears. "I'll meet you in an hour."

"Leave Emily here," Linda said. "I'm keeping her today anyway. Do what you need to do. I'll make sure she's fed."

As much as Cassie wanted to keep Emily with her, she knew it was silly. She'd just have to put her in her crib with toys while she grabbed a shower.

"All right," she conceded, dropping the bag back onto the counter and easing Emily into the wooden high chair next to the wide granite island. "Thanks, guys."

Barely keeping it together, she started for the door. When Tessa called her name again, Cassie raised a hand

and waved her off. She just wanted to be alone for a minute, to compose herself.

How could she be so naive? Of course some big-city bachelor would be turned off by kids, but to act so repulsed by the fact made her flat-out angry.

She'd sworn when Derek had left she wouldn't allow herself to get hurt again. So, what did she do? Sleep with the first man who showed her any kind of affection.

Seriously, she thought she had more self-respect than that.

More angry at herself now, Cassie marched across the Barrington estate to her cottage next to the stables. Swatting at her damp cheeks, she squinted against the bright early-morning sun.

And because of the light in her eyes she didn't see Ian until she was in the shadow of her house. There he stood, resting against one of the porch posts as if he belonged there.

"Don't you have a client who needs your attention?" she asked, not stopping as she brushed past him and slid her key from her pocket to let herself in.

When she tried to close the door behind her, Ian's muscular arm shot out and his hand gripped the edge.

Those dark eyes leveled hers as she reined in her tears. No way would she let him see just how upset she truly was.

Tension crackled between them as Ian stood on the threshold, making no move to come in or leave.

"What do you want?" she asked.

"I want to know why you didn't tell me you had a daughter."

"Do you have kids?" she retorted.

He blinked. "No."

"Why didn't you tell me you didn't?"

"It never came up."

She threw her arms out. "Exactly. We didn't discuss too much personal stuff before…"

Shaking her head, Cassie looked up to the ceiling and sighed. "Just go. I made a mistake—it's over."

When her front door slammed, she jumped.

"I don't like being played." Ian fisted his hands on his narrow hips.

"This is my life, Ian." She gestured toward the Pack 'n Play in the corner and the toys in a basket next to the sofa. "I'm a mom. I'm not apologizing for it, and you won't make me feel bad."

When he continued to stare, muscle ticking in his jaw, Cassie tried her hardest not to wilt under his powerful presence. His gray T-shirt stretched over taut muscles, and she instantly recalled him taking her against the wall.

"Look, you're going to be here for a while," she said, reality sinking in. "I'm going to be here for the most part except during races. We're going to see each other."

His eyes roamed over her as if he were recalling last night, too. A shiver crept through her, but she remained still, waiting on his response.

"I wish you were different," he told her, his voice low.

Stunned, Cassie crossed her arms. "What?"

Cursing, Ian turned for the door. "Nothing. You're right," he said, gripping the handle and glancing over his shoulder. "We have to see each other, so why make this harder than necessary? Last night was a mistake, so let's just forget it happened."

He walked out the door and Cassie resisted the urge to throw something. For a second, when he'd said he wished she were different, she'd seen a sliver of vulnerability in his eyes. But he'd quickly masked it with his cruel, hurtful words. *Fine.* She didn't need anybody, especially someone who acted as if her child was a burden. Emily came first in her life. Period.

And no man, not her ex-husband and certainly not this sexy stranger, would make her feel ashamed.

Cassie turned toward her bedroom and cursed her body. She hated Ian Shaffer for his words, his actions, but her body still tingled from everything he'd done to her last night. How could someone so passionate and gentle turn into someone so hurtful?

Something about Emily had triggered such a dramatic turnaround. Unfortunately, Cassie didn't have the time or the energy to care. Whatever issues Ian had didn't concern her.

Now she just had to figure out how to see him on a daily basis and block out the fact he'd made her so alive, so confident for a brief time. Because now she didn't feel confident at all. She wished she could have a do-over of last night.

This time she'd keep her clothes on.

Seven

Ian may have had the best sexual experience of his life last night, but any desire he felt for Cassie was quickly squelched when he'd discovered her with a baby. A baby, for crying out loud.

It wasn't that he didn't like children. Kids were innocent in life, innocent in the actions of adults. How could he not love them? He just didn't see any in his future. And Cassie having a child certainly wasn't a problem in and of itself.

No, the issue had been when he'd seen her holding her child and he'd instantly flashed back to his mother, who would drag him from sitter to sitter while she went out at night.

But he wouldn't blame his past for his present problems. His body seemed to forget how angry he was and continued to betray him. Cassie was still sexy as hell and he'd forever be replaying just how hot their encounter had been.

But now that he knew she had a daughter, messing

around on a whim was definitely out. He wasn't cut out for the long term, and he refused to be the lover floating in and out of a kid's life the way his mother's lovers had floated through his.

Shaking off the unpleasant memories seeing Cassie with her baby had inspired, Ian approached Max Ford. His client had recently married his high school sweetheart and the couple had adopted a little girl. Ian couldn't be happier for the guy, but he wanted no part in the happily-ever-after myth himself.

"Hey," Max greeted him as he headed toward the makeup trailer. "Coming in with me?"

"Yeah."

Ian fell into step behind Max. The actor tugged on the narrow door and gestured for Ian to enter first. After climbing the three metal steps, Ian entered the cool trailer and nodded a greeting to the makeup artist.

Max closed the door behind him and exchanged pleasantries with the young lady. Ian took a seat on the small sofa across from the workstation and waited until the two finished their discussion of the day's events.

"You're working out in the stables and field today?" Ian asked. "I saw the script. Looked like the scene with you and Lily when the first horses were brought onto the estate after the wedding."

Max nodded as the makeup artist swiped over his face with a sponge full of foundation. "Yeah. It's a short scene. This afternoon and evening we'll be shooting some of the wedding scenes at the small church in town."

Ian settled deeper into the sofa, resting an arm across the back of the cushion. "Everything going okay so far?"

"Great," Max told him. "Raine is planning on joining me in a few days. She was excited I was shooting on the East Coast."

Ian knew Max and Raine had been through hell after years apart before finally finding their way back to each other in Max's hometown of Lenox, Massachusetts. Ian couldn't imagine trying to juggle a family while working in this crazy industry, let alone from across the country. Speaking of crazy, Ian never thought Hollywood heart-throb Max Ford would settle down, much less on some goat and chicken farm in New England, but to each his own and all that. Love apparently made you do some strange things.

"You talking to Lily soon?" Max asked.

Max had been one of Ian's first clients. They'd both taken a chance on each other, the risk had paid off and here they were, at the top of their games. They had no secrets and oftentimes their relationship was more like friends than business associates.

"Yeah. Hoping to get a few more minutes with her today."

The makeup artist reached for a brush and started stroking a shadow across Max's lids. Yeah, Ian would much rather stay on this side of the industry...the side where his face stayed makeup-free.

"I'll keep you posted," Ian said, not wanting to get too detailed since there were other ears in the room. "I plan on being on set for the next several weeks, so hopefully something will come from that."

Something positive. There was no way Ian wanted his ex-partner to get his clutches on Lily. Not to mention Ian was selfish and now that Lily was between agents, he wanted her because she was one of the top Hollywood leading ladies.

Added to that, she was the rare celebrity who hadn't been jaded or swayed by the limelight. Lily was the real deal who made a point to keep her nose out of trouble.

Any agent's dream client.

"I've discussed some things with her," Max stated. "She's

interested in hearing your terms and ideas, so hopefully she makes the right decision."

Ian was counting on it. Lily was smart enough to know the industry. After all, she'd just left her agent, who'd been a bit shady with her career. She'd put a stop to that immediately.

Ian could only hope she saw the hands-on way he worked and how invested he was as an agent. Visiting movie sets was his favorite job perk. Getting out of a stuffy office and being on location was always the highlight. Plus he wanted to make sure his clients were comfortable and there were no glitches.

"I'll be around if you need me." Ian came to his feet and moved toward the trailer door, pulling his phone from his pocket to check his emails. "I plan on being at both scenes today."

"Sounds good. I assume you've met all the Barringtons?" Max asked as the makeup artist ran the powder brush over his neck.

Ian swallowed. "Yeah. I've met them."

Met them, slept with one and still felt the stirrings from the continuous play of memories.

"They're one impressive family," Max went on, oblivious to the turmoil within Ian. "Damon is an amazing man with all of his accomplishments, but I swear, Cassie and Tessa are a force to be reckoned with."

Ian bit the inside of his cheek to avoid commenting on one of those "forces." The image of her in that body-hugging dress still made his knees weak, his heart quicken.

"That's why this movie is going to kick ass," Ian said, circling back to work, where his mind needed to stay. "Everyone loves a story like this, and having it on the big screen with two of Hollywood's top stars will only make it pull in that much more at the box office."

"I hope you're right."

Ian was confident this movie would be one of the biggest for both Max and Lily. Hollywood's heartthrob and sweetheart playing a married couple in a true story? It was a guaranteed slam dunk for everybody.

Which reminded him, he needed to check his emails and hopefully line up another client's role.

"I'll see you in a bit," Ian said as he exited the trailer.

He refused to glance toward Cassie's cottage. He wasn't some love-struck teen who'd slept with a woman and now wondered what she was doing every waking minute.

Okay, so he did wonder what she was doing, but love had absolutely nothing to do with it. His hormones were stuck in overdrive and they would just have to stay there because he refused to see her in any type of personal atmosphere again.

Even flings warranted a certain type of honesty, and getting involved, in any manner, with a woman who reminded him of the past he'd outrun was simply not an option.

A flash of movement from the field in the distance caught his eye. He headed toward the white fence stretching over the Barrington estate. As he neared, his gut tightened.

Cassie sat atop a chestnut-colored horse flying through the open field. Her hair danced unrestrained in the wind behind her and the breeze carried her rich laughter straight to him…and his body responded…work and emails instantly forgotten.

Ian stood frozen and admired the beauty. From behind her came Tessa on her own horse, but Ian's gaze was riveted on Cassie. He hadn't heard that deep laugh. She all but screamed sex with that throaty sound, her curves bouncing in the saddle, hair a wild mass of deep crimson curls.

Her carefree attitude would've been such a turn-on, but in the back of his mind he couldn't forget where he came from. From a father who had standards so high nobody could reach them and a mother who spent her time entertaining boyfriends and husbands, leaving a young Ian a distant second in her life.

He never wanted to go back to that emotional place again.

"You've got an audience."

Breathless and smiling, Cassie turned to her sister as Tessa came to a stop beside her. This felt good, to get out and not worry about training or anything else for a few minutes. Just getting back to their roots and racing was something she and her sister didn't do nearly often enough.

"Who's the audience?" Cassie asked, fully expecting to see some of the film crew. The cameramen and lighting people seemed to be all over the estate, moving things around, making the place their own for the sake of the film. The Hollywood scene was definitely a far cry from the usual relaxed atmosphere of Stony Ridge.

A sense of pride welled deep within her at the fact that Hollywood loved her family's story as much as she did. Horses, racing and family... That was what it meant to be a Barrington, and they excelled at it all because they worked hard and loved harder.

"Your agent," Tessa replied, nodding back toward the fence line. "I saw him stop when you raced by. He hasn't moved."

Cassie risked a glance and, sure enough, Ian stood turned in her direction. He was just far enough away that she couldn't make out his facial expression...not that she cared. But damn, why did he have to be a jumbled mess? He'd wanted her with such passion last night, had made her feel so special and wanted. How dare he pull such emotions out of her when she was still trying to piece the shards of her heart back together after her divorce?

Today when he'd seen Emily, he'd become detached, angry and not at all the same man she'd been with last night. His silence had hurt her, had made the night before instantly ugly.

And after coming home, she'd checked her phone and found a missed call from Derek. Seriously? After months of no contact whatsoever, now he decided to call? Cassie had deleted the message without listening. She didn't care what he had to say, and, after her emotional morning with Ian, she wasn't in the mood.

"He's not my anything." Cassie turned back toward Tessa, turning her back on Ian and willing him to go away.

"He was something to you last night."

Squinting against the sun, Cassie shrugged. "He was my temporary mistake. Nothing more."

Leaning across the gap between the horses, Tessa slid her hand over Cassie's. "I'm not judging at all. I just want you to know people aren't perfect. We all make rash decisions, and beating yourself up won't change what happened."

Cassie knew Tessa would be the last person to judge her, but that didn't stop the embarrassment from settling in her gut.

"I just hate that I gave in to the first man to show me any attention since being divorced," Cassie explained, gripping the reins.

Tessa's warm smile spread across her face. "Honey, Ian is a very attractive man, you're a beautiful woman and you all were locked in an attic all night. Instant attraction is hard to ignore, especially when you have nothing else to focus on."

"Self-control is a beautiful thing," Cassie murmured. "Too bad I didn't have any."

Laughing, Tessa squeezed Cassie's hand before pulling back. "Yeah, well, I didn't have any where Grant was concerned, either, and look how well it worked out for us."

Cassie's eyes darted down to the impressive diamond band surrounding Tessa's ring finger. Grant had gotten a flat band because of Tessa's riding career; he knew she wouldn't want to work with anything too bulky.

And that proved just how beautiful a relationship her sister and Grant had. The man knew Tessa inside and out, loved her and her career. He'd even overcome his own personal demons to be with her.

Cassie couldn't be happier for the two of them, but her situation was different.

"I'm pretty sure my attic rendezvous will not be leading to any proposals," Cassie joked. She had to joke with Tessa, otherwise she'd cry, and she refused to let this experience pull her down and make her feel guilty for having needs. "Besides, I think seeing Emily was like a bucket of cold water in Ian's face. I won't be with anybody who can't accept that I'm a package deal."

"I saw Ian's face when he found out Emily was yours," Tessa said, shoving her hair behind her ear. "He was definitely caught off guard, but the man wasn't unaffected by whatever happened between the two of you or he wouldn't have just stopped to watch you ride by. He may be torn, but he's still interested. You can't blame him for being shocked you're a mother."

Yeah, well, Ian's interest more than likely consisted of getting in her pants again...which she wouldn't allow.

But the memory of last night still played through her mind. His touch had been perfect. His words had seduced her until she'd forgotten about anything else but the moment they were locked in.

No matter how her body craved to be touched by his talented hands again, Cassie knew she deserved better than the way she'd been treated afterward.

So if Ian wanted her, that was his problem and he'd have to deal with it. She had enough on her plate without worrying about some big-time Hollywood agent who was only looking for only a fling.

She had a racing season to finish and a school for handicapped children to get started.

Her soon-to-be brother-in-law, Grant, had a paralyzed sister who used to ride, and her story had inspired Cassie on so many levels. Even though they hadn't met yet, just her story alone was enough to drive Cassie to want more for the next chapter of life. And what better way to teach her daughter to give back and love and care for others? Instilling love in young children made all the difference. She and Tessa were evidence of that.

Throwing a glance over her shoulder, Cassie had mixed emotions when she saw Ian was nowhere in sight. On one hand, she was glad he'd moved on. On the other, she kind of liked knowing she'd left some sort of impression on him.

No matter how things were now, for a time last night, she'd been in a sexy man's arms and that man had been attentive and giving and had made her feel more self-worth than ever.

Having regrets at this point was kind of in vain.

Besides, no matter what common sense played through her mind, she couldn't deny the physical pull she still felt toward Ian. And she was positive she hadn't seen the last of him.

Eight

After shooting wrapped for the day, Ian headed toward the stables to see if Lily was in there. He hadn't seen her for two days, and Max had mentioned he'd seen her heading that way. Ian hadn't had a chance to speak with her yet. The chaos of filming and so many people around had gotten in the way. Other than the usual small talk, he'd not been able to catch her alone.

Hopefully he could find her and perhaps they could arrange for a time to sit down and talk.

The sun was just at the edge of the horizon, casting a vibrant orange glow across the sky. The air had turned warmer as spring approached summer. Soon they'd be off to the Preakness Stakes, where Tessa would try to win the second race on her way toward the coveted Triple Crown.

The entire crew was riding the high of the shoot as well as getting sucked into the excitement of cheering the Barrington girls on toward victory. He had no doubt Tessa and Cassie were a jumble of anticipation and nerves.

Ian shoved his hands into his pockets as he approached the stables. He wasn't letting his mind wander to Cassie, because if he thought of her, he'd think of her sweet curves, her tempting smile and the fact he still wanted her.

Before he could travel too far down that path of mixed emotions, Ian rounded the corner of the open stable door and froze.

Lily was in the stable all right. But she wasn't alone. The groom, Ian believed his name was Nash, had his back to Lily, and Lily's hand rested on his shoulder, a look of concern marring her beautiful face.

She whispered something Ian couldn't make out and Nash's head dropped at the same time Lily's arms slid around his waist and she rested her forehead on his back. The intimate, private moment shocked Ian and he really had no clue what he'd walked in on.

The old-fashioned lanterns suspended from the ceiling cast a perfect glow on them and Ian quickly stepped out of the stable before he could be spotted…or interrupt whatever was happening.

He had a feeling whatever was going on between the groom and the star of the film was on the down low… especially since an affair had nearly cost Grant Carter his job when he'd been sneaking to see Tessa.

But that had all worked out and the two were headed down the aisle in the near future.

Their secret would be safe with him. For one, he wanted Lily to trust him and sign with his agency. And for another, why stir up trouble? Ian couldn't help but laugh. He and Cassie were pretty far-fetched in terms of the possibility of getting together, but look where they were now after a heated night in the attic.

Heading back toward his on-site trailer, Ian stopped when a scream cut through the evening. It was loud enough to have him trying to figure out where the sound was coming from.

He heard it again and moved toward the row of cottages settled beyond the main house. The grounds were deserted now since the entire crew had left for the hotel in town. Only a handful of people were staying on the property in trailers like the one Max had requested for him. The scream split through the air once more and Ian quickly found the culprit.

Just behind Cassie's cottage there was a small patio area and suspended from the pergola was a child's swing.

Cassie pushed her daughter, and each time the child went high, she let out a squeal. Ian's heart dropped at the sight. He didn't recall ever having that one-on-one playful time with either of his parents. Perhaps when he'd been a toddler, but he doubted it, considering they weren't affectionate when he'd been old enough to recall.

The sweet little girl with blond curls blowing in the breeze giggled and kicked her feet when Cassie grabbed the back of the plastic seat on the swing and held it back.

"Hold on," Cassie warned. "Here comes the biggest push of all."

When she let go of the swing, Cassie laughed right along with her daughter and Ian found himself rooted to his spot at the edge of her concrete patio.

The man in him watched, admiring Cassie's laid-back style, with her hair in a ponytail and wearing leggings and an oversize T-shirt that slid off one delicate, creamy shoulder. Her feet were bare and her face was void of any makeup, which was how he'd seen her since he'd arrived. Everything about her screamed country girl.

While the man in him watched, the lost little boy in him turned his attention to Emily. He took in all the delight from the sweet girl still clutching the rope holding up her swing and wondered where her father was. Did the man even know he had a child? Did Cassie have any contact with him?

All the questions forming in his head were absolutely none of his business, yet he couldn't help but want to know more.

Ian's gaze traveled from Emily back to Cassie…and he found her looking right back at him with those impressive blue eyes.

"What are you doing here?" she asked, giving the swing another light push.

Ian tried not to focus on the fact that her shirt had slipped in the front, giving him a glimpse of the swell of her breast.

"I heard screaming." He stepped onto the concrete pad, cursing himself for being drawn in even more. "I wasn't sure who it was."

Cassie's eyes held his for a second before she turned her attention back to the swing. She held on to the ropes, thus bringing Emily's fun to a screeching halt.

The little girl twisted in her seat to look back at Cassie. Cassie went to the front of the swing, unfastened the safety harness and lifted Emily out.

"We were just heading in for dinner," Cassie said, propping Emily up on her hip.

Damn if her tilted, defiant chin didn't make him want to stay longer. Why torture himself? He wanted her physically, nothing more. Yet he found himself being pulled ever so slowly toward her.

"Don't go in just because of me."

Emily stared at him with bright, expressive blue eyes like her mother's. Her hand reached toward him and he couldn't stop himself from reaching back. The moment he looked into those little baby blues something unidentifiable slid over his heart.

Emily's tiny hand encircled his finger as a smile spread across her baby face. That innocent gesture touched so many places in him: the child who'd craved attention, the teen who'd needed guidance and the adult who still secretly wished he had a parent who gave a damn without being judgmental.

Ian didn't miss the way Cassie tensed at the sight of Emily holding on to his finger, but he wasn't pulling back. How could he deny such an innocent little girl human touch? She was smiling, happy and had no clue the turmoil that surrounded her right now.

"Don't you have a client you should tend to?" Cassie asked, her meaning that he was not welcome all too clear.

"I already talked with Max after the shooting wrapped and we came back here." The crew had taken a few shots of the wedding scene in town. "I didn't see you at the church earlier."

Cassie reached up, smoothing away blond curls from Emily's forehead. "I was there. I stayed in the back with Tessa. We didn't want to get in the way."

"What did you think of the shoot?"

Why was he still here talking to her? Why didn't he just leave? He had calls to return, emails to answer, contracts to look over.

Besides the fact a little cherublike toddler had his finger in a vise grip, he could walk away. Cassie had made it clear she didn't like him, and he wasn't looking for a woman with a child.

Yet here he stood, talking to her and eagerly awaiting her answer.

"It was perfect," she said, a soft smile dancing across her lips. "Lily looked exactly like the pictures I've always seen of my mother on that day. My father teared up, so I know Lily and Max hit that scene beautifully."

Ian wiggled his finger, making Emily giggle as she tugged on him. He took a step forward, now being drawn in by two intriguing ladies.

"I think the fans will fall in love with this film," he told Cassie as his eyes settled on hers. "And your family."

The pulse at the base of her throat quickened and Ian couldn't help but smile. Good to know she wasn't so unaffected. What they'd shared the other night was nothing short of amazing. No matter what transpired afterward, he couldn't deny that had been the most intense night of his life.

Damn it. Cassie and her innocent daughter were the exact picture of the commitment he could never make.

So how could he be drawn to this woman?

"I just want my father to be happy with the end result," she told him. "I want people to see what a hard worker he is and that everything didn't get handed to him."

Ian couldn't help but admire her for wanting people to see the other side of Damon Barrington. The man was a phenomenon, and Ian had no doubt whatsoever that this film would be a mega blockbuster.

Emily let go of his finger and started patting her mother's cheeks. Instantly Ian missed the innocent touch, but he stepped back and shoved his hands into his pockets.

"Was there something else you wanted?" she asked.

Clearing his throat, Ian shoved pride aside and nodded. "Actually, yeah. I'm sorry for how I handled the other morning."

Cassie's brows rose as she reached up to try to pull Emily's hands from her face. "I never expected you to apologize."

He hadn't expected it, either, but he couldn't deny the

fact he'd been a jerk. If he'd learned anything from growing up, it was to know when to apologize. He'd never seen his parents say they were sorry to each other, and he'd always wondered if such a simple gesture would have made a difference.

"I can admit when I make a mistake," he informed her.

Those bright eyes darted down as she sighed. "This is a first for me."

"What's that?"

Glancing back up, she shook her head. "Nothing. I appreciate you apologizing. Since you're going to be here awhile, I really don't want tension. Between you working and me training, I just can't handle more stress."

Ian noticed the soft lines between her brows, the dark circles beneath her eyes. This single mother was worn-out and he'd added to her worry because she hadn't wanted any awkwardness between them.

"Who helps you with Emily?"

Great, now he was asking questions before he could fully process them. He needed a filter on his mouth and he needed to mind his own business. The last thing he wanted was to worry about Cassie and her daughter. He certainly wasn't applying for the position of caregiver.

"My family." Her chin tilted as she held his gaze, unblinking. "Why?"

Yeah, why indeed? Why was this his concern? They'd slept together one night after days of intense sexual tension and now he was all up in her personal space...a space that hit too close to home and touched his heart way too deeply.

He pushed aside the unwanted emotions. He would be here only a short time. Even if his past hadn't mixed him all up, he still couldn't get too involved with Cassie Barrington.

Besides, she had her hands full and they'd definitely

done a complete one-eighty since they'd spent the night together. That night had been full of passion and surrender. Now Cassie had erected walls, thanks to him, and the only thing he saw in her eyes was exhaustion.

"I'll let you get in to dinner," he told her, not answering her question. "See you tomorrow."

When he turned away, Cassie called his name. He glanced over his shoulder and found two sets of beautiful blue eyes staring at him.

"We're not having much, but you're welcome to join us."

The olive branch had been extended and he wondered if this was her manners and upbringing talking or if she truly wanted him to stay.

"I'd be a fool to turn down dinner with two pretty ladies," he told her, turning back to face her. "Are you sure?"

With a shaky nod, Cassie smiled. "I'm sure."

Well, hell. Looked as if he was getting in deeper after all. But he followed her through the back door like the lost man that he was.

They could be friends, he thought. Friends ate dinner together; friends apologized when they were wrong. That was where they were at now because Cassie and her little girl deserved a commitment, a family life—things he couldn't offer.

As Cassie slid Emily into her high chair, Ian watched her delicate skin as her shoulder peeked from her shirt once again. Anything he was feeling right now went way beyond friendship and ventured down the path at warp speed toward carnal desire.

Nine

Cassie had no clue what had prompted her to invite Ian inside. She wasn't weak. She didn't need a man and had been just fine on her own for the better part of a year now. But something about Ian kept pulling her toward him, as if some invisible force tugged on her heart.

And when Emily had reached for him, Cassie had waited to see his reaction. Thankfully, he'd played right along. She'd barely noticed his hesitation and hard swallow, but he hadn't disappointed Emily. Maybe kids weren't the issue with him; perhaps he was just upset because she hadn't said anything. But really, when would that conversation have occurred? When she had fallen into his arms that first day or when she'd told him to strip in the attic?

The image of him doing just that flooded her mind. Cassie was thankful her back was to him as she turned on the oven.

"Hope you like grilled cheese and French fries." Cassie

reached into the narrow cabinet beside the oven and pulled out a cookie sheet.

"Considering I was going to probably have microwave popcorn back in my trailer, grilled cheese and fries sounds gourmet."

Her phone vibrated on the counter next to the stove. She saw Derek's name flash across the screen. No and no. If he was so determined to talk to her, he knew where she was.

Right where he'd left her months ago. Pompous jerk.

As she busied herself getting the meager dinner ready for the other man who was driving her out of her mind in a totally different way, she mentally cursed. Ian was probably used to fine dining, glamorous parties and beautiful women wearing slinky dresses and dripping in diamonds. Unfortunately, tonight he was getting a single mother throwing together cheese sandwiches while wearing an old, oversize T-shirt to hide her extra weight.

More than likely he'd said yes because he felt sorry for her. Regardless, he was in her house now. Surprisingly he'd pulled up a kitchen chair next to the high chair and was feeding puff snacks to Emily.

The sight had Cassie blinking back tears. Emily's father should be doing that. He should be here having dinner with them, as a family. He should've stuck it out and kept his pants zipped.

But he'd decided a wife and a baby were too much of a commitment and put a damper on his lifestyle.

In the back of her mind, Cassie knew she was better off without him. Any man that didn't put his family first was a coward. Not suitable material for a husband or father to her child.

But the reality of being rejected still hurt. Cassie could honestly say she'd gotten over her love, but the betrayal... That was something she would probably never recover from. Because he'd not just left her; he'd left a precious, innocent baby behind without even attempting to fight for what he'd created.

Being rejected by Ian was just another blow to her already battered self-esteem.

"You okay?"

Cassie jerked back to the moment and realized two things. One, Ian was staring at her, his brows drawn together, and two, she'd worn a hole in the bread from being too aggressive applying the butter.

Laughing, Cassie tossed the torn bread onto the counter and grabbed another piece from the bag. "Yeah. My mind was elsewhere for a minute."

"Were you angry with that slice of bread?" he asked with a teasing grin.

"I may have had a little aggression I needed to take out." Cassie couldn't help but laugh again. "You're pretty good with her. Do you have nieces or nephews?"

Ian shook his head. "I'm an only child. But there was a set I visited not too long ago that had a baby about Emily's age. He was the cutest little guy and instantly wanted me over anyone else. I guess kids just like me."

Great. Now he had a soft spot for kids. Wasn't that the exact opposite of the image he'd portrayed the other morning when seeing Emily for the first time?

Ian Shaffer had many facets and she hated that she wanted to figure out who the real Ian was deep down inside.

Dinner was ready in no time, and thankfully, the silence wasn't too awkward. Eating and caring for a baby helped fill the void of conversation. When they were done, Ian went to clear the table and Cassie stopped him.

"I'll get it," she told him, picking up her own plate. "It's not that much."

"You cooked. The least I could do is help clean." He picked up his plate and took it to the sink. "Besides, if you cook more often, I'll gladly clean up after."

Cassie froze in the midst of lifting Emily from her high chair. "You want to come back for dinner?" she asked.

"I wouldn't say no if you asked."

Cassie settled Emily on her hip and turned to Ian, who was putting the pitcher of tea into the refrigerator. Okay, now she knew this wasn't pity. He obviously wanted to spend time with her. But why? Did he think she'd be that easy to get into bed again? Of course he did. She'd barely known his name when she'd shed her clothes for him. What man wouldn't get the impression she was easy?

Cassie turned and went into the living room, placed Emily in her Pack 'n Play and handed her her favorite stuffed horse. Footsteps shuffled over the carpet behind her and Cassie swallowed, knowing she'd have to be up front with Ian.

"Listen," she said as she straightened and faced the man who stood only a few feet away. "I have a feeling you think I'm somebody that I'm not."

Crossing his arms over his wide chest, Ian tilted his head and leveled those dark eyes right on her. "And what do you believe I think of you?"

Well, now she felt stupid. Why did he make this sound like a challenge? And why was she getting all heated over the fact he was standing in her living room? No man had been there other than her father and her soon-to-be brother-in-law. She'd moved into the guest cottage on the estate after Derek had left her so she could be closer to the family for support with Emily.

So seeing such a big, powerful man in her house was a little…arousing. Which just negated the whole point she was trying to make. Yeah, she was a juxtaposition of nerves and emotions.

"I think because we slept together you think I'm eager to do it again." She rested her hands on her hips, willing them to stop shaking. She had to be strong, no matter her physical attraction to Ian. "I'm really not the aggressive, confident woman who was locked in that attic."

Ian's gaze roamed down her body, traveled back up and landed on her mouth as he stepped forward. "You look like the same woman to me," he said, closing the gap between them. "What makes you think you're so different from the woman I spent the night with?"

She couldn't think with him this close, the way his eyes studied her, the woodsy scent of his cologne, the way she felt his body when he wasn't even touching her.

"Well, I..." She smoothed her hair back behind her ears and tipped her head to look him in the eye. "I'm afraid you think that I look for a good time and that I'm easy."

A ghost of a smile flirted around those full lips of his. "I rushed to judgment. I don't think you're easy, Cassie. Sexy, intriguing and confident, but not easy."

Sighing, she shook her head. "I'm anything but confident."

Now his hands came up, framed her face and sent an insane amount of electrical charges coursing through her. As much as she wanted his touch, she couldn't allow herself to crave such things. Hadn't she learned her lesson? Physical attraction and sexual chemistry did not make for a solid base for family, and, right now, all she could focus on was her family. Between Emily and the race with her sister, Cassie had no time for anything else.

But, oh, how she loved the feel of those strong, warm palms covering her face, fingertips slipping into her hair.

"You were amazing and strong in the attic," he told her.

He placed a finger over her lips when she tried to speak. "You may not be like that all the time, but you were then. And that tells me that the real you came out that night. You had no reason to put on a front with me and you were comfortable being yourself. Your passion and ability to control the situation was the biggest turn-on I've ever experienced."

Cassie wanted to tell him he was wrong, that she wasn't the powerful, confident woman he thought she was.

But she couldn't say a word when he leaned in just a bit more, tickling his lips across hers so slowly that Cassie feared she'd have to clutch on to his thick biceps to stay upright.

She didn't reach up, though. Didn't encourage Ian in tormenting her any further.

But when his mouth opened over hers so gently, coaxing hers open, as well, Cassie didn't stop him. Still not reaching for him, she allowed him to claim her. His hands still gripped her face, his body pressed perfectly against hers and she flashed back instantly to when they'd had nothing between them. He'd felt so strong, so powerful.

More than anything to do with his looks or his charming words, he made her feel more alive than she'd ever felt.

Ian's lips nipped at hers once, twice, before he lifted his head and looked her straight in the eyes.

The muscle ticked in his jaw as he slowly lowered his hands from her face and stepped back. "No, Cassie. Nothing about you or this situation is easy."

Without another word, he turned and walked through her house and out the back door. Cassie gripped the edge of the sofa and let out a sigh. She had no clue what had just happened, but something beyond desire lurked in Ian's dark eyes. The way he'd looked at her, as if he was wrestling his own personal demon...

Cassie shook her head. This was not her problem. Sleeping with the man had brought up so many complications—the main reason she never did flings.

Was that why she kept feeling this pull? Because sex just wasn't sex to her? For her to sleep with someone meant she had some sort of deeper bond than just lust. How could she not feel attached to the man who made her feel this alive?

Glancing down to sweet Emily, who was chewing on her stuffed horse, Cassie rested her hip against the couch. This baby was her world and no way would she be that mother who needed to cling to men or have a revolving door of them.

Better to get her head on straight and forget just how much Mr. Hollywood Agent affected her mind.

Trouble was, she was seriously afraid he'd already affected her heart.

Ten

"My girls ready for next week?"

Cassie slid the saddle off Don Pedro and threw a glance over her shoulder to her father. Damon Barrington stalked through the stables that he not only owned, but at one time had spent nearly every waking hour in.

Even though the Barringtons' planned to retire from the scene after this racing season, Damon still wasn't ready to sell the prizewinning horses. He'd had generous offers, including one from his biggest rival in the industry, Jake Mason, but so far no deal had been made. Cassie highly doubted her father would ever sell to Jake. The two had been competitors for years and had never gotten along on the track…or off it.

"We're as ready as we'll ever be," Tessa said as she started brushing down the Thoroughbred. "My time is even better than before. I'm pretty confident about the Preakness."

Damon smiled, slipping his hands into the pockets of his worn jeans. The man may be a millionaire and near royalty in the horse industry because of his Triple Crown win nearly two decades ago, but he still was down-to-earth and very much involved in his daughters' careers.

"I know you'll do the Barrington name proud, Tess." He reached up and stroked the horse's mane as Cassie slid in beside her father.

"What are you doing down here?" Cassie asked. "Thought you'd be keeping your eye on the film crew."

Damon patted the horse and reached over to wrap an arm around Cassie's shoulders. A wide grin spread across his tanned, aged face. His bright blue eyes landed on hers.

"The lighting guys are reworking the living room right now," he explained. "The scene they shot the other day wasn't quite what they wanted. They're shooting a small portion again this afternoon."

This whole new world of filming was so foreign to her, but the process was rather fascinating. "I plan on heading into town and picking up some feed later," she told him. "I guess I'll miss watching that."

And more than likely miss seeing Ian again—which was probably for the best. She needed space after that simple dinner and arousing kiss last night. He hadn't been by the stables and she hadn't seen him around the grounds, so he was probably working…which was what she needed to concentrate on.

"I thought I'd take Emily with me and maybe run her by that new toy store in town," Cassie went on. "She's learning to walk now and maybe I can find her something she can hold on to and push around to strengthen her little legs."

Damon laughed. "Once she starts walking, she'll be all over this place."

Cassie smiled. "I can't wait to see how she looks in a saddle."

Tessa came around Don Pedro and started brushing his other side. "Why don't you take her for a ride now? I'm sure she'd love it and it's such a nice day out. We're done for a while anyway."

The idea was tempting. "I still need to get feed, though."

"I'll send Nash to get it," Damon spoke up. "He won't mind."

Cassie leaned her head against her father's strong shoulder. "Thanks, Dad."

Patting her arm, Damon placed a kiss on top of her head. "Anytime. Now go get my granddaughter and start training her right."

Excited for Emily's first ride, Cassie nearly sprinted to the main house and through the back door to the kitchen, where Linda was washing dishes.

"Hey, Linda." Cassie glanced over the island to see Emily in her Pack 'n Play clapping her hands and gibbering to her animals. "I'm going to take Emily off your hands for a bit."

"Oh, she's no trouble at all." Linda rinsed a pan and set it in the drainer before drying her hands and turning. "I actually just sat her in there. We've been watching the action in the living room. She likes all the lights."

Cassie scooped up her girl and kissed her cheek. "I'm sure she does. She'd probably like to crawl all over and knock them down."

Laughing, Linda crossed to the double ovens in the wall and peeked inside the top one. "I'm sure she would, but I held on tight. The cranberry muffins are almost done if you'd like one."

Yeah, she'd love about six warm, gooey muffins dripping with butter, but she'd resist for the sake of her backside.

"Maybe later. I'm taking Emily for her first ride."

A wide smile blossomed across Linda's face. "Oh, how fun. She's going to love it."

"I hope so," Cassie said. "I'll be back in a bit."

When Cassie stepped back into the barn, Tessa had already saddled up Oliver, the oldest, most gentle horse in the stables. Cassie absolutely couldn't wait to see Emily's excitement as she took her first horseback ride.

"He's all ready for you," Tessa exclaimed, reaching for Emily.

Cassie mounted the horse and lifted Emily from Tessa's arms. Settling her daughter in front of her and wrapping an arm around her waist, Cassie reached for the rein and smiled down to Tessa.

"Get a few pics of us when we're in the field, would you?"

Tessa slid her hand into her pocket and held up her phone. "I'm set. You guys look so cute up there," she said, still grinning. "My niece already looks like a pro."

Cassie tugged on the line and steered Oliver out of the barn and into the field. The warm late-spring sunshine beat down on them and Cassie couldn't help but smile when Emily clapped her hands and squealed as the horse started a light trot.

"This is fun, isn't it, sweetie?" Cassie asked. "When you get big, Mommy will buy you your own horse and he will be your best friend."

Cassie didn't know how long they were riding, and she didn't really care. Memories were being made, and even though Emily wouldn't recall this day at all, Cassie would cherish it forever. She thought of her own mother and held Emily a little tighter. Her mom lived in her heart and there was an attic full of pictures and mementos to remember her by.

Turning Oliver to head back toward the front fields, Cassie swallowed as new memories overtook her. That attic wasn't just a room to store boxes and old furniture. Now the attic was a place where she'd given herself to a man...a dangerous man. He made her feel too much, want too much.

And what was with him wanting to eat dinner with her and Emily? Not that she minded, but having him in her house just once was enough to have her envisioning so much more than just a friendly encounter.

She had to admit, at least to herself, that Ian intrigued her. And if she was going that far, she also had to admit that every part of her wished he weren't just passing through. She missed the company of a man...and not just sex. She missed the conversation, the spark of excitement in harmless flirting... Okay, fine, she missed the sex, too.

But it really was so much more than that. There was a special connection, a certain bond that strengthened after being intimate. At least there was for her. Perhaps that was why she couldn't dismiss what had happened between her and Ian so easily.

As she neared the stables, she caught sight of Ian walking toward the main house with the beautiful Lily Beaumont at his side. The gorgeous actress was laughing and Cassie had to ignore the sliver of jealousy that shot through her. Ian wasn't hers by any means, no matter what she may wish for.

And Lily was a very sweet woman, from what Cassie had experienced on the set. As Cassie watched the two head toward the front door, she couldn't help but get a swift kick back into reality. Ian and Lily were from the same world. They were near the same age, for crying out loud.

In comparison, Cassie was just a worn-out single mom. Squeezing Emily tight and placing a kiss on her little mop of curls, Cassie knew she wouldn't wish to be anything else. Being the solid foundation for Emily was the most important job of her life, and for now, all her daughter's needs had to come first. One day, Cassie vowed, she'd take time for herself and perhaps find love.

"I'm actually considering your offer and one other," Lily stated.

Ian rested his hand on the knob of the front door. "You don't have to tell me the other agency. I already know."

And damn if he'd lose this starlet to his rival. They'd ruin her and not give a damn about reputation, only the bottom line, which was money to them.

"It's not a decision I'm going to make overnight." Lily lifted her hand to shield her eyes from the afternoon sun. "I am glad you're on set, though, because that will give us more of a chance to discuss terms and what I'm looking for in an agency."

Good. That sounded as though she was interested in him. "I'm ready to talk anytime you are."

A bright smile spread across her face. "Well, right now I'm needed for a scene, but perhaps we could have lunch or dinner one day while we're both here?"

Returning her smile, Ian nodded and opened the door for her, gesturing her in. "Let me know when you're not filming and we'll make that happen."

Nodding her thanks, Lily headed into the house. Ian wasn't sticking around for the short scene retake. He had other pressing matters to attend to. Like the beauty he'd seen out in the field moments ago. With red hair blazing past her shoulders and a heart-clenching smile on her face, Cassie had captured his attention instantly. So what else was new? The woman managed to turn him inside out without even being near. More times than not she consumed his thoughts, but when he'd seen her taking her daughter on a horseback ride, Ian had to admit that the sight had damn near stopped him in his tracks.

Emily's sweet squeals of delight, the loving expression on Cassie's face... The combination had shifted something in Ian's heart, something he wasn't quite ready to identify.

But he did know one thing. He'd been wrong. He was wrong about Cassie in thinking she was just like his mother. His mother never would've taken the time to have precious moments with him like the ones he'd seen with Cassie and Emily. His mother had been too busy on her quest for love and Mr. Right.

Ian ran a hand over his hair and sighed. He'd turned out just fine, no thanks to Mom and Dad, but getting involved with a woman and an innocent child was a hazardous mistake that would leave all parties vulnerable and in a risky position. What did he know about children or how to care for them?

And why was he even thinking this way? He was leaving in a few weeks. No matter his attraction and growing interest in Cassie Barrington, he couldn't afford to get personally involved.

Hours later, after he'd drafted a contract he hoped would entice Lily Beaumont into signing with his agency, Ian found himself leaving his trailer and heading toward Cassie's cottage.

Night had settled over the grounds and all was quiet. No bustling crew or noisy conversation. Max's wife and baby had shown up earlier in the evening, so they were probably holed up in his trailer for family time. And the producer's and director's families had arrived the day before. Bronson Dane and Anthony Price were at the top 1 percent of the film industry and still made time for their growing families.

Everyone had a family, a connection and the promise of love.

Ignoring the pang of envy he didn't want to feel, Ian stepped up onto Cassie's porch, which was illuminated with a lantern-style light on either side of the door. As soon as he knocked, he glanced down to his watch. Damn, maybe it was too late to be making a social call.

The door swung open and Ian took in the sight of Cassie wearing a long T-shirt and her hair down, curling around her shoulders. Long legs left uncovered tempted him to linger, but he brought his eyes back up to her surprised face.

"I'm sorry," he said, shoving his hands into his pockets. "I just realized how late it was."

"Oh, um…it's fine." She rested her hand on the edge of the oak door and tilted her head. "Is everything okay?"

Nodding, Ian suddenly felt like an idiot. "Yeah, I was working and lost track of time. Then I started walking and ended up here."

A sweet smile lit up her features. "Come on in," she told him, opening the door and stepping aside. "I just put Emily to bed, so this is fine."

He stepped inside and inhaled a scent of something sweet. "Is that cookies I smell?"

Cassie shut the door and turned to face him. "I thought I'd make some goodies for the wives who arrived. This way they can stock their trailers with snacks. I already made a batch of caramel corn."

His heart flipped in his chest. He hated the fact he kept going back to his mother, but he honestly couldn't recall a time when his mother had baked anything or even reached out to others by doing a kind act.

A shrink would have a field day in his head with all his Mommy and Daddy issues. *Jeez.* And here he'd thought once he'd left for L.A. he'd left all of those years behind.

"They will really appreciate that," he told her.

Shrugging, Cassie maneuvered around him and grabbed a small blanket from the couch and started folding it. "I'm no Linda, but I do enjoy baking when I have the time."

She laid the folded blanket across the back of the couch and looked back at him. He couldn't stop his eyes from traveling over her again. How could he help the fact he found her sexier than any woman he'd ever met? She probably wouldn't believe him if he told her that her curves were enticing, her low maintenance a refreshing change.

Cassie tugged on the hem of her shirt. "I should probably go change."

"No." He held up his hand to stop her. "This is your house—you should be comfortable. Besides, I've seen it all."

Her eyes flared with remembrance and passion as Ian closed the space between them and looked down at her mouth. "I've tasted it all, too, if you recall."

With a shaky nod, she said, "I remember."

The pulse at the base of her throat increased and Ian ran a hand over his face as he took a step back. "I swear, I didn't come here for this."

Cassie's bright blue eyes darted away. "I understand."

"No, you don't." Great, now she thought he was rejecting her. "It's not that I don't want you, Cassie. That's the furthest from the truth."

Shoving her hair back from her shoulders, Cassie shook her head. "Ian, it's okay. You don't have to make excuses. I'm a big girl. I can handle the truth. Besides, we're past this awkward stage, right?"

"Yeah," he agreed because right now he was feeling anything but awkward. Excited and aroused, but not awkward. "I don't know what possessed me to show up at your door this late, but..."

Cassie produced that punch-to-the-gut smile. "You can stop by anytime."

How did she do that? Instantly make him feel welcome, wanted...needed. There was so much more to Cassie Barrington than he'd first perceived. There were sides to the confident vixen, the single mother and the overworked trainer he had yet to discover.

Cassie was giving, loving and patient. He'd known instantly that she was special, but maybe he just hadn't realized how special. This woman embodied everything he hadn't known he'd been looking for.

"Why are you looking at me like that?" she asked, brows drawn together, smile all but gone.

Ian took a step toward her. He'd been mentally dancing around her for days and now he was physically doing it as he made up his mind on how to approach her.

"Because I just realized that all of your layers are starting to reveal themselves, one at a time." He slid his fingertips up her arms and back down, relishing the goose bumps he produced with such a simple touch. "I didn't want to see all of that before. I wanted you to be unattainable. I wanted you to be all wrong and someone I could easily forget."

Those vibrant eyes remained locked on his as her breath caught.

"But there's no way I could ever forget you, Cassie. Or us."

He didn't give her time to object. He claimed her lips and instantly she responded—opening her mouth to him, wrapping her arms around his neck and plunging her fingers into his hair.

Ian knew he wasn't leaving anytime soon. He also knew her T-shirt had to go.

Eleven

Cassie had no idea what she was doing. Okay, she knew what she was doing and who she was doing it with, but hadn't she just had a mental talk with herself about the hazards of getting wrapped up in Ian's seductive ways? Hadn't she told herself she'd already been burned once and was still recovering?

But the way his mouth captured hers, the way he held her as if she were the rarest of gems, Cassie couldn't help but take pleasure in the fact that Ian pulled out a passion in her that she'd never known existed.

When Ian's hands gripped the hem of her T-shirt and tugged up, she eased back and in an instant the unwanted garment was up and over her head, flung to the side without a care.

Dark-as-sin eyes raked over her body, which was now bare of everything except a pair of red lacy panties. The old Cassie wanted to shield herself with her hands, but the way Ian visually sampled her gave her the confidence of a goddess.

"I could look at you forever," he said, his voice husky.

Forever. The word hovered in the air, but Cassie knew he was speaking only from lust, not in the happily-ever-after term.

Ian pulled his own shirt off and Cassie reached out, quickly unfastening his pants. In no time he was reaching for her, wearing only a smile.

"Tell me you know this is more than sex," he muttered against her lips. "I want you to know that to me, this is so much more."

Tears pricked the backs of her eyes as she nodded. The lump in her throat left her speechless. She really didn't know what label he wanted to put on this relationship, but right now, she couldn't think beyond the fact that Ian's hands were sliding into her panties and gliding them down her shaky legs.

Cassie wrapped her arms around his broad shoulders and kicked aside the flimsy material. Ian's hands cupped her bottom as he guided her backward.

"Tell me where your room is," he muttered against her lips.

"Last door on the right."

He kissed her on the throat, across the swells of her breasts, all the while keeping his hands firmly gripped on her backside as he maneuvered her down the hallway and into her room.

A small bedside lamp gave the room a soft glow. Ian gently shut the door behind him and looked her right in the eyes. There was an underlying vulnerability looking back at her, and Cassie knew what he was thinking.

"I've never had a man in this room," she told him. "And there's no other man I want here."

As if the dam had broken, Ian reached for her, capturing her lips once again and lifting her by the waist.

When she locked her legs around his hips and they tumbled onto the bed, Ian broke free of her lips and kissed a path down to her breasts. Leaning back, Cassie gripped his hair as he tasted her.

"Ian," she panted. "I don't have any protection."

His dark gaze lifted to hers. "I didn't bring any. I hadn't planned on ending up here."

Biting her lip, Cassie said, "I'm on birth control and I'm clean. I've only been with my ex-husband and you."

Ian's hands slid up to cup her face as he kissed her lips. "I've never been without protection and I know I'm clean, too."

She smiled. "Then why are we still talking?"

Cassie moved her hands to his waist. Before she could say another word, Ian slid into her. Closing her eyes, Cassie let out a soft groan as he began to move above her.

"Look at me," he demanded in that low tone. "I want you to see me and only me."

As if any other man could take his place? But as she stared into his eyes, she saw so much more than lust, than sex and passion. This man was falling for her. He may not even recognize the emotion himself, but it was there, plain as day, looking back at her.

When his pace increased, Cassie gripped his shoulders and arched her back. "Ian...I..."

Eyes still locked on to her, he clenched the muscle in his jaw. "Go ahead, baby."

Her body trembled with her release, but she refused to close her eyes. She wanted him to see just how affected she was by his touch...his love.

When his arms stiffened and his body quivered against

hers, Cassie held on, swallowing back the tears that clogged her throat.

One thing was very certain. The night in the attic may have been all about lust, but this moment right here in her bed, Cassie had gone and fallen in love with Ian Shaffer.

"I have to be on set early," Ian whispered into her ear.

Pulling himself away from the warm bed they'd spent the night in, Ian quickly gathered his clothes and dressed. Cassie eased up onto one elbow, and the sheet slipped down to stop just at the slope of her breasts. All that creamy exposed skin had him clenching his jaw and reliving what had just transpired hours before between those sheets.

"How early?" she asked, her voice thick with sleep.

"I'd like to see Max before he starts."

Okay, so the lie rolled easily off his tongue, but he couldn't stay. He couldn't remain in her bed, smelling her sweet scent, playing house in her little cottage, with her innocent baby sleeping in the next room.

What did he know about family or children…or whatever emotion was stirring within him? His career had always taken precedence over any social life or any feelings. With his parents' example of the epitome of failed marriages and love, he knew he wanted something completely different for his own life, so perfecting his career was the path he'd chosen.

How could he put his career, his agency and the impending addition of Lily to his client roster in jeopardy simply because he'd become entangled with Cassie Barrington? She was the poster child for commitment, and an instant family was something he couldn't get wrapped up in.

Cassie was a beautiful, intriguing complication. His eyes darted to the bed, where she studied him with a hint of desire layered with curiosity.

"Everything okay?" she asked.

Nodding, he shoved his feet into his shoes. "Of course. I'll lock the door behind me."

Unable to avoid temptation completely, Ian crossed the room, leaned down and kissed her lips. Just as her hand came up to his stubbled jaw, he pulled away and left her alone.

He stepped onto the front porch, closed the door behind him and leaned against it to catch his breath. The easy way Cassie welcomed him into her bed—and into her life with Emily—terrified him. Last night she'd accepted him without question and she'd given him everything she had... including love. He'd seen it in her eyes, but even more worrisome was what she may have seen reflected in his.

Because in those moments, when they were one and her bright blue eyes sought his, Ian had found himself completely and utterly lost. He wanted so much, but fear of everything he'd ever known regarding love and family made him question his emotions and his intentions.

Damn it. His intentions? What the hell was this? He wasn't the kind of man who had dreams of driving a minivan or heading up a household. He was a top Hollywood agent and if he didn't get his head on straight, he could lose one of the most important clients he'd ever had the chance of snagging.

Shaking his head, Ian pushed off the door and forced himself to walk toward his trailer. Twenty-nine years old and doing the walk of shame? *Classy, Shaffer. Real classy.*

Darkness and early-morning fog settled low over the estate. He shoved his hands into his pockets and decided he needed to shower and change before seeing Max...especially considering he was wearing the same clothes as yesterday.

He hadn't totally lied when he'd left Cassie's bed. He would talk to Max, but it wasn't dire and they could always talk later. Yet he worried if he stayed, he'd give Cassie false hope.

Okay, he worried he'd give himself false hope, too, because being with her was like nothing he'd ever experienced before and he wanted to hold on to those moments.

But the reality was, he was passing through.

Ian took his time getting ready for the day, answered a few emails and jotted down notes for calls he needed to make later in the week. He hated to admit he was shaken up by this newfound flood of emotions, but he had to come to grips with the fact that whatever he was feeling for Cassie Barrington was most definitely not going away.... It was only getting stronger.

By the time he exited his trailer, he had a plan of action, and today would be all about work and focusing on the big picture and his agency.

Crew members were gathered around the entrance of the stables, and off to the side were Max and Lily, holding their scripts and chatting. Ian headed in their direction, eager to get the day started.

"Morning," he greeted them as he approached.

Max nodded. "Came by your trailer last night to discuss something. Have a late night?"

The smile on Max's face was devilish—and all-knowing.

"What did you need?" Ian asked, dodging the question.

With a shrug, Max shook his head. "It can wait. I'm going to talk to Bronson before we start filming. Excuse me."

Ian figured Max left so Ian could chat with Lily. *Good boy.*

"I glanced over today's filming schedule." Ian stepped in front of Lily to shade her face from the sun. "Looks like after three today you guys are free."

Lily smiled. "We are indeed. Are you available to talk then?"

He'd be available anytime she wanted if it meant persuading her to sign with him. "I am. Would you like to stay here or go out to grab something for dinner?"

"I say go out," she replied. "Hopefully we can talk privately without everyone around."

Before he could respond, Lily's gaze darted from his to a spot over his left shoulder. A smile like he'd never seen before lit up her face and Ian couldn't help but glance around to see who she was connecting with.

Nash.

More confirmation that this Hollywood starlet and the groom on the Barrington estate had something going on.

Ian only hoped whatever was happening with the two of them was kept quiet and didn't interfere with filming or hinder her judgment in signing with him.

"Going out is fine," he told her.

Blinking, she focused back on him. "I'm sorry. What?"

Yeah, definitely something going on there.

"I said we could go out for a bite to eat. I can come by your trailer about five. Does that work?"

"Of course," she replied with a nod. "I'll see you then."

As she walked away, Ian turned and caught Nash still staring as Lily entered the stable. Nash had the look of a man totally and utterly smitten and Ian couldn't help but feel a twinge of remorse for the guy. Nash and Lily were worlds apart.

Exactly like Ian and Cassie.

What a mess. A complicated, passion-induced mess.

Ian stood to the side as lighting and people were set in place to prepare for filming. Bronson was talking with Max, and Lily's hair was being smoothed one last time.

Grant and Anthony were adjusting the bales of hay at the end of the aisle.

Ian wasn't sure what Cassie's plans were for the day, but he intended to keep his distance for now. He needed to figure out exactly how to handle this situation because the last thing she needed was more heartache. And he, who knew nothing about real intimacy, would most certainly break her heart if he wasn't careful.

Damon Barrington settled in beside him and whispered, "Their chemistry on set is amazing."

Ian watched Max and Lily embrace in the middle of the aisle, horses' heads popping out over their stalls. The set was utterly quiet except for Lily's staged tears as she clung to Max. The couple was the perfect image of a younger Damon and Rose Barrington, according to the pictures Ian had seen.

As soon as Anthony yelled, "Cut!" the couple broke apart and Lily dabbed at her damp cheeks.

Damon glanced around. "I can't believe my girls aren't down here. You haven't seen Cassie or Tessa, have you?"

Ian shook his head. "I haven't."

No need to tell Cassie's father that just a few hours ago Ian had slipped from her bed. Best not bring that up.

"I'm sure they'll be along shortly." Damon looked over at Ian and grinned. "My girls haven't let too many scenes slip by. They've enjoyed this process."

"And you?" Ian asked. "Have you enjoyed the Hollywood invasion?"

Nodding, Damon crossed his arms over his chest. "It's not what I thought it would be. The scenes vary in length and everything is shot out of order. But I'm very interested in seeing how they piece this all together."

Ian liked Damon, appreciated the way the man had taken charge of his life, made something of it and encouraged his children to do the same. And when his wife had passed, the man had taken over the roles of both parents and loved his children to the point where both women were now two of the most amazing people he'd met.

Ian had never received encouragement from his father and couldn't help but wonder what his life would've been like had his father been more hands-on.

Shrugging off years that couldn't be changed, Ian excused himself from Damon. If Cassie was going to come watch the filming, he needed to be elsewhere.

Because he had no doubt that if he hung around and had to look Cassie in the eye in front of all these people, there would be no hiding the fact that he'd developed some serious feelings for her.

Twelve

Who was he kidding? There was no way he could stay away from Cassie. All during the business dinner with Lily, his mind had been on Cassie and what she was doing.

By the end of the night he'd nearly driven himself crazy with curiosity about what Cassie and Emily had done all day. Added to that, Lily hadn't signed with him. Not yet. She'd looked over his proposed contract and agreed with most of it, but she'd also said she needed to look over one other contract before deciding.

He was still in the running, but he'd rather have this deal signed and completed so he could move on to other deals waiting in the wings…not so he could focus on the woman who had his head spinning and his gut tied in knots.

After walking Lily to her trailer, Ian crossed the estate toward the two cottages. Only one of Cassie's outdoor lights was on and she was on her porch switching out the bulb in the other.

"Hey," he greeted her as he stepped onto the top step. "Need help?"

"I can manage just fine."

As she stood on her tiptoes and reached, her red tank top slid up over her torso, exposing a tantalizing band of flesh.

"I can get that so you don't have to stretch so far," he told her.

She quickly changed out the bulb and turned to face him, tapping the dead bulb against her palm. "I've been doing things on my own for a while now. Besides, I won't be anybody's second choice. I figured you were smart enough to know that."

"I'm sorry?"

Somehow he was not on the same page as her and she was mad at someone. From the daggers she was throwing him, he'd done something to upset her. Considering he hadn't sneaked out of her bed that morning without saying goodbye, he really had no clue what was going on.

"Forget it." She shook her head and opened her front door, then turned before he could enter. "I'm pretty tired, but thanks for stopping by."

Oh, hell no. He wasn't going to just let her be mad and not tell him what was going on. More than that, did she really believe he'd just leave her when she was this upset?

His hand smacked against the door as she tried to close it. "I'm coming in."

Cassie stepped back and let him pass. Emily sat in her Pack 'n Play and chattered with a stuffed horse, oblivious to the world around her.

"I need to get Emily ready for bed." Cassie maneuvered around him and picked up Emily. "I may be a while."

Code for "I'm going to take my time and let you worry." That was fine; he had no intention of going anywhere.

If Cassie was gearing up for a fight, he was ready. Seeing her pain, masked by anger, had a vise gripping his heart, and he cared too much about her to just brush her feelings aside.

Ian glanced around the somewhat tidy living area and started picking up toys before he thought better of it. He tossed them into the Pack 'n Play; then he folded the throw and laid it on the back of the sofa, neatened the pillows and took a plate and cup into the kitchen and placed them in the dishwasher.

By the time he'd taken a seat on the couch, he found himself smiling. Where had this little domestic streak come from? He hadn't even thought twice about helping Cassie, and not just because she was angry. He found himself wanting to do things to make her life easier.

Ian had no clue what had happened with her life before he'd come along, but he knew she was divorced and assumed the ex had done a number on her.

Well, Ian intended to stick this out, at least for as long as he was here. He would make her smile again, because she deserved nothing less.

Cassie wasn't jealous. Just because she'd heard Ian and Lily had had dinner didn't mean a thing. Really.

But that green-eyed monster reared its ugly head and reminded Cassie that she'd fallen for a cheating man once before.

On the other hand, what hold did she have over Ian? He wasn't staying and he'd never confessed his undying love to her. But she'd seen his eyes last night, she'd seen how he looked at her, and she'd experienced lovemaking like she never had before. How could he deny that they'd formed an unspoken bond?

Cassie quickly dried off Emily and got her dressed in

her footed bunny pajamas. After giving her a bottle and rocking her gently, Cassie began to sing.

This was the time of night she enjoyed most. Just her and her precious baby girl. Cassie might sing off-key, she might even get an occasional word wrong, but Emily didn't care. She just reached her little hands up and patted Cassie's hand or touched her lips.

They had a nightly ritual and just because Ian was out in her living room didn't mean she would change her routine. Before Emily fell asleep in her arms, Cassie laid her in her crib, giving her a soft kiss on her forehead, then left the room.

Cassie took a moment to straighten her tank and smooth her hair over her shoulders before she started down the hallway. As she entered the living room, she noticed that Ian was reclined on her sofa, head tilted back, eyes closed, with his hands laced across his abdomen. He'd picked up the toys and neatly piled them in the Pack 'n Play in the corner.

No. She didn't want that unwelcome tumble of her heart where this man was concerned. She couldn't risk everything again on the chance that he could love her the way she loved him.

Tears pricked her eyes as she fully confessed just how much she did love this man. But he could never know.

Her feet shuffled over the hardwood floors, and Ian lifted his lids, his gaze seeking hers.

"Thank you for picking up," she told him, still standing because she intended to show him out the door.

Shifting to fully sit up, Ian patted the cushion beside him. "Come here, Cassie."

She didn't like being told what to do, but she wasn't going to act like a teenager who pouted over a boy, either.

She was a big girl, but that didn't exempt her from a broken heart.

Taking a seat on the opposite end of the couch, she gripped her hands in her lap. "What do you want, Ian? I don't have time for games."

His eyes locked on to hers. "I don't play games, Cassie, and I have no idea what you're so upset about."

Of course he didn't. Neither had her ex when he'd cheated.

She eased back against the arm of the sofa and returned his stare. "Do you know why I'm divorced?"

Ian shook his head and slid his arm along the back of the couch as if to reach for her.

"My husband got tired of me," she told him, tamping down the sliver of hurt and betrayal that threatened to make her vulnerable. Never again. "The whole marriage-baby thing was cramping his style. Apparently he'd been cheating on me for most of our marriage and I was too naive and dumb to realize it. You see, I assumed that when we took our vows they meant something to him."

"Cassie—"

"No," she said, holding up her hand. "I'm not finished. After Emily was born, Derek left. She was barely two months old. He left me a note and was just…gone. It seems the sexy wife he once knew was no longer there for him, so, in turn, his cheating and the divorce were my fault. I know now that he was a coward and I'm glad he's gone because I never want Emily to see me settle for someone who treats me like I'm not worth everything.

"I want my daughter to see a worthy example of how love should be," she went on, cursing her eyes for misting up. "I want her to see that love does exist. My parents had it, and I will find it. But I won't be played for a fool while I wait for love to come into my life."

Ian swallowed, his eyes never leaving hers as he scooted

closer. He wasn't stupid; he could put the pieces together and know she'd assumed the worst about his dinner meeting with Lily.

"I didn't play you for a fool, Cassie." His tone was light as he settled his hand over both of hers, which were still clasped together in her lap. "I have never lied to a woman and I've never pretended to be something I wasn't."

With a deep sigh, Cassie shook her head. "Forget I said anything. I mean, it's not like we're committed to each other," she said as she got to her feet.

But Ian jumped right up with her and gripped her shoulders before she could turn from him.

"Do you seriously think for one second that I believe you're so laid-back about the idea of me seeing you and another woman?" he demanded. "I had a business meeting with Lily. I told you I've wanted to sign her to my agency for months. She's the main reason I came to the set and why I'm staying so long."

Cassie's eyes widened, but he didn't give her a chance to speak. He needed her to know she didn't come in second… and she should never have to.

"I spent the entire evening trying to win her over, outlining every detail of the contract and all the perks of having me as her agent." Ian loosened his grip as he stepped closer to Cassie and slid his hands up to frame her face. "But the entire evening, I was thinking of you. Wondering what you were doing, how long it would be until I could see you again."

Her shoulders relaxed and her face softened as she kept those stunning baby blues locked on his. The hope he saw in her eyes nearly melted him on the spot. He knew she wanted to trust. He knew she'd been burned once and he completely understood that need, the yearning for that solid foundation.

"I'm sorry," she whispered. Cassie's lids lowered as she shook her head before she raised her gaze to his once more. "I don't want to be that woman. I seriously have no hold on you, Ian. You've promised me nothing and I don't expect you to check in."

Ian kissed her gently, then rested his forehead against hers. A soft shudder rippled through her and Ian wanted nothing more than to reassure her everything would be all right.

But how could he, when he knew he wasn't staying? How could they move forward with emotions overtaking them both?

"I hate what he did to me," she whispered, reaching up to clasp his wrists as he continued to cup her face. "I hate that I've turned bitter. That's not who I want to be."

Ian eased back and tipped her face up to his. "That's not who you are. You're not bitter. You're cautious and nobody blames you. You not only have yourself to think of—you have Emily, too."

Cassie's sweet smile never failed to squeeze his heart, and Ian had no clue how a man could leave behind a wife and child. Ian wouldn't mind getting ahold of Cassie's ex. He obviously was no man, but a coward. Selfishly, Ian was glad Derek was out of the picture. If the man could throw away his family so easily, he wasn't worthy.

"What's that look for?" she asked. "You're very intense all of a sudden."

He had to be honest because she was worth everything he had inside him.

"Where is this going?" he asked. "I care about you, Cassie. More than I thought I would, and I think we need to discuss what's happening between us."

A soft laugh escaped her. "You sound like a woman."

Ian smiled with a shrug. "I assure you I've never said this to anyone else, but I don't want you getting hurt."

Cassie nodded and a shield came over her eyes as if she was already steeling herself. "Honestly, I don't know. I care for you, too. I question myself because I'm still so scarred from the divorce and I told myself I wouldn't get involved again. Yet, here we are and I can't stop myself."

Her inner battle shouldn't make him happy, but he couldn't help but admit he liked the fact she had no control over her feelings for him…. At least he wasn't in this boat of emotions alone.

"I don't want you to be the rebound guy," she murmured. "But I'm so afraid of how you make me feel."

Stroking her silky skin, wanting to kiss her trembling lips, Ian asked, "How do I make you feel?"

He shouldn't have asked. Cassie pursed her lips together as if contemplating her response, and Ian worried he'd put her on the spot. But he had to know. This mattered too much. *She* mattered too much.

"Like I'm special."

She couldn't have zeroed in on a better word that would hit him straight in the heart. *Special*. She was special to him on so many levels. She was special because he'd never felt more alive than he did with her. He'd never let his career come second to anything before her, and he sure as hell had never thought, with his family issues, that he'd be falling for a woman with a child.

Cassie inspired him to be a better person, to want to care for others and put his needs last.

But most of all he understood that need to feel special. He'd craved it his entire life, and until this very moment, he hadn't realized that was what he'd been missing.

"You make me feel special, too." Before now he never would've felt comfortable opening up, showing how vulnerable he was on the inside. "I don't want to be the rebound guy, either."

Her eyes widened as she tried to blink back the moisture. "So what does that mean?"

Hell if he knew. Suddenly he wanted it all—his career, the Hollywood lifestyle, Cassie and Emily. Cassie had him rethinking what family could be.

There was that other part of him that was absolutely terrified and wanted to hightail it back to Hollywood. But for now, he would relish their time together until he could come to grips with this mess of emotions.

"It means for now, you're mine." He kissed the corners of her mouth. "It means you are more to me than any other woman has ever been." He kissed her directly on the mouth, coaxing her lips apart before murmuring, "It means I'm taking you to bed to show you just how much you mean to me."

Only wanting to keep her smiling, keep her happy for as long as he was here, Ian slid his arms around her waist and pulled her body flush against his own.

When Cassie's fingers slid up around his neck and threaded into his hair, Ian claimed her mouth and lifted her off the ground. She wrapped her legs around his waist and he carried her toward the bedroom, where he fully intended to make good on his promise.

Thirteen

The day couldn't be more perfect. God had painted a beautiful setting with the sun high in the sky and the temperature an ideal sixty degrees. The stage was set for Tessa to win the Preakness and take the second step toward the Triple Crown.

But no matter the weather, the thrill that always slid through Cassie at each race had to do with the stomp of the hooves in the stalls as the horses eagerly awaited their shining moment, the thick aroma of straw, the colorful silks adorning each horse, the tangible excitement of the jockeys as they shared last-minute talks with their trainers.

Which was exactly what Cassie and Tessa had just finished doing. Cassie had the utmost confidence that this race would go in their favor, but strange things always happened and they both knew better than to get cocky—especially at this point.

The first third of the Triple Crown was theirs, but this

was a new day, a new race and a whole other level of adrenaline rushes.

Cassie followed behind as Tessa rode Don Pedro from the stables through the paddock and entered the track. No matter the outcome, Cassie was proud of her sister, of what they'd accomplished in their years together.

Soon their racing season would come to an end and Cassie would move on with her goal of opening a riding camp for handicapped children. Training a Triple Crown winner would put her in high demand in the horse-breeding world, but she hoped to use that reputation as a launching point for her school.

And beyond the school worries, her father was getting offers from his most heated rival, Jake Mason, to buy the prizewinning horses. Their season wasn't even over yet, for heaven's sake.

But those thoughts would have to wait until after the competition.

As would her thoughts of a certain Hollywood agent who had stayed behind on the estate to get some work done without distractions. The majority of the film crew had accompanied the Barringtons to Baltimore, Maryland, but today they were spectators, enjoying the race. They'd gotten many great shots from Louisville a couple of weeks ago, so now they were able to relax…somewhat. Cassie knew they were still taking still shots for the ad campaign, but not as many as at the derby.

As Tessa rode onto the track, Cassie couldn't help but smile. There was so much to be thankful for right now in her life. One chapter of her career was coming to an end. Another was going to begin in a few months. Her daughter was happy and healthy and nearing her first birthday.

And, delicious icing on the cake, Ian Shaffer had entered her life. For how long she didn't know. But she did know that, for now, they were together and he had admitted his feelings were strong. But did that mean he'd want to try something long distance? Or would he stay around a little longer after the film was finished?

So many questions and none of them would be answered today. She needed to concentrate and be there for Tessa. All else could wait until this race was over.

In no time the horses were in their places and Cassie felt her father's presence beside her. His arm snaked around her waist, the silent support a welcome comfort. Each race had nerves balling up in her stomach, but nothing could be done now. The training for the Preakness was complete and now they waited for the fastest, most exciting moment in sports.

Cassie glanced toward the grandstands, and the colorful array of hats and suits had her smile widening. Excitement settled heavily over the track as everyone's gaze was drawn to the starting gate.

"You're trembling," her father whispered into her ear.

Cassie let out a shaky laugh. "I think that's you."

His arm tightened around her waist as a robust chuckle escaped. "I believe you're right, my dear."

The gun sounded and Cassie had no time for nerves. She couldn't keep her eyes off the places switching, the colored numbers on the board swapping out as horses passed each other and inched toward the lead.

Don Pedro was in forth. Cassie fisted her hands so tight, her short nails bit into her palms.

"Come on. Come on," she muttered.

Tessa eased past third and into second on the last turn.

The announcer's tone raised in excitement as Tessa inched even farther toward the head of the race. Cassie wanted to close her eyes to pray, but she couldn't take her gaze off the board.

Just as the first two horses headed to the finish line, Cassie started jumping up and down. Excitement, fear, nerves… They all had her unable to stand still.

And when the announcer blared that the winner was Don Pedro by a nose, Cassie jumped even higher, wrapped her arms around her father's neck and squealed like a little girl.

"We did it," he yelled, embracing her. "My girls did it!"

Damon jerked back, gripped her hand and tugged her toward the winner's circle, where Tessa met them. Her radiant smile, the mass of people surrounding her and the flash of cameras all announced there was a new winner.

Grant was right there in the throng of people, his grin so wide there was no way to hide the pride beaming off him.

Cassie's heart lurched. She loved that Tessa had found the man of her dreams, couldn't be happier for the couple. But, for the first time, Cassie was not the first one Tessa turned to after a race.

And that was not jealousy talking…. Cassie loved seeing Tessa and Grant so happy, and sharing Tessa's affection was fine. It was the fact that Cassie still felt empty when monumental things happened. Whom did she turn to to celebrate or for a shoulder to cry on?

Tessa turned her head, caught Cassie's eye and winked down at her. Returning the wink, Cassie smiled to hide her sad thoughts.

Soon reporters were thrusting microphones in her face, as well. Very few ever won the Triple Crown, and a team of females was practically unheard of. History was definitely in the making.

The Barrington sisters had done it again, and with only one more race to go to round out the season and secure the coveted Triple Crown, Cassie knew she needed to focus now more than ever on training for the Belmont.

Which meant keeping her heart shielded from Ian, because if he penetrated too much more, she feared she'd never be able to recover if it all fell apart.

They were gone for days, weeks.

Okay, maybe it wasn't weeks, but Ian felt as if he hadn't seen Cassie forever. Which told him he was going to be in trouble when it came time for him to head back to L.A.

She'd arrived home late last night and he'd known she'd be tired, so he had stayed away to let her rest and spend time with Emily. But knowing she was so close was hard.

As he headed toward the stables just as the sun peeked overtop the hilltops, Ian wanted to spend some time with her. He'd actually ached for her while she'd been away. Like most of the nation, he'd watched with eyes glued to the television during the Preakness and he'd jumped out of his seat and cheered when Don Pedro crossed the finish line for the win.

The familiar smell of hay greeted him before he even hit the entrance. As soon as he crossed the threshold, Ian spotted Nash cleaning out a stall.

"Morning," Ian greeted him.

Nash nodded a good-morning and continued raking old hay. "Cassie isn't here yet," he said without looking up.

Ian grinned. Apparently he and Cassie weren't very discreet...not that they'd tried to be, but they also hadn't been blatant about their relationship, either.

"Hey, Ian."

He turned to see Tessa striding into the stables, all smiles with her hair pulled back.

"Congrats on the win." Ian couldn't help but offer a quick hug with a pat on her back. "That was one intense race."

Tessa laughed. "You should've seen it from my point of view."

Her eyes darted to Nash, then back to Ian. "What brings you out this early?"

Ian shrugged, sliding his hands into his pockets. "Just looking for Cassie."

Tessa's grin went into that all-knowing mode as she quirked a brow. "She actually was up most of the night with Emily. Poor baby is teething and nobody is getting any sleep."

"But Cassie has to be exhausted. You just got back late last night," he argued, realizing he was stating nothing new to Tessa.

Shrugging, Tessa sighed. "I know. I offered to take Emily for the night, but Cassie wouldn't hear of it."

Probably because the last time Cassie had been without her child, she had been locked in the attic with him.

"She's spreading herself too thin," Ian muttered.

Nash walked around them and pulled a bale of hay from the stack against the wall, then moved back into the stall. Ian shifted closer to the doorway to get out of the quiet groom's way.

"Follow me," Tessa said with a nod.

Intrigued, Ian fell into step behind the famous jockey. She stopped just outside the stables, but away from where Nash could overhear.

"This isn't where you tell me if I hurt your sister you'll kill me, is it?" he asked with a smile.

Tessa laughed and shook her head, eyes sparkling with amusement. "You're smart enough to know that goes without saying. I wanted to discuss something else, actually."

"And what's that?"

"Did Cassie ever tell you about the little getaway she and Grant came up with for me? Grant felt I was pushing myself too hard, never taking time for myself to regroup and recharge."

Ian grinned. "Must run in the family."

"Yeah, we Barringtons are all made of the same stubborn stuff."

Ian had no doubt the almighty Damon Barrington had instilled all his work ethic into his girls and that hard work and determination were paying off in spades.

"I'd like to return the favor," Tessa went on. "Are you up for taking a few days away from here?"

Was he? Did he want to leave Lily when they were still negotiating a contract? He didn't mind leaving Max. The actor could handle anything and Ian was very confident with their working relationship.

It was Lily that worried him. But he couldn't be in her face all the time. He'd spoken with her a few times since their dinner meeting. She'd promised a decision once she realized which agency would offer her the most and which one she'd feel most at home with.

He had to believe she'd see that his company was hands down the front-runner.

And a few days away with Cassie? He had deals and meetings to get back to, but after days without her, how could he not want to jump at that chance?

"Should I take that smile to mean you're going to take me up on this offer?"

Ian nodded. "I think I will. What did you have in mind?"

Fourteen

How long could a baby be angry and how many teeth would be popping through?

Cassie had just collapsed onto the couch for the first time all day when someone knocked on her door. She threw a glance to Emily, who was playing on the floor and crawling from toy to toy…content for now.

Stepping over plush toys and blankets, Cassie opened the door and froze. Ian stood on her porch looking as handsome as ever, sporting aviator sunglasses and a navy T-shirt pulled taut across his wide shoulders and tucked into dark jeans.

She didn't need to look down at her own outfit to know she was just a step above homeless chic with her mismatched lounge pants with margarita glasses on them and her oversize T-shirt with a giant smiley face in the middle.

And her hair? She'd pulled it up into a ponytail for bed and hadn't touched it since. Half was falling around her face; the other half was in a nest on the side of her head.

Yeah, she exuded sex appeal.

"Um…are you going to invite me in?"

Cassie shoved a clump of hair behind her ear. "Are you sure you want to come in? Emily is teething. She's cranky more often than not since last night, and I'm…well…"

Ian closed the gap between them, laying a gentle kiss on her lips. "Beautiful."

Okay, there was no way she couldn't melt at that sweet declaration even if he was just trying to score points. He'd succeeded.

When he stepped into the house, Cassie stepped back and closed the door behind him. Emily grabbed hold of the couch cushion and pulled herself to her feet, throwing an innocent smile over her shoulder to Ian.

Cassie laughed. "Seriously? She smiles for you and I've had screaming for over twelve hours?"

"What can I say? I'm irresistible."

No denying that. Cassie still wasn't used to his powerful presence in her home, but she was growing to love it more and more each time he came for a visit.

"Hey, sweetheart," he said, squatting down beside Emily. "Did you have your mommy up last night?"

Emily let go of the couch to clap her hands and immediately fell down onto her diaper-covered butt. She giggled and looked up at Ian to see his reaction.

Cassie waited, too. She couldn't help but want to know how Ian would be around Emily. He hadn't spent too much time with her, considering he stopped by at night and he'd gone straight to Cassie's bed.

Reaching forward, Ian slid his big hands beneath Emily's delicate arms and lifted her as he came to his full height.

Cassie couldn't deny the lurch of her heart at the sight of this powerful man holding her precious baby. Was there a sexier sight than this? Not in Cassie's opinion.

"I know we talked on the phone, but congratulations." A smile lit up his already handsome face. "I'm so happy for you and Tessa."

Cassie still couldn't believe it herself. Of course they'd trained to win, but what trainer and jockey didn't? The fact they were that much closer to winning that coveted Triple Crown still seemed surreal.

"I'm still recovering from all the celebrating we did in Baltimore," she told him. "I've never been so happy in all my life. Well, except for when Emily was born."

"I have a surprise for you," Ian told her as Emily reached up and grabbed his nose.

Cassie went to reach for Emily, but Ian stepped back. "She's fine," he told her. "I love having my nose held so my voice can sound a little more like a chipmunk when I ask a sexy woman to go away with me for a few days."

Shocked at his invitation, Cassie shook her head, trying to make sense of it. "Go away with you?"

Ian nodded as Emily reached up on his head and tugged his glasses off. Immediately they went to her mouth.

"She's still fine," Ian told Cassie as he dodged her again. "They're sunglasses. She can chew on them all she wants."

"They'll have drool on them."

Ian's eyes darted to the lenses, but he just sighed. "Oh, well. So, what do you say? You up for getting away for a few days?"

Oh, how Cassie would love to get away. To not worry or train or do anything but be with Ian because their time together was coming to an end and she was certainly not ready to let go.

"Ian, going away with you sounds amazing, but I can't."

Ian glanced at Emily. "She's going to use you as an excuse, isn't she?"

Cassie laughed. "Actually, yes. But she's not an excuse.

I mean, I can't ask anyone to keep her for days, especially with her teething and upset."

Bringing his gaze back to Cassie, Ian crossed the space between them until he stood so close she could see the flecks of amber in his dark eyes.

"I'm not asking you to hand her off to anybody. I want to take you both away."

Cassie stared back at him, sure she'd heard him wrong. He wanted to take her and a baby? A cranky baby?

"But…but…are you sure?"

Ian dipped his head and gently kissed her before easing back and giving her that heart-melting grin. "I wouldn't have asked if I wasn't sure."

A million things ran through her mind. Could she actually take off and be with Ian for a few days? Did he honestly know what he was asking? Because she really didn't think he knew how difficult playing house could be.

"Stop thinking so hard." He shifted Emily to his other side and reached out to cup the side of Cassie's face. "Do you want to go?"

Cassie nodded. "Of course I do. It's just—"

"Yes, you want to go. That's what I need to hear. Everything else is taken care of."

Intrigued, Cassie raised her brows. "Oh, is it?"

A corner of Ian's mouth quirked into a devilish half smile. "Absolutely. How about I come back and get you in an hour. Just pack simple clothing and whatever Emily can't live without. I'll be back to help you finish up and then we'll go."

"Where are we going?" she asked.

Handing Emily back to Cassie, Ian shrugged. "I guess you'll find out when we get there."

She tried to get the sunglasses away from Emily and

noticed slobber bubbles along the lenses. Ian waved a hand and laughed.

"No, really, keep them," he said as he headed toward the door. "She apparently gets more use out of them than I did."

Cassie was still laughing after he'd closed the door behind him. A getaway with Ian and Emily? How could she not want to jump at this chance?

And how could she not read more into it? Was Ian silently telling her he wanted more? Or was he getting in all the time he could before he said his final goodbye?

Ian didn't know if he was making a mistake or if he was finally taking a leap of faith by bringing Cassie and Emily to his beachfront home. They'd flown from the East Coast to the West and he'd questioned himself the entire way.

Tessa had suggested he take Cassie to Grant's mountain home for a getaway, but Ian wanted Cassie on his turf. Deep down inside he wanted her to see how he lived, see part of his world.

And he wanted to find out how well she fit into his home. Would she feel out of place or would she enjoy the breathtaking views from his bedroom, which overlooked the Pacific Ocean?

Surprisingly, Emily was wonderful on the plane ride, thanks to the pain reliever aiding in her teething process. As Ian maneuvered his car—it had been waiting for him at the airport—into his drive, he risked a glance over to Cassie. He wanted to see her initial reaction.

And he wasn't disappointed. Her eyes widened at the two-story white beach house with the porch stretching across the first floor and the balcony wrapping around the house on the second. He'd had that same reaction when his Realtor had shown him the property a few years ago. Love at first sight.

"Ian, this is gorgeous," she exclaimed. "I can't believe you managed to get a beach house on such short notice."

He hadn't told her he was bringing her to his home. He'd wanted to surprise her, and he was afraid if he told her, then she'd back out.

As he pulled into the garage and killed the engine, Ian turned to face her. "Actually, this is my house."

Cassie gasped, jerking her head toward him. "Your house? Why didn't you tell me we were coming to your house?"

He honestly didn't have an excuse unless he wanted to delve way down and dig up the commitment issues he still faced. His fear of having her reject his plan, his fear of how fast they'd progressed and his fear of where the hell all of this would lead had kept him silent.

"I can't believe you live on the beach," she said, still smiling. "You must love it here."

Yeah, he did, but for the first time in his life, he suddenly found himself loving another location, as well. Who knew he'd fall in love with a horse farm on the other side of the country?

While Cassie got Emily out of the car, Ian took all the luggage into the house. He put his and Cassie's in the master bedroom and took Emily's bag into the room across the hall.

Thankfully, he'd called ahead and had his housekeeper pick up a few items and set them up in the makeshift nursery. Since she was a new grandmother, she knew exactly what a baby would need. And judging from the looks of the room, she'd gone all out.

Ian chuckled. The woman was a saint and deserved a raise...as always.

"Ian, this house is—"

He turned around to see Cassie in the doorway, Emily on her hip, eyes wide, mouth open.

"I had a little help getting the place ready," he informed her, moving aside so she could enter. "I hope you don't mind that I had my housekeeper get Emily some things to make her comfortable while you guys are here."

Cassie's gaze roamed around the room, pausing on the crib in the corner. "I don't know what to say," she whispered as her eyes sought his. "This is... Thank you."

Warmth spread through him. Cassie was absolutely speechless over a package of diapers, a bed and some toys. Cost hadn't even factored into his plan; Emily's comfort and easing Cassie's mind even a little had been his top priorities.

Before he could respond, Emily started fussing. Cassie kissed her forehead and patted her back. "It's okay, baby. You're all right."

The low cries turned into a full-fledged wail and a sense of helplessness overtook him. Yes, he could buy anything for her, but what did he know about consoling a child or what to do when they were hurting or sick?

With a soft smile, Cassie looked back to him. "Sorry. I'm sure this isn't the getaway you'd hoped for."

Ian returned her smile and reached out to slide his hand over Emily's back. "The only expectation I had was spending time with both of you. She can't help that she's teething."

Her eyes studied him for a moment before she said, "I don't know what I did to deserve you, Ian."

"You deserve everything you've ever wanted."

He wanted to say more, he wanted to do more and give more to her, but they were both in uncharted territory, and taking things slow was the best approach. God knew they hadn't started out slow. Working backward might not have been the most conventional approach, but it was all they had to work with.

"Can you get in the side of her diaper bag and get out the Tylenol?" she asked.

While Cassie got Emily settled with pain medication and started to sing to her, Ian watched from the doorway. Had his father ever felt this way about him? Had the man wanted to be hands-on? Because Ian desperately found himself wanting to be more in not just Cassie's life, but Emily's, as well. He didn't have the first clue about caring for children, but he wanted to learn.

How could he ever be what they needed?

But how could he ever let either of them go?

Fifteen

Thankfully, after a round of medicine and a short nap, Emily was back to her happy self. Cassie put on her bathing suit, wrapping a sheer sarong around her waist, then put Emily into her suit, as well.

Why waste time indoors when there was a beach and rolling waves just steps away?

"You ready to play in the ocean?" Cassie asked Emily as she carried her toward the back door. "You're going to love it, baby girl."

The open-concept living room and kitchen spread across the entire back of the house, and two sets of French doors led out onto the patio. Cassie stepped out into the warm sunshine and stopped.

At the edge of the water, Ian stood with his back to her wearing black trunks and flaunting his excellent muscle tone. The fabric clinging to the back of his well-toned thighs, his slicked-back hair and the water droplets glistening on his tanned shoulders and back indicated he'd already tested the waters.

The man was sinful. He tempted her in ways she never thought possible, made her want things that could never be. They couldn't be more opposite, yet they'd somehow found each other. And they'd grown so close since their encounter in the attic.

The night of the lock-in had been filled with nothing but lust and desire. Now, though, Cassie was wrestling with so many more emotions. At the top of her list was one she'd futilely guarded her heart against…love.

She completely loved this man who had brought her to his home, shown her his piece of the world. But the clincher was when he'd assumed Emily would accompany them. He knew Cassie and Emily were a package deal, and he'd embraced the fact and still welcomed them.

How could she not fall hard for this intriguing man? He was nothing like her ex, nothing like any man she'd ever known, really. And that was what made him so special.

Emily started clapping and pointing toward Ian. Cassie laughed. "Yeah, we're going, baby."

Sand shifted beneath her toes as she made her way toward the man who'd taught her heart to trust again. Just the sight of him had her anticipating their night alone after Emily went to bed.

It wasn't as if she hadn't seen or touched him all over, but still, his sexiness never got old.

Emily squealed and Ian turned to face her. His gaze traveled over her modest suit and Cassie tamped down that inner demon that tried to tell her that her extra baby weight was hideous. Ian never, ever made her feel less than beautiful, so that inner voice could just shut the hell up.

"You look good in a suit, Cass."

His low voice, combined with that heavy-lidded gaze, had her insides doing an amazing little dance number.

"I was thinking the same thing about you," she told him with a grin.

"Mom, Mom, Mom," Emily squealed again, clapping her little hands and staring out at the water.

"Can I?" Ian asked, reaching for Emily.

Handing Emily over, Cassie watched as Ian stepped into the water. Slowly, he waded in deeper, all the while taking his hand and cupping water to splash up onto her little pudgy legs. Emily's laughter, her arms around Ian's neck and seeing Ian bounce around in the water like a complete goofball had Cassie laughing herself.

This getaway was exactly what she needed. Coming off the win at the Preakness and rolling right into a special weekend had Cassie realizing that her life was pretty near perfect right now. For this moment, she would relish the fact that Ian had to care for her on some deep level… possibly even love her. If he only had feelings of lust, he wouldn't have brought her to his home, wouldn't have invited a teething, sometimes cranky kid, and he certainly wouldn't be playing in the water with Emily like a proud daddy.

Cassie hated to place all her hope, all her heart, on one man…but how could she not, when he'd captured her heart the instant they'd been intimate in that attic?

Not wanting to miss out on a single moment, Cassie jumped into the ocean, reached beneath the water and pinched Ian on the butt.

The grin he threw over his shoulder at her told her she was in for a fun night.

Rocking a now peaceful baby had Ian truly wishing for so much. He'd convinced Cassie that he could put Emily to bed. He figured the little one was so tired from the day of playing in the ocean and taking a stroller ride around his neighborhood that she'd fall fast asleep.

She'd been fussy at first and Cassie had shown Ian how to rub some numbing ointment onto Emily's gums. He'd given Emily a bottle, even burped her, and rocked her until her sweet breath evened out.

He glanced down to the puckered lips, the pink cheeks from the sun—even though they'd slathered her with sunscreen—and smiled. Was it any wonder Cassie worked herself to death? How could a parent not want to sacrifice herself to make such an innocent child happy?

Cassie worked so hard with her sister, worked harder in the stables caring for horses, and she busted her butt to make a secure life and happy home for Emily...all without a husband.

Oh, she'd be ticked if she knew he worried about her not having someone in her life to help her. Granted, she had her father, Tessa and Linda, but whom did she have at night? Who helped her at home?

God help him, but Ian wanted to be that man. The weight of a sleeping baby in his arms, the sweet smell of her skin after her bath and the thought that this innocent child had complete and total trust in him were truly humbling.

Once he knew she was asleep, Ian eased from the rocking chair and laid Emily into the new crib, complete with pink-and-white-striped sheets. When he stood up, she stirred a little, but she settled right in.

A sigh of relief escaped Ian. He'd mastered numerous multimillion-dollar movie deals, he rubbed elbows with A-list actors and he'd managed to start his own agency at the age of twenty-four. But putting a child to sleep all by himself felt like quite an accomplishment.

He glanced at the monitor beside the crib and made sure it was on before he stepped out into the hall and quietly shut the door behind him.

He barely managed not to jump when he noticed Cassie across the hall, leaning against the doorway to his bedroom.

"You did it," she said with a wide smile. "I'm impressed."

All thoughts fled his mind as he took in the muted glow that surrounded her from the small lamp in his room. Her long red curls slid around her shoulders, lying against the stark white silk robe she wore—and what she wasn't wearing beneath. The V in the front plunged so deep, the swells of her breasts begged for his touch.

"I like your pajamas," he told her, crossing the hallway and immediately going to the belt on her robe. "Reminds me of something…"

Cassie lifted her arms to wrap around his neck. "What's that?"

"The fact I haven't seen you naked in several days."

She shifted, allowing the material to slide from her shoulders and puddle at her feet. Ian's hands roamed over the soft, lush curves he'd come to love and crave.

"You feel so good," he groaned as he trailed his lips from her jawline down the smooth column of her neck. "So perfect."

When she trembled beneath his touch, Ian cupped her behind and pulled her flush against his body. Nothing had ever felt so right. Every time Cassie was in his arms, contentment settled deeper and deeper into his heart.

She undressed him rapidly, matching his own frenzy. Ian had brought other women to his home. Not many, but a few. Yet he knew the second he laid Cassie beneath him and looked down into her blue eyes…he never wanted another woman in this bed.

* * *

He knew she wasn't asleep. The full moon shone through the wide expanse of windows across the room from the king-size bed and directly across their tangled bodies.

Cassie's breathing wasn't even and he'd felt the soft flutter of her lashes against his arm. Whatever thoughts consumed her mind, they were keeping her awake.

More than likely they were the same things that had him awake hours after they'd made love…twice.

Ian trailed his fingertips over her hip, down into the dip of her waist and back again. Goose bumps prickled beneath his touch.

"Talk to me," she whispered in the darkened room.

Words that had frightened him on more than one occasion after sex. But this was so different from any other time. First, Cassie was like no other woman. Second, what had just happened between them was so far beyond sex. And third, he actually didn't cringe as the words hovered in the air between them.

Moreover, he *wanted* to talk to her. He wanted her to know about his past, his life and what had brought him to this point…and why the thought of commitment scared the hell out of him.

Part of him truly wanted to try for her. Never before had he even considered permanent anything in his life, let alone a woman and a child. Cassie changed everything for him, because she was starting to *be* everything for him.

Of course, there was that devil on his shoulder that kept telling him he couldn't just try out playing house with this woman. She was genuine, with real feelings and a heart of gold that she had to protect. If he attempted to try for a long-term spot in her life and things didn't work out, he would never be able to forgive himself.

"My childhood wasn't quite as rosy and enjoyable as

yours." The words tumbled out before he thought better of opening up about the past he hated to even think about. "My father was a military man. Things had to be perfect, and not just perfect, but done five minutes ago. When he was home on leave, if I had a chore, I had better get to it the second he told me or I would face punishment."

Cassie gasped next to him. "He hit you?"

Ian stared up at the darkened ceiling as he continued to trail his fingertips over her lush, naked curves. "On occasion. But it wasn't a beating. He was old-school and a hand to my backside wasn't unheard of. But then he came home less and less because he and my mother divorced. That's when she started bringing her male friends into the house."

Ian recalled how weird it felt having a strange man at the breakfast table when he woke up, but eventually he didn't question his mother...and he didn't ask the names of the men. Would it matter? They'd be gone when she finished with them anyway.

"My mom is currently in the middle of her fourth divorce and I've no doubt number five is waiting in the wings absolutely convinced he's the one."

Cassie's arm tightened around his abdomen. "I'm sorry. I can't imagine."

Her warm breath tickled his chest, but Ian wouldn't have it any other way. He loved the feel of her tucked perfectly against him, her hair falling over his shoulder, the flutter of her lashes against his side.

"Don't be sorry," he told her. "There are kids way worse off than I was. But I always wished I had parents who loved each other, who loved me. A family was everything to me when I was younger, but I wanted the impossible."

A drop of moisture slid down his side. Ian shifted his body, folding Cassie closer as he half loomed over her.

"Don't cry for me." In the pale moonlight, her eyes glistened. Had anyone ever cried for him before? "I'm fine, Cassie. I guess I just wanted you to know what I came from."

Soft fingertips came up to trail down his cheek. Her thumb caressed his bottom lip, and his body responded instantly.

"I'm crying for the little boy who needed love and attention," she whispered. "And I'm crying for the man who fits so perfectly into my family, I'm terrified of how we'll get along without him."

Her declaration was a punch to his gut. The fact that they'd never mentioned his leaving after the film wrapped hung heavy in the air between them. And knowing she not only worried about his absence, but she'd cried over it had him hating himself on so many levels.

"I don't want to hurt you," he murmured as he slid his lips across hers. "That's the last thing I'd ever want."

Adjusting her body so she could frame his face with her hands, Cassie looked up at him with those damn misty eyes and smiled. "I know. I went into this with my eyes wide-open. For right now, though, you're mine and I don't want to think about tomorrow, Ian. I don't want to worry about that void that will inevitably come when you're gone."

Her hips tilted against his. "I just want you. Here. Now."

As he kissed her lips he had a hard time reining in his own emotions, because Cassie was dead-on about one thing.... There would most definitely be a void—the one he would feel without her by his side.

Sixteen

Cassie reached across the bed, only to encounter cool sheets. Quickly she sat up, clutching the material to her chest and glancing to the nightstand clock.

How on earth had she slept until nine? Between having a career set around a working horse farm and being a single mother, sleeping in was a foreign concept and a luxury she simply couldn't afford.

Another reality hit her hard as she jerked to look at the baby monitor on the dresser across the room. The red light wasn't on, which meant at some point the device had been turned off. Throwing the covers aside, Cassie grabbed the first available article of clothing—which happened to be Ian's T-shirt—and pulled the soft cotton over her head. She inhaled the embedded masculine scent of Ian as she darted across the hall.

The nursery was empty. Giggling erupted from downstairs, so Cassie turned and headed toward the sweet sound. At the base of the steps, Cassie froze as she stared into the living room. Ian stood behind Emily, her little hands held high, clutching on to his as he helped her walk across the open space. He'd pushed the coffee table against one wall, leaving the dark hardwood floor completely open.

Emily squealed as she waddled through the area, and Cassie, who still stood unnoticed, had to bite her lip to control the trembling and wash of emotions that instantly consumed her.

Ian Shaffer had officially stolen her heart, and there was no way she could go back to her life before she'd ever met him. The man had opened his home to her and her daughter. He wasn't just interested in having her in his bed. Granted, that was how they'd started out, but over a brief period of time they'd grown together and meshed in such a way that had Cassie hopeful and wishing. Dare she set her sights so high and dream for things that once seemed unattainable?

"Mamamama," Emily cried when she saw Cassie in the doorway.

Cassie stepped toward her daughter and squatted down. "Hey, sweet pea. Are you making Ian work this morning?"

Emily's precious two-toothed grin melted her heart. When she glanced up to meet Ian's gaze, her breath literally caught. He still clung to Emily's fingers and he'd been hunched over so he could accommodate her height, but he just looked so at peace and happy.

"What time did she get up?"

Ian shrugged. "Maybe around seven."

Cassie straightened. "Why didn't you get me up?"

Scooping Emily into his arms, Ian smiled. "Because you needed to sleep, so I turned the monitor off and got her out of the crib. She's been changed and fed—probably not how you'd do it, but it's done nonetheless."

Cassie was utterly speechless. The man had taken such care of her daughter all so Cassie could sleep in. He'd been watching and loving over Emily…over another man's baby, and all without a care or second thought. And now he stood holding her as if the act were the most natural thing in the world.

"Don't look at me like that," he told her. Emily turned her head into Ian's shoulder and his wide, tanned hand patted her tiny back. "I wanted to help and I knew you'd refuse if you even thought she was awake. Besides, I kind of wanted to see how Emily and I would get along. I'm pretty sure she loves me."

Cassie couldn't help but laugh. "I'm sure she does love you. She knows a good thing when she sees it."

Ian's eyes widened, and the muscle in his jaw moved as if he were hiding his words deep within. Had she said too much? At this point, with time against them, Cassie truly believed she couldn't hold back. She needed to be up front and honest.

"I'm not saying that to make you uncomfortable," she informed him, crossing her arms over her chest. "But you have to know this is so much more than physical for me, Ian."

Those dark eyes studied her a second before he nodded. "I'd be lying if I said this was all sexual for me. You and Emily…"

He shook his head as his words died on his lips. Cassie wanted him to go on, but she knew the internal battle he waged with himself and she didn't want to push him. He'd opened up to her last night, bared his soul, and she knew what he'd shared hadn't come easy for him.

Placing a hand on his arm, Cassie smiled. "We don't need to define anything right now," she assured him. "I just wanted you to know this thing between us—it matters so much to me."

With Emily lying against one shoulder, Ian pulled Cassie to his other side and wrapped an arm around her. "Everything in my arms right now matters more to me than I ever thought possible," he told her with a kiss to the top of her head.

Before she could completely melt into a puddle at his feet over his raw, heartfelt words, Ian's hand slid down her side and cupped her bottom beneath his T-shirt.

"This shirt never looked this sexy on me," he growled into her ear. "So unless you want to end up back in bed, you better go get some clothes on."

Shivers of arousal swept through her. Would she ever get enough of him? More so, would he get enough of her?

Tipping her head back, she stared up into his eyes. Desire and, dare she say, love stared back at her. No, she didn't think they'd get enough of each other, which meant whatever they were building wouldn't come crumbling down when he left Virginia after the film was done shooting. But how they would manage was a whole other hurdle to jump.

Extracting herself from his side, Cassie pulled Emily from his arms. "How about we spend the day on the beach?" she suggested.

Emily's little hand went into Cassie's hair, and she started winding the strands around her baby fingers.

"You in a suit?" Ian's gaze raked over her once more. "I'd never say no to that."

With this being their last day of complete relaxation, Cassie wanted to live for the moment, this day, and not worry about what obstacles they faced tomorrow or even next week. She was completely in love with Ian. He wasn't a rebound; he wasn't a filler or a stepping-stone until the next chapter of her life.

Ian Shaffer *was* the next chapter of her life.

Seventeen

"I just need someone who's good with advertising," Cassie muttered as she stared down at the new plans for her riding school for handicapped children.

"How about that hunky agent you're shacking up with?"

Cassie threw a glare across the room at her sister. Tessa silently volleyed back a wicked grin.

"We're not shacking up." Not technically, anyway. "And that's not his job."

"Maybe not," Tessa replied, coming to her feet. "But he'd know more about it than we would, and I guarantee he'd do anything to help you."

More than likely, but Cassie wasn't going to ask. Venturing into personal favors would imply something…something they'd yet to identify in their relationship.

Yes, they'd admitted they had strong feelings for each other, but after the giant leap into intimacy, they'd pulled back the emotional roller coaster and examined where they were going.

And they still didn't know.

Cassie spoon-fed another bite of squash and rice to Emily. Right now she needed to focus on the final race of the season, getting her school properly advertised and caring for her daughter. Ian, unfortunately, would have to fall in line behind all of that and she highly doubted he would want to. What man would? He deserved more than waiting on her leftover time.

"You're scowling." Tessa came to stand beside the high chair and leaned against the wall. "What's really bothering you?"

Sisters. They always knew when to dig deeper and pull the truth from the depths of hell just to make you say the words aloud.

"Ian is out to dinner with Lily."

A quirk of a smile danced around Tessa's mouth. "You're jealous? Honey, the man is absolutely crazy about you. All you'd have to do is see how he looks at you when you aren't paying attention."

The idea that he studied her enough to show emotion on his face for others to see made her way more thrilled than she should be. She wanted to tell him she'd fallen for him—she wanted to tell everybody. But there was that annoying little voice that kept telling her this was too good to be true and that she needed to come back to reality before she ended up hurt.

"He's not like Derek," Tessa informed her as if she were reading her mind. "Ian may be younger, but he's all man and he's only got eyes for you."

Cassie smiled with a nod and scooped up the last bite, shoving it into Emily's waiting mouth. "I know. There's just that thread of doubt that gets to me, and I know it's not Ian's fault. He can't help the mess that is my life."

Laying a hand over Cassie's arm, Tessa squeezed. "Your

life is beautiful. You have a precious baby, an awesome career and the best sister anyone could ever ask for. What more could a girl want?"

To be loved. The words remained in her head, in her heart.

"So where's your guy tonight?" Cassie asked, wiping off the orange, messy mouth, hoping to unearth her daughter. "You two aren't normally separated for more than an hour at a time."

With a smile that could only be equated to love, Tessa positively beamed. "He's going over some things with Bronson and Anthony. I'm pretty sure Dad weaseled his way into that meeting, as well."

Cassie scooped Emily from the high chair and settled her on her hip. "I've no doubt Dad is weighing in with his opinion. I need to give her a bath. You sticking around?"

Shaking her head, Tessa sighed and started across the living room. "I think I'll head home and make some dinner. It's not often I get to cook for Grant, and he's worked so hard lately. He needs to relax."

Cassie squeezed her eyes shut. "I don't want to hear about you two relaxing. Just a simple no would've answered my question."

With a naughty laugh, Tessa grabbed her keys from the entry table and waved. "See you tomorrow."

Once Cassie was alone, she couldn't help that her thoughts drifted to Ian, to the days they'd spent at his home in L.A. and to the fact he'd taken such good care of her sweet Emily.

Yes, the man may be five years her junior, but so what? Her ex-husband had been two years older and look how well that had turned out. Cassie couldn't hang a single argument on age, not when Ian went above and beyond to show her just what type of man he was.

After Emily was bathed and dressed in her lightweight

sleeper, Cassie set some toys on a blanket and let her daughter have some playtime before bed. Settling on the couch, curling her legs to the side, Cassie rested her elbow on the arm of the sofa and watched Emily smack soft yellow and red cubes together, making them jingle.

Exhaustion consumed her, but how could she not be tired? Her plate was not only full—it was overflowing. Physically, mentally, she was drained. Her head was actually pounding so fiercely her eyes ached. Maybe she could just lay her head on the arm of the couch while Emily played for a bit longer.

Adjusting her arm beneath her head, Cassie closed her eyes, hoping to chase away the dull throb.

After the flash of panic in seeing Cassie slumped over the arm of the couch and Emily holding herself up against the edge of the couch by her mama, Ian realized Cassie had merely fallen asleep.

"Hey, sweetie," he said softly when Emily smiled up at him, flashing her two little baby teeth. "Your mama is pretty tired. Why don't we let her sleep?"

Ian scooped Emily up, set her in her Pack 'n Play across the room and made sure she had her favorite stuffed horse. He had to ignore her slight protesting as he crossed back and gently lifted Cassie into his arms. Murmuring something, she tilted her head against his chest and let out a deep sigh. She was exhausted and apparently couldn't even keep her eyes open. It was so unlike her to fall asleep with Emily still up and not confined to one area.

A small bedside lamp sent a soft glow through her bedroom. After gently laying her down, he pulled the folded blanket from the foot of the bed and draped it over her curled form. Smoothing her hair from her face, Ian frowned and leaned in closer to rest his palm across her forehead.

She wasn't burning up, but she wasn't far from it. Careful not to wake her, he peeled the throw back off her to hopefully get her fever down. Her cheeks were pink and the dark circles beneath her eyes were telltale signs of an illness settling in. He had a feeling Cassie would only be angry to know she was getting sick.

He went into her adjoining bath, got a cool cloth and brought it back out, carefully laying it across her forehead. She stirred and her lids fluttered open as she tried to focus.

"Ian?"

"Shh." He curled a hand over her shoulder to get her to remain down. "It's all right. You need to rest."

"Emily..." Cassie's eyes closed for a moment before she looked back up at him. "I don't feel very well."

"I know, baby. I'm not going anywhere and Emily is fine. Just rest."

He had no clue if she heard him; her eyes were closed and her soft, even breathing had resumed.

The woman worked herself too hard. Not that he could judge. After all, he hadn't grown to be one of Hollywood's most sought-out agents at such a young age by playing assistant and errand boy. No, he'd done grunt work, made his career his since he'd left home determined to prove to his free-spirited mother and domineering father that he could manage on his own and succeed way above anything they'd ever dreamed.

And he'd done just that.

But now that he looked down at Cassie resting peacefully, he couldn't help but wonder if there wasn't more in store for him. Work was satisfying on so many levels, but it didn't keep his bed warm, didn't look to him for support and compassion and sure as hell didn't make his heart swell to the point of bursting.

Cassie and Emily, on the other hand...

After clicking off the bedside lamp, he went straight to the hall bath to wash his hands. If Cassie was contagious, he didn't want to get her daughter sick. Granted, the child had been with her mother all evening, but still. Weren't people supposed to wash their hands before dealing with kids?

Yeah, he had a lot to learn. As he lathered up and rinsed, he glanced across the open floor plan to Emily, who had long since forgotten she was angry with being confined. Ian dried his hands on a plaid towel and smiled. Definitely had a lot to learn about little people.

And suddenly it hit him that he actually wanted to do just that. Who knew that when he came out here to sway Lily into signing with his agency that he'd completely get sidetracked by a beauty who literally fell into his arms?

After getting a bottle ready—thank God he'd had those alone days with Cassie and Emily in California so he knew a bit more about Emily's care—Ian set it on the end table and went to retrieve one happy baby.

"Are you always in a good mood?" he asked as he lifted her from the baby prison. "Your mama isn't feeling good, so it's just you and me."

Emily patted his face and smiled. "Dadadada."

Ian froze. *Oh, no. No, no, no.* As if a vise was being tightened around his chest, Ian's breath left him.

"No, baby. Ian."

Emily patted his cheek again. "Dadada."

Okay, he had to put his own issues aside at the thought of someone calling him Daddy because this poor girl honestly didn't know her daddy. She didn't remember the man who was supposed to be here for her and her mother.

Ian held her closer, silently wanting to reassure her that she was not alone. But was he also silently telling himself that he'd be here beyond the rough night right now? Would he be here after the film wrapped up?

Since he was alone with his thoughts he might as well admit to himself that being with Cassie and Emily for the long term was something he wanted and, dare he say... ached for?

As he settled into the corner of the couch with Emily, he slid the bottle between her little puckered lips and smiled as those expressive blue eyes looked back up at him. Eyes like her mother's. Both ladies had him wrapped around their fingers.

Emily drifted off to sleep about the time the bottle was empty. He set it back on the table and shifted her gently up onto his shoulder. If she spit up on his dress shirt, so be it. He hadn't taken the time to change after his dinner meeting with Lily. She was pretty confident she'd be signing with his agency.

And the fact this was the first time he'd thought of that monumental career development since he'd come in and discovered Cassie ill should tell him exactly how quickly his priorities had changed where the Barrington females were concerned.

Once Emily had fallen asleep, he figured it was okay for him to rest on the couch with her. He carefully got up and turned off the lights in the living room, leaving on only the small light over the stove in the kitchen. Pulling the throw off the back of the sofa with one hand and holding Emily firmly with the other, Ian toed off his shoes and laid the little girl against the back of the sofa before he eased down onto his side beside her. Not the most comfortable of positions, but he was so tired he could've slept standing up, and there was no way he'd leave Cassie alone with the baby tonight.

Resting with the baby on a couch was probably some

sort of Parenting 101 no-no, but since he'd taken no crash courses in this gig, he was totally winging it.

The next thing he knew someone was ringing the doorbell. Ian jerked up, taking in the sunlight streaming in through the windows. It was Sunday and the crew was taking the day off. Was someone looking for him? The doorbell chimed again and Emily's eyes popped open, too.

Ian picked her up and raked a hand over his hair as he padded to the door. The last thing he needed was for someone to ring that bell again and wake Cassie. Apparently they'd all slept uneventfully through the night.

As he flicked the lock, Ian glanced out the sidelight, frowning when he didn't recognize the stranger on the porch.

Easing the door open slightly, Ian met the other man's gaze. "Can I help you?"

The stranger's eyes went from Emily back to Ian before the muscle in his jaw jumped. "Who the hell are you, and where is Cassie?"

Shocked at the immediate anger, Ian instantly felt defensive. "I should be asking you who you are, considering you're on the outside."

Narrowed eyes pierced Ian. "I'm Cassie's husband. I'll ask again. Who the hell are you?"

Husband. Ian didn't miss the fact the prick left out the "ex" part.

"I'm her lover," Ian said, mentally high-fiving himself for wiping that smug look off the man's face.

Eighteen

Cassie held on to the side of her head, which was still pounding, but now she had a new problem.

Frozen at the end of her hallway, she had full view of Ian holding Emily and the front door wide-open with Derek standing on the other side looking beyond pissed. This was the dead-last thing she wanted to deal with in her life, particularly at this moment.

"Derek, what are you doing here?" she asked, slowly crossing the room, praying she didn't collapse.

"Go back to bed, honey." Ian turned to her, his face softening as he took in what she knew was impressive bed head. "Emily is fine and he can come back later."

"Don't tell my wife what to do," Derek practically shouted as he shouldered his way past Ian and into the living room.

"She's not your wife." Ian's eyes narrowed. When Emily started to fidget, Ian patted her back and murmured something to her. "I need to feed her and change her diaper."

Derek's gaze darted from Ian to Cassie and back to Ian.

"What the hell is this? You move in your lover to shack up? Never took you for a whore."

Cassie didn't think she could feel worse. She was wrong. But before she could defend herself, Ian had turned back, clenching the muscle in his jaw.

"Apologize," Ian said in a low, threatening tone.

Cassie had no doubt if Ian hadn't been holding the baby, he would've been across the room in an instant.

"This has nothing to do with you," Derek shot back. "Why don't you give me my daughter and get out."

No matter how awful Cassie felt, she raised her hand to silence Ian and moved closer to Derek. Too bad whatever bug she'd picked up couldn't be fast-acting or she'd so exhale all over him.

"You relinquished any right you had when you walked out on us." Cassie laid a hand on the back of the couch for support. She'd be a little more intimidating if she wasn't freezing and ready to fall onto her face. "You can't just barge into my house and try to take control. I don't know why you're here, but I don't really care."

Cassie felt Ian's hard body behind her, his strong hand settled around her waist. The man offered support both physically and emotionally with one simple, selfless touch. And the sea of differences between the two men in this room was evident without so much as a spoken word.

Ian had watched her with care, concern and, yes, even love. Derek stood glaring, judging and hating. When he'd first walked out she would've done anything to get her family back, but now that he was here, she loathed the sight of him.

"I'm here to see my wife and daughter," Derek told her.

"I'm not your wife," Cassie fired back. "And if you want to see Emily, you can contact your attorney and he can call mine. You can't just charge in here after being gone for nearly a year and expect me to just let you see her. Did you think she'd be comfortable with you?"

"She seems fine with him." Derek nodded his chin in Ian's direction.

"That's because she knows who I am," Ian stated from behind her. "Now, Cassie has asked you to leave. She's not feeling good and my patience has just about run out. Leave now or I'll escort you out personally, then notify the crew's security to take you off the estate property."

Derek looked as if he wanted to say more, but Ian stepped around Cassie, keeping his arm wrapped around her waist. He said nothing and kept his gaze on Derek until Derek stepped back toward the front door.

"I plan on seeing my daughter," Derek threatened. "And my wife. I'll go through my lawyer, but I will be getting my family back."

He slammed the door, leaving the echoing sound to fill the silence. Cassie hadn't seen Derek in so long, she had no idea how to feel, how to react. She didn't feel like battling him.

And had he threatened to take Emily? Was that what he'd implied?

Cassie sank onto the back of the couch and wrapped her arms around her waist. Maybe she should have listened to those voice mails.

"Go back to bed, Cass. Don't think about him—just go rest for now."

Cassie looked up at Ian, still holding Emily. The image just seemed so...right. The three of them *felt* right. They'd all been random puzzle pieces and when they'd come together they'd instantly clicked into place without question.

Shoving her wayward hair behind her ears, Cassie shook her head. "I can't rest, Ian. He just made a veiled threat to take Emily. He can't do that, right? I mean, what judge would let him have my baby after he walked out on us?"

Tears pricked her eyes. She couldn't fathom sharing custody of her baby. Emily belonged here.

"She doesn't even know him," Cassie murmured, thinking aloud. "There's no way he could take her. Emily would be terrified."

Ian rested a hand on her shoulder and held on to Emily with his other strong arm. "You're jumping the gun here. He didn't say he was going to ask for custody. I honestly think those were just hollow words. He wants to scare you because he's angry I was here. I guarantee had you been alone, his attitude would've been completely different. One look at me, especially holding his daughter, and he was instantly on the defensive."

Emily started to reach for Cassie, but Ian shifted his arm away. "Go on back to rest. I'll feed her breakfast and then I'll check on you to see if you feel like eating. You're exhausted and working too hard."

Cassie raised a brow. "Working too hard? Are you the pot or the kettle?"

Laughing, Ian shrugged. "Does it matter?"

Cassie pushed away from the couch and sighed. "Thanks, Ian. Really. I don't know what I would've done without you here last night."

After a light kiss across her forehead, Ian looked into her eyes. "There's nowhere else I would've rather been."

As Cassie got back into bed, she knew Ian wasn't just saying pretty words to try to win her over. The man was full of surprises, and she found herself falling harder with each passing revelation.

And now here she was, 100 percent in love with a man who lived on the other side of the country, who would be leaving in a couple of weeks to go back to his life. And, of all the rotten timing, her ex had decided to show up now.

Cassie curled into her pillow and fisted her hands beside her face as the tears threatened to fall. Somehow this would all work out. She had faith, she had hope and, for the first time in her life, she had love. All of that had to count for something…didn't it?

Once Cassie had gotten a little food in her, she seemed even more tired, so Ian insisted on taking Emily for a few hours and then checking back. There was no way he could leave her alone with a baby, but he still had work to do.

Single parents worked while caring for their babies all the time, right? Shouldn't be too hard to send some emails and make a few phone calls.

After fighting with the straps on the stroller and narrowly missing pinching Emily's soft skin in the buckle, he finally had her secured and ready to go. Diaper bag over his shoulder, Ian set out across the estate, pushing Emily toward his trailer.

Bright purple flats covered her feet as she kicked her little legs the entire way. Ian knew he was smiling like an idiot, but how could he not? Emily was an absolute doll and she was such a sweet kid. He was actually looking forward to spending time with her.

Max Ford and his wife, Raine, were just stepping out of their trailer as he passed by. Max held their little girl, Abby, who was almost two now.

"Look at this," Max said with a wide grin. "You seeing how the family life fits you?"

Ian didn't mind the question. Actually, he kind of warmed at the idea of it. "Cassie isn't feeling too great, so I told her I'd take Emily for the day."

Max's daughter pointed down to Emily. "Baby."

Laughing, Raine took the little girl and squatted down to the stroller to see Emily. "Her name is Emily," Raine explained.

"You're pretty serious about Cassie," Max said in a softer tone. "Happened pretty quick."

Ian shook his head and raked a hand over his hair, which was probably still sporting a messy look after sleeping on the sofa all night. "Yeah, it did. But I can't help it, man. I didn't see this coming."

"You plan on staying after the film is done?" Max asked.

Ian watched the interaction between the two little girls and Raine and his heart swelled. "I honestly don't know," Ian said, looking back to Max. "How hard was it for you with the transition?"

Max's gaze drifted to his family, and a genuine smile, not what he used for the cameras or his on-screen love interests, but the one that Ian had seen directed only at Raine, transformed his face. "When you want something so bad you'd die without it, there's no transition. It's the easiest and best decision I've ever made."

Yeah, that was kind of where Ian's mind was going. Having Cassie and Emily in his life made him feel things on a level he hadn't even known existed inside him.

Ian said his goodbyes to Max and his family and stepped inside his trailer. After settling Emily on a pink fuzzy blanket from her house, Ian placed her favorite toys all around her. Standing back to admire his feat of babysitting, he went to boot up his laptop, grabbed his phone and sat at the small kitchenette. Thankfully, the trailer was all open and small, so Emily couldn't leave his sight.

After answering a few emails, Ian glanced at the little girl, who was chewing on one toy and pounding the other one against the side of her rainbow-striped leggings. So far so good.

As he dialed one of his clients, rising star Brandon Crowe, who was on his way to Texas for filming, Ian scrolled back through his emails, deleting the junk so he could wade through and find things that actually needed his attention.

"Hello."

"Brandon, glad I caught you." Ian closed out his email and opened the document with his client's name on it to make notes. "You arrive in Houston yet?"

"About an hour ago. I'm ready for a beer, my hotel room and about five days of sleep. In that order."

Ian chuckled. His client had been filming all over with a tight schedule; the crew had literally been running from one location to another.

"What's up?" Brandon asked.

"I know your mind is on overload right now, but I need to discuss the next script. I have a film that will be set in Alaska and the producer has specifically asked for you. I'd like to send this script to you and see what you think."

Brandon sighed. "Sure. Did you look it over?"

"Yeah. I think this character would be a perfect fit for you. I can see why they want you for the role."

"Who's the producer?" Brandon asked.

Ian told him more specifics and turned to see Emily… only she wasn't there. Panic rushed through him as he jerked to his feet, sending his chair toppling to the floor behind him.

"Emily," he called, glancing around the very tiny area.

"Excuse me?"

Ian glanced at the phone. For a second he'd forgotten about the call. "I need to call you back. The baby is gone."

"Baby?"

Ian disconnected the call and tossed his phone on the

table. Stepping over the toys and blanket, Ian crossed to the other end of the trailer. He peeked into the tiny bathroom: no Emily.

"Emily," he called. "Sweetheart?"

In the small bedroom, Ian saw bright rainbow material sticking out from the side of the bed. He rounded the bed. Emily sat on her bottom, still chewing her favorite stuffed horse. Of course, when she saw him she looked up and gave that heart-melting smile.

"You're rotten," he told her. "Your mom is not going to let you come play with me anymore if you give me a heart attack."

He scooped her up and was rewarded with a wet, sloppy horse to the side of the face. *Nice.*

The next hour went about as stellar as the first, and by the end of hour two, Ian knew he was an amateur and needed reinforcements. There was just no way he could do this on his own.

How the hell did Cassie manage? Not only manage, but still put up the front of keeping it together and succeeding at each job: mother, sister, daughter, trainer. She did it all.

Of course, now she was home, in bed, flat-out exhausted and literally making herself sick.

As Ian gathered up all Emily's things, she started crying. The crying turned into a wail in about 2.5 seconds, so Ian figured she was hungry. Wrong. He changed her diaper. Still not happy.

He picked up the bag and Emily, stepped outside and strapped her into the stroller. Perhaps a walk around the estate would help.

Keeping toward the back of the main house, Ian quickly realized this also wasn't making her very happy. That was it. Reinforcements were past due.

He made his way to the back door, unfastened the very

angry Emily and carried her into the house, where—*thank you, God*—Linda greeted him with a smile and some heavenly aroma that could only be her cinnamon rolls.

"I've done something wrong," Ian yelled over Emily's tantrum. "We were fine." A slight lie. "But then she started screaming. She's not hungry. She has a clean diaper. We took a walk. I don't know what to do."

Linda wiped her hand on a plaid towel and tossed it onto the granite counter before circling the island and holding her hands out for Emily. The baby eagerly went to the middle-aged woman and Ian nearly wept with gratitude that someone else surely knew what they were doing.

"She probably needs a nap," Linda told him as she jostled and tried to calm Emily.

Ian laughed and pushed a hand through his hair. "After all of that, I need one, too."

Smiling, Linda patted Emily's back. "You say you fed her?"

Ian nodded. "She took a bottle. I have some jar food, but Cassie said to save that for a bit later."

"If she's had her bottle, then her little belly is full and she's ready to rest. I'll just take her into the master bedroom. Damon has a crib set up in there for when Cassie is over here."

Ian sank to the bar stool, rested his elbow on the island and held his head in his hands. Good grief, being in charge of one tiny little being was the hardest job he'd ever had... and he'd had the job only a few hours.

Hands down, parenting was not for wimps.

A slither of guilt crept through him. Had he been too hard on his parents all those years? His free-spirited mother who was always seeking attention and his by-the-book father who could never be pleased...were they just struggling at this whole parenting thing, too?

Ian didn't have the answers and he couldn't go back in time and analyze each and every moment. The most pressing matter right now was the fact that he was in love with Cassie and her sweet baby, and the ex had just stepped back into the picture.

Great freakin' timing.

But Ian needed to wait, to let Cassie deal with this matter in her own way. He wasn't stepping aside, not by any means. He'd offer support any way she wanted it, but this was her past to handle, and with a baby involved, Ian had a bad feeling things were about to get worse before they could get better.

Nineteen

Cassie jerked when the loud knock on her door pulled her out of her sleep. Glancing to the clock on the bedside table, she realized she'd slept most of the day. Damn, she'd never slept that much.

Throwing off the covers and coming to her feet, Cassie was thrilled when she didn't sway and within moments knew she was feeling better. Perhaps her body was just telling her she needed to slow it down every now and then. The pounding on her door continued and Cassie rolled her eyes. There wasn't a doubt in her mind who stood on the other side of the door. Ian wouldn't pound on her door. He'd knock or just come on in, and so would her father and Tessa.

And that left only one rude, unwanted guest.

Shuffling down the hall, probably looking even more stellar than earlier today when Derek had stopped by, Cassie actually laughed. Was he really here to plead for his family back when she looked like death and after he'd left her for some young, hot bimbo? Oh, the irony was not lost on her.

Cassie took her time flipping the lock on the knob and opening the door. Sure enough, Derek stood there, clutching a newspaper. Disapproval settled in his eyes.

"Funny," she told him, leaning against the edge of the door. "That's the same look you wore when you left me. What do you want now?"

He slapped the paper to her chest and pushed past her to enter.

"Come on in," she muttered, holding on to the paper and closing the door. "I thought I told you to have your lawyer contact mine."

Derek scanned the living area, then stretched his neck to see down the hall. "Where's Emily?"

"With Ian." Crossing her arms, crinkling the paper, Cassie sighed. "What do you want, Derek?"

"First of all, I don't want my daughter with a stranger."

Hysterical laughter bubbled out before she could even try to control it. "Seriously? If anyone is a stranger to her, it's you. We've already established what you think of Ian, so state your reason for this unwanted visit or that threat of calling security will become a fast reality."

He pointed toward the paper. "Apparently you haven't seen today's local paper. Maybe your pretty boy is a stranger to you, as well."

Cassie unfolded the paper. She'd play his game if it meant he'd leave sooner.

Her eyes settled on the picture of Lily and Ian. Cassie had known they were having a business meeting the evening before, she'd known they were discussing a major career move for both of them, but she hadn't known the media would spin the story into something…romantic.

Her eyes landed on the headline: Hollywood Starlet on Location Still Finds Time for Romance.

The way their two heads were angled together in the grainy picture did imply something more than a business meeting. The intimate table for two complete with bouquet and candles also added to the ambience of love.

Cassie glanced back up to Derek. "What about it?"

She would not give her ex the satisfaction of letting it get to her, of coming between something she and Ian had built and worked hard at.

"Looks like your boy toy has someone else on the side." Derek smirked. "Is this really what you've moved on to?"

"Why are you here?" she demanded. "What do you want from me?"

"If you'd answered my calls or texts you'd know I want my family back. I had no idea you opted to replace me with such a younger man."

Cassie smacked the paper down on the table beside the door. "Don't you dare judge me. You left me, remember? And if we're casting stones, I'll remind you that when you left, you moved on with a much younger woman with boobs as her only major asset."

Fired up and more than geared for a fight, Cassie advanced on him. "You're just upset because Ian is a real man. He cares about me, about Emily. My looks don't matter, my size doesn't matter and he's taken to Emily like she is his own, which is a hell of a lot more than you ever did for either of us."

Derek clenched his jaw as he loomed over her and held her gaze. "I just want you to know that this man, this kid, really, will get bored with the family life. He'll move on, and then where will you be? I'm man enough to admit I was wrong and that I'm willing to try again."

She hated that she felt a small tug, hated that for months

she'd prayed for this moment. But she loved Ian. How could she deny herself the man she felt she'd been waiting for her whole life?

But on the other hand, how could she deny her daughter the bond of her parents raising her in the same house?

Cassie shook her head, refusing to listen to the conflicting voices in her head. She needed to think, needed to be alone.

"I waited for months for you to come back," she told him, hoping her words would make him squirm, make him feel the heavy dose of guilt he was due. "I cried myself to sleep when I thought of Emily not knowing her father. But you know what? After the tears were spent, I realized that Emily was better off. Both of us were, actually. Neither of us needed a man in our life who didn't put us first. We needed a man who would love us, put our needs above his own selfish ones and be there for us no matter what."

When he opened his mouth, Cassie raised a hand to silence him. "I would've given you the same in return. I married you thinking we were both in love, but I was wrong. You didn't love me, because if you did, you wouldn't have found it so easy to leave me."

"I'm back, though." He reached out, touched her face. "I want my family back, my wife back. I know I made a mistake, but you can't tell me you're ready to throw everything away."

When the door opened behind her, Cassie didn't have to turn to know Ian stood just at the threshold. She closed her eyes and sighed.

"Actually," she whispered. "You already threw it all away."

Derek's eyes darted from hers to just over her shoulder before he dropped his hands. "You can keep the paper. Maybe it will give you something to think about."

She didn't move as he skirted around her. When the door shut once again, Cassie turned slowly to see Ian, hands on his hips. Even with the space between them, Cassie saw so many emotions dancing in his eyes: confusion, hurt, love.

"Where's Emily?" she asked, hoping to keep the conversation on safer ground.

"I actually just left her with Linda. She's taking a nap."

Cassie nodded, worry lacing through her. "What you just saw was—"

"I know what I saw," he murmured. "I know he wants you back. He'd be a fool not to. It's just—"

Ian glanced down, smoothing a hand over the back of his neck, then froze when his gaze landed on the paper. Slowly he picked it up, skimming the front page.

Cassie waited, wondering how he would react.

When he muttered a curse and slammed the paper down, Cassie jumped.

"Tell me this wasn't Derek's defense," Ian begged. "He surely wasn't using me as his battle to win you back."

Shrugging, Cassie crossed her arms around her waist. "It's a pretty damning photograph."

Closing the spacious gap between them, Ian stood within a breath of her and tipped her chin up so she looked him in the eyes. "The media is known for spinning stories to create the best reaction from viewers. It's how they stay in business."

Cassie nodded. "I'm aware of that."

Ian studied her for a moment before he plunged his fingers through her disheveled hair and claimed her lips. The passion, desire and fury all poured from him, and Cassie had to grip his biceps to hold on for the ride.

He attacked her mouth, a man on a mission of proving something, of taking what was his and damning the consequences.

When he pulled away, Ian rested his forehead against hers. "Tell me you believe that I could kiss you like that and have feelings for another woman. Tell me that you don't trust me and all we have here is built on lies. Because if that's the case, I'll leave right now and never come back."

Cassie's throat tightened as she continued to clutch his arms. "I don't believe that, Ian. I know you wouldn't lie to me. You've shown me what a real man is, how a real man treats a lady."

Taking a deep breath, she finally stepped back, away from his hold. "But I also know that this is something I'm going to have to deal with if we're together. The media spinning stories, always being in the limelight."

"I'm an agent, Cassie. Nobody cares about me. If I had been out alone, nobody would've known who I was."

Cassie smiled. "But you were out with the breathtaking Lily Beaumont. All of your clients are famous, Ian. There will be other times, other photos."

Shaking her head, she walked around and finally sank onto the sofa. Ian joined her but didn't touch her. She hated this wedge that had settled between them...a wedge that had formed only once Derek had entered the picture.

"I want to be with you, Cassie," he told her. "As in beyond the movie, beyond next month or even next year. I want to see where this can go, but if the idea of my work will hold you back, maybe we both need to reevaluate what we're doing."

Tears pricked her eyes as she turned to face him fully. "You want to be with me?"

Reaching out to swipe the pad of his thumb across her cheek to clear the rogue tear, Ian smiled. "Yes. I know it's crazy and we've only known each other a short time, but I do want to be with you."

"Is this because my ex is back? Are you feeling threatened?"

Shaking his head, Ian took her shoulders and squeezed. "This has nothing to do with Derek. His appearance is just bad timing, that's all. I can't deny myself the fact that being with you has made me a better person. Finding myself wrapped around yours and Emily's lives makes me want more for myself. I never thought about a family before, but I want to see where this will lead and how we can make it work."

Hope filled Cassie as she threw her arms around Ian's neck and sniffed. "I know I'm a hot mess right now," she told him. "I have no idea how I was lucky enough to get you, but I want to see where we go, too. I'm just sorry you'll have to deal with Derek." Cassie eased back and wiped her cheeks. "He's Emily's father, and even though he abandoned us, I can't deny him if he wants to see her."

"What if he wants custody? Did he mention that again?"

"No. I hope he was just trying to scare me, like you said."

Smoothing her hair behind her ear, Ian smiled and settled his palm against her cheek. "No matter what, I'm here for you. Okay?"

For the first time in a long time, Cassie knew there was something to be hopeful about, something more than her career and Emily to fight for. And that was the love of a good man.

Ian was right. Damn if Derek's visit hadn't come at the worst possible time. Not only was the estate covered in film crew and actors, but Ian had settled so perfectly into her life and now the Belmont Stakes was upon them.

The final of the three most prestigious races in the horse world. There was no way Cassie could possibly think of

Derek and his threats right now…and yet he had left her with a doozy last night.

He'd called her and issued an ultimatum—either she take him back and give their marriage another go or he would go to his lawyer with a plea to get full custody. Of course, she doubted he could, but the threat was there, and even if he didn't get full, there was always a chance he could get shared. And then where would she be?

Cassie sank down onto the bed in her hotel room and rested her head in her hands. Crying would be of no use, but she so wished she could cut loose and absolutely throw a fit. Being an adult flat-out sucked sometimes.

The adjoining door to the bedroom next to hers creaked open and Cassie glanced up to see Tessa standing in the doorway wearing a gray tank top and black yoga pants.

"I know you're not in a good spot, and as much as I think you could use a drink, that won't help us any in tomorrow's race." Tessa held up a shiny gold bag. "But I do have chocolates and I'm willing to share."

Cassie attempted a smile. "Are they at least rum balls?"

Laughing, Tessa crossed the room and sank onto the bed, bumping Cassie's hip. "Sorry. Just decadent white-chocolate truffles. You ready to talk about Derek being back and wreaking havoc? Because it's been all I could do not to say something to you, but I figured you'd tell me on your own."

Cassie took the bag and dug out a chocolate. No, the sweetness wouldn't cure all, but it would certainly take the edge off her rage.

"I was hoping if I ignored the fact he was in town he'd just go away," Cassie said as she bit into the chocolate.

"How's that working?"

"Not well. How did you find out anyway? He's only been in town two days."

Tessa reached into the bag and pulled out a piece for herself. "Ian and Max were discussing the problem, and I may have eavesdropped on their conversation."

Swallowing the bite and reaching for another truffle, Cassie shifted on the bed to face her sister, settling the bag between them. "I planned on telling you. I was just trying to focus on Ian, make sure Emily was all settled with Linda before we left and praying Derek didn't try to get back onto Stony Ridge while we were gone. I've got security keeping an eye out for him."

"Can you legally do that?" Tessa asked.

Shrugging, Cassie smoothed her hair back and tugged the rubber band from her wrist to secure the knotty mess. "I have no clue. But if he's trespassing on the property, that's all the guards need to know to have him escorted off. If he wants to play the poor-father card, I doubt he'll have a leg to stand on."

"After the race tomorrow, go on home." Tessa reached in the bag and offered Cassie another chocolate, but Cassie wasn't in the mood anymore. "Nash and I will make sure everything is handled and taken care of. Take the truck Nash brought, and he and I can take the trailer and other truck."

Cassie bit her lip when tears threatened. "I don't want him to ruin this, Tessa. We've worked too hard, come too far, and we're both retiring after this season. I can't let him destroy our dreams of going out on top."

Reaching between them to take Cassie's hand, Tessa smiled. "Derek won't destroy anything. You won't give him that power. He's a jerk and he'll probably be gone when we get back because you weren't falling all over yourself to take him back when he appeared on your doorstep."

"He's threatening to file for custody," Cassie whispered.

Tessa let out a string of words that would've made their mother's face turn red. "He's an ass, Cassie. No judge will let him take Emily."

"What about joint custody?"

With a shrug, Tessa shook her head. "Honestly, I don't know, but the man has been gone almost a year, so I would certainly hope no judge would allow someone so restless to help raise a child."

Cassie had the same thoughts, but life and the legal system weren't always fair.

Flinging herself onto the bed, Cassie crossed her arms over her head. "I just never thought I'd be in this situation, you know? I mean, I married Derek thinking we'd be together forever. Then when we had Emily I really thought my family was complete and we were happy. Derek leaving was a bomb I hadn't expected, but now that he's back, I don't want him. I feel nothing but anger and resentment."

Tessa lay on her back next to Cassie and sighed. "You know, between me, Dad, Grant, Linda and Ian, Derek doesn't stand a chance. There's no way we'd let him just take Emily without a fight. If the man wants to play daddy, he'll have to actually stick around and prove he can man up."

"I agree," Cassie told her, lacing her fingers behind her head and staring up at the ceiling. "I won't deny my daughter the chance of knowing her father if I truly believe he won't desert her in a year just when she's getting used to him. I will do everything in my power to protect her heart from him."

And wasn't that just the saddest statement? Protecting a little girl's heart from her own father. But Derek had given her little choice.

"So, you want to tell me what you and Ian are doing?"

Tessa asked. "Because I'm pretty sure the two of you are much more than a fling."

Cassie laughed. "Yeah, we're definitely much more than a fling."

"Who knew when you got locked in that attic the man of your dreams would come to your rescue?"

"Technically he didn't rescue me," Cassie clarified.

Tessa glanced over, patted Cassie's leg and smiled. "Oh, honey. He's rescued you—you just might not see it yet."

She was right. Ian had come along at a time in her life when the last thing she'd wanted was a man. But he'd shown her love, shown her daughter love. He'd shown her what true intimacy was all about. When she'd been sick he hadn't thought twice about taking Emily, even though he knew next to nothing about babies.

He made Cassie's life better.

There was no way that she could not fight for what they had. Maybe she should look into a riding school in California. With her income and her knowledge, she technically could start it anywhere.

She had to deal with Derek first; then she would figure out how being far away from her family would work.

Tessa's brows lifted. "I know that look," she said. "You're plotting something. Share or I'll take my chocolates back to my room."

"Just thinking of the future," Cassie replied with a smile. "Thinking of my school. I've already started putting the wheels in motion for Stony Ridge, but who's to say that's where it has to be?"

Tessa hugged her. "I was so afraid this is what you'd do. Damn, I'm going to miss you if you move."

"Don't go tearing up on me," Cassie ordered. "Ian hasn't asked me, but if he did, I can't say that I would tell him no. On the other hand, Grant has a home out in L.A., too, so I'm sure you'd spend time out there."

"It wouldn't be the same." Tessa sniffed, blinked back tears. "But I want you happy and this is truly the happiest I've seen you in your entire life. I'll support any decision you make."

Cassie reached out, grabbed Tessa's hand and settled in with the fact she'd move heaven and earth to be with Ian. And now she couldn't wait to get home to tell him just that.

Twenty

Ian had a wonderful surprise planned for Cassie. He couldn't wait for her to get home.

Not only had Tessa and Cassie taken the Belmont Stakes and the coveted Triple Crown, but Cassie was on her way back and Ian had to get the stage set. They had so much to celebrate.

Very few had ever taken home the Triple Crown title, and Tessa was the first female jockey to own the honor. The Barrington sisters had officially made history and Ian was so proud he'd been able to witness a small portion of their success. He hated he wasn't there in person, though.

Ian had opted to stay behind for two reasons. So they could both concentrate on their own work without distractions and to see if he could handle being without her.

He couldn't.

After a perfect morning in which Lily officially signed with his agency, he was now in town hitting up the quaint little florist, about to buy an exorbitant amount of flowers in a variety of colors and styles. He wanted her cottage to be drowning in bouquets for the evening he had planned. Not only because he had high hopes about their future, but because she deserved to be placed on a pedestal after such a milestone win.

He may have also had Linda's help in the matter of planning.

The days they'd been apart had been a smack of reality to the face. He didn't want to be without her, without Emily. He was ready to make a family with them.

He also realized that love and marriage—and fatherhood—weren't scary at all once you found the person who totally completed you.

This family had instantly been so welcoming, so loving, and Ian couldn't be happier. From Linda to sweet Emily, he was so overwhelmed by how easily they accepted him. And now Cassie was about to get the surprise of her life.

As Ian rounded the building that housed the flower shop, he smacked into someone…Derek. *Great.*

"You're still in town?" Ian asked, eyeing the man clutching a massive bouquet of roses.

Derek shielded his eyes from the warm afternoon sun. "I'm not leaving until I get what I want."

Becoming more irritated by the moment, and a tad amused, Ian crossed his arms over his chest. "That will be a while, considering what you want is mine."

"Yours? My family is not your property," Derek clarified.

"They're also not your family. Not anymore. Cassie made her choice."

"Did she? Because the Cassie I know loves family." Derek adjusted the flowers to his other hand and shifted beneath the awning of the flower shop to shield himself from the sun. "It means more to her than anything. Do you think she'd honestly choose some young guy who she just met over the father of her child? Because I can assure you, she'll put Emily's needs ahead of her own."

There was a ring of truth to Derek's words, but there was also no way Ian would show any emotion or allow this guy to step into the life he was trying to build.

"Don't blame me or Cassie because you realized too late that you made a mistake," Ian said, propping his hands on his hips and resisting the urge to take those flowers, throw them on the ground and crush them. "Cassie and I have something, and there's no way you're going to come charging in like you belong. You missed your chance."

Derek smiled. "I didn't miss anything. You see, no matter how much you hate me, I am Emily's father. She will want to know me and I will make damn sure my lawyer does everything he can to get my baby girl in my life. Now, if Cassie wants to come, too, that's her decision, but I'll fight dirty to get what I want. Considering the fact that you are a Hollywood playboy, combined with the perfectly timed image in the paper, I don't see how I can't use that against Cassie. Obviously she's eager to get any man's attention—"

All control snapped as Ian fisted Derek's shirt and slammed him against the old brick building. Petals flew everywhere as the bouquet also smacked against the wall.

"Listen here, you little prick." It was all Ian could do not to pummel the jerk. "I will not be bullied into giving up what I want, and Cassie will not be blackmailed, either. If you want to see your daughter, then go through your attorney the proper way, but don't you dare use your own child as a pawn. Only a sick ass would do that."

Stepping back, Ian jerked the bouquet from Derek's hand and threw it down on the sidewalk. He'd held back long enough and Ian knew full well whom that arrangement was meant for.

Ian issued one final warning through gritted teeth. "Stay away from me and mine."

As he walked away, he didn't go into the flower store as originally intended. He had some thinking to do.

No, he wouldn't be intimidated by some jerk who thought he could blackmail his way back into Cassie's life, but if Ian's presence was going to cause issues with custody of Emily, Ian knew he had a difficult decision to make.

As he headed back to his sporty rental car, the small box in his pocket felt heavier than ever.

Cassie had never been so eager to return from a race, especially one as important as this one.

They'd done it. The Barrington women had conquered the racing world and brought home the Triple Crown. Cassie was pretty sure she'd be smiling in her sleep for years to come. She and Tessa had worked so hard, prayed even harder, and all their endless hours and years of training had paid off.

But beyond the joy of the racing season coming to an amazing end, Cassie couldn't wait to celebrate with Emily and Ian and wanted to get Derek taken care of so he would leave her alone once and for all.

Because she'd gotten home later than intended, Linda had stayed in the cottage and put Emily to bed. Now Cassie was alone, her baby sleeping down the hall and unpacked bags still just inside the door where she'd dropped them.

She had to see Ian now. Too many days had passed since she'd seen him, touched him. Each day she was away from him she realized just how much she truly loved him.

A gentle tap on her front door had her jerking around. The glow of the porch light illuminated Ian's frame through the frosted glass. She'd know that build anywhere and a shiver of excitement crept over her at the thought of seeing him again. She hadn't realized she could miss someone so much.

But the second she flung the door open, ready to launch into his strong hold, she froze. Something was wrong. He wasn't smiling, wasn't even reaching for her. Actually, his hands were shoved in his pockets.

"What's wrong?" she asked, clutching the door frame.

Ian said nothing as his gaze moved over her. Something flashed through his eyes as he settled back on her face…regret?

"Ian?"

He stepped over the threshold, paused within a breath of her and then scooted around her. After closing the door behind her, she leaned against it, unsure of what to say or how to act.

Her eyes locked on to Ian's as silence quickly became the third party present. Moments ago she'd had nothing but hope filling her heart. Now fear had laid a heavy blanket over that hope.

"This is so much harder than I thought it would be," he whispered, his eyes glistening. "I had tonight planned so different."

"You're scaring me, Ian."

Wrapping her arms around her waist, Cassie rubbed her hands up and down her bare arms to ward off the chill.

"I love you, Cassie. I've never said that to another human being, not even my own parents." Ian stepped closer but didn't touch her. "Tonight I thought I would tell you I loved you, show you that I can't live without you and Emily, but I've thought about it all evening and came to the hardest decision of my life."

Cassie wasn't a fool. She knew exactly what he was

going to say. "How dare you," she whispered through tears clogging her throat. "You tell me you love me a breath before you're about to break things off? Because that's what this is, right?"

Ian ran a hand over his face. "Damn it, Cassie. I'm letting you go to make things easier. I can't keep you in my life, knowing I could be the one thing that stands between you and keeping custody of your daughter."

Realization quickly dawned on Cassie. "You bastard. You let Derek get to you, didn't you? I never took you for a coward, Ian."

"I'm not a coward, and if Emily weren't in the picture I would stay and fight for you…and I'd win. But Emily deserves a chance to know her father, and I can't stand the thought of you sharing custody or possibly losing because Derek is going to fight dirty. He said it himself. This way, with me gone, maybe you two can come to some sort of peaceful middle ground."

Torn between hurt, love and anger, Cassie tried to rein in her emotions. "You're leaving me because you're afraid. I understand that you didn't have a great childhood, which makes me respect you all the more for stepping up and loving Emily the way you have. But don't you dare leave now when things get tough. I thought you were more of a man than that."

He jerked as if she'd slapped him. "Trust me, Cass. In the long run, this is the best for Emily."

"What about me?" she cried. "I love my daughter and her needs will always come first, but you say you love me. So what about that? What about us?"

The glistening in his eyes intensified a second before a tear slid down his cheek. He didn't make a move to swipe it away and Cassie couldn't stop staring at the wet track.

Her heart literally ached for the man who was trying

to be strong and, in his own way, do the right thing. But damn it, she wanted more and she thought she'd found it with him.

As she stepped forward, Ian took a step back. And that lone action severed any thread of hope she had been holding on to.

"I'm barely hanging on here," he whispered. "You can't touch me. I have to be strong for both of us. Just think about what I said. You'll know that I'm right. There's no other way if you want to keep Emily. Derek won't play fair, and if I'm in your life, he'll use that against you."

He took in a deep, shuddering breath. "I want to be part of your life, Cass. I want to be part of Emily's. But it's because I want so much to be a part of your family that I must protect you both, and unfortunately, that means I need to step aside."

Cassie hated the emotions whirling about inside her. So much love for this man and so much hatred toward another. Damn Ian for being noble.

"If you're not staying to fight for me and with me, then leave." Blinking back tears and clenching her fists at her side to keep from wrapping her arms around him, Cassie held his gaze. "You've done what you came to do, so go."

Ian slid a hand from his pocket, clutched something and reached out to place it on the end table by the sofa. "What I came to do was quite the opposite," he told her as he took a step toward her. "But I want you to have that and remember that I do love you, Cassie. No matter what you think right now. I'll always love you."

Without touching her, without even a kiss goodbye, Ian stepped around her and quietly walked out of her life. Drawing in a shaky breath, she took a step toward the end table and saw a blue box. Her heart in her throat, Cassie reached for the box. Her hands shook because she knew exactly what would be beneath that velvety lid.

Lifting the lid with a slow creak, Cassie gasped. Three square-cut stones nestled perfectly in a pewter band had tears spilling down both cheeks. Cassie's hand came to her mouth to hold back the sob that threatened to escape.

Ian had put all of their birthstones in the ring...a ring he'd planned on giving her when he told her he loved her.

Unable to help herself, she pulled the band from the box and slid it on. A perfect fit—just like the man who had walked out the door moments ago.

As she studied the ring on her finger, Cassie knew there was no way she would go down without a fight. No way at all. Emily would come first, as always, but who said she couldn't have the man of her dreams *and* her family?

If Derek wanted to fight dirty, well, bring it on, because Cassie had just gotten a whole new level of motivation to fuel her fire. And there was no way in hell Derek would take her child or the dreams Cassie had for a future with Ian.

The depth of Ian's love was so far beyond what she'd dared to imagine. His strength as a man and father was exactly what she needed, wanted...deserved. She wouldn't let his sacrifice go to waste.

Twenty-One

Ian wasn't sure why he didn't book a trip somewhere exotic to just get away. He'd come back to L.A. after breaking things off with Cassie. Max had more than understood his need to leave, but his friend had also had some choice words for him regarding the stupidity of his decision.

Ian wished there'd been another way. He'd had many sleepless nights looking for another way to protect Cassie and Emily, but it was because he loved them so much—because they *were* his family—he knew he needed to remove himself from their lives.

The pain after he'd left was unlike anything he'd ever known. Sharp, piercing pain had settled into the void in his heart that Cassie and Emily had left. But he also knew, in the long run, this was the best for the ladies he'd quickly grown to love.

Now, back in his beachfront home, he saw Cassie and that precious baby. How had two females he'd known only a short time infiltrated every single corner of his life? There wasn't a spot in his house, his mind or his heart that they hadn't left their imprint on.

He'd been home almost a month, and in the phone calls and texts between Max and Lily, he knew the filming was nearing the end. He hadn't asked about Cassie.... He just couldn't. The thought of her possibly playing house with Derek to keep the peace for Emily nearly crippled him.

Ian sank down onto the sand and pulled his knees up to his chest. The orange glow from the sunset made for a beautiful backdrop and not for the first time was he elated to have all of this for his backyard.

But he'd give it up in a heartbeat for a chance at happiness with Cassie. Letting her go was hands down the hardest thing he'd ever done in his entire life.

He hadn't been lying when he'd said this decision was better for Emily in the long run. When he'd been younger he would've given anything for his parents to have stayed together. Perhaps his father would've been a little more relaxed and his mother not so much of a free spirit always seeking attention from men.

Ian couldn't alter Emily's future by coming between her parents. His broken heart was minor in comparison to their safety. All that mattered was that sweet Emily wasn't a pawn, that he gave her the best chance to know her father. A chance he'd never had.

Damn it, he loved that little girl. He missed those little fingers wrapped around his thumb as he gave her a nighttime bottle. He missed that little two-toothed grin she'd offer for no apparent reason.

He missed everything...even the diaper changes.

"Beautiful place you have here."

Ian jerked his head over his shoulder, his heart nearly

stopping at the sight of Cassie in a little green sundress, her hair whipping about her shoulders and Emily on her hip.

"I was just in the neighborhood and was curious if you had room for two more," she went on, not coming any closer.

In an instant, Ian was on his feet. "Room for two? Were you wanting to stay here?"

Cassie shrugged, her face tipped up to hold his gaze as he moved in closer. "Your house, your heart. Wherever you have room."

Ian's knees weakened. She'd come for him. When he'd thought they were finished, when he'd thought he'd done the right thing by setting her free, she'd come to him.

"I'll always have room in my heart for you and Emily." Ian reached out, slid a crimson curl behind her ear. "But my house? That depends on what's going on with you and Derek."

Cassie grabbed his hand before he could pull away from her. "Derek is being taken care of by my team of attorneys. I hired three to make sure he didn't blackmail me, you or use Emily as a bargaining chip. He's agreed to supervised visitation because Emily is young and would view him as a stranger. He's not allowed to take her from the state for any reason and I have approval over any and all visits."

Shocked, Ian merely stared. When Emily reached for him, his heart tumbled. Pulling her into his arms, he held her tight, breathing in her sweet scent.

"I've missed you," he whispered into her ear. Her little arms came around his neck and Ian had to physically fight back tears.

"We've missed *you*," Cassie told him. "But I had to make sure Derek was being handled before I could come to you."

Ian lifted his head, slid his arm around Cassie's waist

and pulled her against his side. This right here was worth everything. The heartache he'd felt, the worry, the sleepless nights.

"If you ever try to be noble again, I'll go to the press with horrid lies." Cassie smiled up at him. "I know why you left—I even admire your decision on some level—but being without you for weeks was a nightmare. I never want to be without you again."

Ian slid his lips over hers. "What about your family? What about the school?"

Reaching up to pat his cheek, Cassie smiled. "Emily and I are staying here for a while. As for the school, I'd really like to open it on the estate, but I'll move it to California if you're needed here."

Ian couldn't believe what he was hearing. She was willing to part with her life, live across the country from her family, her rock, all because of him.

"I'd never ask you to leave your family," he told her. "I actually want to be near them. What do you say we keep this home for our getaways and vacations? We can live on the estate or build nearby. The choice is totally up to you, but I want you to have the school at Stony Ridge."

Cassie's smile widened, those sparkling blue eyes glistening. "Sounds like a plan. Of course, we're missing something, you know."

Curious, Ian drew back slightly. "What's that?"

"Well, I've worn my ring since you left." She held up her left ring finger and the sight had his heart jumping. "I assumed that this ring had a question that went along with it. I mean, I'm assuming the man I've fallen in love with plans on carrying out his intentions."

Ian looked to Emily. "What do you think, sweetheart? Should I ask your mommy to marry me?"

Emily clapped her hands and grinned. "Mom-mom-mom."

Laughing, Ian glanced back to Cassie. So many emotions swam in her eyes. So much hope and love, and it was all for him.

"How did I get to be so lucky?" he murmured.

Shrugging, Cassie said, "I'd say fate has been pushing us together since the moment I fell into your arms."

Pulling her tighter against him, he held the two most precious ladies. "This right here, in my arms, is my world. Nothing will come between us again. Not an ex, not my tendency to be noble, nothing. You're mine, Cassie."

Easing back to look down into her eyes, Ian saw his entire future looking back at him. "Tell me you'll marry me. Tell me you'll let me be Em's dad. That you'll even teach me all about horses. I want to be part of everything in your life."

"I wouldn't have it any other way," she told him, wiping a lone tear that had slid down her cheek. "Besides, I still owe you that horseback ride you've never been on."

Ian laughed. "How about we lay Emily down for a nap and we'll discuss other plans for our family?"

The gleam in her eye told him she hadn't missed his hidden meaning. "*Our family.* Those are two of the most beautiful words I've ever heard."

He kissed her once again. "Then let's get started on building it."

* * * * *

CARRYING THE
LOST HEIR'S CHILD

JULES BENNETT

To Gems for Jules—
the best street team an author could ask for!
You all are so amazing and supportive. I love you all!

One

The masculine aroma. The strength of those arms. The hard chest her cheek rested against...she'd know this man anywhere. She'd watched him across the grassy meadows, dreamed of him...made love to him.

Lily Beaumont struggled to wake and realized all too quickly she didn't have a clue how she'd gotten here.

Or more to the point, where was "here"?

The straw rustled against the concrete floor beneath her. She lay cradled in Nash James's lap, his strong arms around her midsection. What on earth had happened?

"Relax. You fainted."

That low, soothing voice washed over her. Lily lifted her lids to see Nash's bright blue eyes locked on hers. Those mesmerizing eyes surrounded by dark, thick lashes never failed to send a thrill shooting through her. No leading man she shared the screen with had ever been this breathtaking...or mysterious.

But, she'd fainted? She never fainted.

Oh, yeah. She'd been walking to the stables to talk to Nash...

"Oh, no." Lily grabbed her still-spinning head. Reality

slammed back into her mind, making her recall why she was in the stables. "This isn't happening."

Rough, callused fingertips slid away strands of hair that had fallen across her forehead. "Just lie still," he told her. "No rush. Everyone is gone for the day."

Meaning the cast and crew had all either gone to the hotel or into their on-site trailers. Thank God. The last thing she needed was a big fuss over her fainting spell, because then she'd have some explaining to do.

Just a few short months ago Lily started shooting a film depicting the life of Damon Barrington, dynamic horse owner and a force to be reckoned with. The Barrington estate had become her home away from home and the quiet, intriguing groom whose lap she currently lay in had quickly caught her attention.

Before she knew it, she'd been swept into a secret affair full of sneaking around, ripping off clothes and plucking straw pieces from her hair...which led her to this moment, this life-altering moment when she was about to drop a major bomb in Nash's life.

All the trouble they'd gone through to keep their escapades a secret were all in vain. No way could this news stay hidden.

"Nash." She reached up to cup his face, the prickle of his short beard beneath her palm a familiar sensation. "I'm sorry."

His brows drew together, worry etched across his handsome, tanned face, and he shook his head. "You can't help that you passed out. But you scared the life out of me."

Lily swallowed, staring at such an attractive, spellbinding man could make a woman forget everything around her... like the fact that she was carrying this man's child.

"Are you feeling okay?" he asked, studying her face. "Do you need something to eat?"

Just the thought of food had her gag reflex wanting to

kick in again. Weren't pregnant women supposed to be sick in the mornings? What was this all-day nonsense?

Lily started to sit up, but Nash placed a hand over her shoulder. "Hold on. Let me help you."

Gently, he eased her into a sitting position as he came to his feet. Then he lifted her, keeping her against his firm, strong body the entire time. Strong arms encircled her waist again and Lily wanted to seek the comfort and support he was offering. This might have been the first tender moment between them, considering anytime she'd come to meet him after dark they hurried to the loft where their passion completely took control.

How on earth would he react to the news? She was still reeling from the shocker herself, but she refused to keep this a secret. He had a right to know. She honestly had no clue what Nash would say, what he would do. A baby didn't necessarily affect his line of work. Hers, on the other hand…

She'd been burned so badly before and had fought hard to overcome the public scandal that ensued. How would he handle being thrust into the limelight?

Lily groaned. Once the story broke, the press would circle her like vultures—and they would make her private life a top headline. People were starving, homeless, fighting wars and the media opted to nose their way into celebrities' lives and feed that into homes around the world rather than something that was actually newsworthy.

Lily loved being an actress, loved the various characters she got to tap in to and uncover. But she hated the lack of privacy. A girl couldn't even buy toilet paper without being spotted. Lily prided herself on being professional, doing her job and doing it well, and staying out of the media's greedy, sometimes evil, clutches…a nearly impossible feat.

"You okay now?" he asked, his breath tickling the side of her face.

Nodding, Lily stepped away, immediately missing the warmth of his body, but thankful the dizziness had passed.

Over the past couple months she'd actually come to crave his touch, miss him when he wasn't near her. She should've known then she was getting in over her head where this virtual stranger was concerned. Their passion had swept her into a world she'd never experienced before. How could any single woman turn away from a man who touched her beneath the surface, who looked so deep within she was certain he could see in to her soul?

A physical connection was something she could handle. But all of those nights of sneaking around, of giving in to their desires had caught up with them. Now they would have to pivot away from the sex-only relationship and actually talk about the future…a future she'd never expected to have with this man.

With her back to him, Lily tried to conjure up the right words, the words that would soften the blow, but really was there a proper way to tell someone they were going to be a father? No matter how gentle the words were, the impact and end result would still be the same.

"Nash—"

Before she could finish her sentence, Nash took hold of her shoulder, eased her around and framed her face with his firm hands. Hypnotized by those vibrant blue eyes, she said nothing else as his mouth claimed hers.

And that right there was the crux of their relationship. Passion. Desire. Instant clothes falling to the floor.

Some might have said having a secret affair in the stables on a film set was not the classiest of moves, but Lily didn't care. She'd been classy her whole life…now she wanted to be naughty. The secret they shared made their covert encounters all the more thrilling.

Who knew Hollywood's "girl next door," as they'd dubbed her, had a wild side? Well, they'd caught a glimpse of it with the scandal, but she had since reclaimed her good girl status. She certainly had never been this passionate with or for a man. Definitely not the jerk who had used her and exploited her early in her career.

Before she'd become a recognized name, she'd fallen for another rookie actor. He'd completely blind-sided her by filming her without her knowledge. Their most intimate moments had been staged; everything about their relationship had been a lie. After that scandal, Lily had to fight to get to where she was now.

Nash's arms enveloped her and Lily was rendered defenseless as his mouth continued its assault on hers. Her arms slid up the front of his shirt, taut muscles firm beneath her palms.

He eased back slightly, resting his forehead against hers. "You sure you're feeling okay? Not dizzy anymore?"

"I'm okay," she assured him, clutching his T-shirt.

Nash's lips nipped at hers. "I missed you today. I kept seeing you and Max together. It was all I could do to ignore the way his arms were around you. His lips where mine should be."

Chills spread over her body. Tingles started low in her belly and coursed throughout. That hint of jealousy pouring from Nash's lips thrilled her more than it should…considering this was supposed to be a fling.

"We were acting," she murmured against his mouth. "You know we're playing a young couple in love."

Lily had wanted to play the role of the late Rose Barrington since news of the project had first spread, and having Max Ford as the leading man was perfect. She and Max had been friends for years…so much so that he was like a brother to her.

Nash's hands slid between them, started peeling down the top of her strapless sundress.

"If Max weren't married with a baby, I'd think he was trying to steal my time with you."

Baby. Just the word threw a dose of reality right smack-dab in the middle of their minor make-out session.

Lily covered Nash's hands with her own and eased back. "We need to talk."

Vibrant eyes stared back at her beneath heavy lids. "Sounds like you're breaking things off. I know we never discussed being exclusive." Nash attempted a smile. "Don't take my Max joke so seriously."

Shaking her head, Lily took a deep breath and pushed through her fear and doubts. "I didn't take you for the jealous type. Besides, I know what this is between us."

Or, what it had started out being.

"Oh, baby, I'm jealous." He jerked her against his body. "Now that I've had you, I don't like seeing another man's hands on you, but I know this is your job and I love watching you work."

"I can't think when your hands are on me," she told him, stepping back once again to try to put some distance between temptation and the truth.

A corner of Nash's devilish mouth kicked up. "You say that like it's a bad thing. Because I'm thinking plenty when my hands are on you."

Smoothing a hand through her hair, Lily tried to form the right words. Since seeing the two blue lines on the stick this morning and confirming what she'd already assumed, she'd been playing conversations on how to break the news over and over in her mind. But now it was literally show time and she had nothing but fear and bundles of nerves consuming her.

"Nash…"

Abandoning his joking, Nash's brows drew together as he reached for her once again. "What is it? If you're worried about when you leave, I don't expect anything from you."

"If only it were that easy," she whispered, looking down at his scuffed boots, inches from her pink polished toes.

Nash was a hard worker, so unlike the Hollywood playboys who always tried to capture her attention. Money and fame meant nothing to her—she had plenty of both. She preferred a man who worked hard, played hard and truly cared for other people...a man like Nash.

This wasn't supposed to happen. None of it. Not the deeper feelings, not the lingering looks that teetered on falling beyond lust and certainly not a baby that would bind them forever.

"Lily, just say it. It can't be that bad."

She met and held his questioning stare. "I'm pregnant."

Okay, maybe it *could* be that bad.

Pregnant? What the hell? Suddenly he felt like passing out himself.

Nash stared at Lily, knowing full well she wasn't lying. After all, she looked just as freaked out as he felt and what would she have to gain by lying to him? She didn't know his true identity, or how something like this would be perfect blackmail material.

In Lily's eyes, and the eyes of everyone else on the estate, he was a simple groom who kept to himself and did his job. Little did they know the real reason he'd landed at the Barringtons' doorstep.

And a baby thrown into the mix?

Talk about irony and coming full circle.

"You're positive?" he asked, knowing she wouldn't have told him had she not been sure.

Lily nodded, wrapping her arms around her middle and worrying her bottom lip. "I've had a suspicion for several days, but I confirmed this morning."

Well, this certainly put a speed bump in all the plans he had for his immediate future here at Stony Ridge Acres. Not to mention life in general. A baby wasn't something he was opposed to, just something he'd planned later down the road... after a wife came into the picture.

"I have no idea what to say," he told her, raking a hand through his hair that was way longer than he'd ever had. "I... damn, I wasn't expecting this."

Lily kept looking at him as if she was waiting for him to explode or deny the fact the baby was his. Of course, she could've slept with someone else, but considering that they'd been together almost every night for nearly the past two months, he highly doubted it.

Besides, Lily wasn't like that. He many not know much about her on a personal level, but he knew enough to know she wasn't a woman who slept around. Despite that whole sex scandal she'd endured years ago, Nash wasn't convinced she was some crazed nympho.

But he also wasn't naive and he wasn't just an average groom, so he needed to play this safe and protect himself from all angles.

"The baby is yours," she stated, as if she could sense where his thoughts were going. "I haven't been with any-body since months before I even came here."

"I thought you said you were on birth control."

"I am," she countered. "Nothing is foolproof, though. I'm assuming it happened that one time we…"

"Didn't use a condom."

One time in all those secret rendezvous he had thought he'd put one in his wallet, but they'd used it already. They'd quickly discussed how they were both clean, amidst clothes flying all over the loft floor, and they'd come to the mutual decision to go ahead… Thus the reason for this milestone, life-altering talk they were having now.

Emotions, scenarios, endless questions all swirled through his mind. What on earth did he know about babies or parenting? All he knew was how hard his mother worked to keep them in a meager apartment. She'd never once complained, never once acted worried. She was the most courageous, determined woman he'd ever known. Traits she'd passed down to him, which gave him the strength to carry on with his original plans, even with the shocking news of the baby. He would not let his child down, but he had to follow through and take what he had come for.

"I don't expect anything from you, Nash," Lily went on as if she couldn't handle the silence. "But I wasn't going to keep this a secret, either. Secrets always become exposed at the wrong time and I felt you deserved to know. It's up to you whether you want to be part of this baby's life."

Secrets, hidden babies. Wow. The irony kept getting harsher and harsher as if fate was laughing at him. This hurdle she'd placed in front of him really had him at a cross-roads. What started out as a fling had now escalated into something personal, intimate…anchoring him in for the long term. Because now he couldn't keep pretending to be someone he wasn't, unfortunately he couldn't come clean with his identity, either.

He wanted to give his child, and Lily, the absolute best of everything. Even though Lily wasn't financially strained, Nash would be front and center in his child's life in every single way. How the hell could he do that without her discovering his identity?

Damn it. He'd never, ever intended for her to be hurt, but he'd passed the point of no return and now the inevitable heartbreak lay in the very near future.

She was never supposed to know who he really was. She was supposed to be gone well before he revealed himself. But now she would be part of his life forever and there was no escaping that hard fact.

"I would never leave you alone in this, Lily." He stepped forward, sliding his hands up over her smooth, bare shoulders. His thumbs caressed the edge of her jaw as an ache settled deep within him, knowing he would cause her even more pain. "How are you feeling? I assume the pregnancy is why you passed out?"

"I'm feeling okay. I've been very nauseous for several days, but this is the first time I've fainted." Her eyes sought his as a smile tugged at her unpainted lips. "I'm glad you were there to catch me."

"Me, too."

He still craved her, ached for her, even with the stunning news. Nash slid his mouth across hers, needing the contact and comfort that only she could provide. When he'd go back to his small rental cottage at night, he'd long for her even though he'd just been intimate with her. Nash had never been swept into such a fast, intense affair before.

And his attraction had nothing to do with her celebrity or her status as one of Hollywood's most beautiful leading ladies. Lily was genuine, not high maintenance or stuffy. Nash honestly admired her. The fact that she was sexy as hell and the best lover he'd ever had was just a bonus.

Her lips moved beneath his, her arms wrapped around his neck as her fingertips toyed with the ends of his hair. Even though they'd been secretly seeing each other for a couple of months, their passion had never once lessened. This woman was so responsive, so perfectly matched for him that he simply couldn't get enough.

Right now they had more pressing issues to deal with... not to mention the ones he had to face on his own.

Damn it. He'd wanted to keep her out of his own sordid affairs and keep things strictly physical. But now Lily discovering the truth about him was unavoidable. There was no way he could avoid the crushing blow that would eventually come down. He could delay the bombshell, weigh his options, because he didn't just have Lily and a baby to think about...he had another family to consider.

Stepping back, Nash studied her, processing just how vulnerable she was right at this moment and knew the end result of his lies would be the same. Once she figured out who he was, she would want nothing to do with him. There was no way in hell he'd be absent from his child's life, though, which meant Lily couldn't be rid of him no matter how much she would come to hate him.

"I'll walk you to your trailer so you can pack your things."

Lily jerked back. "Pack my things?"

"You're coming to stay with me."

Lily completely removed herself from his touch and crossed her arms over her chest. "Stay with you? Why on earth would I do that?"

"So I can take care of you."

Laughing, Lily shook her head. "I'm not dying, Nash. I'm having a baby."

"My baby," he corrected. "I want you with me, Lily."

"How am I going to explain why I'm living with you and not in my trailer? Nobody knows about our affair."

Nash shrugged. "I don't care what they think. I care about your health and our baby."

"Well I care," she all but shouted, throwing her hands to the side. "The media is just waiting to publish something juicy on me. Don't you understand that I have a career, a life, and I can't throw it away because you want to take charge? I've worked too hard to overcome the reputation Hollywood first gave me. I'm no longer the wild child of the industry. I'm respected and I'd like to keep it that way."

Fine, so he was thinking selfishly, but still, he refused to let her go through this alone. Just the thought of his mother being in this position once upon a time had his stomach tightening. Besides, this was Lily. She was a drug in his system and having her close by at all times would only feed their sexual appetite even further.

Maybe he needed to rein in the testosterone. But only for now and only because he refused to back down. He would still find a way to keep her close whether she liked it or not. Yes, he wanted the sex, but now that there was a child involved...he wanted to be right there every step of the way for his son or daughter.

"Fine. I'll come stay with you."

Lily raised a brow and tilted her head. "Seriously, Nash. I'm fine. I'm not going to do anything but sleep and work."

"That's what concerns me," he retorted. "You're getting tired and you're pushing yourself because the film is almost finished. You passed out, for crying out loud."

"I can't stop working."

Moments ago he'd been ready to take her up to the loft. Now he was struggling with how many more lies he would have to tell before this was all over.

Horses shifted in their stalls behind him, the sunset cast a bright orange glow straight through the wide-open stable doors. The setting epitomized calm and serenity...too bad the storm inside him was anything but.

"What about after you're done filming? What will we do about the baby?"

And there it was. The ultimate question that wedged heavily between them, but he had to throw it out there. He had to know what her plans were. He wasn't ready for a family by any means, but considering he and Lily lived on opposite sides of the country, they needed to figure out how they could both be in this child's life.

Lily smoothed her hair away from her face, turned away from him and sighed. "I don't know, Nash. I truly don't know."

They had time to consider how to deal with the baby. For now, Nash needed to stick with his original agenda and nothing could get in his way. He'd done enough spying, enough eavesdropping to calculate his next move.

He'd had many reasons—professional and personal— for taking on a new identity. But the main reason was the horses he needed from Damon. Those horses were the final pieces in the stable he'd spent years creating. He would move heaven and earth to get them.

As he watched Lily, her worried expression, her still-flat belly, Nash came to the realization that the truth he'd come here to disclose had nothing to do with Lily. Yet, because of a decades-old secret, Lily and his baby might pay the price.

All he had to do was figure out a way to get Damon to sell him the horses, go back to his own estate and keep his child in his life.

One monumental obstacle at a time.

Two

Well, she'd lost only part of the battle. She wasn't going back to Nash's place, but he was escorting her to her trailer. And she was almost positive he intended to spend the night.

A thrill shot through her, but would their cover be blown? He'd promised to be up and in the stables working before sunrise so he shouldn't be spotted. She didn't want him to think she was ashamed, far from it. Unfortunately, her reputation was always at stake and after the scandal from years ago, the press would love to see her "backslide" into bad girl mode. She refused to give them any fodder.

Nash knew of the sex video that had been leaked and he knew how sensitive she was about her privacy. Being a very private, secretive person himself only made their hidden affair the perfect setup. They'd been able to sneak around on the private grounds for months now.

Thankfully, the press wasn't on-site because of the security who kept them outside the gates. Still, she worried. What if a member of the crew spotted them together? What if they leaked a story? She couldn't endure another scandal, she just didn't have the energy to fight it, and she wouldn't put her mother through that again.

"Relax." Nash squeezed her hand. "Nobody can see us. It's dark."

He was right. Nobody was around, but she was used to being in the loft of the stables where she was sure no one would see or hear them. Right now, walking across the Barringtons' vast estate to head toward her on-site trailer, Lily just felt so exposed. Their footsteps were light and all was quiet except for an occasional frog croaking, a few crickets chirping and a horse neighing every now and then. They were utterly alone.

Before discovering the baby, Lily had wanted to talk to Nash about her feelings...feelings that had grown deeper than she'd expected. They'd both agreed that everything they shared was temporary and physical, but somewhere along the way her heart had gotten involved. She didn't want to open up now or he'd probably think she was just trying to get a husband to go along with the baby to keep the gossip at bay.

With Nash's rough fingers laced through hers, Lily had to admit she loved the Neanderthal routine when he'd gone all super protective of her. She'd known from the moment she met Nash that he was a man of power, of authority.

Her stepfather had been a man of power, too, waving his money around to get what he wanted. Nash was different, though. He was type A, without all the material possessions. He appealed to her on so many levels; she just wished they weren't facing this life-altering commitment together when they barely knew each other.

Yes, they were compatible in bed—rather, in haylofts— but that didn't mean in her realistic, chaotic world they would mesh well. Added to that, she didn't know if *she* could handle having her passionate nature back in the public eye. Any serious relationship she took out in the open was subject to being exploited.

When they stepped into her trailer, Nash locked the door behind him. The cool air-conditioning greeted them. A small light from the tiny kitchenette had been left on, sending a soft glow throughout the narrow space.

Nash's heavy-lidded eyes met hers. She knew that look, had seen it nearly every night in person, then again in her dreams later. He could make a woman forget all about reality, all about responsibility.

This was the first time he'd been in her trailer and she realized just how broad and dominating his presence truly was. A shiver of arousal slid through her.

"We really should talk about this," she started, knowing she had lost control of this situation the moment she'd agreed to let him come back to her trailer. "I want you to know I didn't trap you."

"I know." He closed the gap between them, barely brushing his chest against hers. "I also know that I want you. I wanted you before you broke the news and I still do. A baby doesn't change the desire I have for you, Lily."

Oh, mercy. When he said things like that, when he looked at her like that…how could a girl think straight? Just one look from beneath those heavy lids framed by dark lashes had her body reacting before he could even touch her. This was why they had to sneak around. No way could she be in public with this man when he looked at her like he was ready to eat her up, and she knew she had that same passionate gaze when she looked at him.

He smelled all masculine and rugged, and pure hardworking man. A man who was gentle with animals and demanding as a lover was pretty much her greatest fantasy come to life. A fantasy she hadn't even known lived within her until she'd met Nash.

"Maybe we shouldn't be doing this," she stated as his fingertips slid up over her chest and started peeling away the elastic top of her dress. "I mean, we have a lot to talk about, right?"

Nash nodded, keeping his focus on his task. "We do,

but right now you're responding to my touch. I can't ignore that. Can you?"

His gaze met and trapped hers. "Unless you're ashamed to have the groom in your trailer."

Lily reached up, squeezing both of his hands. "I've never, ever hinted that I'm ashamed of you, Nash. I'm just not normally a fling girl and whatever we have going on is nobody else's business. That's all. I'm not hiding anything else."

A brief shadow crossed over his face and Lily wondered if she'd imagined it for a moment because just as fast as it came, it was gone.

"I can't deny you," she whispered. "How can this pull still be so strong?"

Nash dipped down, gliding his mouth over the curve of her neck, causing her head to fall back. The rasp of his beard against her bare skin always had tingles shooting all over her body. On occasion he'd trimmed his beard back, but thankfully he'd never fully shaved, because Lily figured she was ruined for smooth faces forever after being with Nash.

"Because passion is such a strong emotion," he murmured as his lips trailed up her neck. "And what we have is too fierce to sum up in one word."

In no time he'd yanked her dress down to pool at her feet. Lily kicked it aside as he quickly worked her free of her strapless bra and panties.

He reached behind his back and jerked his T-shirt up and over his head, tossing it to the side. Those chiseled muscles beneath a sprinkling of dark hair on his chest didn't come from working out in some air-conditioned gym. Nash's taut ripples came the old-fashioned way: from hours of manual labor.

"I love how you look at me," he muttered as he lifted her from the waist and crossed to the end of the trailer with the bed.

He lay her down and stood over her, whipping his belt through the loops of his jeans. Lily didn't know what on earth they were doing. Okay, she knew what they were doing, but wasn't this a mistake? Shouldn't they be discussing the baby? What their plans were for the future?

But when his weight settled over her, pushing her deeper into the thick comforter, Lily relished in the feel of his hard body molding perfectly with hers. Right here, this was the feeling she'd come to crave—the heaviness of him pressing into her in a protective, all-consuming manner.

Nash was right. *Passion* was such a simple word for the intensity of what they shared. But what label did it have? The impulse with which they'd jumped into an affair had overwhelmed them both. They'd never given anything beyond sex another thought.

The truth was, she had feelings for Nash, feelings she didn't think she'd have again for another man. Could she trust her feelings to stand up to public scrutiny? Could she rely on anything she felt that stemmed from a hidden affair?

Giving up her mental volley of trying to have this all make sense, Lily raked her fingers up his back and over his shoulders as he settled between her thighs. Nash had a way to make her forget everything around her, make her want to lock away the moments in time she shared with him. As he entered her, his mouth claimed hers and Lily had no choice but to surrender. Why did every moment with this man make her feel things she'd never felt before?

Nash's hands slid up her sides and over her breasts as her body arched into his. In no time her core responded, tightening as Nash continued to move with her.

After he followed her lead and their bodies stopped trembling, he lifted her in his arms, tucked her beneath the covers and climbed in beside her.

"Rest, Lily." He reached over and shut off the light. "Tomorrow we'll work this out."

Did he mean he'd still try to get her to move into his house? Although his dominance was a turn-on, she wouldn't let him just start taking charge simply because of the baby.

She was still in charge of her own life. Besides, being intimate with a man and living with him were two very different things.

As much as Nash was coming to mean to her, she still had to face reality. She was going to be done filming in about a week and she had a life in LA to get back to.

So where did that leave them?

Well, what a surprise. They'd ended up with their clothes off again and nothing was discussed or planned.

On the upside, she wasn't nauseous this morning...yet.

As she headed toward the makeup trailer, her new agent Ian Schaffer stepped out of one of the cottages on the Barrington estate. Ian had initially come out to the movie set in hopes of getting Lily to sign with his agency, and she did, but then he had gone and fallen in love with one of the beautiful Barrington sisters.

Sweet Cassie, the gentle trainer, and her precious girl, Emily, were both part of Ian's life now and family had never looked so adorable. Ian caught her eye and waved as he headed her way. At some point she'd have to discuss her own family situation with Ian and what this meant for upcoming films...especially since he was already getting several scripts for her to look over.

Too bad none of those movies called for a pukey pregnant heroine. She'd so nail that audition with her pasty complexion and random bouts of profuse sweating.

"You have a second?" he asked.

"Sure." Lily shifted so Ian's height blocked the morning sun. "We're heading into town today to shoot a scene near the flower shop, but I'm not due in wardrobe for a few more minutes. What's up?"

"I have a really good script that came through yesterday I'd like you to look at it." Ian rested his hands on his hips and smiled. "I know we've only worked together for a few weeks, but you had indicated that you'd like to try something different, maybe break away from the softer, family-style roles and into something more edgy. Are you still up for that?"

Lily tilted her head and shrugged. "Depends on the role and the producer. What do you have for me?"

"How would you feel about playing a showgirl who is a struggling single mother?"

Lily froze. "Um…yeah, that's quite the opposite of anything I've done before."

Oh the irony. Showgirl? By the time the movie started filming Lily figured her waistline would be nonexistent. As far as the single mom aspect? She honestly had no clue. Nash claimed he wouldn't leave her, but he'd only been aware of the baby for less than twenty-four hours. Once reality set in would he still feel the same?

"Lily?" Ian eased his head down until his gaze caught hers. "You all right? You don't have to look at the script if that's too far outside your comfort level, but I will say the producers are amazing and the script is actually very well plotted. Aiden O'Neil was just cast as the opposite lead."

Aiden was a great guy, an awesome actor and would be a joy to work with again. But how could she accept this role knowing she couldn't commit to the grueling hours of exercise and perfecting her body that, no doubt, Hollywood would require in order to portray a showgirl?

Lily's eyes drifted over Ian's shoulder and landed on Nash. Now that was a leading man…and he'd sneaked out of her trailer without her noticing. He'd promised to be gone by morning, and he was, but still she'd been a little disappointed not to be able to wake up next to him. Yes, she was quickly losing control over her feelings for Nash and she feared she'd have a hard time keeping them tucked against her heart.

Ian swiveled, glanced across the estate and turned back to Lily. "I'm not sure why you keep hiding what you two have going on."

Lily jerked her attention back to Ian. "Excuse me?"

Shrugging, Ian smiled. "I won't say anything, and honestly I doubt anyone else has picked up on the vibes you two are sending out."

Lily wasn't sure if she was relieved or afraid that someone else knew about her and Nash. Old images of a video she'd thought private played through her mind. That was another time, another man. Nash was trustworthy...wasn't he?

"What is it you think you know?" she asked, crossing her arms over her chest.

"I caught you two in a rather...comfortable embrace about a month ago. I was looking for Cassie and you and Nash were in the stables. I didn't say anything because I know you value your privacy and it was nobody's business what you two do in your downtime."

Lily had thought for sure no one would've spotted them at night and after hours. Thankfully it was only Ian who most definitely had her best interest at heart. As her agent, he didn't want any bad press surrounding her, either. The limelight would stay directed elsewhere, for now.

Blowing out a sigh, Lily nodded. "I don't know what is going on between Nash and me, to be honest. But just keep this between us, okay?"

Ian smiled. "You're my client, and I'd like to think, friend. We all have secrets, Lily. I won't say a word."

Speaking of secrets, she had a doozy. But for now, she would keep the pregnancy to herself. This was definitely something she and Nash needed to work through before sharing the announcement with any outsiders. They were still riding the sexual high, the excitement of being so physically attracted to each other, she had no clue how to discuss something so permanent with him. They were facing a relationship she didn't think either of them was ready for.

"You sure you're okay?" Ian asked.

Pulling out her most convincing smile, Lily nodded and turned to head toward the wardrobe trailer. "Fine. Just ready to relax after this shoot is over."

"Well, when you get a chance, come find me. I'll let you

look over those scripts." He fell into step with her. "I believe the single mom part would be perfect for you, but that's going to depend on how comfortable you are with playing a show-girl. I also have a part that is set in a mythical world, and that also involves bearing a great deal of skin because from what I can see, the women all wear bikini tops and short skirts."

Lily refrained from groaning because here she was, just discovering her pregnancy and already having to choose between her career and her personal life.

How would she juggle this all when the baby came? Eventually the world would know she was pregnant, then she couldn't keep Nash a secret any longer—couldn't keep her feelings for him a secret. Sooner rather than later, their relationship—whatever it became—would be out front and center.

How would he cope? How would they get through this? As a couple? As two people just sharing a child? With the depth of her feelings only growing stronger, Lily worried she was in for a long road of heartache.

Three

It was after midnight and Lily hadn't come to him. He'd spent the night in her trailer, in her arms. So why wasn't she here?

Turning off the lights in the stables, Nash kept to the shadows of the property and headed toward the back of the estate where Lily's trailer sat. He told himself he just wanted to check on her to make sure she was feeling okay. Nash refused to believe he was developing deeper feelings for her. He couldn't afford to be sidetracked right now, not until his plan was fully executed.

He climbed the two steps and glanced over his shoulder to double-check he was alone before giving her door a couple taps with his knuckles. When she didn't answer, he tried the handle, surprised it turned easily beneath his palm. Even with security, keeping the door unlocked wasn't smart. You never knew what length the crazies would go to in order to snap a picture of a celebrity. Money held more power than people gave it credit for.

"You need to keep this locked," he told her as he entered. "Anybody could walk right in."

Lily sat hunched over the small dinette table, papers

spread all around her. When she glanced up at him, tear tracks marred her creamy cheeks.

Fear gripped him as he crossed the small space. "Lily, what happened? Is it the baby?"

Raking her hands through her long, dark hair, she shook her head. "No, no. The baby is fine."

A slight sense of relief swept through him, but still, something was wrong. He'd never seen such fierce emotions from the woman who always appeared so flawless, so in control…except when she surrendered herself to him and she unleashed all of that pent-up passion.

"Then what is it?" he asked, sliding in beside her on the narrow booth.

Her hand waved across the table. "All of this. I'm looking at the future of my career, yet I have no clue what way to go. I'm at a crossroads, Nash, and I'm scared. There's no good answer."

Nash wrapped his arm around her and pulled her against his side. He'd grown used to the perfect feel of her petite body nestled next against his. What he wasn't used to was consoling a woman, delving into feelings beyond the superficial. This was definitely out of his comfort zone and he absolutely hated it. Hated how he'd allowed himself to get in this position of being vulnerable with the threat of being exposed before he was ready.

More than anything else, he hated lying to Lily. She didn't deserve to be pulled into his web of deceit and lies, but now that she was pregnant, there was no other option. He'd already put his plan in motion and he wasn't leaving until Damon Barrington gave up the horses and Nash disclosed his real identity to the man. Nash couldn't wait to see Damon's face when the truth was revealed.

But now he had Lily and a baby to worry about. He sure as hell didn't want innocents caught in the mix. Things had been so simple before, when Lily planned to wrap up filming and go on her way. Everything in her life from this moment on would revolve around their child and he had to figure out a way to make this right...he just had no clue how.

Angst rolled through him at the thought of his own mother feeling even an inkling of what Lily was going through. And his mother had been all on her own. No way would he ever let Lily feel as if she didn't have him to lean on. He wasn't looking for that traditional family, but he wouldn't abandon what was his.

For so long it had been just Nash and his mother. She'd always put his needs first, rarely dating, never bringing a man to the house until Nash was in his late teens when she got engaged and eventually married. She'd always made sure her two jobs covered their bills and a few extras.

In short, she worked her ass off, purposely setting her own needs aside until Nash was old enough to understand and care for himself.

He didn't want to see Lily struggling as a single mother, juggling a career and a child.

Added to that, she was pregnant with *his* child. It would take death to tear him away from what belonged to him. Did he love her? No. Love wasn't in the cards for him, wasn't something he believed in. That didn't mean he didn't already love this child they'd created. Now Nash had to make sure once she discovered the truth, she wouldn't shut him out.

He knew how she loathed liars, how she'd been betrayed by a man in her past. Surely she would see this situation was completely different.

"What are all these papers that have you so upset?" he asked her.

Lily rested a hand on his thigh, tapping a stack with her finger. "Scripts Ian gave me to look over for the next film. He's so excited because this will be our first film together, but everything here would be impossible for me to do until after the baby is born and that's if I get my body back. Hollywood is ruthless when it comes to added pounds."

He kept his opinion about Hollywood and their warped

sense of "beautiful" to himself. Not all women needed to be rails to be stunning and added pounds didn't take away from a woman's talents. Lily was a petite woman, but she had curves in all the right places.

"Why don't you tell Ian that none of these will work for you?"

Lily lazily drew an invisible pattern over his jeans with her fingertips. "I need to tell him about the baby. This has to be my sole focus. My career will have to come second for a while. I only hope I'm not committing career suicide."

Nash smiled and stroked away a strand of hair from her eyes. "I highly doubt this will kill your career. Ian will understand, I'm sure."

Lily scrubbed her hands over her face. "This is my life. I don't know anything else. What do I know about being a mom?"

About as much as he knew about being a dad.

She slid out the other side of the booth and grabbed a bottle of water from the fridge. Nash watched as she twisted off the cap and took a long drink. An overwhelming sense of possession swept through him. This sexy, vibrant woman would soon start showing visible signs of their secret affair.

"You can't keep pushing yourself right now, Lily. It's best you relax."

Her eyes darted to his. "I don't need you coming in here and telling me how I should be reacting. My life is mine alone, Nash. Yes, you're the baby's father, but I need to figure out what to do here. Even if I take some time off, I'm still in the spotlight. I don't want…"

She bit her lip and glanced away. In the soft light casting a glow in the narrow space, Nash saw another fresh set of tears swimming in her eyes. Damn it.

"You don't want the media to know," he murmured.

After a slight hesitation, she nodded, but still didn't meet his gaze. He climbed out of the seat and came up behind her, cupping her shoulders and easing her back against his chest.

"They're going to find out, Lily. What you need to do is make sure you always stay in control." Sliding his arms down, he covered her flat stomach with his hands, still in awe that a life grew inside there. "Don't let them start the gossip. I'm sure you have TV interviews scheduled. Make a big bombshell announcement then. You'll take the wind right out of the press's sails."

Lily turned in his arms. Her eyes met his as she blinked back tears. "That may be the best plan of action. But, I need to tell my mother first."

Her mother. They'd never discussed their parents. That topic usually meant a relationship was building. He and Lily hadn't planned on building on anything. They were enjoying their time together, not thinking of tomorrow.

Tomorrow, however, had caught up with them and smacked them in the face with a good dose of reality.

The fact they were bound forever now sent a bit of uncontrollable fear sliding through him. Whether either of them liked it or not, they were about to delve into personal territory.

Lily could talk about her mother all she wanted. That was most definitely an area in his life he wasn't ready to reveal.

"Does your mother live in LA, too?"

"No, she lives in Arizona in a small, private community that's run by an assisted living facility. She has her own home on the grounds and she's very independent, but if her health gets bad or as she gets older and needs care, she's already set."

Lily stepped back and crossed her arms. "I don't tell people where she is because I want her to have a normal life and not be hassled by the media."

Nash didn't want another reason to be drawn to Lily, but damn it she was protective of her mother. How could he not relate to that? Nash would do anything for his mother...which was why he was still harboring his secret instead of bursting through Damon's front doors and laying it all out on the line.

Part of Nash wished he'd never kept this secret about his life, wished he'd just confronted his past immediately and moved on. But he'd wanted to protect his mother and wanted to move cautiously without making rash decisions. Lily was a different story. He'd seen her, he'd wanted her. Now, here they were, pregnant and discussing parents.

Irony shot at him from so many angles he could hardly keep up. He had been a secret baby, and Lily was expecting a baby that had to remain a secret for now. The best course of action for him would be to complete his original plans and confront Damon.

"Are you going to see your mom as soon as you're done filming here?" he asked.

He needed her gone. He needed her away so he could have a face-to-face with Damon and not have Lily right there witnessing his confession of every single lie he'd told since meeting her. There was no way he could avoid the outcome, but he could at least soften the blow if she weren't present for the bomb he would drop.

He wanted so much, from Damon, from himself...from Lily. In the end, he would have it all. He hadn't gotten this far in his life by sitting idly by and watching opportunities pass. He reached with both hands and took what he wanted.

"I just need to think." She rubbed her head and sighed. "I need to find a doctor. I have no idea where to go. Obviously I should look in LA, but I won't be back there for a while."

"I'll find you one." When she quirked a brow, he added, "I know people in the area. You need a checkup and then you can see a doctor when you get home."

Assuming she went back home after filming wrapped up. Hell, he had no idea what her plans were. Honestly, all they'd managed to work out was how well they fit together intimately. Any discussion beyond that would be a vast change of pace.

"Just get me a name," she told him. "It's going to be nearly impossible to get in and out of a doctor's office here without word getting out about my condition."

Nash's mind was working overtime. He couldn't say too much or she'd know something was off about him and who she believed he was. She had to keep thinking he was just a groom until he could tell her otherwise. The last thing he needed at this point was her, or anyone for that matter, getting suspicious. Still, money talked and he'd use any means necessary to get her the proper care she needed while she was here.

"I bet we could get a doctor to come here, secretly," he offered. "People can be silenced for a price."

Lily's eyes widened. "You're not paying someone to keep quiet. I know how this works, Nash. We just need to find someone who can be discreet."

From her tone and the worry filling her eyes, Nash knew she didn't like the idea of him spending his money on her health care. Little did she know how heavily padded his accounts were. Even if they weren't, even if he did only make groom's wages, he'd spend every last cent if that meant proper care for his baby.

"I'll take care of it," he assured her. "You won't have to worry about a thing."

Lily leaned her shoulder against the narrow kitchenette cabinet and stared at him. "There are so many layers to you," she muttered. "You're all casual and laid-back, yet sometimes you're all business and take-charge. Makes me wonder who the real Nash is."

She'd barely scratched the surface. All too soon those layers would be peeled back one at a time, revealing things that would change lives forever.

Forcing himself to relax, he hooked his thumbs through his belt loops, intending to keep playing the part of groom. "Which Nash do you think I am?"

With a shrug, Lily continued to stare. "I'm not sure. You

just seem more, I don't know, powerful and composed than I thought you'd be about the baby."

In one stride he'd closed the space between them, snaked his arms around her waist and leaned over her so her back arched. "You saying I wasn't powerful when we were in the loft?"

Lily's hands slid up his chest. "Oh, you were powerful, but you didn't have that serious tone you just used."

Nash eyed her mouth, then traveled back up to her eyes. "Trust me, when it comes to someone I care about, I'm very serious."

Lily's tremble vibrated his entire body. He couldn't let her know anything about his real life, but at the same time he had to use his influences to keep her near, keep her and the baby safe. Everything in his life was at stake—things he hadn't even considered a possibility were now major markers on his journey. He'd started down this path with one vision, now suddenly there were forks in the road. Still, he had to stay on track because no matter which way he went, hearts would be ripped apart. Two life-altering secrets would shatter the trust he'd built with everyone around him over the past couple of months.

Even with the odds drastically stacked against him, with the devil in the corner mocking him, Nash had no intention of failing. He'd have it all: the horses, a family, his baby.

Four

"What do you mean he's still not accepting our offer?"

Nash glanced behind him, making sure he was still alone. He'd stepped out of the stables and around the side where he was sure to have privacy when his assistant had called.

Damon Barrington may technically be his boss here, but Nash had a surprise in store for him.

"I know what they're planning," Nash said in a low tone. "I know exactly what he's willing to let go of and what he wants to hold on to. What the hell will it take to get him to sell to me?"

"I think that's the issue," his assistant replied. "You know how he feels about you. He may sell to someone else."

Nash raked a hand through his hair. Yeah, he knew how Damon felt about him. They'd been ongoing rivals in the horse industry and for the past two years or so, but they'd pretty much used their assistants to handle all business dealings between them. That gap in time had only aided in Nash's covert plans. All he'd done was grow a beard, grow his hair longer and put on old, well-worn clothes. Sometimes the easiest way to hide things, or people, was right in plain sight.

Nash had wanted to purchase several of Damon's prize-winning horses, knowing the mogul was set to retire after this season, but Damon kept refusing. Nash needed those horses, needed the bloodlines on his own estate because he'd not been faring well in the races and losing was not an option.

The most recent offer had been exorbitant and Damon still wasn't budging. Stubborn man.

Like father, like son.

"Let me think," Nash said, heading back toward the front of the stables. "I'll call you back."

He slid the phone into his pocket and rounded the corner. Stepping from the shade to the vibrant sun had him pulling his cowboy hat down lower. He needed to figure out what it would take to get Damon to sell those horses to him because Nash had never taken no for an answer and he sure as hell wouldn't start now.

Pulling the pitchfork off the hook on the wall, Nash set out to clean out the stalls at the end of the aisle. Tessa and Cassie had taken two of the coveted horses out for a bit which gave him time to think and work without distractions.

What if someone else called Damon's assistant and made an offer? Would the tenacious man consider the generous offer then if he knew the horses weren't going to his rival?

Nash shoved the pitchfork into the hay, scooped out the piles and tossed them into the wheelbarrow. He missed his own estate, missed doing the grunt work with his own horses, in his own lavish stables. But he'd left his groom in charge and knew he could trust the man.

Only Nash's assistant knew where he was and that he was trying to spy on the Barringtons in an attempt to buy them out. But even his right-hand man wasn't aware of the other secret that had Nash uncovered here. Nobody knew and until he was ready to disclose his full plan, he had to keep it that way.

If Damon hated him before, how would the elderly man feel once he discovered the real truth?

By the time the first stall was clean, sweat trickled down his back. Nash pulled his hat off, tugged his T-shirt over his head and slapped his hat back on. He didn't often take his shirt off during workdays, but the day was almost done and the heat was stifling. He'd even gotten used to the itchiness of his beard after endless hours of working in this heat.

After both stalls were ready to go, Nash put all the materials away. Damon kept a clean, neat stable—something they had in common.

Nash didn't want to admit they had anything in common, but over the past several months since he had been on the Barrington estate, he'd seen Damon many times, seen how he treated his family, the crew filming there. But Nash hadn't allowed himself to get swept into that personal realm. He was here for a job, both as a groom and as a businessman.

Nash's last order of business was sweeping the walkway, ridding it of the stray straw and dust. The chore didn't take long, but had him sweating even more. He pulled the T-shirt from his back pocket and swiped it across his neck and chest.

"Have you ever thought of doing calendars?"

Nash jerked around to see the object of his every desire standing in the stable entryway, the sunlight illuminating her rich hair, her curvy build.

"What are you doing here?"

"Is Cassie around?"

"She's out riding." He took a step closer, since no one was around and he couldn't resist. So, he'd actually found one thing he had absolutely no control over. "You all right?"

With a soft smile, she nodded. "Yeah. I have a short break between scenes and I needed to ask her something."

Fisting his shirt, Nash crossed his arms over his chest. "Care to elaborate?"

"I'm asking her what doctor she used while she was pregnant, if you must know," she whispered.

"I already found out and you have an appointment." He'd had to do some sneaky digging, or rather his assistant did, but he'd been able to find the doctor in town who Cassie had seen for her pregnancy. "I was going to tell you this evening because I wasn't sure of your schedule today."

Her eyes raked over his bare chest and he didn't mind one bit being the recipient of her visual lick. "Keep looking at me like that and people are going to know more about us than we want them to."

Her eyes snapped up to his. "I can't even think when you're working like that," she muttered, gaze darting back down to his bare chest. "But thank you for arranging the doctor. When is he coming?"

"*She* will be here on Thursday."

Lily nodded. "That will be great. We're supposed to finish filming Thursday, but they may have something else for me to do last minute. I'll make sure I'm free, though."

"We're meeting at my house so there's no question as to why she's here."

"Taking control again?" A corner of Lily's lips kicked up into a grin. "This once I don't mind and if we were alone, I'd show you how grateful I am for you taking care of this."

Damn, his body responded immediately and he couldn't wait to get back to her trailer. "We'll be alone later and I'll let you."

At first all the sneaking around had been exciting, thrilling. Of course, that part was still arousing, but they basically knew nothing about each other. All he'd wanted was to confront his past, secure his future and now he was dealing with a whole new future.

Lily was an amazing woman, there was no denying that fact. But that didn't make him ready to settle down and play house, either. Could he see himself with someone like her? Considering they only knew each other in the bedroom, sure. Reality might be a different story.

Why the hell was he thinking like this? They were having a baby, that didn't mean they had to register for monogrammed towels.

"Hey, Lily."

Nash turned to see the beautiful Barrington sisters as they led their horses into the stalls.

"Hi, Cassie, Tessa." Lily walked around him, sending her signature scent of lilac straight through him. "I had a break from filming and thought I'd come see you guys since I rarely get in here."

Good save.

Nash went on with his duties, trying to ignore the feminine laughter of the three women in his life…only two of them had no clue just how close to him they were.

He'd created a complete and utter mess and he had to gain control and figure out how the hell to keep his plans and deception from blowing up in his face.

As much as he didn't want to admit it, he'd come to care for this family. Even though he hadn't let them in beyond work, he knew these sisters, saw the love their father had for them, witnessed bonding moments when they thought no one was around.

They were a family. A tight-knit, perfectly woven-together family. And when Nash ended up besting Damon, Nash had no clue where that would leave him in the family tree.

Ridding her body of her meager breakfast of dry toast was not a promising start to her day. It was the final day of shooting and Lily just wanted to crawl back into bed and tell the crew to do the scene without her. With her stomach revolting, she didn't care that she was the female lead, she just wanted to lie in her bed and die, because she was positive that's what was happening.

She was already fifteen minutes late for hair and makeup. She was never late. Some actors and actresses had a reputation for being divas while filming, often times making the rest of the crew wait on them, but Lily had prided herself on being professional. Her time wasn't worth any more than any other person's on set.

She slapped her sunglasses on, hoping to hide the dark

circles until she got to the makeup chair. She'd had enough energy to throw on her strapless maxi dress and flip-flops before heading out. But her mind wasn't on filming. Besides the baby, Lily was seriously starting to worry about her and Nash.

Her and Nash? Why did they instantly click like a couple inside her mind?

Because that's the way her mind—and her heart—had started leaning. The man exuded strength, not just in his physical job, but with everything he did. Since he found out about the baby he'd been ready to control every aspect of this pregnancy, to anticipate her every need. And, as much as it pained her to admit it, his dominating presence only deepened her attraction to him.

There was so much to the man and she wanted to discover it all. She completely trusted him with her body, now she wanted to see if she could trust him with more.

What did he want? Did he want more with her? If he did, would he be able to handle the very public life she led? One worry after another cycled through her head.

The overcast clouds were about as cheery and pleasant as she felt at the moment. She really hoped the first trimester passed quickly and she was a textbook case pregnancy because, while she was excited about the little life growing inside her, she was so over feeling carsick, as if she was riding a roller coaster and spinning in circles all at once.

Adding all of that to the uncertainty about Nash and what move they would take next was about to break her.

"I was just coming to check on you." Ian fell into step beside her. "Everything okay?"

Tears pricked her eyes. Was everything okay? Not really. She was pregnant by a man she knew little about and she was falling in love with him. That chaotic mess had somehow become her life and she had no clue how to sort out all these emotions to make sense of things.

Ian stared at her, waiting on her to answer. Shoving her

hair away from her shoulders, Lily blinked back tears, thankful for the sunglasses.

"I wasn't feeling very well this morning."

He gripped her elbow and pulled her gently to a stop. "You're looking a little pale. Are you okay?"

Lily sniffed and shook her head. "No, I'm not, but I will be."

Ian's brows drew together as he glanced around, then focused back on her. "You're crying. That's not okay. Did something happen with your mom?"

"No, my mom is fine."

Lily reached beneath her sunglasses and swiped the tips of her fingers at the tears just starting to escape. Why couldn't she control her emotions? She just wanted to wrap up this day of filming and go back to her trailer where she could think of how to gently let Nash know she was developing stronger feelings for him.

"If you're sick, maybe I should see about putting your scene off. A few more hours shouldn't make a difference."

A few hours? She needed a few weeks, or months, depending on how long this state of feeling like death lingered. Of course by that time she'd resemble a whale which would totally knock her out of playing Rose Barrington.

"A few hours won't make a difference, but thanks."

She sniffed again, desperately needing a tissue. Wow, if the paparazzi could only see her now. Sniffling, crying and looking like pure hell. They'd make up something akin to Starlet Hooked on Drugs or The Girl Next Door Reverts Back to Her Wild Days as their top story.

"Does this have to do with Nash?" he whispered. "You seem really upset for just not feeling well. Did he do something?"

Hysterical laughter burst through her as more tears flowed. Yeah, she was officially a disaster and she was totally falling apart in front of her new agent. An agent who had flown all the way out here to convince her to sign with his agency...the poor man was probably reconsidering his decision even though in the short time they'd been official, they had come to think of each other as good friends.

So instead of letting him continue to think she'd gone completely insane, she blurted out, "I'm pregnant."

Ian's eyes widened for only a second before he wrapped his arm around her shoulder and pulled her into a friendly hug.

"I assume this is Nash's?"

Lily nodded against his shoulder and held on to his arms. "Nobody knows. Please keep the news to yourself until I tell you otherwise."

"Of course." He gave her shoulder a slight squeeze, then stepped back. "Is this why you haven't gotten back to me on either of those scripts?"

His smile warmed her and she nodded. "I'm so torn. I have no clue what work you can find for me and I just don't know how I'll manage with being pregnant or even what will happen when the baby comes."

Ian kept his grip on her shoulders and tipped his head down to look her straight in the eye. "Listen, this news is a shock to you now, but you are a strong woman. Actresses have babies all the time. You will do just fine and I've no doubt I'll find work for you. Never worry about that. That's my job. Okay?"

The strong wind had her hair dancing around her shoulders. Lily shoved the wayward strands behind her ears. "I need to get to hair and makeup. I'm really late now. Thanks for understanding and for keeping my secret."

Ian dropped his hands. "You go on. I'm going to see Nash because he's been shooting death glares at me from the stables since we stopped to talk."

Wrapping her arms around her waist, Lily smiled. "He's a bit protective."

"Looks like a man in love to me."

Love? No. Lust? Yes. They weren't near the stage for love to enter the equation—well, she was teetering on the brink. Their sexual chemistry was completely off the charts, though.

"Tell him I'll see him later and that I'm fine," she told Ian. "He worries like my mother."

With a soft chuckle, Ian nodded. "Will do."

Ian walked toward the stables and Lily paused briefly to stare at Nash. Even from across the wide concrete drive and the side yard, she could see the stone-solid look on his face. That wasn't jealousy. What did he have to be jealous of, anyway? Yes, they were having a baby together, but they'd still made no commitment to each other.

Why shouldn't they try for more? Why couldn't she just tell him what she wanted? She wasn't asking for a ring on her finger. This innocent baby wouldn't be caught in the middle. Lily wanted her child to have security and the love of both parents whether they were together or not. She had to figure out how Nash felt about her beyond the sexual aspect.

But she had a feeling she knew how his mind worked. A man like Nash wouldn't let go of anything that belonged to him and since this baby was his, she knew he wouldn't let go of her, either.

This could be an opportunity to see if she was ready for something long-term with the man who had literally turned her world upside down.

Five

Nash had no idea how nervous he had been about this appointment until he closed the door behind the doctor once the checkup was done. Now he and Lily were alone in his rental house which was only a few miles from the Barrington estate.

The baby was healthy with a good, strong heartbeat. Lily's blood pressure was a bit on the high side and the doctor warned about too much stress and urged her to rest for the next few weeks until the next appointment. Nash vowed silently to make sure Lily was relaxed, pampered and wanted for nothing as long as she was here. And she would stay here for the next few weeks…if not longer. They hadn't really discussed her living arrangements, but Nash wasn't backing down on this matter. His child would stay under his roof for now.

The movie had officially wrapped up yesterday and Lily was free. Which meant he had some decisions to make. This wasn't just about Nash and Lily anymore. An innocent baby would be coming into this world soon and would depend on his or her parents to provide a stable, loving home.

When he stepped back into the living room, Lily was reclining on the leather chaise in the corner, pointing the remote toward the flat screen hanging above the stone mantel. He may be using this home as a prop for his plan, but that didn't mean he couldn't decorate it according to his style and his needs, just on a smaller scale. His designer had done quick work before Nash moved in and everything was perfect for a single groom who splurged only on a few necessities. A large television was a necessity.

When Lily had mentioned how nice his home was, he'd indicated the place came already furnished. A small lie piled atop all the others he'd doled out since he'd put his plan into motion. At this point, what was a white lie about decor in the grand scheme of things?

Lily's vibrant eyes shot to his, a smile spread across her face as he approached. "I know I should still be scared, or nervous, or whatever, but I'm just so happy the baby is healthy."

Resting his hip next to her bare legs on the chaise, Nash settled his hand on her calf and rubbed from her ankle to her knee. "There's no rule book that states you have to feel a certain way."

Lily rested her head against the arm, her hair falling over her shoulder, framing her natural beauty. This was how he preferred her. Not made up for a shoot with perfectly sprayed hair, but fresh-faced, hair down and wearing a casual dress. He loved how she didn't worry about her looks, didn't fuss with herself just because she came from the land where appearances were more valuable than talent.

Small-town life suited her and Nash wasn't immune to the fact he was starting to like how well she blended into his world...or the world he'd created for his charade.

How would she look in his real home? In his grand master suite that had a balcony overlooking the fields? The need to make love to her beneath the dark sky slammed into him. He wanted her on his estate, not in the rental home that was merely a prop for a life that wasn't even his.

"I'm pretty calm right now." She rested her hand on his

thigh, her dainty pink polish striking against his dark denim. "The film is done, the baby is fine."

Lily's hand came up, her fingertip traveled over the area between his brows. "Why the worry lines?"

Where to start? Did he confess now that he'd lied about his identity all along? Did he tell her he had more money than she ever thought possible and that this house, even his name, was one giant cover to keep him trudging forward with his master plan?

Did he truly want to see all that hurt in her eyes when he came clean about his life, that nearly every single thing he'd ever told her had been false?

Damn it, he hated he'd become *that* man. Hated that he would inevitably crush her. He didn't want her to look at him in disgust, but the moment would come and there wasn't a damn thing he could do about it. All he could do was stall, earn her trust outside of the bedroom.

Whether he wanted to face the fact or not, his feelings for her were growing deeper and damn if that didn't complicate things even further.

He'd thought getting her out of his system, then out of his life after the film was over, would be a piece of cake. His secrets could've remained just that from her and he could've revealed them once she was gone.

Yet here he was, tangled in his own web of lies, becoming more and more restricted with each passing day, each new lie, and finding himself sinking deeper into a woman he knew only intimately.

"Just worried about you." And that was the absolute truth. "With your blood pressure on the high side, I just want to make sure you take it easy."

Her hand slid over his stubbled cheek. "I'm taking it easy right now."

Easing forward, craving more of her touch, Nash slid his hand up over her knee, beneath the soft cotton dress and over her thigh. "I intend for you to take it easy until your next appointment."

Lily stilled, her hand falling into her lap. "Nash, I can't stay that long. I have a life in LA, a job, my mother is in Arizona…I can't just stay here and forget all of my obligations."

"You can take a break," he insisted. "You heard the doctor. A month off will be good for you and you don't have another film to get to, right?"

Lily shrugged, her eyes darting to her lap where she toyed with the bunched material of her dress. "I can't stay here with you, Nash. This baby is real. I can't just play house."

"You can." His eyes held hers as he leaned closer, nipped her lips and eased back. "You can stay for today." He nipped again. "And tomorrow."

He wasn't ready to play house yet, either, but he also wasn't letting her go.

"Reality is so hard to face when you're touching me," she murmured against his lips. "I don't even know what to do next."

Nash eased back and winked. "I've got a good idea."

"Does it involve the kitchen?" she asked with a crooked grin.

Giving her thigh a squeeze, Nash leaned back. "I thought you were nauseous?"

"Right now I'm starving."

Nash came to his feet and glanced down to her. The way she all but stretched out over the chaise, her dress hitched up to near indecent level, her hair spread all around her, she was sexy personified and had no clue the power she held.

And she was pregnant with his child. He never imagined just how much of a turn-on that would be.

Mine. That's all he could think right at this moment and the revelation nearly had his knees buckling

"What are you in the mood for?" he asked, trying to focus.

"Grilled cheese."

"Grilled cheese? Like bread, butter and a lot of fatty cheese?"

"You saying I can't have that?" she asked, quirking a brow as if daring him to argue.

"Not at all." With a laugh, he held his hands up in defense. "I'm just shocked that's what you're asking for."

"Grilled cheese is just one of my weaknesses," she told him. "All that gooey cheese and crispy bread."

Something so simple, yet a fact he hadn't known about her. Which just proved he really didn't know much about the mother of his child except how to excite her, how to get her to make those sweet little moans, how to make her lids flutter down just before she climaxed.

"One grilled cheese coming right up," he declared, quickly heading toward the kitchen before he took what he wanted, which was Lily all laid out beneath him.

He was serious about wanting her there, wanting her to stay with him until they figured out a game plan. So that meant he needed to take the time to learn more about her and not just how fast he could peel down those strapless sundresses she seemed so fond of.

As much as he wanted to learn about her, he was terrified she'd be wanting to learn more about him.

Which begged the ultimate question. Did he come clean or continue this farce for as long as possible?

Ever the gentleman, Nash had put her bags from her on-site trailer in his guest bedroom. He was giving her the option of staying in a room by herself or sleeping with him.

This baby had them taking every step carefully, moving from a hot, steamy affair into something more…calm.

Lily slid her hand over her still-flat stomach and took in the cozy bedroom with its pale gray walls, dark furniture and navy bedding. The fact that she was pregnant with his child and trying to figure out where to sleep was really absurd.

Lily turned, smacking into the hard, firm wall of Nash's

chest. His bare, gloriously naked, tanned, taut muscular chest. Would she ever tire of looking at this man? Would her body's fierce response always be so overwhelming? When she was with Nash she couldn't think, let alone figure out a future or make decisions. He aroused her, made her ache and crave his touch, and he'd managed to start working his way into her heart. Strong, firm hands gripped her bare arms in an attempt to steady her as her eyes held on to the tantalizing view before her.

"I'm going to assume by the way you're looking at me that you're not sleeping in the guest room."

Lily's eyes traveled up to see the smirk, the dark lifted brows. "Did you parade in here half-naked on purpose to sway my decision?"

With his focus on her lips, the tips of his fingertips slid over her sensitive breasts and down her torso to grip her hips and pull her flush against his strong body.

"It wouldn't take much persuasion to get you in my bed," he murmured against her lips. "The decision up to you."

She never grew tired of his hard body against hers. Lily flattened her palms against his chest. "I'd love to sleep in your bed, but I need you to know that I have no clue what's happening between us. I mean, I know I have feelings for you that go beyond sex. And that was before the baby. I don't know what to do now and I have no clue how you're feeling."

Great, now she was babbling and had turned into that woman who needed emotional reassurance. She'd also exposed herself a bit more than she'd intended.

Shaking her head, she slid her arms up around his neck and laced her fingers together. "Never mind. I'm not looking for you to say anything or make some grand declaration. I guess I'm just still scarred from trusting the wrong man a long time ago."

Of course she'd redeemed herself, but Lily had no doubt if she slipped up the media would be all too quick to resurrect that footage her then "boyfriend" had taken of her in the bedroom.

"You can trust me," Nash told her, sliding his hands up and down her back. "I know you're worried about the future, but you can trust that I will always take care of you and our baby. Never doubt that."

The strong conviction in his tone had her believing every word he said. "You must've had some really amazing parents for you to be so determined and loyal."

A sliver of pain flashed through those icy blue eyes. "My mother was the strongest woman I've ever known. She's the driving force behind everything good in my life."

"And your father?"

Nash swallowed as he paused. Silence hovered between them and Lily realized she probably should just learn to keep her mouth shut. But she wanted to know more about Nash. He was the father of her child, for pity's sake. They were bound together for life and eventually, little by little, they had to start opening up. "I never knew my father."

Lily's heart broke for him as she smoothed his messy hair away from his face. "I'm sorry. My father passed when I was younger, so I know a little about that void."

Click. Another bond locked into place and her heart slid another notch toward falling for this man.

"So it was just you and your mother, too?"

That scenario would've been better, actually. After all she and her mother had lived through, being alone would've been for the best.

"No." Lily slid from his arms and went to her bag to pull out a nightgown. She hated discussing her stepfather. "My mother was a proud woman, but we were pretty poor and she ended up marrying for financial stability."

A shrink would love diving into her head. The stepfather had virtually ruined her for any man with money and power. Settling down with someone as controlling as that wasn't an option. Lily would rather be alone than to be told how to live her life.

Lily kept her back to Nash as she pulled her strapless maxi dress down to puddle at her feet before she tugged her silky chemise on. For now her sexy clothes still fit.

"She probably wouldn't have married Dan had it not been for me," she told him, turning back around. "Mom was worried how she would keep our house, keep up her two jobs and keep food and clothes coming."

Picking up her discarded dress, she laid it on the bed and crossed back to Nash. "He was a jerk to her. Treated her like a maid instead of a wife. Treated me like I didn't even exist, which was fine because I didn't want a relationship with him anyway. But I loathe him for how he treated my mother."

Nash pulled her into his arms, surrounding her with the warmth and security she'd hardly known. This sense of stability was something she could easily get used to, but could she trust her emotions right now? Passion was one thing, but to fully rely on someone else, to trust with her whole heart… she wanted that more than anything.

"He's probably sorry he treated you like that now that you're famous."

Lily laughed and eased back to look him in the eyes. "I wouldn't know. He left my mother several years ago, just as I was getting my start. He took all the money, even what she'd worked for. He was always a greedy money whore. Money never meant anything to me, still doesn't. It doesn't define me, but I saw the evil it produced."

Nash's arms tightened on her again. "Money isn't evil, Lily. It's what a person chooses to do with it that can be evil."

"Yeah, well I choose to keep my mother comfortable in a nice home that's in a gated community where she can have her privacy and not worry. Other than that, I don't need it."

"So if I were a rich man you wouldn't have looked my way twice?" he joked.

Lily laughed. "Oh, you still would've caught my attention. I've just always promised myself I wouldn't get involved with anyone like my stepfather."

Nash squeezed her tighter. "Not all men are like your stepfather."

"Don't defend him."

Nash's chuckle vibrated through her. "I'm not, baby. I'm defending all of mankind."

Lily snuggled deeper into his embrace, wondering what path they were starting down. The last time her passion had bested her, she'd ended up across the internet, on the news and every magazine willing to make money off her bad decisions. Karma had intervened and her ex hadn't made it very far in the industry. She couldn't help but take a little satisfaction.

Now her passion had cornered her again. This time the consequences were far greater than a soiled reputation. She was going to be in charge of another life. How long would Nash want to be in the baby's life? Would he honestly be a hands-on father? He hadn't grown up with a dad so perhaps he truly did want to give this child a better life.

Lily hated all the unknowns that surrounded them, but her doctor said she needed to relax and she would do anything to ensure a healthy baby. Maybe she hadn't planned on a child, but the reality was, she was going to have one. There was a little being inside of her right now with a heartbeat of its own, growing each and every day. Angry as she may be at herself for allowing this to happen, she couldn't deny that she loved this baby already. If that meant relaxing with Nash for the next several weeks or even months, she wouldn't argue.

She'd wondered how they would work if they tried for something more serious, more than just ripping each other's clothes off at every opportunity. How would they mesh together in reality?

Looked like she was about to get her chance to find out.

Six

He was screwed. Royally, utterly screwed. He'd wanted to open up to her, wanted to start paving the way for an honest relationship. Or at least some type of relationship, considering she was carrying his child and he was developing stronger feelings for her.

Nash still couldn't put a title on whatever they had going because all their "relationship" consisted of so far was hot, fast sex in a stable loft and a surprise baby. He didn't know what the hell the next logical step would be because nothing about the entire past two months had been logical.

But Lily deserved the truth and Nash was too much of a coward to give it to her. He'd had an opening last night when they'd been halfway clothed and just talking. Such an emotionally intimate moment hadn't happened between them before, but that moment slipped by about as quickly as he'd taken off her silky gown. Yet again, he'd let passion override anything else. His need to have her consumed him and he didn't even try to push it aside and reveal his secrets.

Desire was easier to deal with than the harsh realities waiting them both.

Even when she'd spent the night in his bed, he had time to open up. Yet here he was making breakfast on a Saturday

morning like some domestic family man when so many secrets hovered between them.

Soon, he'd reveal the truth—or at least all he was able to.

Damn it. He wanted more from her than sex. He hadn't
expected this…whatever "this" was. The fact so many lies
lay between them only cheapened anything they would start
to build together, but being stuck between the rock and the
proverbial hard place was a position he'd wedged himself
into. And he wasn't going to be able to come out any time
soon.

How the hell was he supposed to know he'd start actually wanting more from Lily? He hadn't planned on a baby,
hadn't planned on Lily being a permanent fixture in his life.
Of course now she'd be part of his life no matter what, but
beyond the baby, he wanted more.

Nash scooped up the cheesy, veggie-filled omelet and
slid it onto the plate. After pouring a tall glass of juice, he
headed toward the bedroom where he'd left Lily sleeping.

Gripping the plate and glass, Nash turned into the bedroom and froze in the doorway at the seductive sight before
him. Those creamy shoulders against his dark sheets had
his body responded instantly. He never had a woman pull
so many emotions from him, have him so tangled in knots
and have him questioning every motive he had for further-
ing his career.

But Lily had a power over him that scared him to death,
because once she uncovered all of his secrets—and there
were many—she'd never want to see him again. Now that
he'd realized he wanted more from her, he also had another
revelation—Lily would end up hurt in the end and because
he was slowly opening to her, he would be destroyed, as well.

He had nobody to blame but himself.

Being cut from her life, from their child's life was not an
option. She may hate men who used money and power to
get what they wanted, but he wouldn't back down, not when
his child was the central point.

Nash moved into the room, setting the plate and glass on the nightstand. Easing down onto the bed, Nash rested his hip next to hers. Those sheets had never looked better, gliding over and across Lily's curves and silky skin, making her look like a pinup model.

The urge to peel down those covers and reveal her natural beauty overwhelmed him. He'd gotten her from the trailer to his rental home. He was easing her into his life slowly. The ache to be closer to her exploded inside him. He had to touch her, had to feel that delicate skin beneath his rough hands.

Nash's fingertips trailed over Lily's bare arm, leaving goose bumps in the path. Even in sleep she was so responsive to his touch.

Lily stirred, her head shifting toward him, strands of dark hair sliding across her shoulder, and her lids fluttered open. For the briefest of seconds a smile spread across her face before she threw back the covers and sprinted to the adjoining bath.

Morning sickness. Nash hated that there wasn't a damn thing he could do to make her feel better.

He pushed off the bed and padded barefoot across the hardwood floor toward the bathroom. He reached into the cabinet beside the vanity, grabbed a cloth and wet it with cold water before turning to her. He may not be able to stop her misery, but he could at least try to offer support.

Nash pulled her hair back, reaching around to place the cold cloth on her forehead. Hopefully that would help the nausea.

"Go away, Nash," she muttered as she tried to take her hair from his grip. "I don't want you here."

Too damn bad. He wasn't leaving.

After a few more minutes, Lily started to rise and Nash slid his arm around her waist and pulled her up. Limp, she fell back against his chest, resting her head on his shoulder. The way her body fitted against his always felt so right, so perfect. Would he ever be ready to let her go?

"I'm sorry," she murmured. "This is not a side of me I wanted you to see."

Splaying his hand across her abdomen, Nash kissed her temple. "Don't hide from me, Lily."

She covered his hand with her own. "I just wish I knew what we were doing. Where we were going."

That made two of them. For now they had a baby to focus on and the passion that was all-consuming whenever they were close to each other. They may not have the ideal setup or even an idea of what to do next, but they had something.

"I'm not going anywhere," he assured her. "And you're going back to bed. You need to keep up your strength and I made you breakfast."

Lily groaned. "I can't eat. The thought of food makes my stomach turn."

"You'll make yourself even sicker if you don't get something in you."

Without a warning, he bent down, snaked an arm behind her knees and another supported her back as he scooped her up and carried her back into bed.

"You're really taking this role of caring for me to the extreme." She slid her arms around his neck and closed her eyes. "But I'm too tired to argue. When I feel better in a couple hours we'll discuss this caveman persona you've taken on."

Smiling, Nash eased down onto the rumpled bed. "I'll take the eggs away if you think you can't eat, but at least drink."

Nash took the plate into the kitchen and dumped the contents into the trash. By the time he got back to her, she was propped up against the headboard, sheet pulled up and tucked beneath her arms. The glass of juice was about a quarter of the way gone.

And she was holding his gold designer watch in her hand.

Her eyes sought his across the room. "This is a pretty nice watch," she told him, setting it back down on the nightstand.

Damn it. He'd completely forgotten he'd left that out.

"Thanks. It was a gift."

Not a lie. One of his own jockeys had bought that for him several years ago after a big win.

"For a groom you have a pretty impressive house, too," she said, settling deeper into the pillows. "You must be really good at managing money."

He knew she wasn't fishing, but he also knew he was treading a thin line here. He had to open up about some things or she'd really start to wonder if he was hiding things from her.

Stepping farther into the room, he shrugged. "I don't really have anything to spend my money on. I'm not married, I don't travel or buy lavish things. I work, I come home."

Okay, that last part was a complete lie. But he really was a good manager of money. Because he came from nothing, watching every dollar was deeply instilled into him at a young age.

"How you feeling now?" he asked, desperate to switch topics.

"Good. You know, I do plan on getting up, showering and possibly doing something today." She took another sip of juice before focusing on him as he sank down on the edge of the bed beside her. "Just want you to be aware that I don't plan on sitting on my butt for the next seven months."

"I'll take you anywhere you want to go."

Lily sighed. "I'd like to go into town. There were some cute little boutiques I saw when we were filming, but if I go, I'll be recognized."

Nash rested his hand on her sheet-covered thigh. "If you want to go somewhere, I'll get you there and you won't be bothered."

Quirking a brow, Lily sat her near-empty juice glass on the nightstand. "And how will you do that? Because I'd love to be able to shop for just an hour."

Keeping his plan of action to himself, Nash shot her a grin. "Consider it done."

With the slightest tilt of her head, Lily narrowed her eyes. "You're planning something."

Easing forward, Nash ran a fingertip down her cheek, her neck and to the swell of her breast. "I am. But your job is to feel better, take your time getting ready and just let me know when you're done. I have nothing to do today but be at your service."

Her wide eyes slid over his bare chest, a smile danced around unpainted lips. "Sounds like I better rest up for an eventful day."

Because his body still hadn't gotten the memo that he needed to chill, Nash came to his feet. "I'm going to clean up in the kitchen. Yell if you need anything."

He cursed himself all the way down the hall. Lust, sex, it was always there, hovering between them. She was pregnant with his child, which was a hell of a turn-on, but this wasn't the time to worry about how soon he could have her again. He had to find a way to lessen this instant, physical pull between them. They'd indulged in an affair for months and where had that gotten them?

Too much was at stake, too many lives hinged on his next move.

He needed to touch base with his assistant, needed to send a final offer to Damon Barrington because Nash refused to settle for anything less than he came here for. He had an agenda and he had to stick with it or he'd lose it all.

She had no clue how he did it, she really didn't care.

Lily strolled out of the last boutique with bags in hand and headed toward Nash's truck parked in the back alley. He'd gone in with her, even helped her shop and offered pretty good advice when she would try on things.

Who was this guy? She'd never met a man who actually added input on a woman's purchases. He didn't sit out in his truck, he didn't ask her if she was almost done and he didn't act bored even one time. In fact, in one store he found a blue dress which he threw over the dressing room door, telling her it would look great on her.

Guess what? He'd been right. Not only that, the dress was stretchy and flowy. Perfect for that waistline that would be disappearing in the very near future.

Still, she was trying to put a label on him and so far there were just too many layers. No way could such an intriguing man be narrowed down to just one appealing trait. She could only assume his eye for fashion, his nurturing side and his patience came from being raised by a single mother.

And it was his take-charge, powerful side that must have stemmed from wanting to care for his mother. How could she fault that? How could she even think he was anything like her stepfather? Control was one thing, being protective was another.

Nash pulled the passenger side door open, took her bags and placed them in the extended cab part of the truck before offering his hand and helping her up into the seat.

Lily smiled, her eyes level with his now. "Such a gentleman."

"My mama raised me right," he told her, grabbing the seat belt and reaching across her to fasten it. His hands lingered over her breasts as he adjusted the strap. "Better keep you safe."

"Well, my boobs are fine so you can stop," she laughed. "I take back my gentleman compliment since you just wanted to cop a feel."

Nash's flirty smile had her heart clenching tighter. "You wouldn't want some stuffy gentleman. You like the way I can make you lose control."

Standing in the open truck door, Nash's hand traveled over her leg to slide up under her cotton skirt. "Boring and mundane isn't for you."

Not at all. She always thought she wanted someone who was down-to-earth, more trustworthy than the jerk who exploited her innocence years ago. She never thought she'd find someone who was so laid-back, loyal and had the ability to set her body on fire with such simple gestures. Finding the complete package had never crossed her mind.

When she'd started the affair, she'd definitely gone for appealing. Now she was discovering there was so much more than she'd ever bargained for when it came to Nash.

Lily's breath hitched as Nash's fingers danced across her center. Instantly she parted her legs without even thinking. His mouth, just a breath away from hers, had her aching for that promise of a kiss. Never had she desired or craved a man with such intensity.

"Did you have fun today?" he asked, his hand still moving over her silk panties.

"Yes," she whispered. "What are you doing?"

His eyes darted down to where she was fisting her skirt with both hands. "Getting you ready."

"For what?"

Nash nipped at her lips before breathlessly moving across her cheek to whisper in her ear, "Everything I've ever wanted."

His confident declaration had her shivering. Her head fell back against the seat as her lids closed. This man was beyond potent, beyond sexy and quickly becoming a drug she couldn't be without.

Seconds later he removed his hand, smoothed down her skirt and captured her mouth with his. Lily barely had time to grip his arms before he eased back, his forehead resting against hers.

"You think I'm everything you've ever wanted?" she asked, worried what he'd say, but unable to keep the question inside.

"I think you're everything I didn't know I was looking for and more than I deserve."

Slowly, Nash stepped back, closed the door and rounded the hood.

Well, that was intense. Now she was achy, confused and had questions swirling around in her mind. There was no doubt he could turn her on with whispered words, the tilt of his head with that heavy-lidded stare or a feather-light touch. But she wanted more. The man obviously cared about her or he wouldn't have gone to so much trouble to get her in his home, get her out of the house without being seen by too many people and care for her while she'd been sick.

He didn't have to do all of that, yet he did, never once asking for anything in return.

Added to that, he'd just hinted at his deeper emotions and she had a feeling he had shocked himself with his declaration, if his quick retreat was any indication.

Lily wanted to uncover so much more because she honestly didn't know a whole lot about the man who would be in her life forever—one way or another.

As he maneuvered the truck toward his home, Lily adjusted the air vents. Summer was in full force and the sun beat right in through the windshield, making her even hotter.

As much as her body ached for his, she needed backstory, needed to know what made this impossible-to-resist man so captivating. While they were driving, this was the perfect opportunity to dig in to his life a bit more.

"Where did you grow up?" she asked, breaking the silence.

His hand tightened on the steering wheel. "Not too far from here."

"Have you always worked with horses?"

"Yes."

He wasn't as talkative as she'd hoped, but most men weren't. Still, he never seemed to open up about his past... which made her want to uncover all he held back.

"So you had horses growing up?"

His eyes darted toward her, then back to the road. "We couldn't afford them."

Lily laced her fingers together in her lap and turned to stare out the window as he turned onto his road. "Sorry if I'm prying. I just want to learn more about you."

"Nothing to be sorry about," he told her. "My mom worked for a farm so I was always around horses. We just didn't own any. I always swore I'd have a farm of my own one day."

He had a vision, dreams. He worked hard and didn't sit back and feel sorry for himself about what was missing from his life.

How could she not be intrigued by this man who was so opposite from any other man who'd captured her attention? Everything about Nash was different. There wasn't a doubt in her mind that he held on to his past because he was embarrassed. He was a groom, she was a movie star, but couldn't he see that she saw them as equals?

She'd had very humble beginnings and she'd tried to express how money meant nothing to her. All she wanted was a man she could trust and rely on. The fact Nash turned her inside out with his seduction was just icing on the proverbial cake.

When Nash pulled to a stop in front of his house, Lily hopped out and grabbed some bags while Nash took the others and headed up the porch to unlock the door. Once they were settled inside and the bags were dropped onto the floor inside the foyer, Lily turned to Nash.

"Do you mind if we talk?"

Tossing his keys onto the small table, he turned back to meet her gaze. "I'd hoped we'd be doing other activities. What do you want to talk about?"

Lily stepped forward and reached up to wrap her arms around his neck. Instantly his strong arms enveloped her, always making her feel safe, protected...loved. Could he love her? Was he even thinking along those lines?

"Anything," she said. "I just feel like all we do is get naked and I think we really have so much to discuss. The future, what we're doing, the baby. I still don't know much about you."

Nash pulled back, literally and figuratively, as he stepped around her and let out a sigh. "You know all you need to right now."

Lily turned and followed him into the living room, refusing to accept his evasive tactics. "I know you grew up around horses and that you are close with your mother. That's all."

Across the room, Nash rested his hands on the mantel, his head dropped as tension crackled in the silence between them. Something weighed heavily on those wide shoulders of his, something he didn't want her to know.

Was he worried she'd think less of him? Did he wonder how much he should share just because they had different pasts?

Dread settled deep in the pit of her stomach. Was he hiding something worse? Endless possibilities flooded her mind.

"Nash, I know you're keeping something from me." She eased farther into the room, skirting around the sofa and coming to stand just behind him. "You're scaring me with the silence. It can't be that bad, can it?"

She hoped not. Had her judgment been so off again? *Please, no. Please let it be something that is in actuality very, very minor.*

"You deserve the truth," he muttered, still gripping onto the mantel so tightly his knuckles were white. "This is harder than I thought."

Lily slid a hand over her stomach. What had she done? She stepped back until her hip hit the edge of the sofa arm. She gripped the back of the cushion for support.

What bomb was he about to drop and how would this affect the life of her and her child?

Nash turned, his eyes full of vulnerability and fear. Raking a hand through his hair, he met her gaze across the room. "Damon Barrington is my father."

Seven

She'd been played for a fool...again.

Her shaky legs threatened to give out. How could she be so foolish? Was she so blinded by men with pretty words and charming attitudes that she couldn't pick out the liars?

Damon Barrington, billionaire horse racing icon, was Nash's father? Her eyes sought his across the room. He hadn't moved, had hardly blinked as he watched her to gauge her reaction. So many thoughts swirled around in her mind she didn't know how she was supposed to react.

"You lied to me."

That was the bottom line.

Oh, no. Nash's father was a wealthy mogul and famous in his own right in the horse racing industry. How would the media spin this story once word got out who her baby's father was?

The muscle in his jaw ticked as he crossed those muscular arms over his chest. "Yes, I lied."

No defense? Was he just going to reveal that jaw-dropping fact and not elaborate?

Lily rubbed her forehead, hoping to chase away the impending headache. She wouldn't beg him to let her in. He either wanted to tell her or he didn't, but he better have a damn good reason for lying to her face.

"I honestly didn't want to lie to you," he defended, as if her silence had triggered him to speak up for himself.

A laugh escaped her. "And yet you did it anyway."

"Damon doesn't know who I am." In two long strides, Nash closed the gap to stand directly in front of her. Those bright blue eyes held hers as if pleading for her to hear him out. "To my knowledge he never even knew my mother was pregnant. I only found out he was my birth father several months ago and that's when I came to work for him. I needed to see what kind of man he was, needed to know if I even wanted to pursue a relationship with him."

A bit of her heart melted, but he'd still withheld information from her, pretending to be someone he wasn't.

"You're the son of the most prominent man in this industry and you didn't even think to tell me?"

Nash reached for her hands, held them tight against his chest as he took another step toward her. "When we first started our connection was just physical. You know that. But then I started getting more involved with you and I worried about disclosing the truth, but I also knew you'd be leaving at the end of the shoot. I wasn't going to say anything to Damon until you were gone and it never would've affected you. But now…"

Realization dawned on her. He'd had to tell her. But the fact of the matter was he only did so when forced to, and that hurt her more than she cared to admit.

"The baby."

Nash nodded, squeezing her hands as if he was afraid she would turn and run. "I truly never wanted you involved in my mess, in this lie, but things were out of my control."

Lily raised her brows. "Out of your control?"

"Fine." The corners of his mouth lifted slightly, showcasing that devastating smile. "I couldn't control myself around you, but I could control how much of my life I let you in on. I wasn't able to tell you before."

"Why now?" she asked, searching his face, finding only vulnerability masked by a handsome, rugged exterior. "You could've kept this to yourself until you talked to Damon."

He held her hands against his heart with one palm and slid his other hand up along her cheek, his fingers threading through her hair.

"No, I couldn't. You've come to mean more, we mean more, than I thought possible. I wasn't ready for you, Lily. I've had this secret living in me, I couldn't just let anyone in."

His heart beat heavily against her hand and Lily knew that him baring his soul was courageous and brave. He could've kept lying to her, he could've gone to Damon first with this bombshell, but he'd opened himself up.

"Besides," he went on, drawing her closer. "I need you. More than I want to admit, and on a level that terrifies me. No matter what's going on around me, in spite of all my issues, I need the passion we possess. I need you, Lily."

Mercy, when he said things like that her entire body shivered, her stomach flopped as nerves settled deep inside her. He wasn't lying now. No man had ever looked at her the way he did. She saw the raw truth in his eyes. Saw how hard it was to expose himself.

"I need you with me right now," he told her, nipping at her lips. "I need to draw from your strength."

The man was twice her size, with his broad, muscular shoulders, his towering height, yet he wanted her strength? He humbled her with his direct, bold declaration.

"Are you going to tell him soon?" she asked, gripping his shirt.

"I really don't know. Part of me wants to, especially now that the film is done, the racing season is over and the girls aren't under as much pressure."

Lily smiled, warming to the idea of Nash being part of such an amazing family. "You have sisters. Nash, this is such a big deal. You have to go to them. They deserve to know. If you want me to go with you, I will. I'll stay back, too. Whatever you want."

Encircling her waist with both arms, Nash pulled her close where her hands were trapped between them. "I'll go soon. But right now, I want to embrace the fact the mother of my child is in my house where there are no interruptions, no schedules to keep. You're supposed to be relaxing and I have the perfect spot."

She eased back, looking him in the eyes. "Don't keep the truth from me again. We're in this together and I can't be with someone I don't trust."

Those bright eyes held hers, the muscle in his jaw clenched and for a second she thought he was about to say something, but he simply nodded.

"Was that our first fight?" she asked.

Nash nuzzled his lips against her neck, his beard tickling her sensitive skin. "I guess so. We better go kiss and make up."

He walked her backward and Lily couldn't help but laugh as she found herself being drawn more and more into his world. Yes, he'd kept something monumental from her, but in his defense he was still working through the new information himself. She couldn't imagine finding your father at this stage in life and she couldn't blame Nash for being confused on how to respond and what steps to take. This was all new territory and they had to wade through it together.

They headed down the hall, his hands cupping her bottom as he led her into the bedroom.

"This is where you'll stay while you're here," he told her as he trailed his lips across her jawline and to her ear. "Clothing is optional."

A thrill shot through her. Being claimed shouldn't be so arousing, yet she found herself wanting Nash more and more each time he threw down that dominance gauntlet.

With a kick of his foot, the bedroom door slammed shut.

* * *

Nash jerked another bale of hay from the stack and moved it into the stable. Frustration and guilt fueled each aggressive movement. He'd lied to Lily, was still lying to her and had worked his way back into a corner he may never find the way out of.

He'd never forget the look on her face when she'd discovered he was Damon's son. But she only knew part of the truth. The rest of his secret wouldn't be so easily defended and the damn last thing he'd ever intended on doing was hurting her.

His plan was to reveal himself to Damon, figure out how the hell to get those horses and get back to his own estate. He was done living these lies, done hurting people he had been around for the past few months.

As much as the guilt ate at him, he still wouldn't leave without what he came for. Otherwise this whole journey would be in vain.

Sweat poured down his back as he stacked the last bale against the far wall. He'd called and checked on Lily several times today and each time she assured him she was fine and if she needed anything she'd call him. Still, he couldn't help but worry. Would he be like this the entire pregnancy? Always worrying?

Nash knew it wasn't just the pregnancy. Everything was closing in on him at once. He needed to confess now that the racing season was over and Cassie and Tessa were focusing on Cassie's new school. He couldn't wait for Damon to sell those horses to someone else.

Nash's assistant should've already proposed the next offer, now Nash just had to wait.

Waiting was about the dead last thing he wanted to do, but he hadn't gotten this far in life by being impulsive. Timing was everything in reaching your goals.

And timing would definitely play a major role in the next steps he took with Lily. It was like walking through a minefield. One wrong move and every plan, every unexpected blessing could all blow up in his face.

He'd spoken with his mother this morning and she was still worried about him exposing the truth, but Nash assured her he wasn't going to disclose everything, only that Damon was his father. Everything else…hell, he had no clue when to drop that bomb. Would Damon look closer and see the man who had been his rival for so long? They'd not been face-to-face in the business world in years and Nash knew he'd changed. Besides the hair, the beard and the clothes, Nash had done more grunt work on his own land, bulking him up quite a bit and changing his physique.

"You may be the hardest working groom I've ever employed."

Nash jerked around to see Damon striding through the stables. Fate had just presented him with the perfect opportunity…but was he ready to take it?

Damn it, this was harder than he thought. Before him stood the man who was his biological father and had no clue. How would he react? Would putting the fact out in the open change Damon's life? Would he care? Would he embrace Nash as part of the family?

In the past several months since learning the truth, Nash had played this scenario in his head a million times. Now that the perfect opportunity had presented itself, he didn't know how to lead into the life-altering conversation.

"Haven't seen you down here much lately," Nash finally said as he tugged off his work gloves and shoved them in his back pocket.

"The girls are done training, so that's freed up my time." The elderly man rested his hand on one of the gates to a stall, curling his fingers around the wrought-iron bars. "I come down more in the evening now. Been spending some of my days playing with sweet Emily."

Nash smiled. Emily was Damon's granddaughter…and Nash's niece. So many instant family members. Actually, with Ian marrying Cassie, that would make Lily's agent Nash's soon-to-be brother-in-law.

His head was spinning. Everything would start unraveling the moment he told Damon the truth, or the part of the truth that Lily knew.

Nash had no clue how Damon would react to having a long lost son, but he knew damn sure how he'd react if he found out the rest of Nash's identity. Epic anger like nothing Nash had ever seen, of that he was positive.

One step at a time.

"You going to be home later?" Nash asked, resting his hands on his hips.

Horses shuffled in the background, one neighed as if trying to chime into the conversation. Nash was starting to love these stables as much as his own. Damn it, he hadn't counted on getting emotionally invested in this place, this family...Lily.

What the hell was happening to him?

"Should be."

"Mind if I come back around seven? I need a private meeting with you."

Damon's silver brows drew together. "You're not quitting on me, are you, son?"

Son. The word was a generic term yet Damon had no clue just how swiftly he'd hit that nail on the head.

"No, sir."

"You've got me intrigued." Damon let out a robust laugh and nodded. "Sure. Come on up to the house about seven."

"Will Cassie and Tessa be around? They may want to be there, too."

He'd made a split-second decision to include his half-sisters. Honestly, Nash wasn't sure if Damon would want the girls to know, but Nash needed them to. The more time he'd spent here, the more he'd gotten involved in their lives and wanted a chance for a family.

"I can ask," Damon informed him. "You've certainly piqued my curiosity, so I'm sure they'll be intrigued, as well."

Nash swiped his forearm across his sweaty forehead, then rested his hands on his hips. "Great. I'll be up to the main house around seven."

If Lily wanted to join him, he wouldn't turn down her support. He needed her, and that wasn't weakness talking, either.

Besides, if he shared everything he could with her now, perhaps the blow that would inevitably come later wouldn't be so harsh. The only other woman he'd let close to him was his mother. Women in his life had come and gone, nobody really fit. Lily fit…as much as she could with all the jagged edges of his life he'd yet to smooth out.

Nash knew he had fallen into a hole so deep, there was no way out and he was starting to wish for things that could never be.

Eight

Lily resisted the urge to throw her phone, and she would pull the childish tantrum if she didn't have to go through the annoyance of getting a new one.

But she wasn't one to waste money.

For pity's sake, she was so sick of certain people in the industry—ahem, producers, actors, etc.—assuming that because they were a big name, she would jump at the chance to work with them. Then when she declined, the offer of more money really set her teeth to grinding. She couldn't be bought, something they found hard to believe.

Thankfully her agent, Ian, had called with the movie options and the ridiculous counteroffers. He was still trying to find her a film that could accommodate her expanding belly, but Lily wasn't sure how work would fit into the life she was envisioning with Nash. The baby was no problem. A relationship with Nash? How would he feel about Hollywood? There was no way she could stay away from the limelight and she knew he was a private man. He'd made no definite declarations to her, yet she found herself hoping everything would work out, because she truly wanted this amazing man in her life, and not just for the baby.

Swinging her legs around, she propped her feet up on the

leather sofa and settled back against the cushioned armrest. This relaxing nonsense was getting really old really fast and she had only been here a few days. If this lasted her entire pregnancy she would go insane.

Added to that, Nash was very attentive to her needs. Okay, wait, that wasn't a bad thing at all. But the man wouldn't let her do anything for herself. He insisted she take it easy and rest until her next appointment when the doctor would come and assess her.

Funny, Lily didn't recall agreeing to stay with him that long. Apparently he'd assumed she would just live here. That was definitely a talk they would be having soon. At some point she'd have to leave, to pack her things and go back to her life. She didn't want all of this uncertainty in her future.

And she was still reeling from the news that Nash was Damon Barrington's son. Even though her first gut reaction was anger, she had to give Nash the benefit of the doubt. The man was obviously torn. He was struggling with this new identity and working as a groom to get close to his biological father. How could she hold that against him?

He hadn't deliberately lied to her and she'd seen the turmoil he'd battled with over revealing the truth to her. What had he done before coming to the Barringtons' estate? Had he been a groom elsewhere? She assumed he worked with horses since he'd told her he did that as a child. Obviously love for the animals and hard work were in his blood.

Had she been in his shoes, she wouldn't have disclosed her secret to a virtual stranger, either.

Oh, how fate had other plans for them. Lily never would've dreamed she'd be living in Nash's cottage, pregnant with his child while he debated on when and how to drop the paternity bomb on the racing mogul.

The sooner the past came out, the better. Wasn't that true for any type of potential relationship?

The front door opened and closed seconds before Nash's heavy footfalls moved through the foyer. He rounded the arched doorway into the living room and offered her a half smile.

"You look like I feel." She rested an arm along the back of the couch, taking in his lean form as he propped a shoulder against the door frame. "Bad day?"

"I'm grabbing a shower and heading back to the estate." Nash ran a hand along his short beard, around to the back of his neck as he let out a sigh. "I'm going to tell him."

Lily jerked up, gripping the back of the couch. "Does he know you're coming back?"

"Yeah."

Lily couldn't believe he was ready to take this step. She knew he wanted to, but she had no idea he was doing it so soon after telling her. Had opening up to her released something else in him? Something that made him want to get his life in order before the baby came? And, dare she hope, for them to move forward together?

"Do you want me to come?"

Nash's eyes met her, his toe-curling smile spread across his face. "I would, but only if you're comfortable going."

Lily came to her feet, smoothing her simple cotton dress down her legs. Rounding the couch, she crossed the cozy living room. Encircling his neck with her arms, Lily answered his devastating smile with her own.

"I don't want to assume anything in any part of your life, Nash. I know our relationship has been a whirlwind, but I don't think you should go through this alone."

"Damn, I want to hold you," he told her, resting his forehead against hers. "But I smell like the ass end of that stable and I need a shower."

Lily laughed as she settled a quick peck on his lips. "I don't mind, you know. But, go shower. I'll throw on my shoes and pull my hair back real quick."

Nash's brows rose. "That's all you're going to do?"

"Uh, yeah, why?" Stepping back and narrowing her gaze, she crossed her arms. "Are you saying I need to change or put makeup on? I know you're used to seeing me all made up on set, but this is the real me, Nash. No fuss and kind of boring."

His hand snaked out, wrapped around her arm and tugged her until she fell against his chest. "I'm a much bigger fan of the no-fuss Lily. I'm just still surprised that you don't care about getting all made up to leave the house."

With a shrug, she laid her palms against his taut T-shirt. "I'm not like most women and I'm definitely not like most Hollywood women. I'm pretty low-key when I'm not working."

Nash's hands roamed down to cup her bottom as he pulled her hips against his. "That's a good thing. Now let me get in the shower and stop manhandling me or we'll be late."

Rolling her eyes, Lily laughed as he kept squeezing her backside. "Yes, of course. What was I thinking?"

As he moved down the hallway, Lily watched him go. The confident stride, the wide shoulders pulling the material of his sweat-soaked T was beyond sexy and his sense of humor only added to his appeal. She found they were growing more and more comfortable with each other outside the bedroom, not that their passion had diminished any, either.

Within thirty minutes they were in Nash's truck, making the ten-minute drive to the Barrington estate. Lily was nervous for him, but he seemed pretty relaxed with his wrist dangling over the steering wheel, his other hand lightly holding on to hers in her lap.

"So what happened with you today?" he asked, breaking the silence. "Are you feeling bad?"

"No, nothing like that." She glanced out the side window, taking in the beautiful farms with the acres of white fencing as far as the eye could see. "I've been on the phone off and on with Ian. He's still trying to find a part for me that will work with this pregnancy. There was one role that would have been a good fit, but I just turned it down before you got home."

"Turned it down? Why?"

"I'm not ready to commit to something long-term just now." She turned to face him, loving the comfortable feel of his hand wrapped around hers, loving even more how fast they were venturing beyond their physical connection. "Besides, the producer is beyond arrogant and he assumed I'd jump at the script. To be honest, if this was another time, with no complications, I would've sucked it up and taken the film."

"Then take it," he told her simply. "Don't let anything hold you back. If they want you, they'll work around the baby."

"I know they will." She wasn't so sure they would work around the fact that she was falling in love and had no clue where she would end up if Nash wanted a future. "It felt good to say no, though. Money is a big part of negotiating contracts, but he just flashes it like it's the red flag and we're the bull charging in after it."

Perhaps that sounded petty, but she wasn't one to be swayed so easily.

"I just have issues with people throwing money around, thinking that will buy them happiness or anything else they want," she went on. "My stepfather kind of ruined me for the rich type. That sounds strange coming from me with what I pull in per film, but I've never thrown my money around and I certainly have never tried to buy someone to get my way."

Nash tensed. "Not everybody with a lot of money is bad and sometimes they have good intentions but things can still go wrong."

Lily wasn't quite sure how to respond and she was quite frankly shocked that Nash was defending the upper class. But it wasn't worth arguing about and she held tightly to his hand as they pulled into the Barringtons' entrance. The wrought-iron gates, with a scrolling *B* on each side, were standing wide-open, inviting them in.

The long, picturesque drive leading back to the property, showcased the horses out in the pasture and led the way to the grand stone stable up ahead. Of course the family famous for their world-renowned success in the horse racing industry would have something that monumental in their lives front and center.

The months she'd spent filming on this farm and in the surrounding area were some of the best of her life. The small-town atmosphere, the intimate setting and getting to know the family of the story she was depicting was icing on the cake. She'd really grown close to Cassie, Tessa and Damon, and even their cook, Linda. The Barringtons might be small in numbers, but they made up for it in love and determination. Lily wanted that kind of family bond, craved it actually.

Her hand went to her flat stomach and she couldn't help but think ahead to the future about what life would be like with a child…and if the man beside her would be part of it.

"You sure you're ready to do this?" she asked when he pulled up in the circular drive and stopped near the front entrance.

Nash pulled their joined hands up to his lips, kissed the back of hers and gave her a big squeeze. "More than ready."

"What reason will you give them that I'm still here?"

Nash shrugged. "What do you want me to say?"

Lily prided herself on the truth, but she still wasn't ready to disclose her pregnancy to the world, yet. She also didn't want this to be about her or the baby at all. This was Nash's moment to possibly connect with a family he hadn't known existed.

And she was still unsure if she would be part of his family once they really sat down and talked about the future.

One monumental moment at a time.

"We can just tell them we met when I first started filming and became friends and I decided to hang around for a while and take a mini-vacation since the shoot was done."

Nash shot her his signature naughty grin. That sexy smile never failed to arouse her because she knew firsthand what that smile looked like as he rose above her just before he joined their bodies.

"I'm pretty sure they'll know we're more than friends," he told her.

"That's fine," she said with a shrug, realizing she truly didn't care.

She trusted this family to keep things private. They understood the way the media worked, considering they were celebrities in their own right with the Barrington sisters making history with their wins. Besides, she'd come to consider them friends and if she wanted to pursue something more with Nash, she needed to get used to opening herself to those that could quite possibly be a big part of his life.

"I'm just not adding any more information than that and I'm not bringing up the pregnancy. Besides, when you tell them the news, I'll be all but forgotten."

"You could never be forgotten." He smacked a kiss on her hand. "I'm not ready to let our little secret out, either. I like having you and this baby to myself for now."

Nash leaned across the center console, slid a hand along her jawline and captured her lips. Those soft, talented lips had been all over her body, yet when he kissed her with such tenderness and care, she couldn't help but wonder if he held back feelings and emotions he was afraid to express out loud.

Because his silent actions were screaming that he was falling in love with her. Heaven help her, she wanted him to be just as torn as she was. She wanted to know that as she entered into this unknown territory of what she felt could be true love, that she wasn't alone.

"Let's go," he murmured against her lips.

Nine

Nash couldn't let his mind drift to the conversation he had with Lily about her career and he sure as hell couldn't think about how his emotions regarding her were tying him up in knots. He was here for one reason and one reason only—to figure out what Damon Barrington would do with the paternity bomb Nash was about to drop.

"Well, we're all here." Damon smiled, crossing an ankle over his knee in his wingback leather chair in the living room as though he hadn't a care in the world. "I'm anxious to hear what you have to say."

Cassie and Tessa sat on the sofa, their matching bright blue eyes locked on his. Didn't they see it? Hadn't they noticed how they all had the exact same shade of cobalt-blue eyes? He'd purposely not worn contacts when he'd come to the estate, perhaps in hopes that someone would mention his eye color.

Nash sat next to Lily on the other sofa across from Tessa and Cassie. A rich mahogany coffee table sat between them, adorned with a perfect arrangement of summer flowers. The Barrington home was just as lavish and beautiful as his own…a home he was itching to get back to. A home he wanted to show Lily.

The Barrington clan had been surprised to see Lily, but had bought the friend story...or at least they hadn't questioned any further.

Even though Lily wasn't touching him, just her presence beside him all the support he needed. Lily was his rock right now.

"I've really enjoyed my time working here," he began, fighting off the nerves that threatened to consume him. "I've gotten to know all of you and was able to witness history firsthand when Tessa won the Triple Crown. I celebrated even though I was here and not at the race. Being on the ranch during filming was pretty amazing, too."

"You sure you're not quitting?" Damon chimed in. "This sounds like a lead into a resignation."

Nash shook his head and offered a smile. "I assure you, I'm not quitting."

"Is everything okay?" Cassie asked, her brows drawn in.

The two women on the opposite couch were so similar, yet so different. Both had long, crimson hair and those striking blue eyes, but where Tessa was lean and athletic, Cassie was curvy and softer. Both were beautiful, dynamic women and he realized just how much he wanted to be part of their lives.

Damn it. He'd never let himself be vulnerable before. Business had always ruled his life and in that aspect he kept control gripped in a tight fist. His mother was the only person he'd ever let affect him emotionally. But, in a sense, he was also here for her. It was time the secret came out. She deserved to be free of any guilt or residual turmoil and he deserved to know where he stood in his father's life.

"Everything is fine," Nash assured them. Unable to stay seated another minute, he came to his feet and paced behind the couch. "This is harder than I thought."

Along the mantel sat photos in pewter frames, some pictures were of the girls as children, some of Damon's late wife, Rose, but they all depicted the family and the love they shared.

He'd missed out on all of that. But he couldn't blame his mother. She'd made the choices she thought best under the circumstances. Besides, what's done was done and now he just had to figure out the best way to deal with the facts he had…and still get all he wanted in the end.

"I need to start at the beginning." He turned to face them, rested his hands on his hips. "My mother used to work on this estate years ago. She actually worked here as a trainer before I was born."

Damon's eyes widened. "Other than Cassie, I've only employed one other female trainer."

Nash's heart beat so hard, so fast. He waited, letting the impact truly sink in as he kept his eyes on Damon's.

"Your mother was Elaine James?" Damon asked, almost in a stunned whisper.

Both Cassie and Tessa turned their eyes to their father. Nash waited, wanting to see how the events would unfold before he continued.

"Who's Elaine James?" Tessa asked before glancing back to Nash.

"She was one of the best horse trainers in the industry at one time," Damon told her, still staring at Nash. "I used her during a period when female trainers were frowned upon, but some owners snuck around that. She kept her hair really short, wore a hat and would come in early in the mornings and late at night to work with the horses."

Nash knew all of this, had heard his mom tell that same story over and over of how women were gentler and less competitive by nature so Damon had wanted a woman for the job.

"When my mother left here to take care of her parents, she went to work at another farm several hours away," Nash went on. He forced himself to keep his focus on Damon. Right now, nothing else mattered but gauging the older man's reaction. "It wasn't too long after she'd left that she realized she was pregnant with me."

Damon's gasp nearly echoed in the spacious room. Lily sat quietly with her hands in her lap, but Cassie and Tessa's eyes widened as if they were putting the pieces together.

"This can't be," Damon whispered, his eyes darting around the room frantically, then back to lock on Nash's. "You—"

"I'm your son."

There. He'd admitted half of the truth that had weighed heavily on his shoulders since first arriving here several months ago.

Now what? He honestly hadn't planned this far ahead. He'd definitely planned on the end result, but he hadn't factored in all the uncomfortable moments—and now was one of them.

Stunned silence settled over the room. Lily hadn't moved, she merely sat with her eyes locked on his as if silently sending him support. When his gaze landed on hers, she offered a sweet smile of encouragement.

"Nash, forgive me, but I'm going to need more proof than just your word," Damon finally said. "Where is your mother now?"

Nash came around the couch, taking a seat next to Lily again. Now that the secret was out, or part of it anyway, he could somewhat relax for the moment. But he still kept the upper hand.

"I don't blame you for not taking just my word," Nash told the older man. "My mom had a stroke about six months ago. She's doing much better now, but right after the scare, she confessed that she used to work for you and the two of you were…involved."

Nash refused to elaborate.

"Why didn't she tell me?" Damon asked, his brows drawn in, shoulders stiff. "Once she left, I never heard from her again."

Even through years of rivalry and more recently while

working here in a more personal setting, Nash had never seen Damon so stunned.

"When she left to take on a new role at another farm, she had no idea she was pregnant." Nash rested his elbows on his knees, lacing his fingers together as he looked from his half-sisters to his father. "From what she told me, by the time she found out and got the courage to come back and tell you, she was about eight months pregnant. She worried you wouldn't believe her, or that you would marry her just for the baby and she didn't want you to feel trapped. But she wanted you to know. She said she came back to town and all the buzz was about you and Rose and your recent engagement."

Nash recalled his mother's watery confession when she'd begged him to forgive her for not following through and going to Damon. She'd apologized for keeping Nash from his biological father and said that the years of seeing them as rivals in the industry had nearly killed her.

But how could Nash blame her or be angry? She was young, alone and scared. He sure as hell had no place to judge anyone keeping a secret.

"She told me she didn't want to ruin your relationship with your fiancée," Nash went on. "So she ended up having me and raising me on her own."

The words settled in the air and Nash had to fight to keep from reaching out for Lily's hand. He wanted her familiar touch for support, but more than anything he wanted to reassure her that their baby would always know her place in a family.

Damon rubbed his forehead as if still processing all this information. "Did she ever marry?"

Was he asking as a man who once cared for Nash's mother or was Damon asking from a father's standpoint, worried about his son having a male role model?

"She did when I was about ten."

"Yet you still have her last name," Damon said, shifting in his seat. "Your stepfather didn't adopt you?"

This was the part of coming clean that was about to get tricky. He had to proceed cautiously because one slip of the tongue and all hell would break loose as the complete truth was finally revealed.

"He did," Nash replied. "I chose to still use my mother's maiden name."

Okay, that was a lie, but Damon couldn't know Nash's true identity...not until Nash was ready to share that fact. And the first person he owed the real truth to was Lily.

Wow, his priorities had definitely shifted since he'd first arrived at Stony Ridge Acres. When the hell did that happen? When did contemplating his next step automatically have his mind shifting to how Lily would react or how Lily would feel?

"So you've been here all this time...spying on us?" Tessa asked, her eyes narrowed as she took both hands and shoved her hair away from her face. "Why not say something right at first? Why the lies?"

Nash cleared his throat. "I wasn't sure I wanted to reveal the truth, to be honest. I've always worked with horses and before I could really make up my mind on how to handle the situation after I learned the truth, the groom position came open. I couldn't pass it up."

"You couldn't have told us who you were before now?" Cassie's eyes were softer, yet still guarded like her sister's.

Yes, he could've, but he'd been busy trying to buy out Damon's prizewinning horses and in his spare time he'd been getting naked with Lily. His priorities had taken a hard turn into unexpected territory.

"I understand this makes an impact on all of your lives," he began, choosing his words carefully. "I had to see if this was even a family that would welcome me, or if I should keep the secret and eventually just leave quietly."

Lily did reach over now and squeezed his hand. The gesture wasn't lost on the Barrington sisters whose eyes darted in their direction.

Nash didn't want to think how that silent action truly spoke volumes for how supportive Lily was and how, right at this moment, his emotions meant more to her than what other people assumed or thought. Damn it. He didn't deserve her loyalty, her kindness and innocence. He was lying to her and no matter how he justified it, no matter how he knew there had been no way around the secrets, he was still in a relationship with a woman who didn't even know his real name.

"And you've deemed us fit to be in your life now?" Tessa came to her feet, tugged the hem of her shirt down and crossed her arms. "I'm skeptical, for sure, but more than anything I'm a little hurt you basically spied on us."

Nash nodded. "I expected all of you to feel that way, but I had to do what was best for me and my mom. My stepfather is gone and I've taken care of her for years. I have to put her wishes and feelings above anything else."

"She was okay with you coming here?" Damon chimed in.

"She left that decision up to me," Nash informed him. "But she was worried that, at this point, I would disrupt your lives."

"I have a brother," Cassie whispered, her eyes filling.

"Cass," Damon warned. "We still need proof, though I'm pretty sure Nash is telling the truth."

"It's the eyes," Cassie said with a wide smile as she swiped her damp cheeks. "He's got our eyes."

Obviously not one to show emotions, Tessa turned to her father. "How could you go from his mother to our mom in such a short period of time?" she asked, throwing her arms wide. She still hadn't sat back down and Nash was pretty sure she really wanted to storm out. She was definitely the more vocal sister.

Damon eased back in his chair, his hands gripping the leather armrests. "Without getting into details you all probably don't want to hear, Elaine and I were attracted to each other, but we never fell in love or even mentioned a relationship beyond the physical. Once she left, I met Rose and love at first sight was something I had believed to be a myth until I saw her. We met one day, went on our first date the next and were inseparable. She was it for me."

Nash swallowed. His mother had pretty much said the same thing. She and Damon hadn't been in love, just young lovers having a good time. And they were from two different worlds, which was probably frowned upon at that time.

The beginning of his mother and Damon's relationship mirrored that of Lily and himself. Only Nash had every intention of a different ending.

"Your eyes," Tessa murmured as she slowly maneuvered around the coffee table and sat on the other side of him. "I knew when you first came here that there was something about you."

Nash nodded, trying not to get too wrapped up in these emotions that threatened to rise to the surface. "I saw it first thing, too."

He hadn't even realized until this moment just how much he wanted the girls and Damon to accept him. He may have more money than he would ever need or know what to do with, but there was one thing money couldn't buy...a family. And deep inside, that's what he'd always wanted.

"You really are my brother?" she asked, her voice cracking.

Nash smiled. "Yeah, I am."

"So what now?"

Nash shifted to focus back on Damon, who still had his silver brows drawn as if he didn't know whether to be confused or angry. This was another part of the plan that he'd have to tread lightly on because as much as Nash wanted to get those horses, he also wanted this family. He just had to figure out a way to cleverly capture it all.

"That's up to you," Nash told his father. "I love working here, but I understand if you aren't able to trust me right now."

"No," Cassie said, shaking her head. "You've proven your-self. Right, Dad? Nash is the hardest working groom we've ever had."

Damon nodded, easing forward in his seat. "You're more than welcome to keep working here, Nash. And, if you own any horses, feel free to house them here."

Oh, the irony. Between the double families, the Bar-ringtons, Lily and his baby, and the horse ownership, Nash was spinning in circles and feared he'd have a hard time keeping all of his lies straight before he could present them in a justifiable manner.

"I actually don't have any right now," he told Damon, which was partially true. Nash's horses just weren't here locally.

"The groom position is yours as long as you want it." Damon came to his feet and Nash assumed that was his cue to do the same. "And if you get a horse, these stables are available to you anytime."

Nash stood before his father, the same man he was try-ing to buy out, and held out his hand. "I appreciate that."

Damon clasped Nash's hand and pulled him into a one-armed man-hug before easing back. The sadness in his eyes matched his tone. "I'm sorry about your mother. If there's anything I can do…"

"Thanks." Absolutely no way would anyone else take care of his mother. Nash was a bit protective of her and right now he wasn't ready to discuss her too much. "She's doing really well, actually."

Damon nodded and released Nash's hand. "You've cer-tainly dropped a bomb I hadn't expected. I hope my stunned silence at times didn't make you feel unwelcome, I'm just still so shocked."

"I understand. I was shocked, too, but I've had several months to process this." Nash glanced down to Lily who was toying with the hem of her dress lying against her tanned thighs. "I think Lily and I will go and let you all talk things over in private."

He extended his hand to Lily and assisted her up. She presented a killer smile to Damon and patted his arm.

"You've really been blessed with this news," she told him. "Shocking as it may be, your family has grown and you've gained a wonderful son."

Damon embraced her and patted her back. "Rose would've loved you."

Nash knew Damon and Lily had bonded pretty well during the filming of Damon's life. Lily had played Damon's late wife and the two had often discussed the late Mrs. Barrington. Damon was all too eager to share stories and memories of his wife.

Guilt and a new set of nerves settled deep in Nash's gut. There was still one more piece of damning information he had to reveal. He'd grown beyond the man who initially settled in here to spy on his rival and to have a heated affair.

Now Nash wanted a family, both families, and he had no choice but to destroy any amount of progress he'd made. Once the truth revealed itself, any hope of having a relationship with the Barringtons or Lily would be gone.

"I just hope once the film is out, people will see how amazing this family truly is, and not just in the racing world." Lily made her way around the room and hugged Tessa and Cassie. "I'll be in town for a while," she informed them. "Perhaps we could go to lunch or something?"

Cassie smiled. "I'd like that. I assume we can find you at Nash's?"

Lily laughed. "Yes, but please don't let that get out."

"We'd never say a word," Tessa assured. "I'm glad you'll be here awhile. Now that Cassie and I have a little more free time, we could use a girls' day out."

Nash watched as the sisters he'd just inherited bonded with the mother of his child.

Failure wasn't an option. Not when he had this much at

stake. All he could do now was wait for his assistant to get back to him on whether or not Damon would take the deal. Until then, Nash was at a standstill and unclear of his next move.

Ten

Insomnia was a cruel, unwelcome friend.

Lily tried her hardest not to make too much noise as she searched the kitchen for her guilty pleasure. Unfortunately, Nash didn't keep cocoa or chocolate syrup on hand.

With the gallon of milk in tow, she closed the refrigerator door and thought how she could get her chocolate milk fix. Being a chocoholic was her downfall, right behind the grilled cheese. Hey, she could have worse addictions. Granted, food obsessions in LA were unheard of, considering women there opted to starve themselves so they were skinnier than their so-called friends. Lily loved food too much for all of that nonsense.

And she had a weakness for chocolate milk.

With a brilliant plan in mind, she jerked open the freezer and instantly spotted a gallon of chocolate swirl ice cream. Perfect backup in a pinch.

Grabbing the largest glass she could reach in the cabinet, Lily found a spoon and scooped a hefty helping of ice cream into her glass before she carefully poured milk over it. She saw nothing wrong with having a chocolate float at two in the morning. One good thing about the pregnancy, she could totally blame her crazy cravings on the baby. Of course, even when she wasn't pregnant she'd wake up in the middle of the night for chocolate milk, but nobody needed to know that.

Using the spoon, she stabbed at the hunk of ice cream at the bottom of the glass in an attempt to break some of it up into chocolaty goodness. She'd just taken her first sip when footsteps shuffled over the tile behind her.

Licking the milk mustache off her top lip, because she was a classy lady, Lily turned to see Nash looking very sexy and sleepy with his lounge pants sitting low on his narrow waist. His long, disheveled hair fell across his forehead and those bright blue eyes zeroed in on the glass in her hand before darting to the ice cream and milk on the counter.

Even with just the small light on over the stove, she could see the amusement overriding the tiredness etched on his face.

"Don't judge me."

She took another gulp and welcomed the coolness as it spread through her body. Who knew being pregnant turned on some sort of internal furnace?

"I don't even know what to say," he told her with a smirk. "Is this something you normally do?"

Lily leaned her hip against the center island. "When I can't sleep I usually get up and have some chocolate milk, but you didn't have any syrup so I had to improvise."

With a slight tilt of his head, his eyes instantly flashed with concern. "What's on your mind that you're not sleeping?"

Clutching her glass, Lily laughed. Where to start? "Everything at the moment."

Remaining in the doorway with his shoulder propped against the jam, Nash crossed his arms over his deliciously bare chest. Would she ever tire of looking at him? Touching him?

The fire that continued to burn between them wasn't all that had her wanting more with this intriguing man. He excited her in ways she'd never felt before, he made her feel as if she was actually meaningful to his life, as if he wasn't only with her for her celebrity status. And he was honest. She needed honesty. Coming from a land where lies flew as quickly as the wind, she needed that stability. She needed him.

Earlier tonight when she'd seen him vulnerable, baring his soul to a family that didn't know he existed had twisted something even deeper within her. There was so much more to Nash than she'd first uncovered and all she knew was she wanted to discover the rest.

"Talk to me," he murmured, that low tone washing over her. "I'm a pretty good listener."

He was good at everything…hence her hang-ups and torments.

"I'm just thinking." *Worrying.* "With Damon knowing who you are now, what will happen next with your life."

She took a drink, thankful for the prop in her hands and the comfort of her guilty pleasure. Having these thoughts occupy her mind was one thing, letting them out in the open was another. But here they were, surrounded by near darkness and silence where they would have no interruptions. Might as well lay out some of her concerns.

"That's not all on your mind."

Lily caught his stare from across the room. He knew her all too well. And here she'd worried they only knew each other intimately. For months everything had been so one-dimensional, which had worked perfectly for them until the shocking baby news. Even after that, though, they'd kept things physical, not delving too deep.

Everything about them had recently shifted. She knew his fears of opening up to Damon and the girls just as he knew her fears of the baby and her career. They were in this together, bonding, growing closer…and that scared her to death.

"I don't want this child to ever worry about where she stands with us." Lily slid her free hand over her stomach, silently vowing protection over her innocent baby. "I saw the torment in your eyes, Nash. I saw the vulnerability when you were talking to Damon. You're a strong man, but family is something that I can see you take very seriously. I guess I'm worried where we're headed, not just you and me, but this baby. I don't want her life torn between ours."

Nash moved farther into the kitchen. The closer he came, the bigger he seemed to get. Those tanned, bare, broad shoulders, wrapped over muscles from working hard on a farm, would make any woman's knees weak and toes curl. She was no exception.

His hand slid over hers on her stomach. "This child will never question how much we love her. No matter where we are, this child takes top priority."

Thrilled that his level of passion for protecting and loving this child was the same as hers, Lily smiled. But she didn't miss the fact he avoided the topic of them as a couple.

One day at a time. She still had months to think things through. Ian was totally understanding in her taking a bit of time off since she'd just wrapped filming and was coming to terms with the pregnancy. She couldn't be happier that she'd taken him on as her agent.

So while he was figuring out her next career move, Lily was trying to get a handle on her personal life and how she could keep her career, raise the baby and figure out her feelings for Nash. Whatever they had went beyond lust, beyond sexual, but she couldn't identify it quite yet.

Without another word, Nash took the cold glass from her hand and took a drink. Milk settled into his mustache before his tongue darted out to swipe it away.

She'd never been attracted to a man with a scruffy beard and unkempt hair before, but something about Nash had been intriguing from the second she'd met him. Lily had actually found his ruggedness sexy and a nice change from all the pretty boys in Hollywood who worried too much about their looks.

"You're right," he told her. "This is good."

Reclaiming her glass, Lily took another drink and made a mental note to go to the store for syrup first thing in the morning. A woman had needs, after all.

Speaking of needs, the way Nash's heavy-lidded eyes raked over her silky chemise made her shiver with arousal. She'd worried about staying with Nash because she'd been afraid all they would do was act on all this sexual chemistry they had instead of figuring things out. But staying with him had forced them to evaluate what was going on between them and open up a little more each day.

The sex was just icing on the proverbial cake.

Without a word, Nash took the glass from her once again, but instead of taking a drink, he set it on the counter. The clank of the glass on the granite echoed in the silence. His strong hands glided over her silky gown at her sides as he eased her closer to him. The warmth of his fingers burned through the thin layer of material.

"I know something else that cures insomnia," he murmured. "It's quite a bit more grown-up than chocolate milk."

With a firm hold around her waist, Nash leaned forward, sliding his lips over her jawline and down her neck. Trembling against his touch, Lily gripped his biceps and tilted her head back as he continued his path on down toward the slope of her sensitive breasts.

Nash cleverly reached up, easing the thin straps of the chemise down with just the brush of his fingertips. Lily lifted her arms, ridding herself of the straps and in a swift whoosh, the flimsy garment puddled at her feet, leaving her wearing nothing but his arousing touch.

Nash quickly took advantage of her state of undress and bent his head to continue his torture with those talented lips. Lily arched into him as he claimed her with only his mouth. While Nash thoroughly loved on her breasts with his hands and lips, she slid her thumbs into the waistband of his pants and shoved them down. A sense of urgency overwhelmed her.

Nash pulled away from her breast and before she could protest, he slammed his mouth onto hers. Wrapping her arms around him, she threaded her fingers through his hair and held him in place. Without breaking contact from her mouth, Nash lifted her off the ground, keeping her flush with his body.

Encircling his waist with her legs, Lily locked her ankles behind his back and clung tighter as he moved from the kitchen toward the hall. Lily clutched at his shoulders, angling her mouth to take the kiss deeper in an attempt to take some control. When he tried to break the kiss, her lips only found his again. She needed his mouth on her, needed that contact with a desire she'd not known before Nash.

He backed her into the wall before they made it to the bedroom door. Grabbing her hands from his shoulders, he plastered them beside her head and held her in place with only his hard, firm body.

"None of that," he whispered against her lips when she tried to capture his mouth again. "You're supposed to be relaxing, which means I'm in control."

Lily smiled, tilted her hips toward him, pleased when his lids shuddered closed as he let out a low groan.

"You would tempt a saint," he growled.

"I only want to tempt you."

Nash's eyes opened, focused on hers as he slid into her. Those cobalt baby blues demanded her attention, held her captivated as he set the pace. Lily couldn't look away if she wanted to.

Everything about Nash was demanding, yet attentive, bold, yet nurturing…in bed and out.

As her hips met his and her hands continued to grip his shoulders, Lily watched Nash's face. A myriad of emotions crossed before her eyes: determination, arousal, need…and love. She saw it as plain as she could feel him. The man loved her, but whether he was ready to admit it to himself was an entirely different matter. He had enough going on right now without professing his love to her.

Still, she couldn't help but feel a bit relieved that he may have developed such strong feelings for her. Because she had already started falling for the simple groom with a complicated life.

Lily continued to hold his gaze as she trembled with release, and as Nash followed suit, he didn't look away. Those bright blues stayed transfixed on her, sending a new wave of shivers coursing through her.

And when their tremors passed, Nash leaned his forehead against hers and whispered, "You're more than I ever thought I was looking for."

Eleven

Nash had no clue what the hell had transpired in the hall just moments ago, but as he lay holding Lily in his arms on the bed they'd shared for a week, he realized two things: one, she was more vulnerable than she wanted him to see; and two, he'd let some of his own feelings slip out when his guard had been let down.

He had to keep his emotions close to his chest. He couldn't afford to reveal just how fast he'd started falling for Lily.

She was right when she'd said family meant everything to him and that's why he had to remain in control. He had to grip tightly with both hands: the Barringtons in one and Lily and his baby in the other.

She shifted against his side, her hand drifted over his abdomen as she slid one smooth leg over his thigh. He'd carried her back to bed after they had frantic sex in the hallway.

Yeah, he was a real classy guy not being able to hold back long enough to take those few extra steps to get her into bed. She didn't seem to mind. Actually if her moans and nails biting into his shoulders had been any indication, she'd rather enjoyed herself.

As frantic and aggressive as they'd been together, something had passed between them…something silent, yet significant. He'd seen so much in her eyes and he worried what she'd seen in his.

Lying in silence for several minutes, Nash knew Lily wasn't going to sleep anytime soon.

"I'm sure you see the parallel in my mother's pregnancy and yours," he told her, breaking the silence. He glided his fingertips along her bare arm across his body. "You're not here because of that. You're here because I want you here."

Lily's body softened against his. "I know. I know we started off as just a private affair and suddenly we're both thrust into a world we have no clue how to face. One day at a time is all we can do right now."

Relieved that she knew that much, Nash wished he could tell her the rest. Wished he could fully disclose his identity. But telling her now would certainly murder any chance he had of being with her. He needed more time.

"But, I do need to make some decisions soon," she said after a minute of silence. "I can't stay in Virginia forever and avoid my responsibilities."

Forever. Was he ready to use such a word when thinking of them in terms of a couple? He'd never considered forever with one woman before, but something about Lily made him reconsider his list of priorities. She made him want to be a better man, not always putting business first and really focusing on life. But he'd already dived headfirst into this plan before he met her and, unfortunately, there was no turning back now.

Damn it. He'd had every intention of coming out of this charade unchanged and besting his rival.

"Have you told your mom about the baby?" he asked.

Her warm breath tickled his side as she blew out a sigh. "Not yet. This isn't something I want to just tell her over the phone. Besides, I'd like to go visit her, anyway. I try to get there between films."

Moonlight filtered through the crack in the curtains, slanting a soft glow across the bed. So many things raced through his mind, from the buying of Damon's horses to the baby, but one thing was certain. He couldn't let Lily go. He kept having images of her in his home, his real home, on his grounds and in his stables. She would fit in perfectly and his staff would be just as charmed by her as he was.

"What do you say we go on a picnic or horseback riding tomorrow…well, today." He stopped, wondering if that was even a possibility. "Are you even allowed to ride horses pregnant?"

She turned, fisted her hand and rested her chin on it. "I'm not sure, really. Are you asking me on a date?" she asked with a smile.

Smoothing her hair away from her face and shoving it behind her shoulders, he trailed a fingertip down her cheek. "Yeah. Kind of working backward, but what do you say?"

"I'd love to go on a date with you. Let's just stick with the picnic for now, okay?"

Why her bright smile and upbeat tone sent his heart into overdrive was beyond him. They were having a baby, they'd been intimate and she went with him to offer support with Damon. Now he decided to ask her on a date?

"If we have a big date planned, I better get some sleep," she told him around a yawn.

"Need more ice cream and milk?" he chuckled.

"Oh, no." Her delicate laugh filled his room, his heart. "Your way worked so much better to cure my insomnia. You wore me out."

Nash couldn't help but smile as he kissed the top of her head. "That's the idea. Now rest."

He pulled the thin comforter up around her shoulders and held her tight until her breathing slowed and her hand beneath his went lax.

Nash couldn't wait for the sun to rise, to get in some time at Stony Ridge, then go on a date with Lily. He needed her to see who he truly was before she found out about the other side to him. He needed her to see that there was so much more to him than his millionaire businessman and millionaire persona. He was still the man who tended to horses and enjoyed the simple ways of life.

But first, he needed to find out where Damon stood on selling those thoroughbreds. Little did Damon know, his newfound son was also his most hated rival in the racing industry.

"You've got to be kidding me."

Lily cupped her hand and scooped up the cool, refreshing water, playfully sending it in Nash's direction.

"Come on," she teased. "You're a country boy. Don't let a little creek water scare you."

After a filling picnic consisting of sandwiches, fresh fruit, lemonade and chocolate chip cookies, Lily had toed off her sandals and stepped into the brisk creek to splash and play around. Nash still lay propped on one elbow on their blanket, watching her with a huge, devastating grin.

"Oh, I'm not scared," he retorted as he sat up and pulled off his cowboy boots and socks. "It's you who should be scared."

Shivers raced across her body at his threat. She slid her toes gently over the creek bed in an attempt to avoid the sharp pebbles.

Nash came to his feet, reached behind his head and yanked his T-shirt off and flung it to the side. Oh, my. Those taut muscles all tanned and perfectly sculpted had her belly quivering. He knew how to fight fire with fire…he poured gasoline on it.

"Keep looking at me like that and I'll clear off that blanket in two seconds and make better use of it," he warned as he stepped closer to the creek.

At the edge, he stopped and rolled up his jeans. Lily propped her hands on her hips, loving this playful, relaxed day. With the sun high in the sky, the warmth of summer was in full swing and the country setting was just what the doctor ordered. Nash had told her about this creek that ran through the back of his rental property. It was simple, private and perfect for them. And from how he kept eyeing her in her short tank-style dress, she figured privacy was going to be to their benefit very shortly.

Would she ever tire of how he watched her? How his eyes seemed to drink her in, in one sweeping glance? Each time she caught him visually sampling her, her need for him sharpened even more.

"Damn, that's cold," he complained as he put one foot in. "You didn't tell me that."

Rolling her eyes, Lily laughed. "It's refreshing. Don't be such a baby."

"I'll show you baby."

He bent down, scooped up handfuls of water and trickled a stream down her bare legs. The coolness did nothing to ease the heat rushing through her. Everything with this man turned intimate and aroused her like nothing else she'd ever experienced.

He made her laugh, made her appreciate how a relationship between two totally opposite people may actually work.

And she found herself wanting that more and more each day. She wanted to be with a man who wasn't afraid to lean on someone else when he needed to, a man who could also protect and take charge without being overbearing. She wanted Nash.

Still bent down, his hands lingered on her legs, those bright eyes came up to hold her gaze. "You're right," he said. "This was a great way to cool off."

"You turn everything into sex," she laughed, even though she wanted him to rip her clothes off and have his way with her on the creek bank.

His hand stilled, that naughty grin widened. "I'm a guy. Of course everything is about sex. It doesn't help you're looking at me like you want to gobble me up."

Lily couldn't help herself. She took her foot and tapped

his chest with just enough force to send him butt first into the water. Crossing her arms, she tried her hardest not to double over with laughter as he glared up at her with a smirk on his face.

"Thought you needed to cool off," she quipped with a shrug.

"Oh, baby, I always need to cool off around you," he told her as he started to come to his feet. Water dripped off his hands, his thighs as he wrapped his wet arms around her and pulled her flush against him. "Don't tell me you don't want me for my body."

Lily's hands were trapped between them, so she laid her palms against his bare chest. "You have a very fine body, Nash. No denying that."

"Gee, you make a guy feel really wanted."

Lily slid her hands up to his shoulders, around his neck and laced her fingers together. "I think your ego needs bringing down a notch sometimes."

Those kissable lips offered up a sideways grin. "And you're the woman to do that?"

"That I am," she said. "I bet you've used this body to get what you wanted from women before. I can't blame you, though, you're a sexy man. All those muscles from manual labor, the scruffy, rugged beard and shaggy hair...you give off a sense of mystery. But I want more than the body, more than the seductive exterior."

She nipped at his lips, loving the sensation of his soft beard feathering over her skin. "I want to uncover the mystery," she whispered against his mouth. "I feel there's so much more to you than what you're showing me."

Nash stiffened in her arms, those bright eyes narrowed in on hers. "Be careful what you wish for," he told her. "What if you don't like what you uncover?"

What started out as playful had taken a turn into an area she wasn't sure about heading into. While she'd been half-joking, his tone implied he was dead serious. Was he implying there was something she wouldn't like about him? Was he hiding something else? Everyone had secrets, but the way he'd issued that warning, Lily couldn't help but wonder what he meant.

"How much more do I need to uncover?" she asked, swallowing the lump of fear in her throat.

Those strong hands on her back slid down to cup her backside. "You could spend a lifetime unraveling me."

Arousal slammed through her, but something else, something akin to love spiraled right along with it. Was he indicating he may want forever? Were they honestly ready for that type of talk?

All of a sudden black dots danced in front of Nash's face as the world tilted. Her heart rate kicked up and her stomach flipped with nerves as she broke out into a sweat.

Lily heard him call her name before her world went black.

Twelve

Cradling Lily in his arms and beating a path through the field and toward his house, Nash said a prayer with each step he took. One second he'd been ready to confess his life to her, the next she'd slumped against his body. A fear like nothing he'd ever known slammed into him.

Never before had Nash been so consumed with worry or gut-wrenching panic. She was pale, too pale. Those pink lips were white and she was deadweight in his arms.

As he reached his patio, Nash laid her down on the cushioned chaise lounge which was thankfully shaded by his house this time of day.

Lily's eyelids fluttered, her face turned toward him and Nash eased down beside her, smoothing her hair back from her face, which was starting to regain some color.

"Nash?"

"It's okay," he assured her, cursing his shaking hands. "You passed out on me. Just lie here for a bit. I'm going to run in the house and get my cell to call the doctor."

Her fingers wrapped around his arm before he could move. "No, please. I'm fine. I think it was just the heat."

"I want the doctor to come and make sure you and the baby are healthy." Uncurling her fingers from his arm, he brought her hand to his lips and kissed her palm. "I need to know."

He didn't wait for her to argue, it wouldn't matter if she did because he was up and in the house in seconds. As he placed the call, he went back out to Lily who was still lying down, now with her arms wrapped around her abdomen.

The doctor assured Nash he would be there within ten minutes. Sometimes money wasn't the root of all evil.

Nash's hand slid over hers. "Are you in pain?"

Shaking her head, Lily squeezed her lids together. A lone tear streaked out, sliding down her temple and into her hair. Nash eased back down beside her, swiping the moisture away.

"Talk to me," he urged, placing his palm against her cheek. "Are you hurting or still dizzy?"

She opened her eyes and stared up at him. "I feel fine. I just got scared. What if something is wrong? I mean, just because I feel fine now doesn't mean something isn't going on inside my body."

He shared her dread, but refused to be anything less than strong for her, for their baby. Had his mother gone through this type of fear and worry? Nash couldn't even fathom his strong, vibrant mother being alone and facing all this uncertainty without support.

"Everything will be fine," he assured her. "The doctor will give you a clean bill of health."

Her dark eyes filled as her chin began to quiver. Damn it, he hated being so helpless. What could he offer her right now but promising words and a shoulder to cry on? Even paying for the best doctor to be at their beck and call couldn't prevent something unexpected from happening.

Nash was used to getting his way, getting what he wanted, whether it be through his power or financial control. But this child and this woman he was coming to deeply care for couldn't be handled in the same manner as his business dealings.

The fact he was putting them above everything else, even his end goal, should tell him he was falling in deeper and deeper with this Hollywood starlet.

"What are we doing?" she asked, her voice trembling. "How can we raise a child when we live on opposite sides of the country and our lives are so different?"

Nash knew enough about pregnancy to know that her hormones were all over the place and with the scare she'd just had, Lily's mind was going into overdrive. Treading carefully with each word was the only way to keep her calm.

"Right now, all we're going to think about is relaxing because our baby is depending on us to keep her safe."

That misty gaze held his. After a moment's hesitation, Lily nodded and smiled. "You're right. As long as she's healthy, we can figure out the rest."

Nash slid her hand between both of his and squeezed. "You know we keep referring to this baby as 'she'?"

Lily's smile widened. "I know. Honestly I don't care what the sex is, but something just tells me this will be a girl."

The image of a baby with Lily's stunning, natural beauty gripped his heart. No matter if the baby had his bright blue eyes or her dark features, Nash knew one thing, this baby would be loved, would know her place in the family and would want for nothing…and he didn't just mean monetary things, either.

After the doctor had come and gone, giving Lily a clean bill of health, Nash had still insisted she lie around and do nothing. Absolutely nothing. This hero act was sweet for about five minutes, but she was really getting tired of him jerking around to see if she was okay with every move she made .

Lily settled deeper into the propped pillows behind her back and crossed her ankles. She probably should warn Nash she didn't plan on staying in this bed the entire time she was here. Tomorrow she would get up and do…something.

Her phone chimed on the nightstand and Lily glanced over to see a text from Ian. She hadn't checked her phone since this morning, considering she'd planned on a more fun-filled day she hadn't wanted to be interrupted. But when the events had turned more worrisome, she'd not even given work a second thought.

Reaching for her phone, she quickly read his text.

Did you get my voice mail?

Lily went to her messages and listened, her heart thumping as she realized Ian was presenting her with a role made for her and she had to make the decision rather quickly. As in, by Monday morning.

After she listened fully to his message, she fired back a text stating she'd listened and she was definitely interested and he would have a decision by tomorrow night. She didn't go into details of her day's events because even though he knew she was expecting, he didn't need to worry she couldn't do her job.

As she was pondering the role and how wonderful the opportunity would be for her, Nash rounded the corner with his phone in hand.

"Still feeling good?" he asked, coming to stand beside the bed.

"I hope you don't think I'm lying in this bed for months," she informed him. "I'm going to have bedsores."

Nash lifted her legs and sat down, placing her feet across his lap. "Yeah, well we had one outing and you went out like a light. I don't think my heart could take too much more of that."

His heart. That was an area they'd yet to explore. She honestly wanted to know what was in his heart where they were concerned.

"I just got off the phone with Damon."

Lily perked up. "Did he call you?"

Nash smiled. "Yeah. He wants us to come out to the estate for lunch tomorrow. You don't have to if you don't want to. Don't feel obligated."

Lily sat straight up. "First of all, that's a little hurtful that you think I wouldn't want to. Second, if you're not comfortable with me around your new family, just say so. I know you're wanting to get to know them and I'm still an outsider."

Nash slid his hands up her legs to her thighs as he gripped her and leaned forward. "I want you there. Never doubt that I want you with me. I didn't want you to feel like I was dragging you through my family drama right now."

"Fair enough." The fact he wanted her there spoke volumes for the direction their relationship was headed. "Are you going to tell them about the baby?"

Nash's thumbs slid back and forth over her bare thighs, making this conversation hard to focus on. But she realized he wasn't even paying attention to the gesture when he sighed and shook his head.

"I'm not sure," he said. "I want to leave that up to you since we're not ready for the media to get wind of it."

"Well, Ian knows, so Cassie may, too. Although he did promise to keep the information to himself."

Lily thought about the Barringtons, about how dynamic this family was and how the media tended to hound them, too. They would understand the need for privacy, especially when an innocent baby was involved. A close-knit family like that knew all about loyalty and protecting those around them.

"I don't mind if we tell them," she said, pleased when his mouth split into a wide grin.

"Seriously?"

"Sure. That will give everyone something positive to discuss, something that takes the edge off the intensity of you shocking them with your identity."

The smile on his face faded, the muscle in his jaw clenched. Something she couldn't identify passed over his eyes.

"You all right?" she asked, wondering what she'd said that had him so worried.

He blinked, and an instant transformation had his smile returning. "I'm good. Just thinking about how I'll fit into Damon's life now, I guess."

Framing his face in her hands, Lily held his gaze. "You'll fit in perfectly. You all already have a love of horses, it's in the blood. Things will all work out, you'll see."

His dark brows drew down as if some worry still plagued him. "I pray you're right."

"That was wonderful," Lily declared as she sat her napkin on the table. "Thank you."

"My pleasure," Damon replied with a smile.

Nash hadn't known what to expect when coming for lunch today, but so far he was pleasantly surprised at how easily he and Lily had slid into the family role…as if they were a real couple coming to his parents' for a gathering.

With Ian, Cassie and Cassie's little girl on one side of the long table and Tessa and her husband, Grant, on the side with Nash and Lily, Damon sat at the head like the grand patriarch he was.

The confident man had no clue he'd just hosted his rival.

Nash wished more than anything he and Damon weren't at odds in the business world. Nash hated lying, hated being someone he wasn't just to get the prizewinning horses to complete his breeding program. He hadn't worried about this when he'd first come onto the scene.

He had Lily to thank for that bout of conscience. When he'd set out to get the inside scoop on Damon's plan after the racing season, Nash had been ready to steal, lie and cheat to get what he wanted. But Lily made him want to be a better man.

Nash had also gotten to know Damon on a more personal level and the elderly man wasn't too different from Nash. They both knew what they wanted, and both went after it full force…how could Nash fault that? Damon wasn't the man Nash had originally thought.

Damon had a passion for the sport, just like Nash. The man cared for his family, would do anything to protect them. Nash hadn't seen that side of him years ago in the circuit. All Nash had known was how ruthless Damon could be. And, honestly, Nash had actually recognized how alike he and his father were.

Trouble now was, Nash was already wrapped so tightly in his own lies. He still wanted those horses, still needed desperately to breed them with his own back on his estate. He'd not had the best seasons lately and he had to do something.

Lily's hand slid over his leg under the table. "You okay?" she whispered.

Pushing away thoughts of business, Nash patted her hand. "Yeah."

"Nash, I'd like to talk with you a moment if you don't mind taking a walk down to the stables with me," Damon said, not really asking. A man like Damon Barrington didn't ask.

"Of course," Nash replied, wondering what the man would want to discuss in private. Had he found out the rest of the truth? Doubtful, but the possibility was always there.

"You're not seriously going to talk work are you?" Tessa asked.

"Not at all." Damon came to his feet and handed his plate to Linda who had just come into the dining room. "Ah, thank you. But I would've taken my own plate in."

Linda, the house cook and all around amazing lady to the family, laughed. "Of course you would've. I trained you years ago."

"Go on," Lily gestured to Damon and Nash. "I'll help clean up."

Both Tessa and Cassie both chimed in their refusal for Lily's help, but Lily stood and started gathering dishes anyway.

"I think we should pitch in, too, Ian," Grant spoke up as he scooted his chair back. "I don't know about you, but I don't want to face the wrath of my wife if I let Lily do all of this."

Reaching into the high chair, Ian pulled Emily out and tucked her firmly against his hip. "Actually, there's a smell coming from our section over here and I'm pretty sure I'm on diaper patrol. You enjoy wrapping up the leftovers, though."

Lily couldn't help but get a bit choked up at the easy way this dynamic family all meshed together so beautifully. What would it be like to live here, to have that connection every day? She had her mother and they were extremely close, but Lily wondered how raising a child in LA and bouncing him or her around from film set to film set would affect the outcome of her child's life.

"Lily?"

Nash's soft tone, his easy grip on her elbow had her turning. "I'm sorry, what?"

She realized the entire room was now staring at her. Great. She'd thought they'd all scurried out, apparently not.

She'd given off the image of a professional actress when she'd been filming on set here for months, but now they were all looking at her as if she'd sprouted another head.

"I asked if you were okay." Ian stared across the table at her and seeing him holding his stepdaughter had Lily smiling and nodding.

"I'm pregnant," she blurted out.

Nash laughed. "Way to break the news, sweetheart."

Inwardly cringing, she turned to him. "Sorry. I'm botching things up here."

He took the stack of plates from her hands and kissed her cheek. "You're fine."

Lily glanced around the room to the stunned faces. Only Ian was smiling and threw her a wink and a nod of encouragement.

"It's okay," she told them with a smile as she blinked back the tears. "Nash and I are both excited about this. While we certainly weren't planning on a baby, we are thrilled."

"A son and a new grandbaby on the way all in one week?" Damon asked as he puffed out his chest and grinned. "This calls for a major celebration."

"How about Wednesday?" Cassie suggested with clasped hands and a wide smile. "That's the fourth. We could have fireworks, grill out and make a big night of it."

Lily's head was spinning as the Barrington sisters started planning, then Linda came in, heard the news and chimed right in on everything she could make, too. As she babbled on, she bustled around the table, took the plates from Nash's hand and kept right on planning without missing a beat.

The moment went from her instant onslaught of tears to a chaotic meshing of voices chattering over each other.

"I think they're excited," Nash leaned over and whispered in her ear.

Damon came around the table and settled his hand on her shoulder. "Congratulations, Lily. I'm really happy for you guys."

Lily couldn't help the lump of emotion that settled in her throat. Nash's newly minted father was already welcoming her and the baby into the family. This was everything she'd ever wanted to give her children...a sense of belonging.

"Thank you."

Nash's hand slid over the small of her back. "We want to keep this private for now," he informed his father. "Lily is taking some time off and staying with me until we figure out the best course of action. If the media gets hold of this news before we're ready..."

"I understand completely," Damon nodded. "If you need anything, let us know. Privacy is something we value here. I promise to only keep Nash a few moments in the stables and then we'll be back and we can continue this celebration."

Nash leaned down, placed a kiss on her cheek. "I'll be back in a bit," he murmured before following Damon and the other men from the room.

Lily looked up to see, Tessa, Cassie and Linda all smiling

at her. Damn it. She wished she could label her relationship with Nash because she didn't want to bond and fall in love even more with these amazing women if it wasn't going to be long-term.

Now that Nash had come clean with his family, would he want to get closer to them? Surely he wouldn't want to just pack up and follow her back to LA. But, she had a job, a life there that she couldn't ignore.

She loved her job, not so much the lack of privacy, but digging into roles and bringing emotion to the screen. She still hadn't decided whether to take the film Ian had sent her way and she had to discuss things with Nash, too.

Lily needed to know what he was thinking, what he was feeling before she fell any deeper in love with this family.

But she was afraid it was too late for that.

Thirteen

Nash entered the stables, like he had many times before, but this time Damon walked silently at his side. The fresh, familiar smell of hay and leather greeted them, while a couple of the horses peeked their heads out to see who their new visitors were.

A tug on Nash's heart irritated him. He couldn't think of this estate as home or as a place where he would be welcome once Damon found out the truth. But he truly loved these grounds, these horses.

"Man-to-man," Damon started as he moved easily down the center aisle, his cowboy boots scuffing against the concrete. "How nervous are you about this pregnancy?"

Nash laughed. "That's not at all what I thought you'd say once we got down here. But, between us, pretty nervous. Not about the baby, and I know Lily will be an amazing mother. The worry more centers around the fact I want her to have a healthy pregnancy."

Damon stopped in front of the stall that housed Don Pedro, Tessa's prizewinning horse that had helped her secure the coveted Triple Crown and put the Barrington sisters in the history books as the first females to accomplish such a feat.

"It's rough being the man in this situation." Damon rested his hand on the top of the half door. "You're used to fixing things, being in control of everything in your life. I know when Rose was pregnant with our girls, I was a nervous wreck until she delivered. But once I held that baby in my arms, I knew for certain I'd never let anyone or anything hurt them if I could prevent it at all. I'd sell my soul to the devil himself to keep my girls happy."

Be careful what you wish for.

"Lily has had a few dizzy spells and she was told to relax and take it easy to keep her blood pressure down, so right now that's all I can concentrate on." Nash reached out, sliding his hand up the stallion's velvety nose. "So, I'm sure you didn't bring me down here to talk babies."

Damon took a step back, crossed his arms over his chest and nodded. "I want to make you an offer."

Intrigued, Nash continued his slow caress of Don Pedro's soft hair. This was where that power and control came into play. No matter what Damon said, Nash had to remember that he held the upper hand, not his father. And it was how Nash chose to play his hand that would determine both of their futures and any relationship Nash hoped to have.

"Tessa and Cassie retired, as you know. Cassie has plans to open a school for physically challenged children here and Tessa will help when she's available. She and Grant have discussed moving." Damon's gaze shot straight to Nash's, held there and demanded full attention. "I've been offered an excessive amount of money for several of my horses and I've yet to take an offer."

It took every bit of willpower Nash had not to laugh. He knew all about those offers...and the fact they'd been turned down.

"I know we just discovered each other," Damon went on. "But I'd like to offer Don Pedro to you. I've thought about this since you were here the other night and I know a gift hardly makes up for missing your entire life, but you're the best groom I've ever had and this is the best horse we've ever had. I'd like you to have him."

Nash barely caught himself before his jaw dropped. Control. He had to remain in that mindset. Damon Barrington was handing over such a remarkable horse? A horse that could pull in more money than any other at this point in time?

"I never expected that," he said honestly.

Here all this time Nash had been dishing out offer after offer only to be rejected and now Damon was hand delivering the horse right to his rival. Had he admitted the paternity months ago, would Damon still have given Nash the horse once the season was over? Or had Damon just come to know Nash well enough to know he would take care of the animal like the royalty Don Pedro was?

The fact that Nash had deceived a man he'd actually come to care about weighed heavily on his heart and his conscience. This would not end well...for anybody.

"What did Tessa say?" Nash asked.

Damon waved a hand, then reached out to stroke the Thoroughbred's neck. "She was well aware we'd be selling him after the race and she's on board. I'm selling a couple, actually, if Cassie can part with them. We all get attached, but that girl is so emotionally invested it rips her heart out to let them go after she's trained them."

Nash glanced at the horse in question, one of his main motivations for coming here. The end goal was in sight, but that last shred of truth still remained wedged between Nash and all he wanted. His goals had changed somewhat, but he still wanted Don Pedro. He just didn't know that he was comfortable using deceit to achieve that end anymore.

"I'm sure you could get a great deal of money for him from other owners who want to breed him," Nash said after a moment. "Are you sure you just want to give him away?"

"I could sell him, sure, but racing was never about money to me." Damon stepped away from the stall and crossed the aisle to show some affection to a horse named Oliver. "I had a passion for riding when I was a young boy. My mother was single and couldn't afford to give me a horse, so I would take lessons at a local horse farm in exchange for working in the barns. It was hard work, but I learned the love of the sport and saved every single penny I ever received because I was going to buy my very own horse."

A slice of guilt slashed right through Nash's heart. Hearing Damon talk of his childhood, wondering how much more their lives mirrored each other, Nash turned to face his father.

"I know hard work," Damon continued, resting his elbow on the edge of the door. "I know it pays off and I want to reward you for all you've done here in a short time. I realize you came here to technically spy on us, but I have to admit, I would've done the same had I been in your shoes."

That damn lump of remorse settled in his throat, making it nearly impossible to swallow. Nash had never expected to have a bonding moment with Damon and he sure as hell hadn't thought he'd nearly get choked up over it. But here Damon was sharing a part of his past, proving why Nash should take the free gesture of love.

Damn it.

Nash glanced back to the coveted stallion in question. Could he seriously go through with this? Just take the prize-winning horse and move on? Everything he'd wanted was right within his reach; all he had to do was grab hold.

What would Damon say once he learned the truth? Deceiving the man was initially the plan, but, now that Nash had actually spent time here and gotten to know this family, he cared for them in a way he never would've imagined.

Turning down this gesture, however, would require an explanation Nash wasn't quite ready to disclose yet. So he tightened the web he'd woven around himself and turned back to Damon.

"I'll take good care of him," Nash said with a smile that didn't quite come from his heart.

Damon's shoulders relaxed as his lips curved into a grin. "Anything for my only son."

The guilt knife twisted deeper, leaving Nash more vulnerable than he'd ever thought possible. He'd officially become the man he never wanted to be. Because in the end, he would tear apart the relationships he'd just started to build, relationships he realized he wanted more than anything.

He hadn't even known how much he longed for a family until he came here. Then when he'd discovered the baby another layer of need was added. So here he was, his heart overflowing with family bonds and relationships and in one second that all could be wiped right back out of his life.

Right now, he had to figure out a way to reveal the truth in the least damning way because that tight fist he'd had gripping all he wanted was slowly coming apart and he could feel the control slipping from his grasp.

Lily didn't remember laughing so hard in such a long time. Having an impromptu girls' day was beyond fun and quite a departure from the cattiness of the women in LA. Lily really didn't have good girlfriends back home and being here with Cassie, Tessa and Linda almost felt as good as being with her own mother.

"So what do you think for desserts?" Linda asked, crossing her leg over her knee and propping her notepad up on her thigh. "So far I only have the main course. What's your favorite dessert, Lily?"

"She's a fan of chocolate."

Lily jerked her head toward the doorway where Nash stood looking all scrumptious in his black T-shirt pulling taut across his wide shoulders and those well-worn faded jeans hugging narrow hips. His gaze zeroed right in on hers.

"I believe chocolate milk is high on the list," he added, his tone dripping in sex. "Ice cream will do in a pinch. Right, Lily?"

Lily suppressed a shudder. The man knew exactly how

to turn her on in a room full of people without so much as stepping into her breathing space.

"Why don't we do sundaes?" Linda asked, oblivious to the sexual tension.

Cassie laughed. "Emily will love that."

"I'm always up for anything chocolate, too," Tessa chimed in, pushing her hair back over her shoulder.

Lily smiled, excited to be pulled into the Barrington family like she belonged there. "Sounds like a great night. What can I bring?"

"Yourself." Cassie leaned over and patted Lily's leg. "Linda gets offended if we try to bring anything to a party she's throwing. And we've learned she's the best and anything we make won't compete so we just let her have at it. Bring Nash and an appetite. That's all."

Lily glanced to Linda who was rigorously jotting down notes, her lips thinned, her eyes narrowed. This woman was all business when it came to meal planning. Lily knew from being on the set that Linda loved to feed a houseful of people and she was an amazing chef.

"Sounds good to me," Lily said around a yawn. "Sorry, I'm so tired lately."

"It's the first trimester," Cassie told her with a soft smile. "You'll regain some energy soon."

Nash came to stand in front of her and extended his hand. "Why don't I get you home? It is getting late."

Glancing out the window, Lily realized the sun had all but set. They'd been there most of the day and time had flown by.

She took his hand and came to her feet. "This was so fun. Thanks for having us over."

"You're welcome here anytime," Tessa told her. "Feel free to come any time Nash is working. We can always use another female around here."

"Good thing the guys aren't nearby to hear that," Linda said as she rested her pad and pen on the coffee table. "But, I agree. Come by anytime."

After saying their goodbyes, Lily and Nash headed home.

Home. Had she really started thinking in terms of his house as her own? She'd spent the majority of the day being welcomed into his newfound family, she was having his baby and her feelings for him were growing stronger every single day.

Yeah, she was starting to feel as if this was home. LA seemed so far away, as if a lifetime had passed since she'd been in her spacious condo. Just the thought of going back to the lonely space depressed her. She'd never fallen in love with a place—or the people—she'd visited on location before like she had at Stony Ridge. Part of her never wanted to leave, the other part had to be realistic and see that she couldn't stay forever. Her job didn't allow her to set roots.

So how could she raise a baby with a man who lived here? How could she leave the man she'd fallen for in such a short time?

Tears pricking her eyes, that tickle in her nose and clogging of her throat had become all too familiar sensations lately. Her hormones were raging all over the place, just like everything she'd read said they would. She sniffed, turning to glance out the window so Nash wouldn't see her sniveling like some crazy, unstable woman...which she was, but still.

"Hey." He reached across the truck console and gripped her hand, giving a reassuring squeeze. "You all right?"

Lily glanced over, catching his quick look her way before he concentrated back on the two-lane country road. "I love it here," she found herself saying. "I mean, it's so nice, so laid-back. And today I felt like a normal person."

Nash's soft chuckle filled the cab. "Sweetheart, you're going to have to clarify that last part."

Staring down at their joined hands, his so large and tan and hers so delicate and pale, she tried to find the right words to make him understand.

"I'm always treated like a celebrity everywhere I go," she began. "I don't mind the pictures, the autographs, that's all fine and comes with my job. But that's just it. I do a job and that's what it is to me. I don't see myself as someone on a level above anyone else. Today everyone treated me like I was just a family friend, they welcomed me into their home and I had a fun time without worrying about work or the pettiness that comes along with the industry."

Nash continued to drive, not saying a word, and Lily started to feel a bit silly.

"I'm sorry," she finally said. "That all probably sounds ridiculous. I'm already worried about the media hounding me when I return to LA. They hover all over, even going through my garbage to get any morsel of gossip they can sell. I have no clue how to resolve that unless I do what you mentioned and make an announcement during a live interview. But this town, these people are so amazing. I'm comfortable here and it's just going to be hard to leave."

There. She'd said it. She really wanted to know how he felt on the matter and it was past time they discussed where they were headed. She was kind of glad her rambling led them down the path to a topic they'd danced around for over a week. The uncertainty of her immediate future was starting to really cause more anxiety than she should be dealing with.

"Do you want to stay?"

That low tone of his produced the loaded question she'd been asking herself.

"I want to know what you want."

Such a coward's answer, but she needed to know where he stood, needed to know what was on his mind because up until now they'd only talked seriously about his past and they'd had amazing sex. That was all well and good...better than good, actually, but there was so much more to be brought out in the open.

"I want you to be happy." He gripped the wheel tighter with one hand and continued to hold hers with the other as he maneuvered the truck around a series of *S* curves. "I want our baby to be healthy and I want us to build on what we've started."

"And what have we started?" she prompted.

She wanted him to label their relationship. Okay, maybe that sounded immature of her, but baby or no baby, she found herself wanting to be part of his world, wanting to see what the long-term outlook could be for them.

Nash turned onto his road, then into his drive before he pulled to a stop, killed the engine and turned to face her. The porch light cast a soft glow into the cab of the truck and his bright eyes seemed to shine amidst those dark, thick lashes.

"You want me to lay everything out for you?" he asked, grabbing her other hand and holding on as if his life depended on this moment. "I want you to figure out what makes you happy. Do you want to go back to LA and have the baby? Do you want to stay here until the baby is born and then see what happens? I'm not asking you to choose between the baby and your career, I'd never do that. But whatever you decide, you better make damn sure I'm part of that plan because I want this, us, a family. I'm going to take what I want and I'm not backing down."

Nash tugged her forward and claimed her mouth like a man starving for affection and staking his claim. With their hands tightly secure in her lap, Lily opened for him, relieved that he'd declared how he wanted to be with her and a bit aroused at the demanding way he'd all but marked her as his own.

Nash and his powerful mannerisms never failed to make her feel wanted and—dare she say—loved.

But she just realized she hadn't brought up the job opportunity Ian had presented her with. She had until tomorrow night to give him an answer.

When Nash eased back and looked her in the eyes, Lily knew she had an important decision to make. And this time her career move would affect the man she'd fallen in love with.

Fourteen

Lily had changed for bed, washed her face and pulled her hair back into a low, messy bun. She hadn't seen or heard a peep out of Nash since they got home. He'd come in, tossed his keys on the entryway table and told her he'd be back inside in a bit.

That was over an hour ago. She'd given him space, but what was bothering him right now? He'd been so open in the truck, then it was as though he waged some inner war with himself and he shut her out…again.

Was he having doubts about what he'd revealed to her in the car? Was he still caught up in the whole Barrington saga? Perhaps he was worried about the baby. Or maybe it was whatever Damon had discussed with Nash in the stables. Nash hadn't even mentioned the man-to-man talk and she wondered if she should ask about it or just let him decide if he wanted to open up.

Whatever had him closing her out right now, she wished he'd let her in. He only opened up to discuss his superficial emotions, but when it came to his fears Nash was a private man.

Well, too bad. If they were going to try to make this work, they needed to have an open line of communication

at all times. The best of relationships struggled sometimes
and they already had so many strikes against them. She refused to let go of the one man who made her feel like love
was a great possibility and there was a chance for a happily-
ever-after.

Wearing only her simple short blue tank-style gown,
Lily padded through the house and slid open the patio door.
Thanks to the light above the door she could make out Nash
sitting out in the yard on a cushioned chaise lounge beneath
a large old oak tree.

The warm summer evening breeze slid over her bare skin
and for the briefest of moments she considered going back
inside and allowing him the privacy he seemed to want. She
didn't want to be that nagging woman who was always trying to get her man to open up. Even though Lily ached for
Nash to talk to her, she hoped he would do so on his own.

Before she could make a move, Nash glanced her way.
Even in the dim light, she saw the angst in those stormy
eyes. The man held so much inside, all that worry he could
be sharing with her. She knew he didn't want to upset her
and he wanted her to be completely relaxed. But, how could
she relax when she was constantly struggling with her own
emotions and wondering what was on his mind that seemed
to always put that worried look on his face?

Without a word, Nash extended his hand in a silent invitation for her to join him. Stepping from the warm, smooth
concrete into the cool, soft grass tickled Lily's toes as she
made her way through the yard.

When she slid her hand into his, he maneuvered her
around until she sat on his lap, her legs over his thighs and
her feet brushing the top of the grass. Her head fell against
his shoulder, a move she'd become so comfortable with.

Nash's deep breathing combined with the crickets chirping in the distance had Lily smiling at another layer of the
simple life she absolutely loved. Relaxing here would be no
problem at all. And raising a child in this calming atmo-

sphere would be a dream. Perhaps she could live here. Why not? Who said she had to live in LA? She was well-known, her agent shopped scripts for her and she would have to go on location regardless of where she lived.

When Ian scheduled her live interview, she could confess her pregnancy, open up about the man she'd developed a serious relationship with and explain they are keeping things private and had purposely kept away from the limelight.

Could the solution be so easy? So within her reach?

"Sorry I disturbed you," she told him, breaking the silence. "I started getting worried when you didn't come back inside."

Nash's arms tightened around her waist. "I lose track of time when I sit out here."

"I can see why." Lily trailed her fingertips along his tanned, muscular forearm. "So quiet and peaceful."

He flattened his palm against her belly, spreading his fingers wide. "How's our girl?"

"Safe and healthy."

He turned his head slightly to kiss her forehead. "And you? How are you feeling?"

"Hopeful," she answered honestly.

The rhythm of his heartbeat against her shoulder nearly matched hers. There was so much going on inside her, so many unanswered questions, but there was something she had no question about.

"I love you," she whispered into the darkness. His body tensed beneath hers. "I know we've really gone about everything backward and I don't expect you to say anything back. But I have to be honest with you because I need you to know how serious I am here."

When he remained silent a little piece of her heart crumbled. While she didn't expect him to return her feelings, she'd had a thread of hope that he would. She wanted to know how deep he was in with her, but he continued to be a man of mystery, because she never could get a good grasp on exactly how he felt.

Oh, he'd said he wanted to be with her, but that didn't necessarily mean love. And she so wanted a family, a real family. She didn't want to settle for less…and she *wouldn't* settle for less.

When the silence became too much to bear, Lily started to push off Nash's lap, but those strong arms around her tightened. "Don't go."

On a sigh, she closed her eyes and leaned back.

"You're everything, Lily," he said after a minute had passed. "I had no idea what my life had been missing until you came into it. But I'm still working through some things, still struggling with my identity."

The fact that she was worried about herself had guilt coursing through her. Nash had a great deal of life's obstacles thrown at him all at once.

"I want to give myself to you completely." His hands covered hers over her stomach as his soft, raw words washed over her. "I want nothing to come between us. This baby we've made is a blessing and I'm not taking our little family for granted. I just need some time to come to grips with everything and get things in order for us."

Easing up, Lily turned in his arms. Tears flooded her eyes. "Oh, Nash. There's nothing you need to get ready for us. I'm sorry I put you on the spot, but I couldn't keep the truth from you any longer. I think I started falling in love with you the moment you first swept me up into that loft."

Cupping her cheek with one of his rough, calloused hands, Nash's eyes zeroed in on hers. "I don't deserve you."

"You deserve everything you've ever wanted," she retorted with a smile as a tear slid down her cheek.

With the pad of his thumb, he swiped the moisture away. "I hope I get it."

Lily laid a kiss on his lips before shifting to lie against him once more. "Am I hurting you?"

"Never."

He may not have been able to give her the words she wanted to hear, but she knew he loved her. All those demons he battled internally kept him from speaking the truth, but Lily knew in her heart that Nash was in love with her.

"I have a film opportunity," she told him. "I think it's a good choice."

His body stilled beneath hers. "Are you going back to LA?"

Lacing her fingers through his, she settled their hands in her lap. "Not yet, but I will have to for a bit if I take the role. I would actually do the entire film there. I also still need to go see my mom, too."

"What's the role?"

Lily laughed. "Something I've never done before, actually. It's an animation and I'm pretty excited about the prospect because I think this will be a really big hit."

Nash stroked his thumb across the back of her hand. "And what does Ian suggest?"

"He said it's perfect, especially since I can record in a studio and not worry about my growing tummy." Lily turned her head to look up at Nash. "But I wanted to discuss this with you before I gave him my answer."

Piercing blue eyes met hers. "When does he need an answer by?"

"Tomorrow night."

Lily's heartbeat quickened. She'd never discussed her career with anyone other than her agent before. Never had anyone else to consider when making a film choice. This new territory was interesting and slightly nerve-racking.

"Do you want to take the role?"

"I think I do."

Nash shifted in the chair, causing her to sit up and look down into his eyes.

"What would you do if you weren't pregnant and you

didn't know me?" he asked, sliding his hand over her bare thigh.

"I'd take the role."

With a squeeze to her leg and a sexy, rugged smile, Nash nodded. "Then that's what you should do. I don't expect you to recalculate your life, Lily. You still need to do what makes you happy."

A weight she didn't know she was carrying was lifted off her shoulders. "Ian said recording wouldn't start for a couple months, but he's getting me the script to look over. Aiden O'Neil is going to play opposite me."

"Wasn't he the guy in one of the scripts you just turned down?"

Lily nodded. "He declined after he heard I wouldn't do it. He's a good friend, like Max. And this will be a good change of pace for me. Hey, no hair and makeup, either."

Nash laughed. "You're stunning no matter what you have on." Those eyes darted down to her lips as his fingers trailed up her thigh and beneath the cotton gown. "Or don't have on."

The man could get her body to respond with the simplest words or lightest of touches.

"You know you're the only man I've let get this close to me since the scandal." She trembled as his hand continued to glide over her skin. "I never thought I'd get this close to someone again, let my heart be exposed to the chance of being ripped apart."

Nash's looked at her seriously. "You humble me, Lily."

"If you want to try to make this work, you're not going to be able to avoid the media. Not once the pregnancy is out there."

The muscle in Nash's jaw ticked. She knew he didn't want to be thrust into the public eye. Resting her hand against the side of his face, rubbing her thumb along his bottom lip, Lily leaned in and whispered, "Take me inside and make love to me."

In one swift move, he had her lifted and turned to straddle his lap. Then his hands were lifting her gown to her waist. Lily leaned forward and clutched his shoulders as he worked the zipper on his jeans.

"Or not," she added as he threw her a crooked grin.

"I don't want to wait," he said, easing a hand between her legs to stroke her until she thought her eyes would roll back in her head. "Do you?"

Lily shivered, holding on tight to him so she didn't fall. "No," she whispered as he continued to torture her. "Please, Nash."

She'd come out here wearing a flimsy nightgown, sans underwear and she thought he could wait to get inside the house? Hell no. Nash wanted her here, now.

He also wanted to not discuss how the media would hone in on them. The last thing he needed was being identified before he could fully disclose the rest of his life.

The little moans escaping her, the way her hips rocked against his hand and seeing her eyes closed, head tilted back as he pleasured her was nearly his undoing. Not to mention the perfect distraction for both of them.

Damn it, he owed her so much…a debt he could never repay because while she was freely handing out her love, he was still betraying her by keeping a lie bottled inside.

The thought of having her walk out of his life once she learned the truth would be the equivalent of taking a knife to his heart. Because he loved her. God help him, he did. And when she'd whispered those sweet words to him, it had taken all of his willpower to remain silent.

He couldn't tell her he loved her, not when there was such a heavy lie that still hovered between them. He could only show her how much she meant to him. Once he revealed himself, after he'd talked with Damon one more time, Nash would truly open up and tell her every single thing she deserved to know.

Nash removed his hand, gripped her hips and eased her down onto him. Making love to Lily with the warm summer breeze embracing them like lovers, Nash wrapped his arms around her and tugged her toward him, capturing her mouth. Her fingers slid into his hair, sending him another reminder that he was living a lie. The longer hair, the scruffy beard, the rental home…all of it was a lie.

All of it, except for the fact he loved her, loved this baby and wanted a lifetime with them both.

As her body started to tremble, Nash felt himself losing control. She broke the kiss, looked him in the eyes, just like when they'd been in his hallway.

Those dark eyes held his as her body tensed. "I love you," she told him as her body broke.

And as Nash followed her over the edge, he wished he could repeat those words back to her.

The food had been amazing and now the entire Barrington clan was gathered on the back lawn, waiting for the fireworks show that Damon had no doubt shelled out a pretty penny for, considering they'd planned this impromptu party very last-minute. But when a man had his financial padding, he could afford to snap fingers and plan such niceties with little notice.

Blankets were lying side by side and some front to back creating the effect of an oversize outdoor carpet. Ian, Cassie and little Emily sat on one blanket. Another quilt had Grant and Tessa all snuggled together. Lily was nestled between Nash's legs, her back leaning against his chest. And surprisingly Damon and Linda were on a quilt together, laughing and…whispering?

Was something going on there?

Nash smiled. Good for Damon if he was seeking happiness. He'd been without his wife for so many years, concentrating on raising his family and climbing to the top of the horse racing industry.

Nash rested a hand on Lily's stomach. He would do the same thing for his child. Nash wanted to give his baby, and Lily, everything they deserved and more.

She'd already made plans to visit her mother this coming weekend. Nash figured while she was gone, he could have a heart-to-heart with Damon and come clean with him.

He kept telling himself he was waiting on the right opportunity. No other time would work to his benefit except while Lily was gone. He could only hurt so many people at a time without crumbling himself. And he had to remain strong or he'd never be able to fight to keep what was his.

When the first spark and boom lit up the sky, Emily squealed and jumped to her feet. "Look! Look!"

Nash watched the adorable toddler with bouncing blond curls. Her infectious laughter had everyone watching her reaction as opposed to the show in the sky.

"She is precious," Lily said.

Cassie grinned. "Thanks. I was afraid the noise would scare her, but obviously not."

With each colorful burst, Emily clapped or jumped up and down. Nash caught Tessa's glance to Grant, a smile tugged at her lips and Grant's hand came around to her stomach, as well.

Interesting. Looked as though they had their own announcement to make.

Yeah, he needed to finish revealing his identity sooner rather than later because he wanted to be part of this family with no lies hovering between them. If they would accept him after all was said and done. He also had to have a long talk with his mother. Lily wasn't the only one who needed to share news about her pregnancy. Nash hadn't wanted to tell his mom over the phone, either.

"I'm going to grab a bottle of water." Lily came to her feet and looked down to him. "Want anything?"

A do-over? A chance to make this all right from the beginning? A lifetime to make it up to her?

"I'm good," he told her. "I would've gotten your water for you."

Lily laughed. "I'm perfectly capable of getting my own water."

As she moved around him, he saw Tessa hop to her feet as well and head in Lily's direction. Within seconds, Cassie and Linda followed.

Emily settled onto Ian's lap and Damon turned toward the others. "Looks like our ladies have deserted us."

The fireworks continued, the thunderous sound filling the warm night.

"I'd say Tessa is telling our news," Grant replied with a wide grin.

"She told me this afternoon," Damon said, his smile matching Grant's.

Ian's head bounced back and forth between the two men. "Well? Do I get to know what's going on?"

"We're having a baby, too," Grant said.

Ian leaned over and slapped Grant on the shoulder. "That's awesome, man. Congratulations."

Nash nodded in agreement. "I'm happy for you guys."

"I'm sure they're all back there chatting about babies and pregnancies," Damon said, leaning back on his hands. "Linda has treated my girls like her own since Rose passed. I'm sure she's all over Tessa, asking about her eating habits and if she's resting enough."

"Oh, I'm making sure of it," Grant supplied. He raked a hand through his hair and sighed. "But her emotions are all over the place."

"Dude, they're not going to settle down anytime soon," Nash informed him. "Lily can go from crying to laughing in seconds."

Ian smoothed Emily's curls down, as they kept blowing in the wind. "Cassie has been wanting another baby," he said. "I'm sure all this baby talk will only speed up the process. We'd discussed waiting another year."

"My family is growing." Damon beamed, glancing up when Linda came back and settled down next to him. "These are exciting times."

"Indeed they are," Linda said as she patted Damon's leg.

Oh, yeah. Something was definitely going on there.

Cassie, Tessa and Lily came back and took their seats. Lily clutched her water bottle and leaned back against him.

Nash leaned over and patted Tessa on the arm. "Congrats on the baby."

Tessa lit up, just like Lily did when they discussed their baby. "Thanks. I'm so excited."

Chatter ensued as the fireworks came to an end. An hour later they were all still discussing babies, due dates, baby showers and growing families. Emily had long since fallen asleep in Ian's arms and Nash felt a tug on his heart. He couldn't wait to cradle his own child to sleep, to know that he was a comfort and security for someone.

Lily tipped her head, kissed him slightly on the lips. "Thank you for bringing me here."

"I didn't bring you," he replied, hugging her tighter against him. "Your movie brought you here."

She ran her hand along his arm. "You know what I mean. You've included me in your life, in your new family even though we're still new ourselves. I feel like I belong here, like I belong with you. You don't know how much that means to me."

Yeah, he did. He knew she valued family just as much as he did. He knew she wanted their baby to have that special bond.

But would Nash sever that bond once he revealed himself?

Nash kissed the end of her nose and squeezed her tight again. "You deserve this."

And he just had to find a way to convince her he wasn't purposely deceiving her and that she belonged there. She belonged with him.

Fifteen

Taking the first step in getting his life back under control was long overdue. He loved Lily. There was no denying the fact anymore. Now with her in Arizona visiting her mother, he was at the Barrington estate about to confront his father and put one hell of a kink in their newfound relationship.

He should've let this out earlier, but he'd just not been ready. Since falling so hard for Lily, Nash knew putting it off any longer would be an even bigger mistake. Starting now, he was going to set things straight and take control of his life.

Here all this time he'd thought he'd been in control. He'd only been controlled by his own lies and selfishness.

Nash paced the living room. He'd already gone into the kitchen and said hi to Linda, who was washing up dishes from breakfast. She'd invited him to stick around for lunch, but Nash didn't make any promises. He highly doubted he'd be welcome at that point.

Nerves curled deep in his gut and a vulnerability he hated to admit he had threatened to consume him. But he wouldn't back down. He wouldn't take the coward's way out.

"Nash, I was surprised to hear from you today." Damon crossed the room and Nash came to his feet. "Not that you aren't welcome anytime. What brings you here on a Saturday morning? Is Lily with you?"

Nash shook his head. "She went to visit her mother in Arizona. I needed to talk to you about something important."

Damon laughed and smacked his hand on Nash's shoulder. "Last time you said that you announced you were my son. What else could you have to tell me?"

Raking a hand through his long hair, hair that he couldn't wait to cut off so he could get back to looking like himself, Nash gestured toward the chair. "You may want to have a seat."

Damon's smile faltered. "Is something wrong with your mother?"

"No, no. She's fine." Nash sank to the sofa, resting his elbows on his knees. "I actually drove down to see her yesterday after Lily's plane took off. She's excited about the baby."

Nervous chitchat would only postpone the inevitable for so long. He'd come here on a mission and he refused to let nerves take over.

"I actually came to tell you that I can't accept Don Pedro from you."

Damon's silver brows drew in as he eased forward in the leather chair. "If you're concerned about the money I could make by selling him, don't be."

Shaking his head, Nash clenched his fists. Damn it, he hated this. "I know you're not concerned with the money. I know this because I've been offering to buy him for nearly three months now."

Confusion settled onto Damon's face as the elderly man drew his brows together in confusion. "I'm not following you."

"You've been getting phone calls from Barry Stallings."

Damon's back straightened. "How do you know this?"

Holding firm to his courage, Nash leveled Damon's gaze. "Because Barry is my assistant."

Damon stared, studied for a minute, then gasped as realization dawned on him. Jerking to his feet, he started shaking his head.

"How can this be?" he whispered, as if to himself. "You—you're…what the hell game have you been playing? The long hair, the beard. You're a bigger man than I remember. Then again I haven't seen you in person in years. How long have you been planning to come here and spy on me? Was the son angle just a convenient reason? Or are you even my son?"

For once in his life, Nash remained seated, wanting Damon to feel in control. Nash had never relinquished power to anyone before, and certainly not to his longtime rival, but right now, rivalry was gone and this was about so much more.

"I haven't lied about the fact I'm your son," Nash began. "I did find out when my mother had a stroke several months ago."

"Jake Roycroft is my son." Damon's jaw clenched. "So, you came in deceiving us from day one with this fake name, long hair and a beard. Your clothes are all worn and even your truck is dated. You sure as hell thought this betrayal out down to the last detail."

There was no other angle to look at it. Damon was dead-on.

"I did," Nash confessed. "I wanted to come in, find out what you had planned for your horses after retirement. I needed a prizewinner to breed with mine and I wanted the best.

"Finding out I was your son was like a slap in the face," he went on, putting everything on the line for the family he'd come to love…the rival he always thought he'd hate. "I couldn't believe it. But my mother's gut-wrenching confession was all the proof I needed. She'd kept the truth from me, from you, because she knew it would tear us up. She'd watched this feud for years, but when she had her stroke, she couldn't keep the secret anymore."

"And what was your plan when you first arrived?" Damon

asked, his tone anything but that of a loving father or the cheerful man who'd walked into this room moments ago.

Now Nash did rise. He needed to pace, needed to get out of here, but he had to stay and continue to unravel this damn web he'd caught himself in.

"I was hoping if I got a good idea of what your plans were for the horses, I could get my assistant to offer enough money to take them."

Nash crossed to the mantel where a new photo of Tessa, Cassie and Damon sat. The trio stood in front of Don Pedro after the historic win of the Triple Crown. Nash hadn't been there, he'd been here at Stony Ridge taking care of the other horses.

Other photos showed Rose holding her two young daughters in front of a waterfall, a teen Tessa atop a Thoroughbred, Cassie in a ring with another horse. The family was tight and Nash wondered if he'd ever truly be able to break in where he longed to be.

"I was also battling whether or not to tell you the truth about being your son." Nash turned back around. Damon hadn't moved, except to cross his arms over his chest. "But the more I got to know you all, the more I learned as the film was being shot, I realized you weren't the enemy I knew over the years. You were a ruthless businessman to me, but with your family...you were a different person."

Nash refused to succumb to those damn emotions that he was nearly choking on. He wouldn't show weakness, not now. Remaining strong was the only way he would get through this.

"Between sneaking around with Lily and battling how to tell you who I was, I was torn. I decided to tell you everything after the film crew left, after Lily and I were finished and after you'd hopefully sold the horse to my assistant."

Damon's eyes narrowed. "That all changed when Lily became pregnant. Right?"

Nash nodded, disgusted by the look of hatred he'd put in Damon's eyes.

Being cut off from the Barringtons would kill Nash, but he would take it like a man. He'd done all of this to himself and had nowhere else to place the blame. Every downfall that was about to happen was nothing less than what he deserved. Nash just prayed the people he'd come to care about had mercy on him.

"Have you been lying all this time to Lily?" Damon asked.

The man may as well have punched him in the gut. Nash rested his hands on his hips, glanced away and nodded.

"So she knows you're my son, but she has no clue you're a millionaire with your own estate, your own spread of horses," Damon repeated as if to drive that knife deeper. "She thinks she's fallen in love with a simple, hardworking, honest groom. You waited until she left town to confront me and, what, you expect this to all be tidied up for when she returns?"

Damn it, why did that explanation make Nash sound more like a bastard than a man who'd started off with good intentions?

"I'm telling her everything when she comes back," Nash replied, forcing himself to hold Damon's angry gaze. "I love her. I didn't come into this expecting to get wrapped up personally with anybody at all, least of all Lily. Then our affair started and spiraled out of control. Then I got to know you all even more and I started wanting more than what I came here for. I started out with a goal to get Don Pedro at any cost. Now, though, I don't want him. I just want Lily, I want my father. You have all the power. You can cut me out of your life or we can try to make this relationship work."

Damon continued to stare through that narrow gaze.

"I understand if you don't want anything to do with me." Nash had laid it all out there, had even offered a meager defense. Now he had to finish up and get the hell out before he started sobbing like some damn fool. "I wouldn't blame you for cutting me out of your life. I mean, I haven't been part of your life for very long, so you could just go back to the way things were before I ever came around. Nothing would change for you, really."

Linda stepped into the doorway. "Damon—"

"Not now, Linda."

She moved farther into the room until she was standing beside Damon. "Don't make a decision you'll regret later."

Nash jerked his attention to the elderly woman who was gripping a kitchen towel in her hands, her knuckles white. He'd never guessed he'd have an ally in any of this, but having anybody at all on his side was a blessing he didn't deserve.

"Linda, you don't know what you're talking about," Damon said between clenched teeth. "This is between me and Nash. Damn it. Jake."

"Nash is my real middle name," he replied, as if that made any of this easier to swallow.

Linda laid a hand on Damon's arm. "I know you're hurt, but if you'll put your pride aside for two minutes, you'll see he's hurt, too. And, he's still your son. That's something he never had to reveal."

Damon's eyes flashed toward Nash's. Odd, now that everyone had been calling him Nash for months, he'd come to think of himself as Nash, the groom, as opposed to Jake, the billionaire.

"I don't want to make this harder for you," he explained. "I wanted to get everything out and I did. I'll go and leave the next step up to you."

Leaving with so much hurt between them, leaving with so many questions still left unanswered would kill him. But Damon needed to come to grips with this just as Nash had. Realizing his rival was also his father had taken Nash months to digest and he couldn't expect Damon to do so in the span of a few minutes.

Silence filled the room as Damon continued to stare at

Nash in disbelief. Linda still clutched the towel as her eyes darted back and forth between the two stubborn men.

"You know how to reach me." Nash raked a hand over his jaw, the beard he'd become so familiar with bristling beneath his palm. "I won't contact you again."

Damon said nothing as Nash headed toward the foyer, but there was one last thing his father needed to know. One last bit of his heart he'd lay on the line, even though he would surely damn himself later for being so open and vulnerable.

Gripping the door frame, Nash turned to look at his father for what would probably be the last time. "For what it's worth, I enjoyed the past several months. I'd wondered about my father my entire life and even though I was shocked that it turned out to be you, I wouldn't trade my time here with you and the girls for anything."

Those threatening emotions choked him as Nash headed out the door, leaving Stony Ridge and his father behind.

That part was over, and as hellish and gut-wrenching as it had been, Nash knew what had transpired between his father and himself was absolutely nothing compared to the hurt and the anguish that awaited him when Lily returned. The thought of causing her pain was killing him.

She deserved to know the truth once and for all. And he deserved nothing less than watching her walk away. Now he had to figure out a way to keep the inevitable from happening.

Sixteen

Being away from Nash for a week had been harder than she'd thought. She'd loved seeing her mother again, but she truly missed the man she'd fallen in love with. Lily found herself missing the Barringtons, as well.

In the two weeks she'd been gone her little belly had pooched out just enough to have her smiling and gliding her hand over the swollen area. Not a drastic change to anyone looking at her, but she noticed and she had no doubt Nash would notice. That man knew her body better than she did.

She'd been careful not to wear anything tight, plus she donned sunglasses and a hat when traveling through the airport. The last thing she wanted was anyone finding out about the baby before she could make an announcement.

Nash's idea of her dropping the bomb before the media could speculate was brilliant. With the Barrington film getting buzz already months before release, Ian already booked her a one-on-one interview with a popular TV anchor. And perhaps by then she'd have some other news to share…maybe even a ring on her finger. Dare she hope that Nash was ready to follow her confession with one of his own?

Lily had changed her flight to a day earlier. She hadn't been able to wait to get back to Nash, to have him see how her belly and their baby had grown. She wanted his hands on her, wanted to share this moment, silly as that may sound.

Lily had rented a car at the airport, eager to surprise Nash since he thought he'd be picking her up the following morning. As she pulled up next to his old truck in the drive, she smiled and killed the engine.

The porch swing swayed in the breeze, as did the hanging ferns. This cozy home was perfect for their family. Images of her lavish condo in LA flashed through her mind and Lily knew that second that she didn't want her child growing up in a town with so much chaos. This porch would be the perfect play area for a toddler, the wide drive would serve as the place where their child could ride a bike or make chalk drawings. The expansive backyard just begged for a swing set complete with slide and maybe a sandbox.

When Lily looked at this house, she didn't see it as Nash's home anymore, she saw it as their future. Even though he was just renting it, she had fallen in love with it and wanted to stay. Perhaps if she offered the owner a fair price he'd sell to them.

One goal at a time, she promised herself as she stepped from the car. A light drizzle had accompanied her drive in and now the rain started falling a bit harder, faster as she made her way to the front door. The luggage in the car could wait. Her need to see Nash couldn't.

The front door was unlocked, such was life in the country, and another reason she wanted to raise her family there.

As soon as she stepped over the threshold, she smelled that familiar, masculine scent that could only be associated with the man she'd fallen in love with. She'd missed that smell, missed the feel of his body next to hers as she slept, missed the way he would hold her, look at her, bring her a random grilled cheese when she hadn't even said she was hungry.

And her body ached to touch him again. She'd gone so

long without sex before meeting Nash, but since that first time with him, she constantly craved more. Nash was it for her.

No longer did she fear the media and what they would say. They'd talk regardless and half the "news" was made up stories anyway. No, she knew Nash would be by her side; he wouldn't let her go through any of this alone. She was that confident in their newfound relationship. They'd come so far from the frenzied affair in the loft. Even their passion had reached another level of intimacy.

"Nash," she called as she stepped into the living room and clicked on a lamp. Dusk was settling outside and the promise of a storm was thick in the air. "I'm home."

Footsteps from the back of the house had her turning toward the hall. The sight of him shocked her, leaving her frozen in her place and utterly speechless.

The sight of him wearing only a pair of worn jeans riding low on his hips and nothing else but excellent muscle tone was enough to have her go silent and just enjoy the view. But, it was the clean-shaven face and the new haircut that had her doing a double take.

Those piercing blue eyes surrounded by thick, dark lashes were even more prominent now. His hair was wet as if he'd just gotten out of the shower. He froze, resting his hands on his hips. Apparently he was just as surprised to see her as she was about his transformation.

"You're early," he stated, brows drawn in. "Is something wrong?"

"Everything's fine." Lily took a step forward, then another until she'd closed the gap between them. Reaching up to cup his face with both hands, she studied this new Nash. "Why the change?"

Not that he looked bad. The Nash with the beard and unkempt hair was rugged and mysterious. This Nash with the square jaw and chiseled cheeks, with more emphasis on those mesmerizing eyes was flat-out sexy and intriguing.

"I needed to," he told her, taking her hands in his. He

kissed her palms before placing her hands on his chest. "It's the first step in getting where I need to be, where we need to be."

Lily couldn't stop taking in the sight of him. Who knew a dark beard and disheveled hair could change someone's appearance so much?

Those worry lines between his brows had deepened and the haunted look in his eyes hadn't been there when she'd left.

"Something's wrong." The feel of his quickened heartbeat beneath her hand confirmed her suspicions. "Talk to me."

Releasing her hands, he slid his own around her waist and pulled her against him. When he froze and jerked his gaze down, Lily smiled.

"I grew a little," she explained, lifting her oversize T-shirt to expose her slightly rounded belly. "One morning I just woke up and there it was."

She wondered how he'd react to her new shape, but when both of his hands came around to cover the swell, Lily knew he was just as excited about their growing baby as she was.

Nash dropped to his knees, laying his forehead against her stomach as his thumbs stroked her bare skin. The thought that this child could already bring such a strong man to his knees was so sexy.

Lily threaded her fingers through his much shorter hair. "I've missed you so much," she whispered.

The first rumble of thunder shook the house, rain pelted the windows harder now. Nash glanced up at her, a storm of his own flashing through his expressive eyes as he came back to his feet and gathered her against him.

He tilted his face against her neck, his lips tickling her skin and sending jolts of need streaming through her...as if she needed any more encouragement to want this man.

"I've needed this," he murmured. "Needed you."

Lily wrapped her arms around his bare waist. "You'll always have me, Nash. I'm in this forever, but you keep holding back. When will you open up and let me in? Finally see that what we have only gets stronger each day?"

Nash pulled back, and lightning flashed through the window, illuminating his handsome, yet troubled face. "I've always known how strong we are, Lily. I've never doubted it, never once thought what we had wasn't real. I didn't want to admit it at first because I knew you'd be leaving and I was going to have to say goodbye, so I was protecting myself. But you mattered to me the second I made you mine up in that loft."

Her body trembled at the memory even though she had a sinking feeling there was more to what he had to say.

"You're right, I've been holding back." He stepped away, raking a hand down his smooth jaw. "I never intended for you to get caught in this war I made with myself. I figured once you were gone and we parted ways you'd never have to know."

Chills crept up her spine. What was he about to confess? Was he married? Did he already have children somewhere? Was he dying? The endless questions swirled around in her head until she thought she'd pass out.

Gripping the back of the sofa, Lily met his gaze head-on. She wasn't about to cower now. Whatever he was on the verge of telling her obviously was tearing him up, too. If they were going to be a couple, they needed to face the crisis together.

"You said that about Damon being your father," she told him. "Is there another secret you've kept from me?"

"I need you to know I never meant for you to be affected by this."

Wrapping her arms around herself to ward off the tremors overtaking her body, Lily held her ground. She didn't move, didn't blink. Whatever this was, it was bad.

"You also need to know that I love you," he continued. "I fell in love with you before you told me about the baby. I've wanted to tell you, wanted you to know."

When he stepped forward and reached for her, Lily took a step back, holding her arms out to her side. "Don't. Don't preface whatever bomb you're about to drop with love and think that will fix this. You're picking an awfully convenient time to express the feelings I've tried to get you to share for a while now."

Nash nodded, drawing in a shaky breath. "You're right. You deserve more than what I've given. Just promise you'll hear me out before you make any decisions regarding us, our baby."

"Just tell me!" she yelled, fear spawning her outcry.

The lights flickered, but came right back on as thunder and lightning filled the night. How apropos for everything that was taking place inside this house, inside her heart.

"My real name is Jacob Nash Roycroft. I'm known as Jake to nearly everybody." He took a deep breath and let it out. "I'm not a groom, I'm a horse owner myself. All of this was a setup to spy on Damon."

Air left Lily's lungs as she stared at the man who was quickly becoming a stranger right before her eyes. "Why?" she whispered.

"Damon Barrington has been my rival for a couple of years now." Nash glanced down, raking a hand over his head before he lifted his tormented eyes to meet hers again. "We both own racehorses and I knew he and his girls were re- tiring. I wanted to go undercover so I could see how to get some of his prizewinning horses because he wouldn't sell them to me. I also wanted to see him as a man outside of the business world. I didn't even know going in if I would tell him about being his son. Every single day I battled this and before I knew it, we were in an affair and by then I was in too deep."

Everything he told her weighed heavily on her heart. He'd lied to her from the beginning. He had his own horse farm, he was a racehorse mogul.

Which meant he had money. Plenty of money and he

was used to getting his way. Which would explain his take-charge attitude, his beautifully appointed home, the doctor who made house calls, no doubt because Nash had paid her a hefty sum.

There was no way to describe the level of hurt that spread through her, leaving her cold, empty. Everything she'd known...no, everything she'd felt had been a lie based on nothing but a man who was only looking out for himself. Anything she felt was for a man who didn't even exist...except in her heart.

"You bastard," she whispered, hugging her midsection. She refused to look at him, she wouldn't give him the satisfaction of seeing her broken.

"My name may be different and my bank account bigger than you thought." Nash's bare feet shuffled across the hardwood floor as he came closer. "But I'm still me, Lily. I'm still the man who wants to be with you. I'm still the man who fathered that child."

His palm cupped her chin, lifting her face so she had no choice but to look him in the eyes. "I'm still the man who loves you."

There was no way to stop the tears from spilling over. She didn't even try. She hadn't wanted him to see her vulnerable, but she'd quickly changed her mind. He deserved to see the results of his lies, his betrayal. He deserved to hurt just as much as she was hurting. If he loved her so much, then she'd hate to see how he treated his enemies.

Swatting his hand away, Lily pushed off the back of the couch and stood straight up. "Don't touch me. Never touch me again. You don't love me, you love yourself. I don't think you're capable of loving me, Nash...or whatever the hell your name is."

She'd thought being deceived years ago had been bad, but this was a whole new level of crippling pain.

She'd take public humiliation any day over having her heart shattered into so many pieces she feared she'd never find all the shards. She'd been so sure she could trust him with everything.

"Hear me out."

"No." There was no way she would listen to more lies. "I'm done here. You had ample time to tell me the truth, but you started everything off with a lie."

Her heart ached and she feared the cracks and voids would never be filled.

"You want to know what's worse?" she asked, her words wretched out on a sob. "I still love you. Damn you, I can't just turn off my feelings. I can't be cold to someone I care about and I never thought you'd be so heartless to me. How dare you make me feel again, make me think I could trust you after you know what I've been through? How dare you make me love, make me believe in a family I've wanted for so long?"

Nash's eyes shimmered and Lily had to steel herself from feeling any pity. She had no room in her heart for him...not anymore.

"Please, Lily." He started to reach for her again, but as soon as her eyes darted to his hand, he dropped it. "I'll do anything to make this right. Anything so you can see how I've changed since we started seeing each other. You need to know that you are the reason I changed, the reason I told everyone the truth. I did it all because I love you. I want to be with you with nothing between us. Tell me what I can do, I'll do it."

Even hearing him pour his heart out, bare his soul, Lily couldn't trust that what he said was true. How could she? For months he'd found it so easy to lie. Not only to lie, but to sleep with her, make a baby and pretty much set up playing house, all while lying straight to her face.

He was used to getting what he wanted and now that she was done, he was pulling out all the pretty words he thought she wanted to hear. Nothing could fix what he'd done, what he'd destroyed.

"I can't be here."

She pushed him out of the way and headed toward the foyer. She'd just scooped the keys to her rental up off the entry table and placed her hand on the knob when Nash, Jake...whatever, placed his hands on either side of her head and caged her against the door.

The warmth of his chest against her back had her sucking in her breath. Damn her body for responding to his nearness. Her heart was broken, but her hormones hadn't received that message.

"We can work this out," he whispered in her ear. "I can't lose you."

Lightning illuminated the sky, the electric flickered, once, twice. Darkness enveloped them, the silence mocked them. There was a time they would have made use of this raging storm, the power outage. Right now, though, they were strangers, back to square one. Because she definitely didn't know this man standing so close to her she could feel the breath on her cheek.

Being deceived once in a lifetime was enough, but this was the second man to lie to her face and make a complete fool out of her. And even though this time had been just the two of them, the pain and anguish was beyond intensified compared to the first time.

"Let me go," she whispered as her throat clogged with more tears. "Just...let me go."

One hand came around, cupping her stomach and Lily choked back a sob. "Never," he rasped, nuzzling her neck with his lips. "I'll never let go of my family. I'll give you space, I'll do anything you ask me to. But not that. I love you too much."

Lily shook her head, circled his wrist and eased his hand away. "You don't understand," she said, turning to face him, his mouth just a breath away from hers. "This is one thing you can't buy back. You can't control or manipulate with money or power. You're dealing with real people, real feelings. I hope you were able to get those horses you wanted to so damn bad."

She jerked on the door handle behind her, causing his hand to fall away. "And I hope losing me and this baby was worth it."

"You can't go out in that storm."

Lily laughed as the sudden wind whipped her hair around her face. "I'd rather face this storm than stay one more second with a man who thought he could keep my heart in one hand and his secrets in the other."

Jake stood on the balcony of his master suite looking out over the land on his estate. He'd sneaked into his own home after midnight as the raging storm died down. He couldn't stay in the rental cottage another second. Every room smelled like Lily, held memories of their passion. The few bottles and potions of hers she hadn't packed for her trip dominated the vanity space in the bathroom, her small clothes hung next to his in the closet and she'd left a pair of sandals by the back door.

He had nowhere else to go but home...a place he'd always wanted her, but where she would never be. The rain had reduced down to a drizzle, but he didn't care. He felt nothing. Not the cool rain, not the emptiness in his heart, not even a yearning to go to his own stables and look things over since he'd been gone for months.

There was nothing left for him now. On a mission to see his father, gain prizewinning horses and not hurt Lily, Jake had managed to damage everything he'd set out to obtain.

Money wouldn't buy his way out of this because Lily was right, he was dealing with people's feelings and all he'd done was trample all over them in his quest to be number one.

Droplets of rain ran down his smooth face and Jake swiped the moisture away as he turned to go back into his bedroom. The second-floor master suite was impressive in size, but that damn king-size bed dominating the middle of the floor mocked him. Sleeping alone would be hell. Knowing he'd never reach for her again, feel her curvy body against his or her soft breath as she slept…at least if she had her way about it.

But he hasn't been lying when he'd said he would give her space. He'd do whatever it took to get his family back. He knew she'd be hurt from the truth, he didn't blame her. He just didn't know how gut-wrenching seeing her emotional breakdown would be.

Jake jerked off his clothes and shoved them into the hamper in the corner of his room before heading on into the open shower. He couldn't sleep, wasn't even going to attempt it.

As he stood amidst all of the showerheads pelting him with scalding water, Jake wondered how much time Lily would take. He would give her space, but he'd be damned if he'd let her go without a fight and there was no way in hell he'd ever let his child go.

Jake flattened his palms against the tile wall, dropping his head as the water pulsed against his neck. He had a fight ahead of him, a fight he'd never had to take on before. Business, horse racing and training, that's what he knew.

What he didn't know was how to fix all the broken hearts he'd left scattered all over his life.

Seventeen

Lily felt like an absolute fool. When she'd left Jake's home three days ago, she'd not been thinking of anything but how to get away from him. There was only one place she could think of to go and here she sat in the Barringtons' kitchen, sipping orange juice and wondering what in the world she should do next.

"Honey, you're going to have to eat something," Linda said.

The woman had been an absolute comfort these past couple days. She'd not asked questions, she'd merely opened the home up and Damon had even told Lily she could stay as long as she needed.

Problem was, she needed support, comfort, a shoulder to cry on and she didn't want to admit it. But they had fussed over her; even Tessa and Cassie had come over to comfort Lily. They'd brought some clothes when they found out she'd left his house with nothing but the suitcase that had still been in the trunk of her car.

To be coddled and pampered wasn't why she had come, but she had to admit, nursing wounds with people who weren't going to stab you in the back was a refreshing change from her LA life. She could stay there—okay hide there—until she figured out what to do.

Today, though, her doctor was coming by the estate to give her a checkup. Since leaving Jake's house, she hadn't been feeling well. Of course, she'd not been eating a whole lot, either. She made herself eat for the baby, but in reality she probably needed more.

Insomnia had become an unwelcome friend, too. She was in a strange bed, alone and heartbroken, but she'd keep that to herself. The last thing she wanted was pity from anybody. All she wanted was to make sure her baby was healthy and then she needed to confront Jake. As much as seeing him again would kill her, she needed to discuss the baby. He was the father and there was nothing she could do to change that cold, hard fact.

"Maybe just some toast," Lily told Linda, trying to avoid eye contact with the caring woman.

"After the doctor leaves, I expect you to eat a full lunch." Linda put a piece of toast into the toaster and turned back around. "No excuses. You need your strength for that baby and to fight that stubborn man of yours."

"He's not my man."

Linda laughed. "Oh, honey. Of course he is. He made some major mistakes, but you love him. You just need time and so does he. He should suffer for what he's done, I agree with you there, but don't make any major decisions right now."

Lily took another drink and smiled. "I couldn't agree more about the suffering, but I don't think time will make this hurt any less. He lied to me, Linda. Twice. I can't forgive that."

The toast popped up just as Damon entered the kitchen. The man looked about as rough as Lily felt. His silver hair was a bit disheveled, the dark circles beneath his bright eyes proved he wasn't getting sleep.

Join the club.

"Sit down," Linda ordered. "I want to talk to you, too."

Damon jerked his gaze toward her, but Linda wasn't looking at his shocked expression as she was lathering a generous amount of butter onto the thick slice of toast.

The older man remained standing, crossing his arms over his chest. "Say what you want to say so I can get out to the stables."

As calm as you please, Linda crossed to Damon, pointing her finger in his face. "You are being pigheaded. I know Jake hurt you, that's understandable. However, have you thought about what you would've done in his situation? Would you have opened up to your greatest rival and bared your soul? No. You would've treated it like a business move. You would've been just as calculating and secretive."

Guilt churned in Lily's stomach. So many people were hurting all because Jake felt he'd had no other choice.

"Maybe I would've." Damon nodded slightly. "But we're not talking about me." His attention turned to Lily. "What about her? What excuse does he have for deceiving her?"

Linda's eyes softened as she took a slight step back from Damon. "She was an innocent bystander who got caught up in the family drama. Jake loves her, I've seen how he looks at her."

Linda smiled, resting her hand on Damon's cheek. "Just as he's come to care for you and all of us. He's hurting, too, Damon. Can't you reach out to him? See if there's any way you can work on this relationship? He's your son. You can't forget that."

Lily cupped her stomach with both hands, wanting this nightmare to be over, wanting to go back in time and make Jake open up to her. But he hadn't trusted her enough to let her in. Hadn't trusted what they had together to share his life in full.

"Why are you so hell-bent on being in Jake's corner?" Damon asked.

With a slight shrug, Linda moved to take Lily's now-

empty glass and put it in the sink. "I'm on the outside looking in. I can see people I care about in pain and I don't like
it. This family is too close and life is short. You above all
people should know that."

Lily winced as Damon's shoulders fell, and he blinked his
eyes as if trying to gain control of his own emotions. Linda
had gone straight to the heart with that veiled hint at Rose's
unexpected death.

The doorbell rang before anyone else could say a word.
Lily was all too eager to step away from this emotional battle
because beneath all of this chaos, Linda and Damon shared
something much deeper than the standard employer-em-
ployee bond.

"That will be the doctor," Lily said as she escaped. "I'll
get it."

Lily was anxious to see how the baby had progressed,
eager to hear that sweet heartbeat that made the whole world
seem perfect and right. She had to focus on her child right
now. Her love life, or the love she'd falsely believed in, would
have to wait because this innocent child came before lies,
deceit and broken hearts.

Entering the open wrought-iron gate flanked by stone
pillars, Lily steered her rental car into the long drive lined
by pristine white fencing.

She couldn't believe she was actually there. Nerves had
her hands shaking as she maneuvered up the drive toward the
impressive two-story colonial-style home. White columns
extended up from the porch, stabilizing a second-story balcony that stretched across the house. A separate three-car
garage sat just behind the house, and off to the left of the
drive were the massive white-and-green stables.

Horses out in the field swished away flies as their tails
swiped back and forth. An old oak dominated the front yard,
but the tire swing dangling from a sturdy branch caught her

attention. Why would Jake have a tire swing on a tree? He was single and didn't have any children...yet.

The landscaping around the wide porch had to have been professionally done with the perfectly placed variegated greenery and pops of color from various buds.

She should have turned around. The house was too inviting and the last thing she needed was to be drawn into this part of Jake's world.

As easy as it would be for her to convince herself to turn around, she had things to discuss with him. They were bound forever, whether she liked it or not, and the doctor had expressed some minor concerns with the baby. Jake deserved to know. Unfortunately, she needed his help, too. As much as she hated to admit it, she couldn't impose on the Barringtons any longer. She'd been there nearly a week and, after her appointment, she knew she needed to stand strong and take control back in her life.

Lily stepped out into the summer heat and made her way up onto the wide porch. Colorful pots filled with various greenery decorating each side of the door made for a picturesque entry. Everything about Jake's home looked like something out of a magazine.

This was not what she'd expected at all. Jake's rental house had seemed homey, but that had been a stage, a prop in his game. His real home was just as inviting, if not more so.

Lily rang the bell before she could change her mind and race back to her car. Moments later a young lady, probably somewhere in her early thirties, answered the door. The beautiful woman with long, blond hair had eyes the color of emeralds and a pleasant smile. Jealousy punched Lily straight in the gut.

"Hello," the lady greeted. "Can I help you?"

Whoever this woman was...

No. Lily had left Jake, so what he was doing now was none of her business. But seeing that he'd moved on so fast only intensified the hurt she'd lived with for the past several days. Or had this woman always been here waiting on Jake?

"Wait…aren't you Lily Beaumont?"

Celebrity status strikes again. "I am," she replied, trying to find fault with the stranger, but her beauty was flawless. "Is Jake here?"

The young woman nodded with a smile. "He's down in the stables," she said, pointing across the way. "He won't mind if you go on down. He told us you may stop by."

Anger slid through her veins, gliding right through the hurt he'd caused. "Oh, he did, did he?" she asked, raising a brow. "Thank you."

Turning on her heel, Lily's sandals slapped against the concrete as she marched her way toward the stables. The heat was nearly unbearable and Lily had to focus on the open doorway to the stable. Once she had her say, she could get back in her air-conditioned car and cool down, then this wave of dizziness would subside.

Of course, trying to keep her blood pressure down was a bit difficult at the moment. How dare Jake alert…whoever that lady was that Lily would be coming by? What a cocky, ego-inflated—

The rant died a quick death in her mind when she stepped through the open door and found Jake shirtless, holey jeans riding low, sweat glistening over every bare spot her eyes took in as he cleaned out one of the stalls.

He hadn't seen her yet, which gave her the opportunity to appreciate the beauty of his body. Just because she was pissed at him for lying didn't mean she was dead. Jake had the sexiest body she'd ever laid eyes on…which is how she ended up in this predicament to begin with. Saying no to a man like Jake was impossible.

Stepping farther into the stables, she stopped halfway up the aisle and crossed her arms. "Don't you have a staff to do this for you?"

Jake jerked around, bumbling with the pitchfork in one

hand before he caught it with the other. Gripping the top of the handle, his eyes drank her in, his chest heaving from obvious exertion. Lily had to remember she was here for one reason only…and it wasn't to appreciate the beautiful male form standing before her.

"What are you doing here?" he asked.

Holding her ground, Lily shifted her stance. "Why are you acting surprised? Didn't you tell the pretty blonde that there was a possibility I'd come by?"

Damn it, she hadn't been able to hold back that stab of jealousy in her tone, and from his amused smirk he'd picked up on her green-eyed monster, too.

"She's my maid," he informed her, swiping his forearm across his forehead.

Lily rolled her eyes. "I don't care what she is. What you do in your time now isn't my business."

Silence settled between them until a horse shifted in its stall. She hated the uncomfortable cloud that seemed to hang over them.

"You do care," he told her, dropping the pitchfork into the stall. "You wouldn't be here if you didn't."

Oh, that ego she once found attractive was so damn maddening right now.

Tilting her chin and taking a step forward, because Lily knew who really held the power here, she stopped only a few feet from him and cursed herself when her eyes dropped to that sweaty, chiseled chest. She couldn't hold on to her control if she was being tempted by the devil himself.

"Actually I'm here because I just had a checkup." Lacing her fingers just below her stomach, Lily held his gaze. "She said my blood pressure is still high and I need to start taking precautions to keep it down. There's some concern with me and the baby, so she said she wants to see me again in two weeks instead of the usual four to make sure the condition is under control."

"Damn it." He raked a hand through his damp hair,

rubbed the back of his neck and met her gaze. "What can I do? I know I've caused you more stress, that can't be helping. Tell me what I can do to fix this."

The worry etched over his face almost moved her. But that worry was for the baby.

"Actually I'm not here to get help from you," she said. "I'm here to ask what you paid the doctor to care for me. I'm reimbursing you."

"Like hell you are." Jake closed the gap between them, the tips of his boots nearly touching her bare toes. Those bright eyes were now blazing, the muscle in his jaw clenching. "You're not paying me a dime. This is my baby, too."

"I had a feeling you'd say that," she muttered as a wave of dizziness swept through her. Lily closed her eyes for just a moment, waiting for it to pass before she opened and met his still-angry gaze. "So I'm at least paying half."

"I pay for what's mine," he all but growled. "I will take care of my family, no matter what the needs are. It's best you realize that now."

Black dots danced before her and Lily shook her head, wiping the sweat from the back of her neck. "Could I get some water?"

In an instant Jake's hands were on her shoulders, touching her face, brushing her hair back. His eyes instantly held concern and worry. "Are you dizzy?"

Damning herself for showing weakness the one time in her life she needed to be the strongest, Lily could only simply close her eyes and nod.

Before she knew what was happening, Jake had swept her up into his arms and was carrying her out of the stables.

"Don't," she protested, but even to her own ears the plea sounded feeble. "I just need water. I'll be fine."

Ignoring her completely, Jake reached the back door to his house and squatted down far enough to turn the knob. Once inside where the cool air-conditioning hit her, Lily was already feeling as if the world had stopped tilting so much.

Jake closed the door with his foot and took her straight to the living area where he laid her on the oversize leather sofa.

"Jake, is everything all right?"

Lily didn't open her eyes, but she recognized the female voice from the lady who had answered the front door. Tossing her arm over her eyes, Lily wished she would've just phoned Jake instead of coming there. She'd wanted to show him she was just fine without him, wanted to prove she could get along alone.

And here she was, flat on her back, depending on him and now his girlfriend/maid was taking part in Lily's humiliation.

"Could you get a bottle of water, please, Liz?"

"Of course."

The cushion next to her dipped and Jake's hand covered her stomach, then his fingertips were at the base of her throat. She missed those hands, missed how they could go from showing strength caring for horses to dominating her body in the bedroom.

"Your pulse is out of control."

"I just got hot," she defended, ignoring her betraying hormones. "Once I get some water and sit for a minute, I'll be fine."

"What have you eaten today?"

Shifting her arm to behind her head, Lily glanced up at him. "I had some orange juice and toast a couple hours ago."

His eyes narrowed. "Lily—"

"Mom said you wanted some water."

Lily jerked her attention just beyond Jake's shoulder and saw a young boy with honey-wheat hair tousled by the wind or just the lack of a comb. He came closer, extending the bottle to Jake.

"Thanks, buddy."

The boy smiled, showcasing a couple of missing teeth. "Hi," he told her. "I'm Tyler."

Lily couldn't help but smile back. The boy had no clue who she was and that was just fine with her. He was adorable, but Lily couldn't help but wonder who he was to Jake. The boy looked nothing at all like Jake, but he didn't resemble the lady he'd referred to as mom, either.

"Tyler is Liz's son," Jake informed her as if sensing where her thoughts had gone.

"Hi, Tyler. I'm Lily." She took the water from Jake and sat up a little higher as she uncapped the bottle. "Thank you very much."

"You're welcome."

He turned and ran toward the back of the house, obviously finding nothing exciting with the new arrival.

Taking a long drink, Lily welcomed the cool liquid as it slid down her throat. She needed to get out of Jake's house. The longer she stayed, the more questions she had and she really had no business asking them since she'd left Jake. Well, she physically left him. Emotionally had they ever truly been vested? When a relationship was built on lies it was really difficult to say who left whom first.

When she twisted the lid back on, Jake took the bottle and set it on the coffee table. "Lie down. I'll get you something to eat."

Remaining upright, she shook her head. "I'm not staying, Jake. I just need to pay you and I wanted to let you know about the baby and my appointment. I'll never keep secrets from you."

His shoulders fell and he gave a curt nod. "I deserved that."

Lily laughed. "Oh, Jake. You haven't begun to get what you really deserve."

"Then let me have it," he challenged, his chin tipped up now. "Say what you want, ask whatever you want. Don't shut me out, not when we have so much between us."

He was serious. He truly thought talking would place a bandage over the hurts and they'd go on their merry way to make a family and happily-ever-after. If she started on her rant of how hurt and angry she was now, she feared she'd never stop.

"Whatever we had between us was a lie," she reminded him. "No matter how much you wish you'd done things differently, you still chose not to come clean with me, with Damon. You can't claim to care about us when you hurt us so deeply."

Jake stared at her for a minute, his eyes penetrating straight to her heart. Smelling him, sitting this close to him, within reaching distance of his bare torso, was pure hell. She missed the man she knew, the groom. The man before her was a stranger, a millionaire, but still…he was the man she'd fallen in love with.

Jake jerked to his feet and walked out of the room, leaving Lily confused. He wasn't going to fight? Was he done here?

Seconds later he came back in and stood beside the sofa. "I know you hate me, I know you want nothing to do with me, but I have a proposition for you."

Lily stared up at him. "You've got to be kidding me."

He settled back down beside her, taking her hands in his. Lily tried to ignore how the simple gesture still made her heart beat faster, how she wanted to keep that familiar touch locked away forever. She wanted to tug her hands back, but she wouldn't be childish. Whatever he wanted to say, she'd hear him out. Fighting at this point was moot. The damage was done and she'd officially steeled her heart…okay, she was in the process of doing so, which was why he needed to stop touching her.

"Where have you been staying?" he asked.

"At Stony Ridge."

"I figured," he muttered. "I want you to stay here."

"I don't want to be here at all, let alone to stay."

"Give me one week," he pleaded, his eyes never leaving hers. "That's all I'm asking. One week for you to see the side of me I wasn't able to show you. After seven days if you still want nothing to do with me, I'll let you go. I will still want to be part of my baby's life, but I won't pursue you anymore. I just want you to see the man I've become, the man who loves you and wants to show you he's not the selfish bastard who originally came to Stony Ridge."

Lily needed to tell him the rest of what she'd learned at her doctor visit, but she hated admitting she needed anything from him.

When she remained silent, Jake squeezed her hands. "Don't listen to your mind, Lily," he murmured. "Listen to your heart. You even told me yourself that you couldn't turn off your feelings. I'm only asking for a week. Let me take care of you, show you how we could be with no secrets, no lies."

One week. It was a drop in the bucket compared to the time she'd already spent with him. But how would her heart be at the end of that time? Resisting him was hard on a good day and she had no doubt he'd pull everything out of his arsenal to win her back.

She just had to be smarter, stronger and remain the one in control. Jake couldn't know how much he still affected her.

"The doctor also told me I needed to stay off my feet and let others do things for me." Lily closed her eyes, sighed and refocused on Nash. "I can't keep imposing on the Barringtons. Looks like you get your wish. I'll give you one week, but that doesn't mean I'm falling back into the way we were before."

Liz chose that moment to step into the room carrying a plate and a glass. When she set them on the table, Lily laughed as Jake thanked her.

"Grilled cheese and chocolate milk?" Lily asked, quirking a brow.

"Your favorites."

Why did he have to be so damn sweet at times? This was the same man who purposely betrayed her. She had to remember that. Who's to say he wouldn't resort to those tactics again?

"You owe me nothing," Jake continued, picking up where he'd left off before Liz had come and gone. "But I'm willing to give you everything. I'm laying it all out there for you to see."

Determination poured from him; he was serious and he wasn't backing down. It's not as if he could break her heart any more than he already had, and at the end of the seven days she'd leave. She'd go back to LA or even Arizona to visit her mother and then on to the set to record the animated film she'd just signed on for.

Lily continued to hold his gaze. "I won't sleep in the same bed as you."

Jake opened his mouth, but Lily cut him off. "That's my nonnegotiable. I'm not here to play house."

His eyes darted to her lips, then back to her eyes. "Deal. But, do you really think you can be here any amount of time and not fall back into my bed?" He eased forward, laid his hands over her stomach and feathered his lips across hers. "Now who's the liar?"

Jake came to his feet, set the plate on her lap and walked out of the room. Her lips tingled from the barely there kiss and she cursed her body for the ache that spread through her, begging for more.

Only an hour into her seven-day stint. Why did she feel as though she'd just fallen right into his perfectly laid trap?

Eighteen

Lily had chosen the bedroom upstairs at the opposite end of the hall from Jake's. That was as far away as she could get.

Day one down. Only six more to go and she would be free to leave for Arizona to see her mother again before heading home to LA. The thought of going back across the country both thrilled and worried her. She was eager to get going on that animation film, but going back to all the shallow people, the chaos of daily living and the lavish lifestyles just didn't appeal to her anymore.

Last night before bed, Lily had sent off a quick text to Ian, letting him know where she was. More than likely the Barringtons knew, but she figured she should at least let her agent know what was going on.

Not that it was anybody else's business, but she didn't mind if Ian shared where she was staying. These were complicated circumstances, after all.

Lily was thankful for the adjoining bath and it would serve Jake right if she spent the rest of her seven-day term in her room. No doubt Jake would show up at her door with trays of food so she didn't have to get up. He'd take the bed rest seriously and he'd use it to his advantage—best she knew that going in. She was allowed to get up and move around, but for the most part, she was supposed to be down with her feet up.

She'd showered and changed into the dress Jake had picked out that day they had gone shopping. Damn it, he'd see this as a sign she was giving in. Little did he know most of her clothes were still back at the rental house and this dress just so happened to be in her suitcase…a suitcase he'd had Linda pack up and bring out to the estate. He was still taking control and she wasn't sure if she was warmed by the fact or ticked that he still felt he had a right to be in charge of her life.

Pulling her wet hair up into a clip, she slid on her flip-flops and made her way downstairs. Before she could hit the landing the doorbell chimed, echoing throughout the house.

When Lily hit the bottom step, she glanced through to the foyer where Damon stood, hands in his pockets and glancing around as if he was just as uncomfortable being there as she was.

Was he here to see Jake or her?

Lily remained on the steps as Jake's footsteps fell heavily on the hardwood floors.

"Damon," Jake greeted. "This is a surprise."

"I apologize for coming by so early," Damon told him. "Is there somewhere private we can talk?"

Jake nodded. "Liz is in the back making breakfast. We can go into the living room. Should I tell her to set an extra place at the table?"

Lily gripped the banister, feeling like perhaps she should slink back upstairs and not eavesdrop on this conversation. But she didn't move.

"I can't stay long," Damon replied.

Jake nodded, leading the way into the living area. Lily slid down and sat on the step, grabbing the slender post for support. Damon was here for one reason: he was either ready to forgive Jake or he was letting him go. A portion of Lily's heart broke for Jake. Even with all the lies and deceit, she worried how he would cope if he lost his father forever. Jake was a strong, determined man, but just discovering your parent and then losing him would be crushing.

"I'm not sure if I should be worried or glad that you showed up on my doorstep."

Damon let out a brief chuckle. Lily couldn't see the men now, but she imagined the elderly mogul shaking his head as she'd often seen him do when he laughed.

The silence fueled the tension. Lily's heart beat so fast, she couldn't even imagine how Jake or Damon were feeling right now.

"To be honest I'm not sure how I feel myself," Damon admitted. "Your latest bombshell really spun me around so fast I didn't know how to react. But I've had several days to think about it."

Nerves fluttering in her stomach, Lily closed her eyes and waited.

"I hate being played for a fool," Damon went on. "I hate that you were that clever and I was so blinded that I didn't see through the disguise and the act."

"Damon—"

"Hear me out."

Lily took in a deep breath sliding her arms around her swollen midsection.

"We were adversaries for so long and I know finding out I was your father was a blow you didn't see coming. Your actions were made out of fear first and foremost. But I also know you're driven to succeed. How can I fault a trait you obviously got from me?"

"I still went about this the wrong way," Jake said, his tone low. "Once I started caring for you, the girls and Lily, I should've said something immediately."

"Yes, you should've," Damon agreed. "But you didn't and what's done is done. I believe everyone should have a second chance and I believe that being without my son for over thirty years is long enough. Life is short."

More silence fell and Lily was dying to know what was happening in that room. She'd listened in long enough. As quietly as she could, Lily came to her feet and headed back up the steps. Once she'd closed herself in her room, she sank back against the door.

Damon had fully accepted Jake for who he was, obviously forgiving the lies and mistakes. Even though he didn't come out and say the words, Damon wouldn't be there if he hadn't.

Lily didn't know if she could be that forgiving. Yes, she figured eventually she'd forgive him. But forgiving him didn't necessarily mean she could let him back into her life, her heart again.

Lily had only been at Jake's estate a short time, and she struggled with her emotions for him every single moment. One second she wanted to talk to him, try to figure out if they could get beyond this hurt. The next second she wanted to leave, wanted to get away because she worried she couldn't trust her feelings.

She wished she had the right answer and prayed for a miracle to guide her to where she needed to be.

Naps while pregnant were beyond amazing. Napping was a luxury she couldn't afford when home in LA or on location filming, but here in Virginia where the pace was slower and she was ordered by her doctor to take it easy, Lily fully embraced a good afternoon rest.

Besides all of that, she was tired. Tired from the pregnancy, tired from the roller coaster ride they'd been on and utterly exhausted from worrying about the future of this child. After spending time on Jake's turf, she was mentally drained and ready to pull her hair out.

Sexually, the man frustrated her. She wanted him, no matter how much her heart still hurt. He'd given her space, he'd not touched her since that slight kiss when she'd first agreed to stay, and damn if that wasn't driving her out of her ever-loving mind.

He'd never even mentioned Damon coming by the other day. Was he keeping that to himself, as well?

As Lily came down the steps, she realized she'd slept much longer than she'd meant to. The antique grandfather clock in the corner of the living room chimed four times, echoing into the empty space.

Lily glanced around, noting the photos along the mantel of Jake with his arm around a beautiful older woman, more than likely his mother, photos of him with jockeys and horses at various winners' circles. In every photo he was smiling.

She'd thought that smile was devastating with the beard, but without it, she could fully appreciate the intrigue, the devilish attitude and the power behind the man.

Laughter and squeals sounded from the front yard and Lily moved to the wide windows, shifting the simple linen curtains aside.

The tire swing swayed back and forth, Tyler held on, his legs dangling out of the hole. And Jake was pushing him.

Lily couldn't deny how the scene clenched her heart. Jake wrapped his arms around the boy's shoulders and pulled back, pausing for a moment before giving another big send-off. The wide grin across Jake's face spoke volumes for how much the lazy evening activity delighted him.

He was going to be an amazing dad. No matter what had happened between them, Lily knew that Jake would always put his child first and be hands-on. But, she couldn't help but wonder about this unique relationship he seemed to have with his maid and her son. Another layer he'd kept from her.

The fact he'd never let her fully in was the main point in that sharp blade that had pierced her heart.

Liz suddenly appeared beside Lily. "Tyler adores him."

"The feeling seems mutual," Lily replied, watching Jake's face light up each time Tyler laughed.

"Jake has been a good influence for Tyler since my husband passed away."

Stunned, Lily turned to Liz. "I'm so sorry."

A soft grin spread across Liz's face, but she kept her gaze on her son. "It's been hard, I won't lie. My husband was a groom here for several years. When he was killed four years ago, Jake asked if I'd like to work for him. I didn't know much about horses, so he asked if I could cook and clean. I know he was just looking out for us, and I could never find a way to repay him because he didn't have to take on a widow and a young child."

Swallowing the lump of remorse, Lily turned her attention back to the front yard. So many facets made up this man. Some were bad: the lies, the betrayal. But the others were so good, so…noble, that Lily hated that he'd damaged his image just to get ahead in the horse industry. Had the breeding, the prospect of winning and generating more money been that important?

"I know it's not my business," Liz went on, shifting to face Lily. "I have no idea what's going on with the two of you, but if it matters, Jake has never brought a woman here before. I can see how much he cares for you."

"He does." She couldn't deny that, but that also didn't mean they were meant to be. "He went about showing me the wrong way, though."

Liz nodded and offered a genuine smile. "Just don't shut him down, yet. Okay? Give him a chance. He's all work and traveling to see his mom. But with you, I see a different side to him and he'd hate me if he heard me say this, but he's vulnerable where you're concerned."

Lily closed her eyes, trying to block out the honest words coming from a virtual stranger. "You care for him."

"Not in the same way you do," Liz corrected. "He and my husband were good friends and had a strong working relationship. But my husband was killed during a robbery. He'd been in the wrong place at the wrong time. Jake didn't hesitate to see to all of my and Tyler's needs. I think of Jake as a friend and a hero when I needed one."

A hero. Lily opened her eyes, her focus shifting instantly

to the man serving as a little boy's hero. A man who had faults and had hurt her so deeply she didn't know how to forgive him.

"I need to get back to cooking dinner." Liz started to walk away, but laid her hand on Lily's arm. "I just wanted to make sure you knew where I stood with Jake because he loves you. He's a powerful man, but you've brought him to his knees. You're in control here."

Liz's footsteps echoed through the room until there was nothing but silence once again, other than the ticking of the grandfather clock in the corner.

Dropping the curtain back in place, Lily went out onto the front porch. The beautiful wide porch with sturdy wooden swings at both ends just begged for a lazy, relaxing day. She took a seat, curled her feet up on the deep red cushions and propped her elbow up on the back, resting her head on her fist. The gentle sway relaxed her.

Lily continued to watch the interaction in the yard, thankful she hadn't been spotted yet. Jake had invited her to stay for a week, had wanted her to see the real man he was with no pretenses, no secrets.

She was already seeing a deeper side to the person she'd fallen in love with. But could she ever get past the fact he thought it was okay to deceive her? Who's to say the next time he wanted something he wouldn't lie to get it?

Between Damon's visit the other day and seeing Jake with Tyler, Lily found herself wanting more. She just worried they were too far gone to get back on stable ground to build anything that could match the fire they had before.

A light flutter in her stomach had her pausing, her hand cupping her belly. The odd sensation happened again and Lily knew she'd felt her baby. Their baby.

The doctor had told her the first feeling she'd get in her stomach would feel like butterflies floating around. The description was pretty accurate, considering that for just a second the shocking sensation had tickled. The movement had only lasted the briefest of moments, but enough to have her smiling.

When she glanced back up, Jake's eyes were on her, and Tyler was hopping out of the hanging tire and racing around to the back of the house. Lily's smile faltered. So much tension stretched between them, so many words that needed to be spoken, so much emotion needing to be released.

Jake made his way toward the porch, and with each step Lily's heart beat faster. He stopped in front of the swing, took her feet from the cushion and sat down, placing her legs across his lap.

"Don't," he told her just as she started to shift away. "Let's just pretend this is a normal day and we're enjoying this late afternoon breeze."

His warm hands gripped her ankles, holding them securely on his lap. She hadn't felt his touch for so long, she knew she'd missed it, but she had no idea just how much his warmth affected her.

"We're not normal people and this isn't just a normal family afternoon," she whispered, hating how true her statement was.

His fingertips trailed from her shin to the top of her foot, back and forth until she couldn't control the tremors that slid through her. That powerful, seductive touch of his would be her undoing.

Jake tipped his head just slightly, focusing those bright eyes right on her as he always had, as if he could see straight into her soul. "You always say you want to be a regular person, not the celebrity when you're off location. Relax, Lily. We're both simply going to be ourselves, nothing fake, no acting. Just Jake and Lily."

Jake and Lily. As if they were an official couple. But she didn't have the energy to argue and she would remain calm to keep her blood pressure down for their baby's sake. And she was done fighting…fighting him and fighting herself.

"I think I felt the baby move a bit ago." She hadn't thought about telling him, but the words tumbled out of her mouth before she could stop them.

Jake's eyes darted to her stomach, a wide grin spread across his face. "What did it feel like?" he asked, his hand pausing in mid-stroke over her leg.

"Like someone was inside tickling me," she explained. "It was faint. The sensations happened twice while I was sitting here watching you and Tyler."

He brought his gaze back up to hers. "How long were you watching us?"

"Long enough to know you two have a special bond."

"I love him," Jake said without hesitation. "I'd do anything for him."

Lily nodded. "Liz explained the situation. I can't imagine being a single mom."

The smack of reality hit her before she realized what she'd said. Jerking her legs off Jake's lap, she came to her feet. Crossing the wide porch, she rested her hands on the white railing at the edge of the structure.

"You won't be alone." Jake's hands slid around her waist seconds later. She hadn't even heard him get up and move toward her. "I'll never let this baby feel neglected and I'll never let you feel like you're doing it all by yourself. No matter what happens with us."

Lily dropped her head between her shoulders and sighed. "There is no 'us,' Jake," she whispered. "Letting you back in…I don't know if I could survive being hurt again."

Tears pricked her eyes behind her closed lids as his fingers splayed across her abdomen. "I'm not giving up on us, Lily," he murmured in her ear. "And I won't let you give up, either."

As much as she wanted to resist him and back up her words with actions, she found herself leaning back against his chest as a tear slipped down her cheek.

"I'm not leaning on you," she told him with a sniff. "I'm not weak and I don't need you. I'm just tired, that's all."

Rubbing her stomach with gentle motions, he kissed the side of her head. "I know, baby. I know."

Nineteen

Jake swirled the whiskey around in the glass tumbler. Staring at the amber liquid wasn't taking the edge off, but he didn't want to lose himself in the bottom of a bottle, either. Right now he needed a clear head, needed to process what the hell was going on with Lily.

Keeping his hands off of her the past few days had tested restraint he didn't even know he possessed. But being with her on the porch, witnessing such raw emotions from her had nearly broken him. The damage he'd caused her was inexcusable, yet she'd leaned on him for a moment and he'd taken that as a sign of hope. At this point, he was grasping at anything she'd throw out.

She'd eaten dinner with him, Liz and Tyler and had gone to her room afterward. He hadn't seen or heard from her all evening and it was nearly eleven. More than likely she was asleep, curled up in that four-poster bed he'd bought from an antiques dealer. The clear image of her dark hair spread all around the crisp white sheets had him clenching the glass before finally slamming it down onto his desk.

If he ever wanted a chance with her, he needed to be open about everything from his life to his emotions. He needed for her to see that he'd changed, he put her first and nothing would come between them again. He couldn't let more time pass without telling her exactly where she stood in his life.

Standing just outside her door, he pondered for a minute if he should wait until morning. She was supposed to rest, after all, but he couldn't. He'd given her space and it was time she realized just how serious he was about winning her back.

Tapping on the door with the back of his knuckles, Jake swallowed and tried to ignore his frantic heartbeat. Nerves consumed him, but being a coward now would certainly secure a future without the woman and child he loved.

The knob rattled just as the door eased open. Lily stood before him, her hair spilled over one shoulder, her eyes wide. Apparently she'd been just as restless as he had. A small light glowed from the table lamp beside her bed.

"Can I come in?" he asked. When she said nothing, he added, "I have some things I need to say."

He worried she would slam the door in his face, a definite right she had, but she opened the door a bit wider and he realized her slamming the door would've been a blessing. Now his penance was having this conversation while seeing her dressed in a silky chemise, the same one he'd slid off her body many times before.

Only this time, her belly rounded out the midsection and her full breasts threatened to come out of the lacy top.

He glanced to the unmade bed, the sheets all twisted in the middle. "I'm sorry if you were sleeping."

Lily shook her head as she sat on the edge of the bed. "I wasn't asleep."

Jake remained by the door because if he even took one more step into this room he wouldn't be able to keep from touching her. Between her tousled appearance and the inviting bed that mocked him, he seriously deserved a damn award in self-control.

But he was here to lay it all on the line. Never before had he done anything so important and so terrifying.

"Damon came by the other day," he began, shoving his

hands into the pockets of his jeans. "We've come to an agreement to work on our relationship."

Lily rested her hands next to her hips. "I know. I was coming down the stairs when he arrived. I listened for a few minutes, but came back upstairs. I'm sorry I eavesdropped. I couldn't make myself leave until I knew what he wanted."

Jake smiled. "It's okay. He said the girls were upset, but they understood my angle and they wanted to get to know their only brother. Damon actually invited me over this weekend for dinner."

Lily's smile hit on every nerve Jake had. He missed that smile, missed the light in her eyes...a light he'd diminished and was desperately trying to get back. He didn't just want that brightness back for only himself, but for her. He wanted her to be that vibrant woman he'd fallen in love with, the stunning light he'd met months ago.

"I'm really happy for you, Jake."

"He asked if you'd be joining me."

Lily's eyes widened before her gaze darted down into her lap. "I don't think that's a good idea."

"I told him I was giving you time to make your own decisions," he went on, not letting her refusal deter him from his goal. "I hadn't planned on telling you about his visit because I didn't want you to think I was trying to sway your decisions."

Her dark eyes came back up to his. "And aren't you?"

"Not by telling you his choice to give me another chance." Jake pulled his hands from his pockets, massaged the back of his neck and took a deep breath. "I've time, Lily. I told you to stay for a week and I've truly tried to keep my distance. Knowing you're here, within my reach, has been one of the hardest things I've ever faced."

"I know," she whispered.

That spark of hope he'd had earlier on the porch grew stronger at her quiet confession—apparently she'd been battling the same war. Jake took another step into the room, then another.

"Tell me you're ready to give up," he told her, damning the tears that threatened to clog his throat. "Tell me the thought of living without what we have is more appealing than fighting for us."

He didn't miss the way her fingers curled into the sheets on the edge of the bed, nor did he miss her shaky intake of breath.

Her silence was invitation enough to move closer, so close he knelt in front of her, taking her hands and holding them in her lap.

"Tell me that I've got no chance with you," he went on. "Because I won't give up on us as long as there's hope. I have to believe you're not ready to give up or you would've left here before now."

Lily's chocolate eyes filled as she bit her unpainted bottom lip. "I can't tell you that."

Relief flooded him, but he was still not in the clear.

"I know we have a lot to work through," he continued. "I know I deserve nothing, but I'm asking for everything. I want you in my life, Lily. I want us to be a family. I don't care if I have to live in LA part of the time and we can come here to get away. You call the shots here."

"I'm scared, Jake. I've never loved like this before, never been so hurt because of it."

Easing forward even more, he let her hands go and wrapped his arms around her waist as he looked up into her teary eyes. "I've never loved like this before, either. That's no excuse for hurting you the way I did, but I can swear on my life that I'll never hurt you again. I want a lifetime to love you, Lily. I want forever to be the man you deserve and the father our children deserve."

She threaded her fingers through his hair. "I'm risking everything by letting you back in."

"My heart is on the line, too," he told her. "If you walked

out again it would kill me. I love you, Lily. I know when I said it before the timing couldn't have been worse. But I love you so much I ache when you're not with me."

The smile that spread across her face had tears gliding down over her cheeks. "I love you, too, Jake."

Every bit of tension and fear left his body as he leaned his head forward, resting it against their baby. Lily's fingertips caressed the back of his neck as he breathed in her familiar scent.

"I won't keep anything from you again," he murmured as he lifted his head.

"I know. You've shown me the man you are. I want to give us another chance." She stared into his eyes, and his heart swelled with love at the light shining back. "I do have one stipulation, though."

"What's that?"

Her hands framed his face, stroked his jaw. "Maybe a little scruff? I fell in love with a rugged man who turned my insides out that first night in the loft. Maybe you could not shave for a while?"

Jake laughed. "Anything you want. Besides, I'll be too busy to shave."

"Oh, really?" Lily lifted her brows. "And what will you be doing?"

Jake's hands traveled up the silky chemise to the thin straps barely containing her breasts. "I plan on keeping you in bed for the next several days."

Her body trembled beneath his. "Well, the doctor did tell me to rest."

Sliding the straps down, he peeled the lacy material over her breasts and palmed her. "Oh, you'll rest. You can just lie there while I take very good care of you."

Lily's head fell back as she arched into his touch. "You have the best ideas."

Epilogue

The grounds were as immaculate as always. The early fall sun shining high in the sky beamed down onto the intimate ceremony. The handsome groom held the bride's hands as their smiles beamed off the other. There was nothing fancy, nothing over-the-top for this outdoor wedding. An arch covered with white buds and sprays of greenery covered the stone walkway, white rose petals sprinkled over freshly cut grass and a family surrounding the happy couple.

Reaching over, Jake took Lily's hand in his. When she sniffed and swiped at the moisture threatening to slip down her cheek, Jake squeezed her hand and leaned over.

"I love you," he whispered. The man knew just how to press on every single hormonal button she had. He palmed her rounded belly with his other hand. "I love her, too. I can't wait to make you my wife."

Lily tipped her head to rest on his shoulder as she watched the couple standing before her pronounced husband and wife by the minister.

Damon kissed his bride, sealing his bond with Linda. Only Tessa, Grant, Cassie, Emily, Ian, Jake and Lily were in attendance. The quaint family ceremony was perfect. Every detail taken care of by the Barrington sisters and

Lily. For once Linda didn't lift a finger. The younger girls had wanted her to just show up and enjoy her special day.

As everyone came to their feet, Jake pulled Lily into his arms. "I can't wait to marry you next weekend."

They'd opted to hold off on their own plans until Damon and Linda were married so everybody's focus and celebration wouldn't be torn. They'd also opted to marry just before her exclusive interview in ten days, which would reveal the pregnancy and her marriage all in one shocking swoop. At nearly seven months, Lily had more energy than ever and they'd just found out the baby was a girl…as they'd thought all along.

They'd both immediately known the name—Rose. How could they name their baby after anyone but the woman who, in a roundabout way, brought Lily to the estate?

While Lily loved how private she and Jake had been for the past several months, she was eager to introduce him to her world, to show everyone that true love existed and she'd found it.

They'd visited her mother and she and Jake had clicked perfectly. Lily couldn't be happier with how her family was growing, how she was being welcomed into the Barringtons as if she'd always been part of them. Damon had fully embraced Jake, as well. The two men were already power planning for the upcoming racing seasons. Just because the girls were retiring and gearing up to open a riding school for disabled children didn't mean Damon was ready to let go just yet. Especially with his son breeding Don Pedro. The families were truly meshing in every way.

Linda and Damon turned, moving from one family member offering hugs and smiles to another. So much happiness enveloped them. Each couple had fought through pain, through obstacles that could break most others.

With three more children in the Barrington clan taking off, Lily knew this dynasty was truly just getting started.

* * * * *

COMING SOON!

We really hope you enjoyed reading this book. If you're looking for more romance, be sure to head to the shops when new books are available on

Thursday
12th July

To see which titles are coming soon, please visit
millsandboon.co.uk

LET'S TALK
Romance

For exclusive extracts, competitions
and special offers, find us online: